P9-EDD-065

09/17

3/17

The Nature of a Pirate

ALSO BY A. M. DELLAMONICA

Indigo Springs
Blue Magic
"Among the Silvering Herd"
"The Ugly Woman of Castello di Putti"
"The Glass Galago"
Child of a Hidden Sea
"Wild Things"
"The Color of Paradox"
"The Cage"
A Daughter of No Nation

The Nature of a Pirate

A. M. DELLAMONICA

A TOM DOHERTY ASSOCIATES BOOK
NEW YORK

This is a work of fiction. All of the characters, organizations, and events portrayed in this novel are either products of the author's imagination or are used fictitiously.

THE NATURE OF A PIRATE

Copyright © 2016 by A. M. Dellamonica

All rights reserved.

A Tor Book
Published by Tom Doherty Associates
175 Fifth Avenue
New York, NY 10010

www.tor-forge.com

Tor® is a registered trademark of Macmillan Publishing Group, LLC.

The Library of Congress Cataloging-in-Publication Data is available upon request.

ISBN 978-0-7653-3451-0 (hardcover)
ISBN 978-1-4668-1237-6 (e-book)

Our books may be purchased in bulk for promotional, educational, or business use. Please contact your local bookseller or the Macmillan Corporate and Premium Sales Department at 1-800-221-7945, extension 5442, or by e-mail at MacmillanSpecialMarkets@macmillan.com.

First Edition: December 2016

Printed in the United States of America

0 9 8 7 6 5 4 3 2 1

For Don DeBrandt, man of many names.
We should have become friends sooner.

The Nature of a Pirate

CHAPTER 1

Kitesharp was bleeding.

The wounded ship was fifty feet long, with a crew of fourteen sailor-mechanics, and when dawn rose over the Fleet of Nations, her blood trail was just a thin line of crimson threaded into her wake. It twisted against the blue of the sea, a hint of pinkish foam that might have gone unnoticed for hours if it hadn't begun attracting seabirds and sharks.

The whole Fleet watched as the birds shrieked and *Kitesharp*'s captain raised a warning cone up her mainmast. Soon—presumably after her bosun had been below for a look—a sphere was raised, too. From a distance, both cone and sphere would appear as flat shapes, seeming to onlookers to be a triangle and circle. It meant *Ship in distress. Help required.*

This particular distress call had gone out twice before.

By midmorning the blood trail was a foot wide and the ship had taken on enough water to raise her bow well above the surface.

The greatest of the Fleet rescue vessels, *Shepherd,* was ready. Her crew brought her alongside the craft as traffic flowed past. Working with military precision, *Shepherd*'s crew lowered a walking bridge to *Kitesharp*'s deck and boarded personnel: twenty workers, first, to help the crew load the doomed ship's tools and fixtures, to strip whatever they could. Yards of hang glider silk were waiting to be off-loaded, along with the flexible boards that made up the skeletons of the gliders' wings. There were bright streamers that carved the kites' paths through the sky, above the sails of the Fleet, and pots upon pots of dyes, glues, and needles. Everything that wasn't bolted down, including the sailors' personal trunks, was already packed.

Shepherd also brought soldiers, fit young adults bearing stonewood swords and a grim sense of purpose. They would search the boat from main deck to bilge, looking for intruders. They brought a spellscribe, who was tasked with seeking anything that might tell them about the intention—a curse, some whispered—that had been worked upon the vessel.

For this third sinking, they also brought Sophie Hansa.

Raised in San Francisco and trained as a biologist, Sophie had been working as a marine videographer until she fell into . . . Well, she was essentially applying twenty-first-century science to puzzles the locals couldn't work out, here on Stormwrack. She had come in search of her birth parents, following them to a society that lived largely at sea, on a world whose existence had been concealed from Earth.

Since then, she'd done everything from hunting for a newfound aunt's murderers to determining international ownership rights over a species of migrating turtles.

The locals were strangely hampered by a cultural taboo against curiosity. Sophie had realized that her best chance of being allowed to stay was by channeling her natural desire to ask questions in ways that earned her political goodwill.

Lately she had been mining the judiciary's warm case files, seeking out little mysteries that might be cleared up with a bit of fact-finding or a basic application of science.

But now someone was sinking small civilian ships that followed Stormwrack's Fleet, the great oceangoing capital city that circled the world, keeping the peace and policing piracy. Knowing the sinkings were caused by magicians wasn't helping the authorities. So, here was Sophie, in her wetsuit, with her tanks and camera and a solar-charged LED lamp, about to take an exploratory plunge through a sinking ship.

"What will you need from us?" asked the head of the *Shepherd* rescue crew, a twentysomething woman, Southeast Asian in appearance (although that meant little here, on this world of tiny island nations), named Xianlu. She was all business. "Kir Zophie?"

Right. Concentrate. "Ship's already taking water—do you know where it's coming from?"

"The aft hold."

"I'll start there, before it gets any deeper."

The officer summoned one of her crew, a broad-shouldered guy with the build of a high school quarterback, clad in a tight-fitting uniform designed for swimming. He looked familiar; after a moment, Sophie realized she had seen him at a disastrous Fleet graduation ceremony she'd attended after she had first arrived here, in the spring, eight months ago.

"Escort Kir Zophie below."

He bobbed his head in assent and gestured for Sophie to follow.

"Get the sails down, move and double," Xianlu ordered, turning her attention to the crews waiting at the ropes.

Kitesharp had a high, snub profile in the water that reminded Sophie of a modern towboat, despite her sails and rigs. Her bow was tilting up as she continued to take water in the stern.

"What's your name?" Sophie asked the boy as they worked their way past a work crew busily sealing the tins of hang glider dye.

"Tenner Vale, Kir."

"Tenner" was a ranking for cadets. It meant he had a full ten years left on his term of service. "Graduation was a while ago, wasn't it?"

He nodded. "In four months, after my exams, I'll be a niner. Xianlu is a septer."

"Do you stay a tenner if you fail the tests?"

He did a double take, probably thinking, *How can you not know that?* Then, having apparently decided she wasn't joking, he said, "A decade is a decade. Niners who've failed their exams are given posts with less responsibility."

"Drop and stow, one, two!" The crew lowered the mainsail. The canvas and rigging loosened and fell to the deck with a sound like a hundred drumbeats. The ship had already been given up for lost. *Kitesharp,* but for the ropes that bound her to *Shepherd,* was now at the mercy of the waves.

"Like a wounded animal," Sophie murmured.

Vale looked frustrated, almost ashamed. "We would fight to save her, if we understood how she's being sunk."

They had to be desperate to turn to me, Sophie thought. Stormwrackers were ambivalent about science. Much of it they labeled atomism and dismissed as unreliable, even dangerous. People preferred to believe in a patchwork of disciplines with as much merit as astrology or dowsing.

Wrackers could navigate ships by the stars. They built and used barometers. But they also thought that observing the flame from a yellow candle would tell them the emotional state of a prevailing wind, and that aspirin worked by "encouraging the spirit to bend like a willow around its hurts."

Sophie was getting away with working for the courts by rebranding her skills. What she was bringing to the table wasn't atomism at all—that was the story. It was a shiny new discipline dubbed "forensic."

Same old wheel, shiny new rim.

Vale opened a hatch, revealing a ladder. Giving him what she hoped was a reassuring smile, Sophie stepped into the hold. The tilt of the ship was more obvious here; she crab-stepped her way down the inclined deck and opened another hatch, peering into a flooded chamber.

"Thanks." She put on her flippers and descended alone. The hold was half full of waist-high salt water. She took a careful stance on the deck, set her light, and began filming, taking a shot of the whole room first, just in case. She captured everything visible above the waterline.

"It is water," she noted.

That look again: of *course* it's water. "Your pardon, Kir?"

"The ship's gushing blood, but filling with salt water. There's no blood here, so where's it coming from?"

He gave the half shrug, a bob of shoulders that was the unofficial Wracker ward against curiosity.

Having filmed it, she took time to look with the naked eye. "You know if anyone has schematics for the ship? Plans?"

"I believe so, Kir."

"To work out how fast the water's coming in, we'll need an accurate measurement of cabin volume."

"A sailing master can do the calculations, if it's important."

She didn't bother to say that, with the right measurements, she could do it herself. "While I'm down there, I want you to record how long it takes the water level to rise from here . . ." She put her hand on one of the ladder rungs. "To this one. Do you understand?"

He made a gesture, indicating rising water. "Sink rate per ten count?"

"Exactly. Do you have something that counts seconds for you?"

Vale nodded. "And a measuring rope, Kir."

"Good. As accurate as you can, please." She set her watch to record the diving time.

"Understood, Kir."

Something in his tone made her think of Captain Parrish; she felt a pang of something that was equal parts longing, loneliness, and frustration.

Forget Garland. It's time to focus on the not-so-smart dive of the day. Still with a hand on the ladder, she checked her camera's waterproof housing, put on her mask and rebreather, took a few breaths, and then bent her knees to bring her face below the level of the rising water. Shining the light around the narrow space, she looked for floating debris or loose rope—anything that might knock or entangle her. But the crew had worked upward from the compromised stern when they began emptying out their ship; the space was empty. Sophie half swam, half crawled to the low point, camera and light at the ready.

She hoped to find a gaping hole in the hull, of course, something to account for whatever was hemorrhaging into the seas behind the ship. But at first glance, there was nothing. No hole, no bubbles, certainly no blood.

Nothing to patch. If she could be patched, she could be saved.

The answering thought came in her brother's voice: *If it had been easy, they wouldn't have asked you to help, Ducks.*

Taking out a bulb filled with blue-black squid ink, she squeezed out a drop, then another, working her way along the floor. The first two drops swirled lazily. The third moved and dispersed, propelled by a current coming up from the boards.

She put out a hand, discovered the pressure of inrushing water, and worked her way toward it, seeking its source by touch.

Here, on the hull. She pushed in close. On the wood there was a waxy mark, dark red on the oak boards, barely visible.

It was the outline of a hand.

She held her position, working the light and camera together to get a decent shot of the outline. It was biggish, with a stubby, truncated pinkie.

The red looks waxy, like crayon, she thought.

Releasing her camera—it was tethered—she dug into her tool kit again, selecting a steel scalpel she'd imported from home. Working carefully, she tried to scratch some of the waxy stuff into a test tube. It didn't want to come.

She tried again, pushing harder. If she could pry up a splinter of the wood . . .

Softness, like flesh.

The blade broke a chip of the wax-marked wood loose, but the force of Sophie's hand drove it inside the outline of the hand. Instead of glancing off of more wood, it dug into something with the give of meat.

All at once, the outline came to life, fingers flexing blindly to grab at the scalpel. As it did, the hull gaped and cracked. A surge of cold water pushed inward. The back of the hand, the part that had been outside the ship, was covered in shreds of bloody tissue.

Like Cousin It from the Addams family. No, It's the one with all the hair. Like Thing, just a hand—eww, hand—but grab that splinter . . .

Sophie caught the chunk of wood with its wax smear, tucking it into her sample tube. Kicking, she put some space between herself and the hand. She reeled her camera back, aimed the light, and started recording video.

The incoming water had more force now. She could feel it gushing past, the sensation reminiscent of water jets in a hot tub. As the hand curled in, leaving a deep, five-fingered hole in the hull, Sophie's diving light picked up barnacles, streamers of seaweed, and gory, spongy-looking masses on the back of the hand, the side that had been in the water.

Sophie snagged a hunk of red tissue, too, clipping it into another specimen flask without taking her eyes off the hand.

The outline on the boards was growing now, the drawn edges of the wrist extending as if someone was there, drawing in both lines with crayon. The hand grew a wrist, then a forearm. It bent at the elbow, and the boards of the hull reshaped themselves into an arm. It lashed about as it groped at the inside of the ship.

Sophie swam farther back. The thing, as it detached itself, was ripping ever-greater holes into the bottom of *Kitesharp.*

What happens when it grows a head?

It'd be dumb to wait around and find out, wouldn't it? She kicked back to the ladder. The tenner, Vale, was timing seconds and measuring water rise.

"Anything, Kir?"

She spat out her rebreather. "Found a monster! Up, up!"

A shudder ran through the ship, accompanied by a sound of splintering wood so loud it drowned out Vale's reply. He offered Sophie his hand.

The incline of the deck grew more steep by the minute as they charged to the nearest ladder out of the hold.

"You first, Kir." The kid drew a shortsword.

Sophie fought an impulse to argue. What was she going to do, fight a monster in her diving rig?

Another splinter. The deck below them cracked, splitting up the middle. The ship listed sharply to starboard.

"Teeth!" Vale cursed. "Ship's cross-cut!"

They scrambled out onto the deck.

The blood slick around *Kitesharp* had become a dense red puddle, a crimson smear broken by tissue and bits of debris. Shark fins stirred in the murk. A boarding plank, extended from *Shepherd,* was stretched across the gap between the two ships. A half-dozen of Xianlu's crew stood ready, waiting for Sophie and her escort.

The ship began to buck, as if something big had taken hold and was shaking it.

"There!" Sophie pointed, as the wooden hands rose to the main deck, one after another, the leading edge of a wooden body covered in gore and seaslime, pushing up through the hatch as if it were forcing itself through a birth canal.

"Wood fright!" someone shouted.

"This far asea? How did it seed?"

The deck heaved. The hatch broke in zigzag fissures. As the hands came down onto the deck they seemed to stick—roots grew from the wooden palms into the planks, and the fright had to rip them out, causing more damage.

It did not breathe. A person would have been panting with effort, but this, whatever it was, had the eerie stillness of a store mannequin.

Sophie trained her camera on it as it raised its head.

Are its eyes covered in moss?

The thing began to stride across the crumbling deck of *Kitesharp,* ripping holes in the boards as its feet fell and rooted, rose and tore loose. It made straight for *Shepherd.*

Sophie could feel the bridge underfoot moving as they pulled away. Vale and Xianlu were guiding her so she could keep filming and still move backwards in her flippers. Unless the thing could jump a hell of a long way—*Why couldn't it?*—there was no chance it'd catch them.

"Someone called this a wood sprite?" Xianlu asked.

"Wood *fright,* Septer," someone else corrected. "Used on Mossma, before the ban, to guard forests. And for murders, sometimes."

"Frightmaking's illegal," Vale said.

"I said *before* the ban."

"Was anything like this aboard the other ships?" Sophie asked.

"If so, it sank with them," Xianlu said.

"I think I woke this guy before he was fully baked," Sophie said.

It *was* a guy; the body was unmistakably male, and on the slender side. He had a limp.

A limp and . . . a foreshortened pinky? She zoomed in on its hands.

The thing began to run toward them.

"Gunner battery one! Fire!"

Stormwrack didn't have cannons. They used magically transformed specialists instead. Three sailors stepped up and hurled flaming spheres at the wood fright.

It pulled up short, throwing both arms up to defend its head—giving Sophie a good shot of all ten fingers—and then disappeared in a burst of fire, leaving an appalling stench of scorched meat and campfire behind.

As the smoke from the cannons dispersed, the remains of the sailing mechanics' shop, *Kitesharp,* fell to pieces and vanished beneath the waves.

CHAPTER 2

DEAR BRAM:

SO I'M SITTING ON *CONSTITUTION,* WAITING ON THE BOSS LADY TO GET AROUND TO SEEING ME AND HOPING TO CONVINCE HER TO GO FORWARD WITH OUR FINGERPRINT PROJECT. SHE MIGHT ACQUAINT ME WITH SOME DIVERS, SO THAT I CAN FIND A PARTNER. THEY'D BE MERMAIDS—HOW COOL IS THAT?

I HAVEN'T FOUND ANYTHING TO CONCLUSIVELY INDICATE WHETHER STORMWRACK IS SOME RADICALLY ALTERED FAR FUTURE OF OURS OR A PARALLEL DIMENSION. I'M STILL HOPING WE CAN SEND ARCHAEOLOGISTS TO A SITE ON LAND WHERE SOMETHING FAMOUS HAS BEEN FOUND AT HOME. THERE'S AN ISLAND NEAR THE LATITUDE/LONGITUDE OF THE VALLEY OF THE KINGS. WE COULD TRY TO TALK SOMEONE INTO SEARCHING FOR KING TUT'S TOMB. IF ALL THAT STUFF LORD CARNARVON AND HOWARD CARTER DUG UP IN 1922 WAS WAITING, UNDERGROUND—THAT WOULD DEFINITELY PROVE WE'RE IN A PARALLEL WORLD, RIGHT?

IT WOULD BE TRICKY—WHAT ISN'T TRICKY HERE? WE'D NEED SOMEONE WITH EXPERTISE WHO WANTED TO DIG THEM, NOT TO MENTION PERMISSION, BUT IT'S THE BEST IDEA I'VE HAD SO FAR.

Figuring out whether Stormwrack was simply the future was important, because whatever had wiped out or submerged most of the Earth's continental landmass had obviously been devastating. Was their home staring down the barrel of a bunch of massive comet strikes? The chances of those hypothetical strikes happening within their own lifetimes was vanishingly small—she and Bram estimated a ten-thousand-year window for such an event—but neither of them could let go of the possibility.

HOW ARE MOM AND DAD DOING? DID YOU GIVE THEM MY LETTER? YOU HAVEN'T SAID—

"Kir Sophie?"

She looked up from the letter she was writing into the impassive, big-eyed face of a government functionary from the nation of Verdanii. "Hi, Bettona."

"Convenor Gracechild will see you now."

Annela Gracechild was part of the government of the Fleet of Nations, a congress of two hundred and fifty sovereign countries, island nations clinging to the archipelagos of land that remained within the enormous seas that covered most of the world.

Sophie hadn't set out to abandon ordinary life in San Francisco, to forge a path, alone, on a strange world. But six weeks earlier she'd been given a choice: stay, now, and make a place for herself . . . or never come back.

Stormwrack's very existence was a whopper of a scientific discovery. And given the lingering chance that it was Earth's future, that a disaster was on the horizon . . . Despite the risks, she'd stayed.

Her brother had returned to San Francisco to follow up their research into the connection between Earth and Stormwrack and—just as important—to ensure their parents didn't report them both missing.

As for Sophie's half sister, Verena, and the crew of the sailing vessel *Nightjar*: Annela had sent them off on an unofficial diplomatic mission.

Sophie had been working to endear herself to Annela, who clearly had veto power over Sophie getting the Stormwrack equivalent of a green card. Agreeing to poke into the serial attacks on the Fleet's civilian ships had seemed, at the time, like a good way to make her case.

It hadn't occurred to her that she might fail.

Now she got up, exchanged bobs with the assistant—she was getting better at the Fleet bow—and followed her belowdecks to a cabin that looked, to Sophie, like an autumn-colored bordello. Orange silks hung from the walls, hiding the boards. Dark-brown cushions, embroidered with fallen leaves, covered most of the surfaces.

Annela Gracechild lay at the center of the nest. She was in her sixties, tall and curvy, with copper skin and so much self-confidence it barely left room in the cabin for air.

"Welcome," Annela said, declining to rise. Bettona set out a tray—tall cylindrical cups of thrown pottery, a steaming pot of anise-scented tea, and a plate of fresh-baked apricot biscuits and salted walnut sticks that reminded Sophie of pretzels. One of Bettona's cuffs was dusted with flour, hinting she had done the baking herself.

"Sit, girl."

Sophie said, "Are you sick?"

Annela gave her a flat look that might have meant anything from *Thanks a lot for saying I look like crap* to *Not in front of the servants, dear.*

"Fasting," she said. "Now, what of *Kitesharp*?"

Sophie filled her in on the morning's events, holding out the camera so Annela could see the wooden fright with its mossy green eyes. "I'm not sure how much I can offer—it's obviously magic at work."

"Reminds me of the salt creatures you fought on that bandit ship, *Incannis,*" Annela said. "Short lived, somewhat mindless, used for mischief—"

"This one can't cross the deck of the ship without rooting into the wood," Sophie said. The tea wasn't the usual, she noted—the anise flavor was strong. "If a thing like this has an intended habitat, I'm guessing this isn't it."

Annela nodded. "Yet tearing apart the ships' hulls and sinking them seems to be the point."

Sophie braced herself for a reprimand for having hastened the ship's demise. When none came, she went on. "The drawn outline of the hand is off—there's something wrong with the little finger. I suggested Septer Xianlu have a glance at all the *Kitesharp* crew."

"In case someone's missing a digit?"

"And walks funny. The fright had a limp."

Annela looked at Bettona, who made a note.

"I also have a sample of the waxy stuff. It might be testable."

"Your brother can send you instructions for performing an alchemical knowing, can he not?" Annela asked.

"Chemical identification," Sophie corrected. "Maybe. If the supplies exist here. There's also this." She held up the plastic container containing the bit of bloody tissue, preserved in denatured alcohol. "It's gross, but I wonder if this might not be uterine tissue."

Annela looked it over. "Looks like it. I suppose there's no way to be sure."

"There might be," Sophie said. *There's no way to be sure* was rapidly becoming her least favorite phrase. "I'll need to talk to a doctor."

"An outland doctor?"

"You must have obstetricians here," Sophie said. "The whole thing had an icky birth vibe to it. The blood trail, the way the fright pushed its way up through the ship—"

"The Fleet decries frightmaking; there was an international effort to stamp out the known inscriptions, perhaps fifty years ago. There'd been an incident, on Tug Island, I believe. Thousands of them, running riot." Annela handed back the sample. "I seem to recall the spells require a subject, someone to provide a . . ." Her hands moved, shaping a figure.

"A template?"

"Yes."

"Is there anyone who'd know?"

"You could ask that last bandit from *Incannis,* the one who attacked you. He's aboard *Docket,* awaiting trial," Annela said. "Request a visitor's pass from the judiciary."

Sophie nodded without enthusiasm. Her birth father had captured the sailor in question, while slaughtering all of his crewmates. She could do without any hard reminders of that particular bloodbath. "Yeah. Or . . . is there a listing or index of spells? Something that would talk about frightmaking?"

"Perhaps some trial minutes persist, from the cases related to the effort to eliminate the practice. You want your pet memorician to look at them?" Annela said.

"Is that a problem?"

"As far as I can tell, you can find a reason to want access to every piece of information, true or false, ever recorded."

"It's not my fault everyone here thinks curiosity's some kind of personality defect," Sophie said.

"Cultural flaw, rather," Annela corrected.

"So I'm not broken, I'm just—"

"Savage. Just so."

"Thanks a lot, Annela."

"To get back to your wood fright: I mentioned the bandit ship and the salt frights because of the effort to stamp out such spellwriting. There can't be that many active frightmakers."

Based on what evidence? "You really believe that whoever made that ship with the salt zombies might be the same person who attacked *Kitesharp*?"

"It's the same behavior, isn't it? Sinking ships and attacking their crews?"

Sophie nodded. "How to prove it, though, that's the thing."

Annela gave a little shoulder twitch, the common gesture that seemed to mean *Don't know, don't care.* "Seems probable enough."

"It's *probable enough* and *we'll never know* that are gumming up your court system," Sophie said. "The point of using me is supposed to be about bringing a little *definitely* and *for sure* into the mix. Not to mention *case closed.*"

Annela tsked. "How much progress have you made? This Forensic Institute of yours promised great things to the peoples of the Fleet, but what you've accomplished is little more than a well-trained agent of the Watch might have managed."

"And yet didn't." Sophie didn't quite hide her sense of insult. It was Annela's way, she knew, to look at a horse-size success and complain because it wasn't an elephant. "Anyway, since you ask, I have a proposal."

"Do you indeed?"

Snagging an apricot biscuit, Sophie pulled out a wad of two-page briefs—a tiny fraction of the Fleet's ongoing bureaucratic logjams.

"What are these?"

Sophie passed them to Bettona, who started leafing through the pages.

"Five or six times a year, someone disappears from Fleet," Sophie said. "They desert, or fall overboard, or whatever. And about every three months, bodies turn up in the ocean. Sometimes they're identifiable, sometimes not."

Annela nodded. "That's life asea."

"These files are petitions by families," Bettona said. "Requests for death benefits for Fleet recruits who've gone missing but are not proved dead."

"And?"

"I've learned that the Fleet takes handprints from its new cadets," Sophie said. "You've even used them a couple times to confirm someone's identity. But it's basically been a matter of getting lucky. Some random officer compares the corpse's prints with the ten most likely missing people. If it happens to look like a match, then hurrah. If not, you're all 'Alas, we can't figure it out.' Eventually, you get one of these lawsuits."

"Petitions," Bettona corrected.

"You can do better, Sophie?"

"Fingerprint identification is an established forensic practice, back home. What if I got the Fleet fingerprint files on the missing people, took the prints of the 'found sailors,' as you call them—"

"The bodies, you mean."

"Yeah. And trained some Watch people so they could create the beginning of a fingerprint bureau?"

"What's to keep you from falsifying matches?"

"Excellent question," she said, managing to hang on to her smile. "The answer is, the Fleet gives us the prints of all the missing individuals but mixes them into a number of other handprint samples. Say five hundred or a thousand. They don't tell us who's who."

"You believe you can pick the missing individuals out of the larger pool?"

"Totally."

"Without magic?"

"Say the Watch gives me a few people and I train them in dactyloscopy. If each of us comes up with the same matches, independently, and if the personnel files they match correspond to missing individuals instead of Joe Random Sailor—"

"That would be convincing," Annela conceded.

"Convincing?" Sophie said. "Get excited, Annela! It'd be impressive!"

Annela couldn't quite hide a smile. "This is something you know how to do?"

"Ah. There's the catch." She laid out how far they had gotten to date. Bram had assembled information on the procedures. They were both pretty sure Sophie could pick it up. "When the technique originally propagated on Erstwhile, a lot of cops managed to work it out by using textbooks and writing to each other."

Annela glowered at the apricot biscuits. "Then this is a ploy to get a transit visa to your home nation."

"It's not a ploy," Sophie said. "I don't ploy. You already know I want to go home."

"And come back. And go again."

"I'm happy to bring forensics to Stormwrack, but it's not all up here." She tapped her head. "You can't ask me for help, cut me off at the knees, and then carp about lack of results."

"Is that what I do?"

"If I can teach the Watch to identify fingerprints, it'll have tons of other uses. At home, prints are used to solve crimes, not just identify bodies."

"How?"

Sophie picked up one of the cookies. It was warm, moist, just a bit oily. Then she rolled her thumb over the teacup, leaving a visible print. "You can find prints like this everywhere. The natural oils in our skin make them. This one's visible, but the Watch can learn to pick up prints that can't be seen."

"To what end?"

"A print match can prove where someone's been, or whether they touched a . . . say, a weapon. It can place someone at a crime scene after they've sworn they were never there."

"Impossible!" Bettona said.

"Seriously. It's a whole thing, back home. Very reliable." Reading the doubt on their faces, she scooped up a carefully polished letter opener, made of lacquered wood, with a visible—if smudged—partial print on it. "This is probably yours, Bettona. Want me to see if I can prove it?"

"No parlor tricks. Not now." Annela rubbed her temples. A clock ticked loudly, somewhere close, and the seconds clunking by made it seem as though the older woman was taking forever. To hide her impatience, Sophie ate another of the cookies.

Finally, Annela said, "It seems a more comprehensible procedure than the identity coding you tried to explain."

"There's no way you can do DNA analysis here. Anyway, about the sailors' bodies. Wouldn't that be good PR? If you start paying out pensions to the families, instead of wrangling over it while they suffer?"

"Mm-m-m," Annela said.

She's going to say yes. Sophie was elated. "There are things I have to go home and learn. Plus, I can't just vanish on my family."

"What will you bring to Erstwhile, while you're landing there to acquire esoteric knowledge on uterine tissue and corpse fingers?"

Sophie fought to keep her mouth shut. She could protest that she'd keep Stormwrack's existence a secret, but Annela would just come back with the inconvenient truth: Sophie had told her brother, the first chance she got. Besides, she *was* hoping to talk the government here into loosening up on the secrecy. Sooner or later, she and Bram had to get more experts from Earth in on researching this world.

First things first. This was the first step, and she sensed, at long last, some give in Annela.

"You've shown this new branch of study has its uses," Annela conceded. "The Watch has a few lamentably curious work pairs who are excited by your results. If they like this proposal of yours, they'll recommend it to the court. You would work with the adjudication branch, continuing as you have been, investigating stalled cases that might be resolved by . . ."

"Evidence? Proof?"

"You would have increased accountability and a higher degree of support.

Salaries for you, your memorician, these apprentice fingerprint investigators you ask for, perhaps a clerk or two."

"What about a role for Bram?" She wasn't eager to expose her brother to Stormwrack and its dangers, but it wasn't her call, and she'd promised to ask.

"Depending on the cases in question. You would also be permitted to make periodic visits to Erstwhile."

"Awesome!" A flood of relief—she almost teared up. Remaining in Fleet had been a gamble, but she'd been afraid to go home until she had official permission to travel between the worlds.

There had always been a chance Annela would never let her go home.

"Before you get too excited, you should know you would have to take the Oath of Service to the Fleet of Nations."

Wrackers and their oaths and agreements. "Which promises what?"

Annela nodded at Bettona, who said, "You would be, in essence, an agent of the court. You would report to the judiciary, act in their interest, enforce the law, maintain government confidences—"

"Doesn't sound too major."

"The consequences, when you break oath, will be severe," Annela said. "You couldn't recover from them as you have from your other blunders."

Blunders. Telling Bram about Stormwrack and magic. Returning when she'd been told to stay away. Getting into a big fight with her birth father over his stupid country of origin and its evil laws—

"What makes you think I'd break oath?"

"You broke your contract with your father within weeks of leaving for Sylvanna," Annela said.

"Yeah, because you didn't tell me he was taking me to the Old South slave plantation from hell!"

"Hell . . . ?"

Sophie sighed. Thanks to magic, she was perfectly fluent in the language of the Fleet, but on occasion she spat out an English euphemism that confused people. Hell, here, was the capital city of another island nation.

Parrish's island nation.

"Forget it," she said, unsure if she was responding to Annela or to the inner voice that brought up Garland at every opportunity.

"One can only fight nature for so long, Sophie," Annela said. "You've freely shared your opinion that the Fleet's values are antiquated and ridiculous. You are bound at some point to prefer your judgment over our rules—"

"How can you say that? I lived just fine in the outlands, as you call them, without ever once going on a crime spree. I barely even break the speed limit when I drive!"

"What will you do when one of your experiments benefits your enemies?"

"I don't have enemies."

"No? There are the men who kidnapped and tortured your brother."

"I—" It was a slap. "Science doesn't lie. Innocent's innocent. Guilty's—"

"I'm not trying to be unkind, Sophie. You've said yourself you have no talent for discretion."

"I said I'm a bad liar. That's different."

"Is it? I believe you will always put how you feel before the facts and rule of law. I fear, deep down, you are contemptuous of our system."

I'm not gonna cry. Sophie toyed with another of the apricot biscuits. "Then why let me go forward?"

"I cannot punish you for oathbreaking until you do it."

"That's how it is? 'Here's a rope. Let's see how long it takes you to hang yourself.'"

"We'd say, 'Here's a rope. Go loop a sinking anchor.' But yes."

This woman is going to be out to get me until the day I die.

"So, what? Can I do this now? I raise my hand and solemnly swear to—"

"Your lawyer must read the documents. We need assurance that you understand what you're agreeing to. After that, there's a swearing in every two days."

"Fine."

A hint of concern etched itself on Annela's face. "You shouldn't do this."

"You shouldn't have promised me I'd fail."

"Striving to prove me wrong is a childish reason to take an oath. But I won't stop you. Do you want to interview that bandit about frights?"

Reluctance rose again, but Sophie quashed it. "Yes."

"I'll file an application. Is there anything else?"

"We talked about me checking out one of those mermaid training drills." Ever since she'd come to Stormwrack, she'd been diving without a proper partner . . . emphatically not a trend she wished to continue.

There was an expression, back home: *Dive alone, die alone.* Sophie liked an adventure as much as anyone, but she didn't want to become an object lesson in the truth of catchy safety slogans.

"Bette, go find that note of introduction for the diving captain."

"At once, Convenor." Bettona disappeared, taking the thumbprinted letter opener with her.

"Well, Sophie? Are we done?"

"Why are you fasting?"

Annela's head came up, barely showing surprise. "It is," she said, "an ordeal set by the Verdanii people."

Religion, then? "Oh. Um. Thanks for telling me."

"It's common knowledge, or I wouldn't."

"The cookies and nut sticks were all for me?"

"Take them with you. I'm not sure why Bettona made so many, but I'd prefer they didn't go to waste. Calm seas, girl."

" 'Bye," she said, bowing herself out.

Constitution was a ship of bureaucrats, which meant that to her fore there was a law library. It was a bright room, filled with small desks and plush velvet chairs. Half of these were pointed at the smoky obsidian portals of the lounge, revealing a tinted view of the ocean. Two ships were visible to *Constitution*'s fore. *Temperance* was the flagship and iron fist of the Fleet, a sharkskinned behemoth with smokestacks rather than sails and almost no glass at all. She was an important symbol of the peace that had reigned between the two hundred and fifty island nations for more than a century. Her captain could sink any ship afloat, simply by speaking its full name aloud.

Step out of line, start a war with your neighbor, and glug, doomed, sunk. A deterrent.

The second ship was *Breadbasket*.

Each nation had one official Fleet ship, and *Breadbasket* was Verdanii, the representative ship of Annela's people. Sophie's birth mother and half sister were Verdanii. She might be, too, if she hadn't repudiated citizenship in a weird government hearing eight months earlier. She was officially persona non grata on her birth mother's home island.

As for her birth father . . .

No. She wouldn't think about Cly.

Where *Temperance* was sharky, *Breadbasket* was a whale ship of sorts—she had a baleen and a tail. Her masts were live trees, red-trunked palms skirted in sails of woven corn silk and inhabited by jewel-toned insects that served some kind of pollinating function for the crops growing on every available deck of the ship.

She was a great oceangoing farm, in other words—a floating cornucopia, a symbol of her nation's great wealth. Verdanii was the nation with the most landmass, the agricultural giant of the world.

Rooting in her satchel, Sophie started, as she often did, with the notebook filled with questions about Stormwrack and Earth.

Opening it, she paged through, scanning the endless list of mysteries before adding a couple new thoughts: HOW DO YOU ID UTERINE TISSUE IN AS? AS, her abbreviation for Age of Sail, was an imperfect description of Stormwrack's technological state—except when it meant Age of Superstition or Age of Just Plain Stupid.

ARE THE BUGS IN *Breadbasket's* SAILS ACRIDIDAE OR NEUROPTERA? WHAT'S A VERDANII ORDEAL? WHAT'S THE VERDANII BELIEF SYSTEM?

IS IT AN EARWORM, OR AM I STILL HEARING THAT DAMNED TICKING CLOCK FROM ANNELA'S OFFICE?

When she ran out of things to wonder, she pulled out the letter she had already begun to Bram.

The note was written on messageply. As soon as she had written the words, an hour ago, they'd turned up on a twin sheet in San Francisco, where her brother was. He had obviously read them in the meantime; there was an answering message right below the spot where she'd stopped.

> GOOD IDEA RE THE ARCHAEOLOGIST. WILL LOOK OVER THE MAP AND READ UP ON EGYPTIAN SITES. BTW: 5.

BTW: "I miss you." With a number, five out of five. To save messageply, they'd stopped putting the words in.

Sophie found herself smiling. Like him, she skipped the "I miss you" and started with:

> 5 TO YOU TOO. I S/B VISITING SOON IF ALL GOES WELL. AG AGREES I NEED FINGERPRINTING INFO.

A shadow fell between her and the tinted view of the sea.

Looking up, Sophie found herself staring at the official government representative of Isle of Gold.

Convenor Brawn looked ancient: he was bald, with skin cured to leather by years under a hot sun. His longcoat was made of red velvet, embroidered in gold and, today, belted with a chain of dangling gold skulls. His seven-foot frame was balanced on high boots and a cane that looked like ivory. His fingernails were four inches long—that seemed to be an Isle of Gold thing—and had been artificially straightened to resemble knife blades. Opals were embedded in the nails.

OMG, what do you want? Sophie managed to strangle the impulse to say this.

Take that, Annela. I can be discreet.

Had Annela arranged this? She'd thrown Bram's kidnapping in Sophie's face only half an hour before. Now here was the man who'd almost certainly ordered it.

They'd shoved a black pearl under Bram's thumbnail with a needle.

Rage gnawed at her resolve to keep quiet. To gather herself, she looked past Brawn, taking in the Fleet page attending him. She seemed to be Golder, too. She had extravagantly long red hair, curly and colored black just at its fringes, and enormous brown eyes. She was about Sophie's age, which seemed old for a page. Maybe she'd failed her exams.

Sophie turned on her camera, out of habit, taking a few shots of them both. Neither of them showed the least curiosity about what she was doing.

"Kir Hansa," Brawn purred into the silence. "We haven't met formally. I am Convenor Brawn from Isle of Gold."

"Uh-huh." She slapped her notebook shut and stood. *If I knew all the nuances of bowing, I could give him some kind of snooty "screw you" half-bob.* Out of perversity, she curtsied.

As he was bowing himself, he missed it, or affected to. "May I offer you a glass of wine? Perhaps you prefer Verdanii beer?"

"I'm—um—full."

"Straight to business then, *oui*?"

"We have business?"

He pointed a claw at a chair and the girl moved, sliding the seat under Brawn's bony backside as he perched on its cushion. "I am following your career. This forensic practice, and the court cases you've been grooming."

"Uh . . . thank you?"

"Isle of Gold is a great nation, and we are fastidious about certain cultural practices. One such is self-reflection. I've concluded that you bested me in the Convene eight months ago."

"I certainly kept you from getting what you wanted," she said. There had been a plot to disenchant *Temperance,* to destroy the spell that made it such a lethal ship-killing weapon.

"Indeed. You threw my plans to dry dock."

She had mixed feelings about having preserved the government's big military deterrent. But back in the day, when *Temperance* first set sail, she had driven Brawn's people out of the piracy racket. The ship had been the instrument by which hundreds of lives were saved.

"It is our tradition to offer someone who has bested us a boon."

Sophie laughed. "You want to do me a favor?"

"Best me one time, I reward you. A measure of respect. Best me twice, and we are enemies *toutta demonde* . . . forever."

"You kidnapped my brother."

"Careful. Openly declaring me a foe would be unwise."

She clenched her fists under the table, taking him in, looking for hints of secrets, of weakness, anything that might tell her what he wanted, or how she could . . . how had he put it? Best him again.

Brawn's eye had fallen on Sophie's book of questions. She fought the urge to close or hide it. He almost certainly couldn't read English, and there were no secrets there anyway.

Instead of snatching it away, she said, "This is a ritual way of saying . . . what? 'No hard feelings'?"

"Yes, nicely put. No hard feelings." He rolled that around, as if tasting it. "It is an opportunity for both parties to sail away from bloody feud."

"What if I never collect on the favor but I cross you again?"

"Then, in the moment before your destruction, I shall offer you a kindness. The traditional choice offered is between painless death or payment to your kin. It's a matter of honor—a concept, I'm given to understand, that you don't cherish."

Maybe he was trying to provoke her so they could go straight to the feuding. "What could you possibly have that I'd want?"

"A Golder spouse and citizen's papers?"

"You want to marry me into the Piracy?" She couldn't help it—she began to laugh. "OMG."

"It's rumored, Kir Sophie, that cased in that self-righteous exterior of yours is the heart of a rogue. It's said you take after ye *perre* . . . your father."

"My father the Supreme Court judge?"

"Your father the killer."

You are trying to pick a fight. Sophie's gaze dropped to the book of questions. She should send the guy packing.

But if he knows stuff . . .

"How about this? I first came here after John Coine traveled to the . . . outlands to buy grenades and assassinate my aunt."

"What's that to me?"

She leaned forward. "What if I wanted to know how he got there? The Verdanii seem to think they're the only ones who—" She wasn't allowed to talk about Earth explicitly. But Brawn was involved. He *had* to know. " Who know the route to the grenade store."

"You're asking for information."

"Yep."

"If I cut you, girl, will you bleed knowledge?"

Gooseflesh rose on her arms. "Do you know?"

He got up, sweeping his lace sleeves over the table as he levered himself upward. "I will do as you ask, soon as you've taken the Oath."

That didn't go how you thought it would, did it? Sophie thought. She knew why, too: suddenly everyone's big predictions about what she would or wouldn't do had fallen into place. Annela figured she'd break her oath because Annela assumed Sophie would think like a Verdanii. Or, perhaps, like a savage outlander.

Brawn had expected her to go into some kind of emo fit, insulting him sufficiently that he could move forward with his vendetta. Now, instead . . .

He uttered a few words in yet another new language, one with a few tantalizingly French-sounding cadences, and then said, "Sophie Hansa, child of outland, daughter of Sylvanna, I hereby commit. Once this boon is delivered, the two of us may sit in comfort and declare a peace." With that, he caned himself away, drawing in his wake the curly-haired page—who shot Sophie a glare as she went.

Heart pounding, Sophie collapsed back into the reading room chair. Now she needed more legal advice: if Brawn was willing to tell her something after she got herself oathed up, it might mean she couldn't legally act on it.

I should just learn the Fleet laws.

When she had first arrived on Stormwrack, it had been by accident. She'd washed up on an island of poverty-stricken fishers, with her half-dead aunt in tow. The island spellscribe had written an inscription to teach her the language of the Fleet.

The spell made her perfectly fluent. She spoke the language without a trace of an accent; she spoke it better than many lifetime residents of the oceangoing city, most of whom had learned it as a second language. All it had cost her was a ripping headache.

She added LEARN THE LAW? to a new page in her notebook and began to consider routes that would take her in the direction of her lawyer. In a city where every block was a ship on the move, even the simplest errands were a series of hops, complex exercises in logistics. If you took an airborne taxi here, you could catch lunch while waiting on a ferry to somewhere else. Residents called it footwork: if you could do ten errands in three transits, you were "light on your feet."

Bram had jotted another note onto the messagepy: CAN U C A STICK FIGURE?

She replied, NO. WHY?

Him: TRYING TO PROJECT TEXT ONTO MESSAGEPLY WITHOUT WRITING.

Her: NOTHING THERE.

Should she tell him about her encounter with Brawn?

What about now?

She scratched the word STILL in front of the "Nothing there" from earlier.

Then, instead of making for the legal quarter, she packaged up Annela's paperwork, took up a page of cheap, unmagical paper, and wrote to her lawyer, Mensalohm, explaining about the offered deal and her idea of learning the law. She flagged a page and asked him to have it delivered.

She sent a second note to Krispos—her "pet memorician," as Annela had called him:

> GOOD NEWS—YOU'RE OFFICIALLY ON THE JUDICIARY PAYROLL. PLEASE READ UP ON ISLE OF GOLD TRADITIONS ABOUT BLOOD FEUDS, FAVORS, AND CHALLENGES. ALSO, SEE WHAT YOU CAN LEARN ABOUT FRIGHTMAKING.

She took a moment to savor that. Krispos was a magically enhanced speed-reader with perfect recall. He had been foundering in a state of impoverished semi-unemployment for about five years. Even the *prospect* of having a real job within Fleet made the old fellow tear up.

She'd done all she could aboard *Constitution*. Taking her note of introduction from Annela, she caught a ferry to *Vaddle,* the diving vessel.

CHAPTER 3

Dear Sophie:
Bram says he can forward you the occasional short message. I can't say either Dad or I understands why you can't use e-mail. It makes me imagine you're on a compound, somewhere remote like Bora Bora, diving the Great Barrier Reef. Still . . . no access to Internet? Is mail truly coming in bundles by boat or something whenever someone putt-putts out to civilization?

If this seems preposterous, you'll have to send a few facts to sharpen up my imaginings. Surely we could be permitted to know which hemisphere you're in?

You know, when I left home to go to university in Oxford, I did this all the time—wrote paper letters home to Grandma and Grandpa. I don't remember it being this difficult. Well. All's fine here. The main thing is, I suppose, that Dad and I are thinking of going to Peru in late August. If there's any chance you'll be back then, let us know so we can make different plans. We don't want to miss you.

Love,
Mom

PS from B—Sorry this is dull, Sofe—I told her no guilt and no questions or I wouldn't send it.

Mermaid training turned out to be rather horrifying.

The Fleet used a leaky-looking sailing vessel called *Vaddle* (which apparently meant "hatchery," in one of the Fleet's many tongues) for its undersea soldiering detachment.

It was a ship of swimming pools. One was square, divided into lanes, where ordinary two-legged cadets swam lengths, practiced rescues, and worked on their endurance. There was also a resistance pool in which senior cadets worked on becoming even stronger swimmers.

Belowdecks were the transforms.

The training master was a sunburned veteran with a desiccated fish tail, Sollo Mykander. Out of the water, she seemed to live in a peculiar hammock chair, carried wherever she wished by a strapping six-foot sailor. The remains of her tail were a mix of silver and rust; the tattered scales put Sophie in mind of an old pat of steel wool. A damp silk tank top clung to her sagging breasts and belly.

"The great 'Nella Gracechild says I'm to tour you about," Sollo said. As she talked, she sponged salt water onto the salmon gills under her chin. The skin was spotted and unhealthy looking.

Keeping her eyes on Sollo's face, Sophie explained, "I'm a diver from the outlands. I want to see how it's done here."

"We've a treat for you, then. We're making a new mer today, if you're interested."

New? "Totally interested!"

"You—Octer Weld—show this curiosity to the birth tank. I'll be down momentarily."

The cadet led Sophie down through the stench of rotting timbers and dying fish to a candlelit room where a complicated spellwriting operation was ramping up. A flaxen-haired six-year-old—Sophie wasn't sure whether it was a girl or a boy—was waiting on a beige couch. Nearby, a pair of individuals who looked to be a spellscribe and his apprentice were prepping a writing table. The material for the inscription was a yard-square sheet of sedimentary shale. Sophie saw a small coelacanth fossil within it.

Fossils! She added a note to her book of questions. ARE THERE FOSSIL VENDORS? WHERE DO THEY DIG? WHAT ELSE HAVE THEY FOUND?

Was there a way to use the fossil record to better understand the link between Stormwrack and Earth?

The cadet spoke to the scribe, clarifying Sophie's observer status.

He offered her a gap-toothed smile. "Best view's over there, Kir."

"Thank you." Before retreating to the designated viewing spot, she took a few photos of the spellwriting space. It contained an assortment of materials—picks, brushes, inks, and paints.

As she came around the sheet of shale, she saw that the remainder of the chamber was dominated by a pair of deep, cylindrical tanks, one of which held a healthy merman.

Merman!

Pick your jaw up off the floor, Sofe. She'd seen stranger things, but how could anyone tire of the miraculous? She raised the camera again.

The second pool contained a circling fish—bluefish, Sophie thought. A forty-pounder, at least.

Sollo arrived in the hammock-chair, still hefted by the strapping sailor. "Are we set?"

Everyone nodded.

She bent to take the child's hands. "What do we say?"

"Endure the dark." The kid was calm, almost disturbingly placid. "*Questi ordeale,* and dawn again wondrous."

Ordeale, Sophie thought. Annela had been fasting for an ordeal.

"Pearl?"

One of the spellscribes handed Sollo a pearl, dime-size in diameter. She shined it with a soft rag, showing it to the child, who examined it solemnly before nodding. Then the big guy carried Sollo over to Sophie's corner.

"Let us begin." Sollo tossed the pearl into the tank with the fish.

A splash. The scribe chipped letters into the stone tablet. The kid rolled off the couch.

He's paraplegic, Sophie realized as the blanket fell away. He began to drag his withered legs, using arm strength, to the pool containing the fish and the pearl.

"It can be hard to watch," Sollo said. Sophie's face must have showed her reaction; maybe she'd made a noise. "We're young when we change. It makes the intention easier to bear. But to watch a child do this . . ."

Record and observe.

She swallowed. "Was he born paralyzed?"

"Yes. On Ualtar. Many nations expose their imperfect young, but children with this particular trouble are welcomed aboard *Vaddle* at birth. Not me, though. I was injured in an accident at age two. I had to apply."

"There must be other birth defects, then, that have . . . magical uses?"

"Oh, yes. There are intentions one can work on a deaf baby, or one with not much mind."

"No choice offered to them, I suppose."

Sollo shrugged. "Magic fashions the otherwise unfit."

Unfit. She had disabled friends, at home, who'd have plenty to say about that attitude.

Her doubts must have shown on her face, because Sollo added, "I'd rather have had my life asea than none at all. Or to have spent years being hauled about, as I am now, like a sack of salt."

By now the boy had crawled to the edge of the pool. With a practiced move, he rolled his lower body into the water.

The bluefish struck, rising out of the tank, glomming on to the boy's barely submerged feet, driving itself up his legs, gulping.

Sophie cried out. The child's eyes were swimming with tears, but he clenched his jaw—*Brave little guy!*—and actually pushed himself into the water, shoving himself farther down the fish's gullet.

The bluefish was distended now, stretched. Sophie could see the shape of the child's legs, the fish sleeved over them, more a rubber suit, less a living thing. With a final thrash, it struggled to reach the boy's waist and bit—really bit—down. Curls of blood swirled in the water, and Sophie thought of the wounded ship *Kitesharp.*

The weight of the fish tipped the boy off the edge of the pool. He treaded water for all he was worth.

The merman in the adjacent pool uncoiled, catching the boy's hands.

Dust and chips of stone flew in every direction, clattering on the deck, as the scribes carved text into the shale.

The merman checked the edge of the bluefish's lips—the punctures left by the teeth. He had a look to see that the boy's navel remained exposed, then folded the fish's flesh upward at the boy's pelvis. He bandaged the join with something that looked like seaweed.

Sophie was reminded of her mother straightening Sophie's dress on school picture day.

But Mo-o-om, I want to wear my soccer uniform.

They murmured together, man and boy, checking everything. The boy was pale, but Sophie was struck again by his courage.

When they seemed to agree that the fit of the fish was correct, the merman looked at the scribe.

"Ready?"

"Proceed."

Using a curved stone knife, the merman cut into the bluefish's head, scooping out its brain.

"Big breath," he said, and the kid sucked air. Then, turning awkwardly in the water, his paralyzed legs weighted with forty-odd pounds of dying fish, the boy dove, making for the pearl at the bottom of the tank.

He didn't come up.

"Here is where our nerve most commonly breaks," Sollo said. "To wait, until breath fails, to take the mouth of the sea . . ."

"He's gonna drown?" *Freaking out, Bram,* she thought. *Five out of five freaking—*

"If he tries to rise before the spines join and the gills move up . . ." Sollo drew her fingers over her own throat, then Sophie's. "Sittler will hold him under."

"That's awful!"

"Yes, but necessary. If he fails now, he bleeds to death of his wounds. I had to be held," Sollo said. "It's a badge of pride to have the nerve, but . . ."

The boy had made it to the bottom and was searching for the pearl amid the bits and pieces of shell.

Sophie fought the temptation to look away. She had felt like this before, on shoots, when she was recording predators. Witnessing the death of an animal—holding a shot in focus as orcas bumped seals off ice floes, for example—had never been her favorite part of the job.

It's truth. You're capturing an important truth, she told herself. *Count to thirty. Hold the shot.*

The boy wrapped his arms around a jutting piece of stone and blew air out of his lungs.

"Oh, brave! Brave!" Sollo said approvingly.

Sophie felt her teeth grinding. The boy thrashed once more before transforming, in a single liquid shudder. Nearly invisible gills slashed their way into his throat, pink, fresh, and healthy. The length of fish on his spine writhed, tightened. Movement and vitality extended in both directions until the tip of the tail was a live thing and there was no transition anymore, no difference between boy and fish.

Indisputably a single creature now, he surfaced, bursting up into the waiting embrace of the merman with a gush of water from his mouth that turned into a triumphant crow as they hugged.

"Is it done?" Sollo asked.

"Ten minutes for final notations," came the word from the writing desk.

They would finish writing out the intention and then store the tablet somewhere safe. If it was broken, the boy would revert to his earlier state.

"Belowdecks, they're doing agility drills," Sollo said. "If you're interested, Kir?"

Sophie took the hint, packing up and leaving them to finish as the boy tore around the tank, reveling in his transformation.

She observed the agility drills and rescue practice, plus a lecture on hunting. When mers got separated from the Fleet, they could live almost indefinitely by foraging in the wilds of the ocean's photic zones.

DO MERMAIDS DESERT THE FLEET? she wrote in her book. WHERE DO THEY GO?

"Haven't you guys been involved in the bumboat sinkings?" she asked as she was waiting for a ferry to take her on to the rear.

"First boat went down before we could deploy. We were on another mission, the second time, and *Shepherd* had 'er in hand. We thought."

"And *Kitesharp*?"

"I got two in the water for her. Hard seeing, all that blood and growth coming off her stern . . ." Sollo spread her arms. "They saw your fright rip itself off the hull. We'll know what to look for, next time. Ah, there's your taxi!"

Sophie climbed aboard, grateful to be on her way back to the residential block at last.

The block was an apartment building at sea, and Sophie's rented berth within it was a smallish cabin with whitewashed boards, a bunk, and few amenities. The ship had mess halls, reading rooms, a bar, and communal baths. A service brought linens and a jug of fresh water daily, giving the block a faint semblance of a cruise ship. You could pay someone to come in and make the bed, but Sophie had declined to subscribe to a maid service.

They did bring mail, though. Her heart thumped as she pounced on an envelope sealed with navy-blue wax.

It was from *Nightjar*'s captain, Garland Parrish. It began, ever so formally:

Gracious Kir Sophie,

I would generally begin any letter to you with pleasantries about the ship and what we are all doing in your absence, but where we are bound, and why, is no matter for the public post.

I can tell you the seas are calm, and everyone is well. Our new medic, Watts, is popular with the crew, perhaps especially Kir Sweet.

"Why you gossipy thing, you," she murmured.

The cat and ferret are getting along. The crew misses you.

I miss you.

Sophie could hear him saying it, in his serious and too-formal way. The image sent a hum of energy through her. She thought fleetingly of her notes to Bram, the game they'd made of assigning numbers to their feelings: "I miss you . . . seven. Ten. Fifty."

I wish our respective duties had not contrived to separate us so soon after our trip to Issle Morta. We'd barely begun to discover what courting might mean for a pair such as we, and since then I have continued to think about what you've told me about outland "dating" (have I the Anglay correct?).

Perhaps we could go to the outlands and try it there, if either of us could get travel papers for an extended visit to your home.

"It might be easier to get some alone time in San Francisco," Sophie muttered. Shipboard living meant being in other people's pockets constantly.

I know many things remain unsettled between us: our cultural differences, the question of destiny that bothers you so, and the awkwardness with your sister.

Know, if it helps, that I believe we can resolve everything, if only we can devote a little time to each other. Words make a poor measure of how badly I wish to begin.

Verena is bound for Verdanii aboard the great ship Fecund, *and* Nightjar *has set a course for the Fleet. I hope, therefore, to see you soon.*

Yours in bright spirits,
Garland Parrish

She read it twice, then turned it over in her hands, treasuring it. Letting the sensation—rough paper on skin—sink into her consciousness.

The seal of wax, so like something out of a history play, caught her eye.

She pulled out her samples from *Kitesharp*, finding the crumb of red and laying it on her desk. It was just a smudge on the splinter of broken deck. Still, the texture was similar.

Digging in her berth's tiny writing desk, she found her own stick of sealing wax. She bent to the floor of the room, rubbing it on the deck, then trying to draw the outline of her hand.

It wasn't easy, as it would have been if it were actually a crayon, but it worked. The marks had a similar shape—wobbly at the edges, the stroke growing wider as the friction wore down the corner of the stick of wax—and the color seemed identical.

By the time she had taken pictures and made some notes on what she'd done, Bram had run his messageply through someone's old-fashioned typewriter.

YOU SEE THIS, RIGHT?

YES, she wrote.

Next was a printer. AND THIS?

YES, she replied.

KTHXBAI. It took her a second to remember this meant "Okay. Thanks. 'Bye."

Linguistic displacement was happening more and more. She said "Seas!" and "Teeth!" nowadays, in place of English exclamations, which required translation.

Bram would be deep in yet another think about quantum entanglements and how the messageply worked. She glanced at her other page, which was far less active. No word at all from Verena.

She had been fighting the urge to pester her sister, rationalizing that Verena needed space, a little time to get over things, lick her wounds. Now Sophie couldn't hold off anymore:

> GARLAND SAYS YOU'RE NOT ON *NIGHTJAR*—WHAT'S UP? I KNOW EVERYTHING'S PROBABLY FINE BUT CAN YOU LET ME KNOW?

Verena was seventeen and the only other daughter of the woman who had given up Sophie at birth. She had spent her short life training to replace their aunt Gale, a seagoing diplomat-spy for the Fleet, and when Gale was murdered—

Sophie thought of Convenor Brawn again, flashing his long fingernails and offering favors.

Verena had taken over Gale's job. She wasn't especially great at it, not yet, but that hadn't kept Annela from sending her off on *Nightjar* to see if she could convince some rigidly protocol-bound aristocrats to recall a convenor who was clearly suffering from severe mental illness.

Verena was smart, and an amazing swordswoman. She also had a hopeless crush on *Nightjar*'s captain, Garland Parrish.

Garland. Sophie burrowed into her blankets, taking up the letter again, running her finger over the signature. The page was like something from a movie: lettered with perfect scoops and swirls.

"*How badly I wish to begin,*" she read aloud.

Rather than do something schoolgirl silly, like kiss the letter, she turned on the small vid screen on her camera. From there she skipped back—past the boy's transformation to mermaid, past the wood fright chasing her, past stills of her growing collection of coral samples—to her one bit of live footage of Garland.

He hadn't known she was recording him.

Garland Parrish was a stunningly handsome man, with walnut-colored skin, unruly black curls, and a smile that had the tendency to hit Sophie with the mind-stopping intensity of a Taser. In this shot, which she'd viewed so many times she had every frame and hiccup of sound memorized, he was engaged in a deceptively girlish round of jump rope.

Also, he was shirtless.

"We learn this as Fleet cadets," he said, unaware that she'd hit the video setting on her camera and set it on a barrel nearby as he started with just a brisk hop-hop-hop. It was good enough cardio conditioning, a practical form of exercise for the deck of a small ship. "Then, of course, we cross the arms, loop, loop, so . . ."

"Boxers do this, at home." Her own voice, disembodied and distant, emanated from the camera.

Garland looked past the lens. There was the smile—zap!

"Up the ramp . . ."

The ramp was a board set on a wooden fulcrum—a teeter-totter, basically—

and he nimbly skipped, forward and back, from one side to the other, as it tipped back and forth under his weight. "Front, backward, sideways."

His skin started to shine as he worked up a sweat, but he wasn't breathless. Jumping on the midpoint of the teeter-totter, perfectly balanced, he looped the rope around his wrists, taking in slack until he was hopping in a tight crouch. From this lowered position, he crabbed sideways down the inclined plane and back across.

Finally, he flipped in midair, handspringing out of the crouch and letting the rope unspool as he came up. From there, with only one hop to recover his momentum and balance, he leaped up to the narrow rail of the ship.

The grace of him was breathtaking, but the clip ended there—he'd jumped right out of the frame. Sophie shut off the camera, set it aside, and burrowed into bed, thinking back to Issle Morta, to kissing him.

"I would very much like to court you," he had said.

It hadn't gone well after that. Verena's jealousy had interfered, and then Sophie learned that he thought the two of them were fated to be together, which was just so *weird* she still didn't know what to do with it, and now that the ship had been dispatched to who knew where . . .

Sophie groaned a little, reliving the memory of the kiss again, mentally skimming through the jump rope video, cutting in her memories of him climbing *Nightjar*'s rigging, and then letting imagination take over—picturing the two of them swimming a shallow reef, warm lagoon, salty water, and nobody around for miles. Perfect water temperature for fooling around. Getting another taste of that lush mouth . . .

She let herself chase that thought to its logical conclusion, running the imaginary footage forward, from kissing to a meeting of tongues, and skin, his dexterous, well-formed muscles.

Hands, she thought, *here and here, and then we'll* . . .

Concentration tightened into wordlessness. She focused, imagined, her breath catching, the feeling so intense it was almost like pain . . .

Garland . . . *Garland* . . .

A rise, a crest, and release.

Burrowing deep under the wool blanket in her bunk, Sophie let the last semblance of coherent thought mumble its way out of her mind, until it quieted. Even the *tick-tick-tick* clock earworm that had been bothering her all afternoon became silent as she drifted, without even noticing it, into sleep.

CHAPTER 4

HI, SOPHIE,

SORRY YOU WERE WORRIED. I SHOULD'VE REALIZED GARLAND WOULD TELL YOU I TRANSFERRED TO *FECUND* AND THAT HE WOULDN'T TELL YOU WHY.

BASICALLY, I ASKED THE FELIACHILD MATRIARCHS IF I COULD VISIT THE CAPITAL FOR SOME VERDANII SPIRITUAL TRAINING. GARLAND SUGGESTED SOMETHING CALLED A DETACHMENT RETREAT. THE IDEA IS I'LL GET OVER BEING IN LOVE WITH HIM AND JEALOUS OF YOU. I DON'T KNOW IF THAT'S POSSIBLE, BUT IT GIVES ME A CHANCE TO GET TO KNOW MY RELATIONS HERE, AND GET THEM USED TO ME HAVING GALE'S POSITION.

"Detachment retreat," Sophie mumbled. Verena's crush on Garland had driven her into a dramatic, almost dangerous outburst when he and Sophie began . . . well, he'd used the term *courting*. How typically discreet of him to not say that Verena was going on some kind of spirit quest to deal with her feelings.

Sophie was rereading the letter on the upper deck of a passenger ferry bound for *Constitution,* enjoying the weak winter sun as it toasted her legs and overly cool feet. Her boots from home had gone missing, and she was still adjusting to the lighter construction of a locally made version. The messageply had come through during the night. She'd scanned it once, quickly, over a hurried breakfast of leftovers: Bettona's apricot cookies and a side of goat's-milk cheese.

The letter went on:

I HADN'T THOUGHT THEY'D SEND A SHIP FOR ME. WHAT DO THEY CARE IF I'M HEARTBROKEN, RIGHT? SOMETHING ELSE IS UP—THE VERDANII SEEM UNSETTLED. ANNELA'S DOING THIS RITUAL FAST TO SEE IF SHE'S WORTHY TO TAKE OVER WHEN THE ALL-MOTHER DIES. MAYBE THE ALLMOTHER'S SICK. IF SO, NOBODY IS ADMITTING IT.

THEY'RE ALSO ASKING QUESTIONS ABOUT ERAGLIDING, THEY'RE THE SAME ONES YOU'VE BEEN ASKING: WHO TOOK GALE'S MURDERERS TO SAN FRANCISCO?

SINCE MOM AND I ARE ON THE SHORT LIST OF PEOPLE WITH THE ABILITY TO TRANSPORT ASSASSINS, MY GUESS IS THEY'RE INVESTIGATING US BOTH.

YOU PROBABLY ALREADY KNOW THAT THERE ARE PEOPLE WHO'D LOVE FOR YOU TO BE THE GUILTY PARTY. GOOD THING YOU DON'T KNOW THE FIRST THING ABOUT ERAGLIDING, RIGHT?

TAKE CARE,

VERENA

It wasn't the subtlest hint she'd ever seen, but Sophie knew that the warning was a kindness.

As far as it went, Verena's statement was almost true. Sophie had seen that timepieces were involved in eragliding. She even had one—Beatrice, her birth mother, had given her tacit permission to hang on to Aunt Gale's old pocket watch.

The Verdanii believed that the power was limited to genetic members of the Feliachild family. As for whether that was true . . . well, like everything on Stormwrack, it seemed to be more a matter of anecdote and tradition than experimentally verified proof.

Timepieces, Sophie thought, listening for the ticking earworm she'd picked up the previous day. A faint residue of varied clock sounds sifted up from her memory, but nothing stuck.

IS IT JUST FELIACHILDS WHO CAN EG? She added the question to her ever-growing list of mysteries to tackle later. The task for right now, meanwhile, was to get through the ceremony for people taking the Fleet oath.

Everything Sophie had done on Stormwrack, so far, had seemed to require a storm of paperwork and bureaucracy. She piled in, expecting the days and even weeks to pile up, but to her surprise the procedures were simple: she was greenlighted to take the Oath only one week after her audience with Annela.

Granted, it had been an insane stretch of days. She'd visited her lawyer twice and had added to her pile of deadlocked Fleet lawsuits, gathering up a few more cases that might, in time, be solved using fingerprint evidence. She'd begun making notes for a forensic manual in Fleetspeak, some of which boiled down to explaining the how and why of procedures she'd been seeing on TV mysteries since she was a kid.

Much of the obvious-seeming cop show stuff wasn't in practice here. Wrackers had no concept of preserving a crime scene, much less of taking a meticulous look at everything in it. The whole idea smacked, the bureaucrats told her, of exercising undue curiosity. These comments had been delivered in tones that suggested that curiosity was a muscle to be weakened, through disuse, until it was as flaccid as a piece of veal.

Sophie had also made it back to *Vaddle* to talk to the divers and to pretend to be a drowning victim in a couple of their mermaid rescue drills. With luck, she'd ingratiate herself and someone would volunteer to be her diving partner.

Paging through her notes, she found her latest failed attempt at writing a fancy old-fashioned not-quite-love-letter in reply to Garland. The problem there was finding something to say that didn't sound like (or wasn't, in fact) the lyrics to a pop song:

I believe in miracles, (bom chicka bom) *you sexy thing . . .*

You make my pants want to get up and dance . . .

I wanna hold your ha-yah-yand . . .

Not that Garland would know if she plagiarized the Beatles.

Is love a binary state? You either are or you aren't? Is it more of a quantum thing, where you can be in love and out at once? There's a comedian, at home, who says love grows out of the trauma of shared experience. . . .

Trauma. She crossed that out. Definitely not a word for something that was meant to be romantic.

Some prophet once predicted that your best friend would die if you ever fell in love. We met, she died . . . I'm afraid you believe I'm your one true girl because of an accident of timing.

She'd never bought into the idea of boy meets girl, true love always. Garland knew that, and seemed to accept it. Even so, she was pretty sure he wouldn't appreciate it if she started a letter with "Dear Obsessive Love Object . . ."

So far, she'd wasted a lot of paper getting nowhere.

"*Constitution* ahead! Disembarking passengers, all starboard. Snap to!"

She joined the throng transferring from the ferry to the whitewashed, red-trimmed bulk of *Constitution,* following the crowd until they'd led her to a corral of sorts, an array of thirty folding chairs fenced in by red ribbons. The chairs were mostly filled, presumably with her fellow oath takers. Takees?

As she scanned the group, Sophie fought back a surge of dismay. She was the oldest person there, by about ten years. Her choice of jeans from home and a cotton tunic meant she was radically underdressed for the occasion. And . . .

Her heart sank. Her birth father had turned out to see her take the Oath.

Clydon Banning was Duelist Adjudicator for the Fleet. When parties to one of the court system's thousands of unresolved lawsuits wanted to grease the judicial wheels, they'd petition him to set up a trial by combat.

Some of the fights were ceremonial—negotiated out-of-court settlements, basically, with a perfunctory clash of swords. Others were deadly earnest. Duelists could be appointed to weigh in on either side, if a contest was judged unfair.

Cly could appoint anyone to fight the duels, or he could take them himself.

Basically, he had a license to kill.

Her birth father was whippy, handsome, and dressed impeccably, as usual, in a black Fleet uniform with a red and gold cape. A big wood chipper of a sword hung at his side. He bowed formally to Sophie as she filed in with the other candidates.

Sophie tensed, unable to make herself bow back. Pretty much the most important question in her notebook was IS CLY A SOCIOPATH?

The memory rose again: Cly, killing the *Incannis* crew, one after another, until nobody was left but the bandit, Kev, who'd grabbed her.

If someone who is a sociopath gets a job ruling on criminal court cases and executing the losers, doesn't that essentially make him a variety of serial killer? She hadn't even dared to write that one down.

Swallowing, she took her assigned seat, turning her back on her father. She tried to listen as a wizened and uniformed old lady lectured her and the rest of the class about the solemnity of oath taking.

"You must put the rule of the Fleet above your own inclinations and nature," the woman droned. "Keeping a century of peace afloat weighs more, in the balance, than your happiness. Than your very lives."

The peace of the many outweighs the good of the few or the one. The mangled *Star Trek* quote arose unbidden, threatening to make Sophie giggle.

She remembered Annela saying, *You shouldn't do this.*

Too bad, Annela. I'm not going to screw this up.

Seas, I miss Bram. Times five.

"People of the Fleet, stand and take the Oath."

Her voice was one among dozens: "I pledge my mind to the service of the Nations, my heart to the Nine Seas, my bones and skin to the ships of the Fleet. I promise to be faithful in all things to the rule of law, the Nations, the Fleet Compact, and the Cessation of Hostilities."

Soon the audience was cheering. Sophie braced herself to face Cly.

As usual, he was holding court; every cadet who didn't have parents to hug after the big ceremony was approaching him, hoping to catch a word. He cleared them away with a gracious celebrity's wave as Sophie approached.

No embrace this time, no kiss on the top of the head. Sophie didn't know how she looked, but there was steel in his gaze.

The last time they'd seen each other, she had embarrassed him at a party attended by the social cream of his hometown.

"Congratulations, daughter. This makes me very happy." There was a trace of the customary warmth in Cly's voice, that affection that made it so hard for her to entirely write him off.

What if she was wrong?

There were things she could ask him.

Not here, though. Not amid a throng of admirers.

"Does it?" she said, realizing he'd been waiting as she churned through her conversational options.

"Why should it not? You're becoming a woman of the Fleet, a member of civilized society—"

She must have made a face.

"No rapprochement today, I see," he said softly.

She swallowed. "What do you want, Cly?"

The warmth coming from him was gone, suddenly. He held out a packet of papers bound in a black folder.

She opened the folder and felt her knees turn to water. "Is this is a Sylvanner birth certificate?"

"Proof of citizenship. You are Sophie Hansa of Sylvanna now." A hint of warning sharpened his voice. "To say otherwise would be a lie."

"Even if I chuck this overboard?"

"You are of Stormwrack, a daughter of Sylvanna, and lawful expert witness to the Fleet. Offering disrespect to your motherland's writs will not change who you are in the eyes of the law."

"You know I didn't want this!"

That does it. I'm getting the whole Fleet code zapped into my brain the minute I get off this ship.

"I was, initially, prepared to respect your wishes regarding Sylvanna." Cly lived in the Fleet, but back on his home island he had an Old South–style estate, complete with fruit orchards, ostrich ranching, beehives . . . and frigging *slaves* to tend to it all. "As you've taken it to mind to introduce adversarial elements to our relationship—"

"You went and made me Sylvanner as payback for one argument?"

Maybe I should ask him if he screws his slaves, right here in front of the whole assembly.

I've got to shake that idea. Beatrice says he doesn't.

"Don't be ridiculous," Cly said. "I declined to ask the population office to do me the immense favor of withholding status papers they were preparing for you as a matter of course."

"Oh, and you're not enjoying this at all."

"Believe me, child, were I petty enough to seek revenge for the appalling scene you created at the Highsummer Festival, you would be in no doubt of the situation."

She looked up at him, simmering. There was something in that phrase—"you would be in no doubt"—that smelled of threat.

"You need the passport. Your father is Sylvanner. Stop trying to deny something neither of us can change."

"Yeah," she said. "We're helpless pawns of fate."

Cly went on: "As I've been reduced to a courier . . . your travel visa from Convenor Gracechild is also in the folder."

"I can go home?" She reopened the folder, interested now.

"You might wait," he said. "Kev Lidman, the bandit from *Incannis,* is coming to trial soon."

Her throat closed. "Do I have to be there? To be a witness, I mean?"

"Do you have something to say about his assault upon you?"

She shook her head—too quickly, perhaps.

"I'm empowered to tell the court what happened," he said.

She could just hear it: *May it please the court, I slaughtered one bandit, then I killed another, and I got a bit of the third one on my shoe—terribly inconvenient, don't you know, getting gore out of the leather. As for the final miscreant, he was so scared he tried to use Sophie as a human shield. . . .*

"Annela wanted me to ask him some questions," she said.

"You need only visit him in prison. As for the trial, that can certainly proceed without you, if you'd rather be elsewhere."

"I'd definitely rather." She all but stroked the travel visa, letting the idea of home—home!—wash away the bloody roil of memories.

Cly took in the deck, the celebrating cadets, and their families. "Speaking of your Verdanii relations, I note they seem to be boycotting this ceremony."

"Don't try to distract me from the point."

"Which is . . . ?"

Oh. She tried to remember. "Can it be undone? The Sylvanner citizenship?"

This, at least, got a startled—and obviously genuine—reaction. "Not that I'm aware. Sophie, the question of who you are, your value as a human being—you cannot think it rests on the peculiarities of my home nation. Or your mother's, for that matter."

"Will you look into it?"

He laughed. "Why should I?"

I am learning Fleet code as soon as I can find a spellscribe with the right color of crayon.

"You wouldn't have any other fun surprises in store for me, would you?" she asked.

A "Halloo!" from the direction of the taxikite dock interrupted her. Their lawyer, the sleepy-eyed, middle-aged Mensalohm Bimisi, came padding down the deck.

Sophie had never seen Mensalohm out of his office; she had begun to question whether he ever left it. He was a soft-looking fellow with a sweet face, a round head covered in white-blond stubble, and a savage reputation among litigators.

Now he inclined his head in lieu of bowing. "Kir Sophie. Your Honor. Sorry I missed the ceremony. I've never had the gift of punctuality."

"No prob," she said.

"That is indeed a grave flaw," Cly said at the same time.

"You've already changed, Sophie. Am I later than I think?"

"She didn't dress," Cly growled, but Mensalohm pressed his lips together, not quite hiding amusement.

There weren't many people prepared to needle the fearsome Cly Banning. Sophie gave him a quick hug.

"Which of us are you seeking, Bimisi?" Cly asked.

"Both, as it happens. I'm trying to be light on my feet for a change. I have papers regarding your divorce, Your Honor, as well as some items for Sophie. It's just a question of who wants to take me on first."

"I hardly need you to walk me through a nuptial dissolution." Cly plucked the folder from his hand. "Daughter, if we're done . . . ?"

Ask him the other thing, her inner voice said. *Forget about whether he sleeps with his slaves. Ask him about his best pal Captain Beck and her magical prosthetic hand.*

She couldn't force the words out.

"Yes? Then I can only hope your feelings about me soften, in time."

With that, Cly bowed and went back to his adoring fans.

"I'd thought you two were getting along," Mensalohm said.

"When? For the ten minutes after I met him?"

"Love is always windy when it bridges port and starboard," he said.

She wasn't in the mood for platitudes. "The captain of his sailing vessel lost her arm as a kid. She's got this prosthetic . . . I don't know what you'd call it. A ghost arm . . ."

"The arm came from a slave?" At her surprised look, Mensalohm said, "It's a common enough spell. He may have been compensated in some way. Did you talk to the donor?"

"Didn't know I needed to, at the time."

"Have you asked His Honor?"

"No." She sighed.

"Why not?"

"He gave me a Sylvanner passport."

Mensalohm laid a hand on her shoulder. "It is who you are, legally speaking."

"Legally schmeegally. I'm thinking I need to learn the Fleet code of law."

"You mentioned that in your note. For your institute? Or the bandit's trial? Or just to more effectively frustrate His Honor?"

"His Honor's schemes. I'm not trying to frustrate him, just to be annoying. If he's going to go fixing me up with portside passports whenever I cross him . . . Plus there's the issue of me not tripping over—" She stopped herself from saying "dumb," remembering Annela's comment about her having contempt for Fleet law. "Over the rules, every time I open my mouth."

Mensalohm considered it. "You could, I suppose. If you mean what I think, it's an expensive scrip."

"I'm told I have a budget now."

"Oh, yes, there's a fat invoice in there from me to the court. Your contract's a big catch, I'm happy to say. But a complete grasp of Fleet law is a heavy intention. To absorb a decade of learning in a matter of hours—no reputable scribe will embark on it without assurance you aren't already loaded."

Magic had a quality that Wrackers referred to in terms of weight—there was a limit to what a person could bear without becoming physically or mentally ill. "What kind of assurance?"

"A list of intentions you're already carrying. I can prepare the documents."

More red tape. "There's only the one spell."

"Get your mother to affirm it. She's the only person who knew of your existence until recently, am I right?"

"Her and Gale."

"She'll need to vouch for Gale Feliachild's not having enchanted you. You'll be seeing Beatrice anyway."

"I will?"

He nodded. "Divorce papers, by definition, come in pairs." He handed her a packet identical to Cly's. "Would you mind delivering these? I gather you're headed back to her mysterious outland refuge."

She nodded, taking it, and then walking him back to where the ferries were coming to take people to other parts of the Fleet. By the time he was gone, the oath-taking party had broken up. Most of the newly sworn kids had gone off with family and friends to celebrate. Scatterings of confetti, seaweed based and biodegradable, were sprinkled on the deck.

"Faithful to the rule of law and the Cessation," she murmured, feeling a low-key sense of melancholy as she took in the seagoing city around her. For just a moment, the weight of responsibility was crushing, as if one hundred and nine years of peace here on Stormwrack was really hers to preserve.

But that was grandiose. She was an outsider, passport or no. One who was going home—to her brother, her parents, and a world with ready electricity.

She cracked open her journal, found the messageply, and jotted Bram and Verena both a note: HEADED BACK TO SFO!

CHAPTER 5

Feuding Customs of the Piracy

1. *LOOK YOUR* ANTAGONISTE *IN THE FACE WHEREVER POSSIBLE: DECLARE FEUD OPENLY, AND DEMAND SURRENDER. NO HONOR BLOWS IN THE SAILS OF THE LICKSPITTLE, THE BACKSTABBER, THE BASE* TRAITRE, *OR THE BELLY-CRAWLING DOG.*

2. *RECOGNIZE, EVEN REWARD, THE PROWESS OF THOSE WHO HAVE DEFEATED YOU, IF THEY ARE SO FOOLISH AS TO ALLOW YOU TO LIVE. SHOULD THEY CONFRONT YOU AGAIN, PURSUE THEM TO THE ENDS OF THE KNOWN WORLD, TO THE OUTLANDS, TO THE VERY STARS, AND DO NOT CEASE TO CLAMOR* GUERRE *UPON THEM UNTIL NAUGHT IS LEFT OF THEIR MEMORY BUT COLD ASH ON THE WIND.*

Krispos, the memorician Cly had hired for her as a weird sort of gift, was booked into the cabin next door to Sophie's rented bunk. He was, as usual, nose deep in a book. Memoricians were speed-readers with perfect recall; he was as close as Stormwrack came to having something like a flash drive.

Because half his cache was filled with obscure poetry Sophie couldn't use, Krispos was also trying to make himself useful by acting as a sort of assistant.

As she returned to the cabin, he handed over a slim bundle of notes—a sort of executive summary on blood feuds—lettered like a medieval manuscript, sans gold, in a coil notebook she'd brought from home. "You wrote this?" she asked.

"I found a spellscribe to intend me for speedwriting." He had been sitting with his feet in a small basin of foaming water; bending, he toweled each of them dry with care. The feet had no nails—it was a mutation, occurring naturally in about one fifth of the people here.

There was nothing natural about the scars on the bottoms of his feet, furrows like the marks of enormous teeth, tracks of scar tissue that he'd flatly refused to discuss.

Don't stare. Instead of dwelling on his wounds, she said, "It looks like the inscription hurt."

He raised his head, huffing a little as he strapped his second sandal. "Does it?"

"One of your eyes is bloodshot." *And you're haggard,* she didn't add.

"It wasn't too bad." He laid a finger over the eye. "And the notes—are they useful?"

She looked at a page.

3. ACT OPENLY, CHALLENGE YOUR FOES, BUT NEVER LAY YOURSELF OPEN TO EASY DEFEAT. HANG A SWORD AT YOUR HIP SO YOUR OPPONENT KNOWS YOUR WILL BEARS A SHARPENED BLADE. IF THEY DO NOT MARK THE KNIFE IN YOUR BOOT, THE FAULT LIES IN THEIR GRASP.

"Very useful," she said, trying to keep her voice breezy even though the hair had come up on her arms.

Krispos briefed her on his day's reading: three hundred pages on the development of magic in the years before the Fleet; a history of the Sylvanna Spellscrip Institute, which controlled patents for a significant number of the world's most important spells; and a long list of the ships reported missing or sunk by mishap in the past three or so years.

By way of trade, she handed him the bureaucratic pile establishing them as expert witnesses within the court system.

"Now to prove our worth," she said. "I'm gonna go home and get what we need for the fingerprint operation. But I want to keep working on these sinkings. Can you put together a list of commonalities between the sunk vessels? Anything that's the same for all three? Oh—and someone called the monster a wood fright. Did you learn anything about that?"

"Frightmaking is an intentionally lost art. It's a matter of treaty. According to the Spellscrip Institute histories, giant frog frights attacked Tug Island sixty years ago. Whatever is known might be forbidden."

"Get whatever you can find. You're doing great, Krispos. Outstanding work."

A bright smile lit his creased, pale face. The bloodshot eye made it a little gruesome.

Sophie managed to meditate her way into sleep that evening, but excitement had her up well before dawn, rattling around her tiny cabin like a pea in a can. She dressed and packed her things far too early, leaving everything she wasn't bringing with her to clutter up a corner of Krispos's cabin. Then she went up to the main deck so she could stretch and wait for the tardy November sun to rise over the Fleet.

Shepherd prowled to the rear, shining a spotlight on the seas and on the straggling ships chasing the bigger blocks of the city-size convoy. Gulls circled restaurant ships and fishers, calling out as the sky lightened.

Sophie was on the first ferry to *Constitution,* one of a great crowd of commuters: Fleet personnel, government workers, and diplomatic officials arriving for what they called the dawn shift. A couple of cadets beside her speculated quietly about the sinking of *Kitesharp* and the others. Their voices held a note of tension. The taller of the two, a young octer, insisted that nobody in the government would care to find out who was responsible.

"The bandits from this summer are dead, aren't they?" his companion replied.

"Was a Sylvanner saw to that, nobody starboard," the octer said. "And they haven't yet brought the survivor to trial—" He broke off, apparently having noticed that Sophie was listening.

Usually, traveling between Stormwrack and the land the people here called Erstwhile was something she did with Verena. With her half sister on Verdanii, it fell to Annela's assistant to do the honors.

It was Bettona who had deported Sophie the first time she arrived in Stormwrack. Another of the Feliachilds, she was a delicate stick of a woman, neither as voluptuous as Beatrice nor as tough and weathered as Aunt Gale had been. The only genetic feature they all shared was the slightly enlarged brown eyes—anime eyes, Bram called them—that Sophie had inherited from her birth mother.

A smell of baking wafted through the front rooms of Annela's office—

more anise and apricot—as Bettona bowed, bidding Sophie welcome. "I can transit you in about ten minutes."

"Waiting on the angle of the sun?" Sophie asked. Verena had mentioned this once.

Bettona nodded, holding out a cup of tea. "This is a traditional libation for traveling."

Sophie took a sip, expecting something like chai but finding just a breath of liquor in the mix, which was otherwise all rose hips and cinnamon. "The first time I came here, it was spontaneous—no waiting, no angle."

"Kir Gale had been stabbed, hadn't she?" She offered a tray of the anise and apricot biscuits; they were oven warm. "And you landed in open ocean."

"Admittedly, that sucked." Sophie nibbled a biscuit, trying to hide her expression. She was excited, and she had no poker face whatsoever. Usually, Annela turned up and ended these conversations before they could properly begin.

Play it cool, she thought. "Okay, but when you sent me back that first time, I ended up on my butt in an alley near Beatrice's, around where I'd vanished before."

"You jerked away from me, as I recall." There was no rancor in Bettona's tone. "Nothing like that will happen again."

"Unless I move, presumably?"

Bettona nodded.

"Where is Annela?" Sophie asked.

"The convenor is occupied." Bettona's inflection was neutral, giving away nothing.

Still fasting then. "But she's okay?"

Another nod.

Sophie had been expecting the usual scrutiny: search and seizure, dire warnings about secret-keeping and all her so-called spy equipment. She'd brought a bag of stuff—data chips for her camera, along with biological samples and a variety of things Bram had requested—but she'd been expecting to have to turn it all over to Annela.

Ah, but now I'm Oath Girl, she remembered. *If I spill the news about Stormwrack to anyone on Earth, I can be prosecuted.*

Annela wants me to step out of line. She said so.

Never mind that. Things to learn.

Sophie gave Bettona her friendliest smile. "We're genetic cousins. You're a Feliachild, right? You've got those big eyes that seem to be a family trait, and you can eraglide."

Slight surprise from Bettona. "Yes."

"You're not another aunt, are you?"

"No. My father and your grandmother are siblings."

A grandmother and a great-uncle. Sophie's breath caught. "*Are* siblings? They're alive?"

"*Neneh*. Apologies." Bettona shook her head. "Ennatrice Feliachild died by ordeal, years ago. My father, Pharmann—it was his heart. Last Febbraio."

"Oh. Sorry." Died of ordeal. And Annela was ordealing. "Does that mean Annela's in real danger?"

"The convenor is strong." That neutrality again. "I am sure she will come through the dark and into wonders."

Sophie took a closer look at the woman. She was expensively clad, as any Verdanii official would be. Healthy looking, but not an athlete. She was left-handed. Her age appeared to be midthirties. "Are they grooming you to replace Annela?"

Bettona smiled thinly. "The convenor is irreplaceable."

"If she ends up Allmother, which I gather is like being president, she'll go back to Verdanii?"

"Of course."

"If not you, who gets her job here?"

"I'm not considered any great gift to the civil service," Bettona said. "Generally this position, convenor, goes to a Gracechild."

She's been found wanting. The Verdanii do that a lot. Okay, this is awkward. . . . "What do you government types do here when you're not working? Is there a book club or what?"

"Pardon?"

"There must be a few hundred people just like you. Young, up and coming, talented, connected, away from home, with a boss who isn't ready to retire."

"The Fleet becomes home, after a time."

"Do you knit? Shop? Raise and trade tropical fish? I can see that you garden: you've got a little pollen in your hair and some dirt under your nails. But that's kind of a cultural requirement, isn't it? Verdanii are big on the farming."

Bettona let out a dry-sounding laugh. "I do my customary duty by the

Breadbasket food cooperative, yes. Now you mention it, there is . . . I wouldn't have called it a club, but the younger functionaries of the starboard side do gather and socialize informally."

"Starboard. The free-state folks have one group and the slavers drink somewhere else. That makes sense."

"Yes, the portside bureaucrats keep to themselves."

Something about that made Sophie think of the conversation she'd overheard on her commute, the young octer complaining that nobody would do anything about the sinking of *Kitesharp* and the other vessels.

Bettona broke in on that thought before it was fully formed. "It's time, Sophie. Stand here, please. And—"

"No jerking away." Sophie obeyed. "Could you bring me to your not-club sometime? Would that be allowed?"

"Maybe," Bettona said. She was concentrating now on a tiny gold pocket watch. As before, she set it on Sophie's palm.

Sophie felt a rush of heat, as if her heart had suddenly pumped a wash of blood directly to her face. For a second, her vision swam. The ticking of the timepiece was very loud; each stroke tapped against her temples like drumsticks. *Tick, tick, tick.*

That's what I was hearing before, she thought, and as she listened, the sound doubled. She could hear the bigger clock in Annela's office, keeping time with the smaller one. *It started here. . . .*

Her vision cleared and the ground steadied underfoot. She, her dive tanks, and the bundles of paperwork were in her birth mother's basement in San Francisco. She listened as the *tick tick bong* of the grandfather clock striking nine replaced the sounds of Annela's wall clock and Bettona's timepiece.

It's not an earworm. I'm actually hearing all three clocks.

She was alone in a stranger's house. It was a weird feeling, as if she were a burglar.

"Hello?" She stepped out into the hall, peering in through the first open door. A converted laundry room, from the look of it—she could see the space where the washer and dryer had sat, and a barely used sink. Near the door was a big cupboard labeled "Garments" in both English and, interestingly, Fleetspeak. She cracked the door. It held generic street clothes: stuff for men, stuff for women, and a bunch of unisex sweaters and rain coats.

In case someone comes from Stormwrack dressed in a weird outfit or a

Fleet uniform. The thought took her to a memory of Garland Parrish, dressed in one of Bram's leather jackets.

"Rowr," she murmured.

The rest of the room was dominated by a cabinet with seven cupboards, each with a locking door, none actually locked. Sophie opened the first door. Inside was a picture of Verena's pewter timepiece, the one Sophie thought of as the pancake clock.

She opened the rest, one after another. Each had a few personal-looking items, more clothes, and a sketch of a clock. One depicted the clock she'd seen Beatrice use to come home from Stormwrack. Bettona's tiny pocket watch was there, too.

There was a sketch of Gale's watch, which Sophie had found and had yet to return.

Seven cupboards. Seven eragliding Feliachilds? She thought again about John Coine and the guns he'd bought in San Francisco. She had taken the Oath now; Convenor Brawn had offered to tell her about that. She took photos of each door.

A door slammed upstairs, startling her. She jumped, wondering if she should just try to sneak out of the house. Because, you know, she was so good at tiptoeing around. *Crawl not behind the back of your antagoniste,* she thought, remembering the pirate customs. As advice went, it wasn't bad. Forcing a smile, she walked back out into the hallway. "Hello?"

Footfalls sounded overhead. A big barrel of a man, fiftyish and fuzzy haired, clad in a white shirt and suspenders, rounded the corner and peered down at her from the top of the stairs.

He broke into a grin. "You'd be Sophie."

English! A surge of feeling brought tears to her eyes. Hearing a real American accent, after weeks of speaking Fleet, seemed to do this to her every time.

"I'm Merro Vanko, Verena's father. This . . ." He turned, revealing a second man, laden with grocery bags, standing behind him. "Is my son, Shad."

Shad was African-American, in his early twenties, with a physique that put Sophie in mind of a baseball player. Sophie realized she had seen a picture of him once, with Gale and Verena. "Hi. Um, I have papers for Beatrice."

"Beebee's not here," Merro said.

Beebee? "When's she back? I need to talk to her, if it's possible."

"It isn't," Shad said. "One of her cancer babies is dying today. She's with the family."

Cancer babies. Beatrice's Verdanii relatives thought of her as a histrionic wimp, but here in San Francisco she ran a pediatric hospice. That had to take a soul of iron.

Merro said, "I know she's expecting to see you. Do you want to hang around and wait? It could be a day or so. If you don't have anywhere to go, we have a guest room."

"No. Thanks though. I'll leave my number, if that works," Sophie said. "I need to see my brother. But I'd love to get together with her. Or all of you. I don't mean to rush off. . . ."

She'd only been living among the overly mannered Fleet folk for six weeks, but apparently it had gummed up her sense of what was polite, how not to hurt any feelings. Now she floundered. What did you say?

If finding out he had a stepdaughter he'd never known about had been difficult for Merro, he had either processed it already or was great at hiding his emotions. "It's complicated. I know."

Sophie opened her notebook, pulled out her Bram page, and wrote HERE! on it. Then she tore out an ordinary scrap of paper, jotted down her mobile number, and handed it over.

"Speaking of a phone, do you need to use our landline?" Merro asked.

"Nope. My brother's got a phone for me." She waved the messageply, which was already showing a reply: I'M IN THE CAFÉ AROUND THE CORNER FROM B'S.

"You and yours know all about us, I guess," Shad said.

"Shad," Merro said. A warning?

Plastering on a bright smile, Sophie shook hands with her . . . birth stepfather? And brother? "Maybe I'll see you?"

Merro nodded. "You're welcome any time."

She all but raced to the café and flung herself into her brother's arms.

"Holy crap," he said. "It's good to see you."

"Five good!"

"Well . . . three."

"Only three?" She pretended to be insulted.

"Not every feeling can be full-on, Sofe," he said, but he'd given her a good once-over and was beaming. "Leave room to dial it up."

"When has that ever worked?"

Sometime in the past couple of weeks, Bram had gotten a haircut. The tan he'd picked up while sailing from Sylvanna to Issle Morta—roughly the distance from Memphis, Tennessee, to Seattle—and back again had begun to fade. He hadn't done anything about getting the pearl removed from underneath his thumbnail, and he wasn't wearing glasses or contacts. . . .

"You get your eyes lasered?"

He nodded.

"And you're hitting the gym?"

"Running less, lifting more. Something called functional training."

"That's very athletic of you." Bram had always had a grudging attitude toward exercise. Maintenance and upkeep, he called it—a task performed out of a sense of obligation to keep his body running, without any tie-in with fun.

"Sailing's strenuous, Ducks. I want twenty-twenty vision and more muscle."

"Don't call me Ducks," she said happily as he handed her a coffee and a slice of lemon pound cake in a waxed paper envelope and led her out in search of the car. "You look good, Bramble."

"Happy, healthy, and wrestling the mysteries of the universe."

"Still single?"

"No. In six months I've married and spawned two kids. What do you think?"

"Just asking." *For Tonio,* she didn't add.

"Come on, Sofe, what have you learned?"

She decided not to lead with her glancing encounter with Verena's father and half brother. Instead, getting into the passenger seat, she mentally rifled through her bag of camera chips. "Pick a discipline."

"Biology."

"I've got a list going of animal species I'm positive we haven't got here in Erstwhile. I got to know a taxidermist and he's going to start saving blood and hair samples for me. Supposedly to start an archive for the court, but maybe one day—"

"Maybe one day we can get someone to run the DNA?"

"Dare to dream, right? And I'm collecting and studying unusual feathers, because they're light."

"No plants?"

"Seeds and some more pressed leaves. It's been tougher. The Fleet's reviewing procedures on anything that might get loose and propagate on an island where it doesn't belong."

"Especially now, I bet." He, Sophie, and Verena had proved that Sylvanna's nearest neighbor was infecting Sylvanna's swamps with a vine that was a variant of kudzu. It had blown up into a political scandal. "What was the best?"

She leaned back, savoring her latte and pound cake. "Fall's coming and we've been making our way southeast, toward where the Horn of Africa would be. And there've been these—well, I'll show you. But remember the bevvies?"

"How could I forget?" The seagoing serpents had looked like Chinese dragons and had the ability to sing chords that amplified human emotions. It was their influence that had nearly driven Verena—who had been at the peak of her heartbreak over Garland—to fling herself into the sea.

"They shed their skin in the fall. All those huge iridescent scales, and a ton of biomatter. They pick up mussels and bits of seaweed and chunks of dead fish. They're filthy like you wouldn't believe; they don't even look like the same creature.

"They all descend to the bottom of the ocean in a specific location—I have the latitude and longitude, so we can figure out the equivalent map coordinates here on Earth—and they inflate their skin to break it loose, to shed it. These fleshy balloons float to the surface, all this food—"

"Calorie bonanza," Bram said.

Sophie nodded. "Fish, mostly tuna and that thing called butterfish, show up. Then birds come in to catch the fish. There are algal blooms. The sea turns green, and the birds come out of the water stained green from their dives, and at the end of the cycle the skins get torn and it turns out they're full of little golden bevvies, tiny and toxic. They frisk in all that soup, whistling—"

They caught an exit to the freeway, and displacement hit her, a million things at once: the speed of the cars, set against the stillness of being on land rather than on the rolling deck of ship after ship after ship, the flavor of oily petrochemicals in the air. She groped for Bram's phone, hit Play, and giggled a little maniacally as a Mika song obligingly burbled out of the car stereo.

Commercial electronics and billboards and jet engines and MRIs and television—

"What are you thinking?" Bram asked, and she realized she'd stopped telling him about the bevvies.

"Is there an opposite to homesickness?" It was a weird feeling—less like pain, more like being spaced out, or stunned.

"Homewellness?" he said. "Good timing, anyway."

"What?"

"Because we're here," he said, taking the exit to his place.

CHAPTER 6

Bram lived in a rented seven-bedroom heritage home, in indifferent repair, called the Dwarf House. He shared it with a dozen or so other graduate students from Stanford and Berkeley.

He parked, got out and popped the trunk, and then unzipped her bag right there.

"Bram," she muttered. "Secrecy, remember?"

"They let you take your chips out?"

"Every last frame and sample." Sophie grinned.

He looked wary. "What'd you have to promise?"

"You know, the usual. Arm and a leg, my firstborn child. Loyalty to the Fleet and respect for its laws."

"Heh."

"That last part's true. I'm officially sworn to defend the Cessation." Stormwrack had been free of war for just over a century, but they'd never written a treaty. On paper, the peace was merely a so-called Cessation of Hostilities.

"I bet you'll keep that promise for at least a week . . . well, depending on how soon you go back."

She punched his arm, stung.

"Oh, did I strike a nerve?" he asked.

"I'm rising above," she said. She hadn't let Annela or Convenor Brawn bait her. Bram, at least, knew her well enough to be allowed to tease.

He kept looking through her things. "Did Tonio get the kits I asked about?"

"Tonio would *never* fail to do you a favor."

He missed—or ignored—the hint. "Ooh, he did."

"Are we going to sit here taking inventory?"

"Okay, okay." He shouldered the duffel, heading through the yard. "How long are you in town?"

She shrugged. "I've sold the Watch on the fingerprint project, so I need resources on the filing system and identification process. Loops and whorls and arches and all that jazz. There's some chemistry I need to relearn. I want to learn to dust for latent prints and do one of the rooms at Beatrice's place."

"So you can try to figure out who brought John Coine here?"

"Yeah. Also refill my oxygen tanks, obviously. Buy real bras for about a dozen women—"

Something—worry?—crossed his face when she mentioned shopping. "That can wait until tomorrow?" he asked.

"Totally."

They climbed to the attic, murmuring greetings to two of Bram's roommates, a pair of physicists. To her surprise, he'd put a serious electronic lock on the trapdoor leading to the attic.

"How did you explain that?"

He punched in a seven-digit code. "They think I'm designing the next breakout video game, remember?"

The security didn't end at the attic door. Bram's computer and external hard drive were living in a heavy-duty safe. He keyed in the combination and retrieved his laptop, then took the camera bag from her and settled in for a long session of downloading and scanning her files.

Sophie, meanwhile, plugged in all her electronics, recharging her batteries with a feeling of giddy greed. No single solar-powered charger here.

They worked in companionable silence, moving files, sorting data, connecting her various gadgets to the wireless network. Bram dove into Sophie's duffel again, examining the kits from Tonio, ripping open the first of them and fishing for what was obviously an instruction sheet.

"What's *verfrite* mean?" He was still learning Fleet, whereas she'd had it magically uploaded into her brain.

"This awful thing they drink on some of the islands. Sort of buttermilk and ginger."

"Oh." Disappointed noise.

"Why?"

"Spell component."

Unease sifted through her. "You're determined to learn magical inscription?"

"We'll never understand what magic is until one of us can work it." He sounded as though he was using ninety-nine percent or more of his kid genius brain to think about spellscribing, and all of one percent to carry on this conversation.

It's a good idea. Why does it bother you?

She wasn't sure.

"How far have you gotten?" she asked.

Still reading, he jerked his head to indicate something in the safe. She opened it, pulling out a sketchbook. Inside he had lettered the magical alphabet, spellscrip, over and over until it was perfectly rendered. His first attempts were in pencil, and sharper, but more recent pages bore the marks of a calligraphy brush. The alphabet then gave way to actual text, words incomprehensible to her, again brushed repeatedly.

"What does this say?"

"It's the scrip for these." He held up one of Tonio's gifts, and she recognized some of the components. It was exactly like a kit she'd picked up in a market, months earlier. She hadn't known it was a spell; what had caught her eye was a carrier pigeon skin among the ingredients.

"What's it do?"

"It's like a kid's kit, educational. Easy spells to try at home, all components supplied."

He passed her the instruction sheet. The pigeon had been someone's pet and had a name. In life, it carried messages. The page directed would-be spellscribes to line a stone box with its skin, using glue made from fish bones. Supposedly, if it was done correctly, the box couldn't be lost. If you moved house, it went too. The crate it was packed in couldn't be mislaid, the box's contents couldn't get lost, and at some appropriate point, later in life, it turned up just when you needed the contents.

Before she could ask if he'd pulled it off, Bram handed her a brownish onyx box the size of her fist. Its interior had the iridescent sheet of pigeon feathers, and the text he'd been practicing glowed at her, in impossibly tiny letters etched into the inside of the lid.

She sat there, blinking at it. Her little brother had worked magic.

"If I can get my hands on the skull of a ram—"

"Shouldn't that be easy?"

"A ram with a name," he said. "Also, saw grass from a country named Colland."

"For what?"

"I can make an outer box to put this in. Supposedly that makes it indestructible. The two, together, are the perfect message in a bottle."

"All you need then is a message." She thought fleetingly of Garland and her failed attempts at love letters.

"How about this: *Dear Me: If you're reading this, Stormwrack is literally a future Erstwhile. Very best wishes, from Me*?"

"You're resorting to magic to prove whether we're time traveling or going to an alternate universe?"

"We have to start somewhere," he said. "If I can figure out the science behind inscription and then use it to determine if we're time traveling, we'll at least know. It was your idea, sort of. We talked about digging up the Valley of the Kings."

She could see his train of thought. "If we leave ourselves a message here, on Earth, in an indestructible followbox, and it turns up you-know-where—that would argue they're two time periods, not two worlds."

"It's a start," Bram said.

"But if we're in one of an infinite number of nearly identical universes, then wouldn't Mirror Sophie and Mirror Bram also leave a mirror time-capsule for . . . argh . . . for mirror future us to find?"

His expression indicated he'd thought of that. Of course he had. "One thing at a time, okay?"

"Yeah. It's a good idea."

"I'll get a goat head next time I'm in Fleet."

"Right." Instead of imagining or pretending that she could stop Bram from pursuing exactly the same path she was taking, Sophie made her way through a maze of piled texts, most on theoretical physics, and hit the bathroom.

I could get the goat. If she brought him enough spell ingredients, maybe he'd sit here in San Francisco and scribe things forever. Studious, safe, and sound.

It wasn't her call. Bram had made it abundantly clear that he was just as eager to study Stormwrack as she was. But anything that kept her baby brother far from pirates, emotion-tweaking bevvies, and sword fighting was just great with her.

She filled the tub with the hottest water she could handle, sliding in with a groan.

"Nice?" Bram called through the door.

"Yeah. But weird, too. Being in the real world feels more like a vacation than . . . I dunno, being home."

"Of course it does. You aren't spending your time flipping through court documents and ferrying from ship to ship and sucking up to mermaids for dive partners. You've been working your ass off."

She thought of the little ship *Kitesharp*. "Why would anyone sink a mechanics' garage?"

"I downloaded a couple books on victimology," he replied, in that voice that said he'd gone back to multitasking.

Sinking victims. The other two ships had been a glass seller and a shared home, something of a dormitory, really, for medical apprentices.

Was it merely a crime of opportunity? Were they choosing ships that had some quality that made it possible to infect them with a fright?

Still need to find out about frights. Gonna have to suck up talking to that jailed bandit.

Drying her hands, she reached for her smartphone. Months of e-mails began queuing up and she gave herself over to the mindless ritual of information triage: open, scan, delete; open, scan, mark as spam; open, scan, save for later . . .

Bram had sent her links on Victorian-era forensics, along with a question: WILL THE FORENSIC INSTITUTE HAVE PROPRIETARY RIGHTS OVER FINGERPRINTING IF WE "DEVELOP" IT?

Patents and copyrights. That's another area of red tape where my knowing the law will help. If Island A is the only source of verfrite *and Island B wants to make some, for a spell, how does the ownership of the inscription get resolved?*

She marked a link for further reading so she could start working on a fingerprint database.

"Did you say something about a mechanics' shop?" Bram asked.

"Twenty minutes ago." She ran more hot water, then told him about *Kitesharp* and the other sinkings.

"Isn't that more a criminal case? Or terrorism? Less of a lawsuit?"

"They asked my opinion. But I can't begin to pretend I know why some rogue frightmaker would sink a glass store or a hang glider repair shop.

Annela said it might be the same person who made the salt frights that attacked *Sawtooth*. Which made it piracy, according to her."

"Because pirates sink ships," Bram said.

And Convenor Brawn had showed up the day after Sophie went out with the *Shepherd* crew to study the *Kitesharp* sinking. He'd offered her a favor, but it was also some kind of ritual warning to stay out of his way.

"Those fuckers," Bram muttered. She'd have bet he was rubbing the pearl embedded in his thumb. An echo of her own anger, over that, pinged through her.

She decided not to tell him about the encounter with Convenor Brawn. Not yet anyway. Instead she said, "I wonder if they're gearing up for another run at sinking or disabling *Temperance*?"

"I—Hold on, Sofe. Hi there. . . . What? No! Again?"

His phone must have rung.

"We'll be right over," he said, which sounded like a cue to get out of the tub if she'd ever heard one.

"What's up?" She set her own phone out of stomping distance and reached for a towel.

"The folks have had a break-in," he said.

Within minutes they were headed out to their childhood home, driving in the direction of Stanford, where their father taught English literature.

"I have to tell you something," he said as they turned onto their street. "The parents—"

"It's happened before," she said.

He paused as he was downshifting, and then let out a little hiss. "I said 'again,' on the phone."

"You said 'again,'" she agreed, elbowing him in a companionable, bratty-sister way. He stuck out his tongue as he parked the car.

There were a half-dozen police on the front lawn, along with a huge black dog whose every hair crackled with not-quite-antagonistic alertness. The person in charge appeared to be a tall African-American woman in a snappy suit. She wore a pricey-looking engagement ring—diamonds and sapphires—and her eyes were watering slightly as she came out of the house.

Allergic to cats, Sophie thought as she took in the yard of her childhood home. There was a shiny new alarm sticker on the back door, which had been punched in by something big and heavy.

"Bramwell," the woman said, shaking his hand. "This your sister?"

"Sofe, this is Inspector Bettel."

"Ella's fine." She scrutinized Sophie. "It looks much the same as last time."

Saying that to see if I know about the last one. "Bram just told me there'd been another break-in."

"Your house appears to have been searched."

"Searched?" She blinked. "Not robbed?"

"First time, they got the family laptop."

With copies of all her Stormwrack footage. Sophie felt a spike of anxiety, then forced herself to let it go. She had backups in the cloud, and this was probably the work of people from Stormwrack anyway.

Wrackers. In our house.

"Sophie?" Her parents were just emerging from the house. "Sophie!"

"Miss Hansa?"

"Hang on a second, okay?" she said to Bettel, and dove into her parents' arms.

CHAPTER 7

Cornell and Regina Hansa were career academics who had adopted Sophie from Beatrice twenty-five years earlier. They didn't know she'd found Beatrice and Cly—and she couldn't tell them, or anyone, because telling them about her birth parents would mean telling them about Stormwrack.

Oh, yeah, this isn't gonna be tricky.

The ironclad closed adoption had, as far as she could tell, suited her parents just fine. They'd never wanted to help Sophie explore her past.

Bram got out of the way as their mother swept in, crushing Sophie into a hug. "Oh! Honey, we've missed you."

She was tearing up. "Are you guys okay?"

"Dad?" Bram said, echoing her question.

"Unscathed," Cornell said. "We were out when the alarm company called."

"Police catch them?"

"*Her*, apparently. Missed by the skin of her teeth."

A sledgehammer lay just beyond the door.

Sophie took it in: a well-used, dirty tool. Splashes of old paint adorned its handle, and there was clay ground into its head. Picked up, maybe, from a nearby construction site? What if her parents had been home when who-ever it was used that to smash in the door? She tried to swallow. Her throat felt like it was full of sand.

"That's not very subtle," Bram said.

"Why bother with subtlety?" Regina said.

Sophie turned a slow circle, taking in the yard and the police. "They didn't take anything?"

"I'm hoping you can tell us." Bettel ushered Sophie through the kitchen; Dad gave her a smile and an arm squeeze as she went past.

"Your parents tidied up after the first time, but—" The inspector was making straight for her bedroom.

"Teeth!" Sophie's possessions had been strewn out into the hall. The intruder had smashed in the walls. Two floorboards had been pried up. So had the windowsill.

Searching for something.

It wasn't her biosamples—Bram had most of those. The few she had left here, a few slides and packets of seeds, lay untouched among the scattered stuff.

"She got out using your parents' balcony," said Bettel. "Ran down the hall, right through the screen, and jumped down to the yard. Outran the police dog. Whoever it was, she was very fit."

"You're positive it was a woman?"

Instead of replying, Bettel said, "Any idea what she was after?"

Sophie could feel her face turning red. She knew, all right, and she was a terrible liar.

Stay in the vicinity of the truth, then.

"I'm a videographer," she said. "The most valuable thing I own is hardware. Dive equipment, cameras. For making footage of . . ."

Wooden, ship-destroying monsters?

Pink narwhals? Red froglike amphibians with tails?

" Animals," she finished. "Engaged in animal behavior."

"Anything proprietary in your video files?"

"You wouldn't steal it. Anyway, my material's backed up online. If someone wanted it, they'd be better off hiring—"

"You think this was a hired job?"

Dammit! For the briefest of seconds, she wished she could just give the inspector the patented Wracker *Don't care, shut up, don't be so curious* brush-off. "I dunno. But hiring, you know, hackers."

"You've been out of town and out of touch, I understand."

"I didn't know this was happening." She shot a dirty look through the window at Bram, who was in the yard, chatting with the dog handler.

"If I asked for your movements—ports, dates, countries visited?"

This was a trap. Her U.S. passport was among the heaps on the floor, where both of them could see it.

Oh, this looks suspicious. What to say?

"This kind of search isn't a random hunt for jewelry or some easy-to-sell music player." Bettel's gaze was all-encompassing, like the searchlight on *Shepherd.*

"Look," Sophie said. "If it was my house and not my folks', I'd say search the place top to bottom. Bring in sniffer dogs, bomb dogs, whatever . . ."

"But?"

"But my mom's a bit of a hippie, if you know what I mean."

"I'm not interested in your parents' weed stash. You're the focus here, Sophie. It's your room they've searched. Twice."

"My point is there was nothing to find. I'm not smuggling drugs. Or doing anything—smuggly. Promise."

"Why would you bring that up, I wonder?"

"Because it's what you seem to suspect."

Bettel joined her at the window, pointing at her parents, who were down on the lawn with Bram. "What happens when whoever she is comes back?"

"There's nothing I can tell you. I'm sorry." She probably looked every bit as worried and terrified as she felt. Or maybe she looked shifty and guilty.

Five guilty.

However she looked, Bettel seemed to read her intention to keep her mouth shut. "Okay, Sophie. If you change your mind, give me a call."

"I will. Thanks. Um, did you send a fingerprint tech?"

Raised eyebrows. "He's in the master bedroom. Why?"

Sophie made her way down the hall. Her parents' room was untouched, but for a few clumps of mud and the screen door being knocked out. She took a whiff of the air, scenting for the reek of the assassins that killed Gale.

Police saw the thief running away, she reminded herself. Nobody had called it a freakish monster with claws.

An athlete. Her half sister, Verena, fit that bill.

She shoved the thought to the back of her mind, along with the guilt seeping from its source, and focused instead on the uniformed officer with a miniature feather duster who was taking prints off the glass of the French doors.

It was easier to say sorry than to ask permission. Sophie raised her camera and took shots—including a close-up—of the powdered prints on the glass.

He glanced over his shoulder. "What are you doing?"

"I've got a shiny new interest in crime science," Sophie told him. "That powder—graphite, right?"

The print technician nodded.

"Do you only identify prints using computers nowadays? Is there a room somewhere where guys with indexes and card catalogs and magnifying glasses do the work?"

The tech laughed. "Mostly computers. Why?"

"I'm researching Victorian procedures for print identification."

He went back to dusting. "I know a retired instructor you could talk to."

Bettel had followed her. Upon hearing this, she threw up her hands and strode away.

Sophie pocketed the fingerprint tech's contact info and rejoined her family. Mom had already decided a house full of cops meant they had to go out for dinner. "Any excuse to not cook," she declared.

"Sounds good to me," Sophie said, and soon they were on their way, in two cars, to a Greek place in the Mission District.

Sophie hadn't realized how much her diet had been limited to seafood until someone offered her moussaka. Restaurant fare was amazing. Normal industrial window glass was amazing. A world that ran on electricity and Wi-Fi, without a single flicker of spellscrip anywhere in sight? So amazing.

As was having a dad who taught poetry instead of wading around in puddles of blood that he'd shed himself.

Her delight in all the conveniences and familiar comforts didn't change the fact that family dinner made for an awkward couple of hours. Bram had obviously convinced their parents that there was no point in quizzing the two of them about where they had been vanishing off to.

Unfortunately, that left a yawning chasm in the conversation.

Sophie cajoled a good fifteen minutes of national politics and local news out of her father. Then everyone fell silent.

"That police detective thinks you're smuggling drugs," her father said.

Sophie snorted.

"I told her rare animal parts were, statistically, more likely."

"Am I deluded, or are you happy about this?" Sophie asked.

"Your father thinks that I'll cave on getting a dog now." Regina had always been a cat person. Unlike Dad, the prospect of more break-ins obviously did not amuse her.

Sophie searched her mother's face. She had left abruptly, without explaining anything, and she'd been gone for months. Her departure had been an awful scene.

Five awful, tears all around.

Now, though, Mom seemed resigned.

Should I feel better about that, or more guilty?

"We'll move me out," Sophie said. "Make my room into a guest room. Box up everything I own, put it in storage—"

"And pay for that how?" Mom said.

"What do you mean?"

"Once you take a look at the papers scattered on your floor, I think you'll find some rather terse notes from credit card companies."

"Oh." She hadn't meant to be gone so long, and the fact that she'd spent everything the credit gods would give her to buy camera and scientific equipment had halfway slipped her mind. She wondered if she'd had any money in the bank before she left. "Well, it doesn't matter. I obviously need to move out."

At the same time, Dad said, "You do think Sledgehammer Sally will be back, then?"

"Teeth," she muttered, out of habit, in Fleet. When she looked up, her father was mouthing the word.

"Was that 'tits'?" her mother asked.

"I—" She looked to Bram for help.

"You can move your stuff to the Dwarf House, Sofe."

"Then they'll break in there!" their mother objected.

"Mom's right about that, son."

"There's nine of us, Regina—someone's always home. Besides, we do have dogs."

"Whatever you're sitting on, kids, it better be worth it. For what you're putting us through? I expect to retire on a mound of diamonds." Mom snapped open the dessert menu. "Baklava to go? Who's in?"

They headed home to find the police were done, and plunged right into straightening up the house and boxing everything Sophie had left. Packing barely took an hour. After, Bram drove a load back to his place while Sophie stayed with her parents. They downloaded a costume drama to avoid talking.

She expected to spend the night awake, in a stew over it all: the break-in, the threat to her family, Inspector Bettel's obvious suspicions—even the money shortage. But the familiar softness of her childhood bed and something about being home—the smell of fog and damp that seemed to come through the window, the mutter in the pipes, and the bed-hogging presence of her mother's six-toed cat—lulled her into a deep sleep.

It was broken, near dawn, by a dream of the bandit Kev, on his knees. Skinny, smelling of fear, he was fumbling teeth out of a mixing bowl filled with watered-down blood. With frantic movements of his red-stained fingers, he tried to arrange them to fill one of the punched-out gaps in her bedroom walls.

Sophie jolted, hard enough to send the cat scuttling across the room. Sitting up, half awake, she clamped her hand over her mouth as she gagged, remembering Cly's blandly focused expression as he skewered one of the bandits. The surprise on the woman's face, the gush of blood between her teeth, from her nostrils . . .

Alive, and then instantly *not.*

Distraction. She lunged for her phone, diving into her backlogged in-box. By the time she was calm again, her parents were moving, and she stumbled downstairs for breakfast and fractured conversations about jobs, break-ins, and guard dogs. It was a relief when Bram arrived to save her, helping to load the last two boxes of her worldly goods and then driving her all of two blocks away, out of sight of home. He parked in front of an old Victorian surrounded by temporary fencing and covered by a tarp. "I was thinking that sledgehammer could've come from here," he said.

"Or a dozen places just like it. You should've told me."

"You were gone. Stuck."

She rocked in place, banging her head against the padded headrest—not quite hard enough to hurt. "Teeth!"

"What are we gonna do?" Bram asked.

She handed him her phone, on which a notes app displayed a string of numbers.

"What's this?"

"Legal description of the parents' property. If we can find you a spell and ingredients for a Don't Break Into This House inscription, I was thinking you could try it out, using this as the house's name."

"That's our go-to now? Magic?"

"Burglar alarm didn't work, Bramble, and we can't be honest with the police. Anyway, it's practice, isn't it? That's why you're making treasure boxes in the Dwarf House attic, right? Now you can practice this."

He acknowledged this with a grunt. "I'm doing schoolkid magic. What if the spell's too hard?"

"Then I'll hire a scribe—once I'm back in Fleet, where I'm actually solvent."

He waved the property description. "What if lot five, parcel twenty, civic tax code mumbo jumbo doesn't work?"

"We get the parents to name the pile of bricks? Hansa Estates?"

"House of Usher," he said.

"Knowing Dad, it'll end up Thornfield."

He reached into her bag, fishing out her notebook. Finding a new page, he wrote, WHAT IF A PERSON, PLACE, OR OBJECT IS GIVEN TWO NAMES?

"That's not a communal to-do list."

"It's a book of questions, isn't it? Keeping them in one place makes sense." He had that mulish expression on: *This isn't just your thing, Sofe. Not anymore.*

She didn't want a fight, not now. "Okay."

Satisfied, he pulled back onto the street. "Where to?"

"The horologist's, to pick up Gale's pocket watch. It's gotta be what our thief was after."

It had belonged to Gale, who had fumbled it in a San Francisco alley, the first time she and Sophie had transited to Stormwrack together. Sophie had searched it out after Bettona sent her back.

"You're not keeping it with you?" Bram asked, after he'd paid the repairman and they were back on the road.

Sophie opened the watch, revealing its painted white face. It had black numbers and impossibly fine hardwood hands. She wound it, just a little.

Tick, tick, tick. The sound filled the car, beating in her eardrums. It had an echo—a heavier, more resonant mechanism. The grandfather clock at Beatrice's?

"I can't be caught with it," she said. "Verena said her people would love to blame me for John Coine coming here to kill Gale."

"My place then?"

"What about a big old bank vault?"

Their parents hadn't been wrong about the cost of paying for storage. Sophie had bought a bunch of camera equipment before her first long sojourn to Stormwrack, and what savings she'd had—which had never been much—were tapped out.

Bram shelled out for the safe-deposit box while she endured a stern lecture from the bank manager about timely payments, debt consolidation, and big *R* Responsibility before they got to leave.

She only stopped hearing the ticking when they were about six blocks from the bank.

CHAPTER 8

Sophie spent the next few days at Bram's, researching forensics and chemistry and hanging out with her parents in the evenings. She managed to connect with the elderly fingerprinting expert, who was only too happy to walk her through the basics of distinguishing whorls from arches, ridgecounting, and other arts of manual print identification.

She loaded as many science texts onto her phone as she could, got her birth control implant refreshed, sold her bike for cash to placate the credit card company, and paid a couple of bills. She trimmed her father's roses and took Mom shopping for clothes for the planned trip to Peru.

She was talking to a dive shop owner about maybe running a quick marine photography workshop, when Beatrice phoned.

"Can you talk?" Her birth mother didn't bother with a preamble.

"Of course."

"I have a message from the family. There's an emergency of some kind. We're expected as soon as we can get back."

Sophie felt a mixture of emotion: twinges of guilt over Mom and Dad, the pull of her half-finished research. She had missed being in Fleet, but sometimes it had seemed like a faraway dream. She and Bram had barely begun sifting through the data she'd brought back.

"I'm in the middle of a bunch of stuff."

"It's not a request. According to this note, you took the Oath."

Ungracious as always. "So, what? I'm at the Fleet's beck and call?"

"E-mer-gen-cy," Beatrice repeated, drawing out the word, as if Sophie were four. "If it's trivial, I'll bring you right back."

"I'll pack and come over." She texted Bram, grabbed her stuff, and headed across the city on Muni.

Beatrice was tall and voluptuous, where her sister Gale had been weather-beaten and compact. Her accent and style of dress were utterly American. She had a black and white fox tattooed on her right shoulder, but only a Wracker would recognize its style or suspect that it meant she was from Verdanii. When she and Sophie first met, she had been appalled to realize that her secret firstborn daughter had tracked her down.

In fact, she'd had an epic freak-out.

Time and a bit of acquaintance had taken the edge off her—the greeting she gave Sophie, this time, was barely nettled. "You missed our window," she said. "We'll have to wait sixteen hours."

"I thought we were in a flaming rush."

"I'm not a practiced eraglider anymore. Unless they send Verena, we're waiting until morning."

"What about that clerk of Annela's . . . Bettona?"

"I wouldn't let Bette drive a bus," Beatrice said scornfully.

"I can tell my brother we're delayed?"

"Knock yourself out."

As she texted Bram, Sophie said, "Someone's been busting into my parents' house."

Beatrice didn't blink. "They've guessed you have Gale's watch."

"Who?"

She shrugged—a real shrug, not the Stormwrack *You're way too curious* shoulder-bob.

"Could it be Annela?"

"Nah. You're sworn to obey the law; she'd demand you give it up. If she even knows you have it."

"Haven't you told her?"

"If anything Verdanii is rightly yours, it's that," she said.

"It hasn't crossed Annela's mind?"

Beatrice tilted her head and Sophie felt her skin crawl: she'd seen herself in the same pose, in pictures. "There may be some 'Don't ask, don't tell' there."

"See if I loop a sinking anchor," Sophie grumbled.

"Or that, yeah." They had been standing in the entryway of the house. Now Beatrice turned, leading the way into a dinky, dated-looking kitchen. She poured two cups of coffee, held one out, and sat at a bar stool alongside the counter.

Sophie sat across from her, taking it in. The place looked as though it had been built in the 1970s, but everything was in good repair. A big window dominated the kitchen sink. Out across a narrow rectangle of yard, Verena's half brother, Shad, and a couple other student-age adults—a couple, from the look of them—were staining a newly erected cedar fence.

The woman who broke into the house had been a track star of sorts; Inspector Bettel said she had jumped from the second-floor balcony to the ground, and had outrun a police dog. But she hadn't been strong enough to knock in Sophie's parents' door or to punch holes in the walls—for that, she'd needed the sledgehammer. "The intruder was either someone from Stormwrack operating here," Sophie mused, "or someone from San Francisco who's helping them. How many people know about Erstwhile?"

"I'm not sure I should tell you."

"I'm oathed up now, remember?"

"Good point. In that case . . . Seventy or so, most of them high government officials. All sworn to secrecy and most too old and creaky to get up to home invasion."

"To come here, people need travel permits from Annela's office. How many of them have come lately?"

"I've got the list." Beatrice pulled it out of a valise. Already prepared . . . Sophie wasn't the only one asking. There were a dozen names, each with an island nation beside it.

"All Wrackers? Nobody from Erstwhile goes to and fro?"

Beatrice shook her head. "Bram's the first true Erstwhiler who's been allowed to return."

"Someone took John Coine gun shopping." A memory of her credit troubles surfaced, and Sophie added, "And paid."

"Maybe there's another way to eraglide. If it's not just the Feliachilds, all bets are off."

"I am going to spend the rest of my life trying to prove negatives: 'Can anyone else eraglide?' 'Probably not, Kir.' 'How do you know?' 'Well, nobody's been caught at it.'"

"There's always you."

"Yeah. Maybe I can be arrested for helping someone terrorize my parents."

"You're in the clear. There are ceremonies tied to eragliding. You haven't been blessed, or trained."

"Would blessing give you a ticking watch earworm? Or does that come with the watch?"

Beatrice's mouth dropped open. "What did you say?"

"I can hear your clock downstairs—actually, if I listen, I can pick up Gale's watch now. Or maybe I'm just imagining that because I know how it sounds. I started hearing your clock when I was halfway here . . ." Sophie held up her phone, displaying map coordinates. "I marked it at a mile and a half distance."

"Mile and a half." Beatrice opened a locked wooden wardrobe, rummaging around for a silver-plated cone lined with what looked like lacquered birch leaves. She laid her hand on Sophie's and said, "Hold this up to your ear."

"Why?"

"It's an ear trumpet. Go ahead."

Sophie raised the cone. Gale's pocket watch came through at once. Hadn't it wound down yet? The clock downstairs bonged, deafening, and Sophie jerked her head away. "Ow!"

"I'll stop ours. Stay here." Beatrice went downstairs and the bonging stopped. "Try again."

"Bossy Verdanii matriarchs," Sophie groused, obeying.

"Well?" Beatrice called from the stairwell.

"I hear Gale's pocket watch."

"Anything else?"

"No-o-o . . ." Sophie started to say, but it wasn't true. There was a thrum, more a heartbeat than anything mechanical. *Brrum, brrum, brrum.* A sense of time passing, a great weight of years reverberating across a yawning distance, calling to her with a voice made of millions of days and nights, of electrical current and crashing waves.

Beatrice took the horn, gently, and the call dissipated.

Sophie had turned, without realizing it, to face the northeast corner of the room. Her shadow fell in that direction and sun warmed her back, even though they were indoors, even though San Francisco was foggy and overcast.

"You can. You can hear the Worldclock. It should be impossible!"

Sophie steadied herself on the counter. "So I can get arrested for treason after all?"

"I don't know about that," Beatrice said. "But you could potentially learn to eraglide."

Sophie led her down to the room with the lockers and started opening doors, exposing the clocks and watches etched inside each door. "This is basically a locker room for Feliachilds who can go back and forth to Stormwrack?"

"Did I say that?"

Sophie decided to take that as permission to go on. "This one's yours—I've seen your clock. Here's Gale's, here's Verena's, and this belongs to Bettona."

Beatrice nodded.

"Who are the other three?"

"Why?"

"Pirates and religious maniacs came here to buy guns, remember? If they have their own way here, we'll never catch them. But the other possibility is—"

"One of the seven brought them?" Beatrice frowned. "My mother was one."

"Ennatrice. She died by ordeal," Sophie remembered. "And there's Pharmann—dead too. Who got his?"

"They're accounted for . . . They're waiting for Verena and Bettona to have children, basically." She tapped a sketch of a wristwatch. "This belongs to Bettona's great-uncle; he maintains our mailhouse in London."

"That cousin's above suspicion?"

"He can't eraglide with anything but himself. He keeps a house and clock. We can go to him, but when he wants to come here, either he takes a commercial flight or I fetch him. Otherwise, he shows up buck naked."

Sophie wondered if that was something a person could fake. "If someone from Verdanii brought John Coine and the other guy here, it can only be one of these seven?"

"Yes."

"Can't anyone can use one of the watches? I mean, if someone's trying to steal Gale's from me—"

"Supposedly it's just a Feliachild."

"As defined by . . ."

Beatrice said. "The customary answer probably isn't scientific enough for you."

"I'll take superstition if that's all you've got," Sophie said. "Nobody else is going to tell me this stuff."

"Indeed." Beatrice laid out the rules briskly. Eragliding was supposedly limited to members of her genetic family, which was one of nine family lines directly descended from the original Allmother's direct descendants.

Family membership depended on who was married to whom, the theory being that if someone strayed too far from that gene pool, they'd have to marry another person from the right family to maintain their status.

"I'm feeling an inbreeding joke coming on," Sophie said.

"Believe me, I've heard them all. Even if you are a true Feliachild, you're supposed to break bread with the Allmother before you can hear the Worldclock." Beatrice frowned. "You seem to have skipped that step."

Maybe this was why Annela had jumped all over the chance to have Sophie repudiate Verdanii citizenship. In promising to stay away from Verdanii, Sophie limited her chances of learning to eraglide. "If it's genetic, and I'm only half Verdanii, maybe I won't be very good at it?"

"Verena's an amazingly talented eraglider, and her father—You met Merro?—is from Oakland. Some have the knack, some don't."

There was so much here to unpack. She thought of her Sylvanner passport. The Verdanii wouldn't want a portside eraglider. No, Annela wouldn't like that one bit.

Now you're thinking like a Wracker, Sofe. Bring it back to the here and now. "In the meantime, people are breaking into my parents' house."

"If it helps, they're probably not in danger," Beatrice said. "I scribed them against casual misfortune when I gave you to them."

"Casual *what*?"

"Please," Beatrice said. "I've been in a car with your mother."

Sophie opened her mouth to defend Mom, thought of all the times she'd come within a hair of whiplash, and shut up.

"It's a light intention. No car wrecks, no house fires, no swindlers—"

"They just got broken into!"

"That was targeted, not casual. And they were out of the house when it happened, both times?"

"Hold on. You? *You* scribed? Or you paid?"

Beatrice's cheeks pinkened. "I'd taken up inscription when I was married to Clydon. It was another reason why marrying him seemed like a good idea. Mother wouldn't let me apprentice."

"He got you into the Spellscrip Institute?"

"Bumped me to the head of the registration list."

"Of course he did. Were you any good?"

"Has your mother wrecked her car? Which reminds me . . . If they're asking a lot of questions and you want me to take the edge off their curiosity—"

"No! Teeth—they're academics! Are you nuts? You can't go playing around with my parents' heads."

"It was just a suggestion."

"What about me?" Sophie demanded. "Did you do anything to me?"

Beatrice's expression froze a little.

"You totally did! What was it?"

With a sigh, Beatrice crossed to an abandoned and rickety-looking baby-changing table propped up against the wall, looking for all the world like it hadn't been moved in two decades. She pushed it aside, then levered up a panel on the floor, revealing a safe.

"Now I know why you don't bother locking the lockers," Sophie said. She felt as if she'd been given Novocain. Her pulse, slamming in her ears, had that whoosh of waves and the Worldclock again. *Brrum, brrum, brrum.*

"It'd be an expression of mistrust," Beatrice said. "We're family, remember?"

A *chunk* as the lock opened. Beatrice started pulling scrolls out of the safe. One. Two. Three.

"You have to understand," she said. "I was never going to see you again. And you were living here . . ."

Four. Five. Six.

"You were never going to be enchanted by anyone else. It didn't matter if I laid on a bit of a magical load. You were never going to find yourself getting into the pain."

Into the pain. Sophie remembered the headache she'd gotten when they taught her Fleetspeak—flawless, accent-free Fleetspeak, in an hour.

Seven.

Paper, parchment, a knitted scarf, all of them glowing with spellscrip. Sophie stared at them, cotton-mouthed.

"What are they?"

"This one's the same ward against misfortune I worked on your parents," Beatrice said. She unrolled another. "Oh—physical vitality. And this one's charm—persuasiveness." Sophie held out her hands for the first three and was staring, jaw slack, as her birth mother glanced over more crumbly looking pages. "Brains, looks, fertility—"

"What? Oh my God!"

"That one's traditional. They teach it in motherschool."

"So I can plan on busting out Feliachild triplets one day, because—" She ran aground as her thoughts turned, inevitably, to Garland. Garland Parrish and babies. *Bzzt.* Before she could completely short-circuit, Sophie said, "What's the seventh?"

Beatrice unrolled it—a fine, crisp sheet of birch bark the color of cream, covered in bright-green calligraphy. "A friend taught it to me before I left Sylvanna. I meant it to bond you with the Hansas. To keep you—"

"From looking for you?"

"I never fit well with my own kin," Beatrice said. There was an apology in her tone. Defensiveness, too. "I wanted you to fit."

Sophie looked at the seven scrips. "Without all this, what? I'd have been an unlucky, clumsy, stupid, butt-ugly pig baby with no social skills?"

"No! You were a beautiful—"

"Don't." She felt the raw edge in her voice. "Don't do that."

"Sophie, they're small intentions. Tiny little—"

"If I go to a spellscribe with all these, plus I was taught Fleet overnight eight months ago, and now I want to learn the legal system upside and downside so I stop falling afoul of Annela and the Fleet's arbitrary dinky picky stupid rules, he'll say no problem?"

Beatrice balked a little. "You're studying law? Law?"

"This isn't about Cly, Beatrice. And it's so not the point."

"Fine. I've screwed everything up, okay? Is that what you want to hear?"

"I want the truth."

"You're too loaded to absorb the code of law. You shouldn't have been loaded for Fleet. These backlands inscribers . . ."

"Oh, go blame the foreign guy?" Sophie was horrifically, deeply, intensely upset. Snatching up the scrolls, she stuffed them in the first thing she found, a plastic grocery bag that had been sitting on the clothes dryer. "You don't even understand how the last one works!"

"Those should stay in the safe."

"I'll be back in fifteen hours to catch that ride to Stormwrack," Sophie said, not even sure it was true, before she stormed out.

CHAPTER 9

She ended up crying in some nameless park on the waterfront, twisting and stretching the handles of the grocery bag that held the inscriptions, and watching a bunch of gulls worrying the body of a desiccated fish on the edge of a litter-encrusted stretch of tidal flat.

It was *everything.* How she looked. The way people tended to let her talk them around to what she wanted. She'd been in tight spots on climbs and dives and had always believed it was a clear head and resourcefulness that had brought her through.

She pulled out the ward against random misfortune. It was stitched on the red scarf, and though the letters were in black thread, they had the glimmer of active magic. The seventh scroll, the one whose purpose Beatrice apparently didn't even *understand,* had been lettered with a fine brush in green.

She couldn't read anything on them but her own name.

She had been weeping for more than an hour when Bram showed, easing his car into the narrow half space beside hers and joining her on the bench. He glanced over the scrolls, one after another, and said, finally, "Whatcha doing, Ducks?"

"Trying to work up the courage to toss 'em?"

"That would be deeply—"

"Idiotic? Impulsive?"

"Unwise. Why don't you let me lock them in that shiny new safe-deposit box with Gale's watch and—"

"Oh, no. No way."

"Sofe." His voice was infuriatingly careful. "I get that you're upset—"

"Do you get why?"

He opened his mouth.

"I don't want to hear what your therapist would say."

"Just . . ." Bram took a breath. "Tell me."

She jumped to her feet, wiping an already sodden tissue over her cheeks. "All this. I'm barely a real person. I'm a made thing. A windup doll—or, who was that statue? Galatea? I'm the image of what Beatrice wanted. A designer baby."

"At most, you're a transform." He used the Fleet word; it meant someone with job-specific magical enhancements.

"Not an oddity?"

"Technically . . ."

"Beatrice did the spells herself—did she tell you that? She was on the run here in Erstwhile. She barely knew what she was doing. Dabbling out of a spell book—"

"She told you this?"

She waved the birch scroll. "She doesn't even understand what this one does!"

He took it, his grip unusually firm as he pried it from between her fingers. "We should work that out, then, before you go pitching it in the shredder."

"Maybe."

"Copy them, Sofe. I'll write out the scrips so we can study them and safely lock up the originals."

"No, no, no." What was most upsetting was that he was looking at the text—running a parallel baby-genius-think about spellscribing—even as he tried to calm her down.

"Sofe, you're not thinking clearly."

"She gave me good luck and brains. Did I tell you the brains part? Mom and Dad could've been stuck with some klutzy, hideous, learning-challenged—"

"Do you honestly want to test that? Tear up the brain scroll and hit Mensa for a new IQ test?"

"The looks could go, couldn't they? Stupid, cosmetic, frivolous—I'm all loaded up with magic. What if I'm chasing pirates and I break my leg?"

"We bring you back here for X-rays and a cast," he said. "You know you don't get the load back by tearing up previous spells. And adding to the parents' trauma by doing something that might change your appearance—"

She laughed. "When we first got to Stormwrack and I learned about magic, I thought Garland had gotten his face done. I was all *Wow, how vain!* There's irony for you."

"Did Beatrice give you your curiosity?"

"Smart people are curious," she said.

"What about the generosity? Don't huff, Sofe, you *are*—"

"Maybe the tendency to freak out is all me. Wait, no—Beatrice is a drama queen."

"Or your interest in nature?"

"I'm just a construct."

Bram had bagged the spells by now, packing them in his own duffel. Even as he talked to her, he'd pulled out his phone and was typing with one finger.

"I've been mooching off the parents," she said.

"Now you're casting around for sticks to beat yourself with."

She wrenched the bag from his grasp. "I hunted down Cly and Beatrice to sort out my origin. My nature, I guess. And he's probably sociopathic and she fine-tuned herself a designer spawn, only to dump it on—"

"Sofe, you know Mom and Dad love you."

"Then she made them lucky, and—whoop!—previously infertile couple gets pregnant. With a baby supergenius."

Bram's thumb froze midtext.

"See. Prospect's not as comfy when you're the changeling monster pixie baby in question." She'd wound herself up enough to power another storm of tears, so she strode away, arms wrapped around the duffel, sobbing as angrily as some toddler who'd gotten her ice cream stolen.

The gulls didn't so much as glance at her.

A small, cool, inner part of her was standing back from all of it.

He's not saying so, but I'm being ridiculous. So Beatrice gave me some gifts as she sent me on my way out of her life. Wouldn't I have done the same? I should be grateful, but damn it, I should've been the one to choose. And now I can't shortcut my way to law—which was maybe lazy, or a bad use of magical loading anyway. . . .

She cried harder. She didn't want to be rational. "This sucks."

Bram had followed her. "She's not wrong about Mom's driving."

She couldn't even rouse a smile.

"Look," he said. "There's some big deal brewing in Fleet, right? You have to go?"

"I'm all oathed up and bound to obey. Besides, if I stay here, that banker will probably drag me off in chains to debtors' prison."

"Debtors' prison's not a thing anymore."

"That cop who thinks I'm a smuggler could have a go at incarcerating me."

"Beatrice is leaving in twelve hours?"

She nodded.

"So we go home, finish turning your room into a guest suite, plant a few webcams, drop your remaining stuff at my place . . ."

She sniffled. "Get Dad a pit bull puppy?"

"Yeah."

"What's the rush? You could do that anytime." She rubbed her eyes. "Oh. You're coming along."

"I'm not leaving you alone, Sofe."

"Bram, that'll make everything here worse. With Inspector Bettel, and—"

"I'm not leaving you with all this, not in a scroll-ripping mood."

"You don't have to—"

"Really? You're over it? You'll let me take the inscriptions to the bank?"

Her jaw set.

"Yeah," he said. "I'm coming. You bet your magically engineered ass I'm coming."

Why couldn't Beatrice have given me a poker face instead of dimples? She was too wrung out to argue. "Fine," she said, and stomped her way back to the parking lot.

CHAPTER 10

Beatrice brought them back to Stormwrack the next morning, into the heat of Annela's clock room, which had been left to get stuffy.

Sophie had cried off and on through the night, and now her sinuses were packed. Her whole body, from the eyelids out, felt incredibly raw, as if she'd been skinned.

She was puffy-faced and unkempt, and it didn't help that, when Beatrice rapped out a summons and a clerk came running, the boy's reaction, at the sight of her, that said she looked as though she'd been run over.

Beatrice bowled past him, into Annela's sumptuous nest. The bed was empty. Through the portal, Sophie saw rumpled bedclothes.

Bram raised a hand to his nose. "Someone's been sick."

"Where are my cousins?" Beatrice demanded.

The clerk, who was maybe sixteen, stammered a reply in Verdanii.

"Use Fleetspeak," Beatrice said, in a voice of iron, but instead of waiting for him to obey, she translated: "'Nella's ordeal is going badly. She's been ferried to the hospital."

"Bettona go with her?" Sophie asked.

"Of course, Kir," said the boy.

Forget the scrolls for a minute, she thought. *Get your head out of your navel and work.* She made herself take a slow breath, pulling air between her teeth, forcing it out again. She bunched the muscles in her hands, arms, shoulders, then relaxed them.

Institute business. Make a good impression. Don't just find the truth; prove it. Make it unassailable.

Following Beatrice into the cabin, she unslung her camera and shot the bedclothes, the walls, and floor. The cabin was filled with cushy luxuries: velvet bolsters, incense burners, ornate paper fans.

"Bram—test tubes."

He began digging.

"For what?" Beatrice said.

Sophie sampled some ash from the incense, then began examining the carpet. A circular patch about six inches in diameter had been scrubbed so hard its dye had faded a little. She looked around for a bucket. "Maybe we can test the vomit for poison."

"You can't be poisoned when you're fasting, Kirs," said the clerk.

"Sure you can," Sophie and Bram said simultaneously.

Beatrice folded her arms. "Bettona's high on your list of suspects, then?"

"Process of elimination." Sophie switched to English. "If there is an eraglider working for the pirates, and it's not you, the London uncle, or Verena . . ."

"Or you?"

Sophie found the trash can. There was nothing in it but more ash and bits of shredded paper. "Bettona's undervalued, and her career prospects are in the bilge."

"'Nella seemed to think she was beyond suspicion."

"If it occurred to you to ask, you wondered about her, too," Bram said.

"I asked," Beatrice conceded. "But she has an alibi. They were drafting new legislation, pulling all-nighters, when Gale was stabbed. Bette couldn't have slipped off to transport Gale's assassins to Erstwhile."

Sophie tried a desk drawer. Locked.

"Confidential papers, Kir," the clerk said.

"We should get a blood sample from Annela," she said.

Bram made a pretense of searching his pockets. "I neglected to pack a phlebotomist in here, Sofe."

"Beatrice? Can Wrackers take blood?"

"*I* can take blood," she said, and Sophie remembered that she worked in a hospice. "I don't know about screening it for poisons."

"If we don't have it, we can't even try. I guess she might throw up again."

"Live in hope," Beatrice said drily. "This doesn't have to be sinister, kids. 'Nella's stubborn and ambitious. She might have pushed the fast too far."

"You believe that?"

"I'll talk to her. If I can get over not being a spellscribe, she can get over not growing up to be God."

I'm not sure that follows, Sophie thought. She turned to the young clerk, who was taking in their activity with an air of astonishment. "Are Bettona's rooms here?"

"No, Kir. She lives aboard *Breadbasket.*"

"Okay. We'll all go to the hospital ship, and then . . . maybe Bram and Krispos can go look at Bettona's place?"

"Actually, Kir, you're wanted most urgently." The young clerk held out a bunch of sealed envelopes.

"I'll watch Annela like a hawk," Beatrice promised. "I'll even take one of your test tubes in case she pukes."

"You're a suspect too."

"Do you want the disgusting body fluids or not, kid?"

"Fine." Exchanging the sample kit for her stack of mail, Sophie cracked open a black-bordered envelope. It was addressed to SOPHIE HANSA E LOW BANN, SYLVANNA. The designation made her skin crawl.

"What?" Bram peered over her shoulder.

"What the clerk said. That cranky old dude, Salk, from the Watch, wants to see me."

"And the rest of the paperwork?"

She did a quick flip. "Red tape. Budget appropriation for the Forensic Institute. Payroll stuff."

"Payroll?" Bram said. "As in, an answer to your cash flow—"

She interrupted. "For the fingerprinting project."

Before he could ask anything else—she didn't fancy Beatrice hearing about her burgeoning credit card debt—she charged out into the maze that was *Constitution*'s lower decks, obliging Bram to keep pace. Soon they were in a dimly lit corridor, on the twelfth level, peering at an unmarked hatch.

"You sure this where Annela took us before?" Bram asked.

"Maybe. All these hatches look the same." She raised a hand to knock, but the door opened before she reached it, yanked aside by a familiar, wizened man wearing a malevolent expression. He smelled, she noted, of vinegar.

"You took your time, child."

"Something about the angle of the sun," Sophie said. She was too depressed to be argumentative.

"And brought your memorician," he said.

"Technically, I'm her autodidact," Bram said in his accented Fleet.

"Has the convenor died, girl? You look like overwarm butterfish."

"I'm pretty sure my oath covered showing up, not looking good."

"Fortunately for us all," he said, gesturing to indicate his own timeworn face. "I am sorry about your cousin Gracechild."

"Is that why you summoned me? Because I need someone to go to *Breadbasket* and search Bettona Feliachild's quarters. In case she poisoned Annela."

"Do you truly believe it a Verdanii domestic matter?" He looked as though the prospect delighted him. "Send your new forensic assistants . . . Selwig and Humbrey."

"I haven't even met them."

"They're up to turning over a residential berth," he said. "Believe it or not, the Watch caught a few criminals during the Cessation without your assistance."

"Sorry."

"We have other business. Come in."

They trooped in and took seats in the uncomfortable desks that gave the room its schoolhouse appearance.

"Here's the wind, girl. This summer past you were aboard your father's ship, *Sawtooth,* when she boarded a small ship run by bandits."

"Retrograd Incannis." Sophie shuddered.

"Since your return to Erstwhile, the surviving bandit has been put to trial and sentenced to death."

"So fast?" Sophie wasn't any kind of fan of the death penalty, but *Incannis* had been sinking other boats and murdering their crews—nobody was disputing that.

Sinking smugglers, she thought. There were things about that that had never made sense.

"The trial was scheduled for next year, but the courts pushed up the date just after you left the Fleet," Salk said. "Now then. The condemned—Kev Lidman's his name—has invoked Fleet law to stave off his execution."

"Typical. Always a loophole, right?"

The old man bared yellow teeth. "If you're proposing to enforce the law, girl, you might pretend to respect it."

"What clause?" Bram said.

"A citizen forfeits his right to life by committing capital crimes asea. But a slaver may assume possession of said individuals by intervening in their dispatch."

"I'm not following this."

"You saved Kev Lidman from a quick skewering at the hands of His Honor the duelist adjudicator. In the eyes of the law, said skewering would have had the same force as legal execution."

Killed a bandit, killed another bandit, got some of the third on my shoe . . . She fought back an inappropriate giggle that half felt like it might lead to throwing up.

"Sophie didn't save the guy," Bram objected. "He put a knife to her throat."

Salk continued: "Lidman and the duelist adjudicator agree that she intervened in his dispatch. She, therefore, asserted primary ownership rights over his person."

"What?" Sophie said.

"Sophie's not a slaver," Bram objected.

"She's Sylvanner, isn't she?"

"She's Sylvanner? Wait, you're Sylvanner now?"

Red tape and loopholes. Was it any wonder she thought Fleet customs were stupid? "Well, I'm an oddity; I might as well be a slaver, too. What happens now, Kir Salk?"

"You can give Lidman back to the court and we'll pass him to another claimant, or behead him in a threeday. As he chooses."

"Beheading? That is *horrifying*."

"Technically, you can behead him yourself."

"And again, twice as hard, with the horrifying. Horrifying five."

"Sofe," Bram said. "This would be the guy who attacked you."

"For a nanosecond!"

"He helped kill the sailors aboard the ships they raided."

"Yeah, he's a bad guy. But you're saying let's add a fun beheading to my list of personal accomplishments?"

"He's basically a pirate."

Ah. Pirates. A justified sore point with Bram. Still . . .

"I don't believe you'd even consider . . . Anyway, wait. What are my other options, Kir Salk? Give him up or . . ."

"It's illegal to keep the bonded in Fleet," the old man said. "If you don't surrender Lidman to the court, you must take him home."

"Home. Sylvanna?"

"Certainly not to Erstwhile." He gave her a canny look. "Well, girl?"

"Teeth! Can I talk to him before I decide?"

"I'd expect no less." He handed her a sheaf of pages. "He's on *Docket*. Your brother will not be permitted to accompany you."

"Understood."

"Go, then. Out of my sight."

They left.

"What the eff, Sofe?"

"Someone will be behind this," she said. "Cly, maybe?"

"How do you figure him?"

She shook her head. "Either it's revenge, because I made such a scene at that festival, or he wants me back on Sylvanna, or—I dunno. Just what we needed. Another level-five pain in our—"

"What can I do?"

Despite the overall trampled feeling, she felt a wave of love and gratitude. "Lots. Get us berths in the apartment block, make an appointment with Mensalohm the lawyer so we can find out how many snakes are in this fun new pit. And, remember Krispos?"

"Mister Memory?"

"I had him reading up on frightmaking inscriptions and Isle of Gold customs for me. See how he's doing."

"What about these new forensic techs?" He flipped through the pages. "Ragan Selwig and Mel Humbrey?"

She peered at the résumés. "Annela probably handpicked them to tell her when I break my oath."

"Now you're getting paranoid."

"Only because everyone's out to get me."

"They're like . . . cop partners, it says."

She nodded. Humbrey apparently came from a free nation; his partner, Selwig, was from the slaveholding island Cardesh. "Wonder if there's any way to reassign or trade in the portside guy?"

"Seems like they're a matched set. Cop married. Like Starsky and Hutch."

Heads together, they browsed the write-ups. The senior of the two, Humbrey, had suffered serious hearing loss on the job and they'd both been reassigned. Salk wrote that they were smart, hardworking, and regular in their habits. Whatever that meant.

"Isn't managing staff rather a lot to take on?" Bram asked.

She shook her head. "If Annela's been poisoned, the Age of Stupid Science needs us on our game. We solve this—"

"It's a feather in our cap?"

"I was thinking more that it'd be, like, we caught a would-be assassin."

"Yeah. Of course." He cleared his throat. "Speaking of bad guys, you don't owe this Kev Lidman person anything."

She remembered vividly how scared he had been. How starved and afraid. She'd been avoiding the issue, pushing away every mention of Kev and his trial, promising herself she'd deal with him later.

What she said was, "Bram, come on. Do you really truly honestly believe I should let a human being get beheaded without first talking to him?"

Bram struggled visibly. "No. Of course not, no. Do you have messageply so we can text?"

She opened her book of questions. "There's the page. And—oh!"

"What?"

"This one says *Nightjar*'s on her way back with—"

And that was when she stepped up to the main deck of *Constitution,* looking like day-old butterfish apparently, and walked straight into Captain Garland Parrish.

Garland was looking ever so slightly disheveled. His black frock coat was the older and more worn of his two, and he had a goat under one arm, a long-haired and woolly beast with twisting horns. It was hanging placidly in his grip, but Sophie could see bite marks on his wrist.

His handsome features lit up when he saw Sophie. Which was especially flattering considering her face had a puffy full-night's bawl all over it.

"Sophie," he said, with every evidence of both pleasure and relief. "You wouldn't by any chance have a rope, would you?"

She set down her camera bag, unclipped the nylon strap from its loops, and held it out. Garland shifted the goat, which promptly sank its teeth into his arm. Ignoring it, he dug into its dreadlocks to reveal a collar.

Sophie clipped the strap on.

"Hold tight," he said, before setting the creature down.

With a clatter of hooves, the thing trotted to the yard's worth of distance the makeshift leash allowed, yanking.

Garland let out an unmistakably relieved sigh and reached for Sophie. Before she had time to object, she found herself enfolded against him.

Damn, it felt good.

He kissed her, and *that* felt even better.

"Apologies," he said. "I no doubt reek of goat."

"It's fine. Why do you have her? She's not another rescue, is she?" Garland had a tendency to liberate and rehome animals who'd been experimented on by spellscribes.

"No, thank the Seas." He shook his head. "The people of Glysta have declined to retire their convenor. They say there's a spell they can work, using the goat hair, to offset—" He broke off as one of the uniformed pages passed nearby.

The convenor had severe mental illness, Sophie remembered. "To fix it?"

"So they claim."

He didn't smell of goat. He smelled of sandalwood and maybe a bit of linseed oil, and he was warm, and he'd been glad to see her, though she looked like a train wreck on legs.

Yeah, and you're magically beautified and charming. The thought came like a fire-hose blast of ice water. She extricated herself from his grip the next time the goat tugged on her.

"Verena told me you went home," Garland said, taking the opportunity to offer Bram a bow.

"Is she still on Verdanii?"

"As far as I know. But you're back sooner than expected. Is something wrong?"

With a huff, Sophie told him quickly about Annela. Then she handed him the sheaf of pages about Lidman, letting him read for himself.

"What will you do?"

"I'll see him, anyway. Then—"

"It's not your responsibility."

"That's what I told her," Bram said.

"If I just let him get guillotined without at least asking why . . ."

"I'd do the same," he assured her, and again she felt that warmth. "You must allow *Nightjar* to take you to Sylvanna."

"You sure you want to—"

"This man did threaten you," he said. "I wouldn't trust you with anyone else."

"She'll take it," Bram said. "Say thank you, Sofe."

"Thank you, Garland." Anyway, being away from him wasn't what she wanted. She pushed aside the swirl of interior objections, all the reasons why she shouldn't be pursuing him or letting him pursue her.

"Is His Honor behind this?"

"I've been wondering." It had come so fast on the heels of him sticking her with the Sylvanner passport. "Judiciary rushed him to trial as soon as I went home."

"I'm sorry."

"Totally not your fault."

"Do you want me to come with you, to talk to the prisoner? You'd have to wait until . . ." He gestured at the goat, who had half stood on its hind legs and was trying to climb onto a stanchion.

"No," Sophie said. "Can you maybe go to *Breadbasket* and meet up with the two Watch guys who are supposed to be searching Bettona Feliachild's quarters?" After all those years of spying with Gale, she would bet Garland knew how to poke around a place looking for clues.

"If you're sure—"

"I'll be okay, really. Bram and I were going to take lodgings—"

"Come to *Nightjar*."

"Tomorrow. Maybe . . ." *Maybe what? We can clean up and I can be magically pretty and charm you to pieces?*

"It will be all right, Sophie."

He leaned in to kiss her again, but she pretended not to see him coming.

"Kaythanksbye." She handed him the goat leash and made for the ferry launch.

CHAPTER 11

Dear Cousin Sophie,

Mumma will be furious when she works out I am writing you, after that scene you caused at the Highsummer Festival. But I am often at the Institute lately, and my mentor Autumn Spell says a child my age should consult her own conscience on questions of friendship.

Since you left Sylvanna, I have been volunteering with the group commissioned by the Spellscrip Institute to enact your study of the annual turtle migration. This has brought me into contact with our neighbors Rees and Fralienne Erminne and we have talked about their abolitionist views on bonded labor. I cannot say I am convinced by their arguments, but I am listening, and thinking a lot.

Since you proved that the nation of Haversham was responsible for perpetuating the throttlevine infestation in the swamps, our efforts to eradicate the vine have been more successful. I thought you would want to know that cousin Clydon kept his word to you, freeing the throttlevine-eating slaves of Low Bann, tearing up the inscriptions that made them into oddities, and helping them settle in a village near Hoarfrost. Other swamplands estate owners have done less, and it has been a contentious local issue. Fralienne Erminne is therefore running for governor of the Autumn District. She would be the first anti-bondage governor in our nation's history. If she can marry her son to someone respectable, she may win, as the current governor has lately been found to have wealthy and powerful friends on Haversham.

Everyone is very much on edge.

I hope this finds you well, busy, and happy. I am keeping some mail for you that has come to Low Bann. If you want me to send it on, let me know where to ship it.

Your cousin,
Merelda Fenn Banning, chile y Low Bann, Sylvanna

Docket, the ship that served as a brig for the Fleet judiciary, was, to Sophie's surprise, a galley. It had two levels of red and black oars bristling from its lower decks and a strange red-and-black exterior that made it apparent the whole craft was, like *Breadbasket*, as much magical organism as construct. The masthead was insectile—a millipede's face. The crew was mostly fivers, older cadets, and many of them were heavily muscled. They were fitter and more stone-faced than most Fleet cadets.

Jailers, Sophie thought.

She braced herself for the prospect of seeing prisoners down in the hold, pulling oars, but her escort conducted her to an interview room divided by a panel of a fine-looking glass substitute, a lightly frosted substance with the shimmer and look of insect wings.

Lidman was already there.

He didn't look as though he'd been hauling oars. He'd been sunburned, starved, and on the verge of scurvy when they caught him. Since then he had put on weight, though not muscle. His hands were encased in translucent red carapaces, the fingers and thumbs protruding.

"Are those casts? Did someone break your hands?" Sophie demanded.

Lidman showed his teeth and said, a bit loudly, "You have a kind heart, mistress."

"No! No, no, no. None of this slave-and-owner crap or I walk."

He lowered his voice. "My life depends on behaving correctly."

Sophie folded her arms tightly across her chest, hoping that she looked stern, not shaky. "Tell me about your hands."

"It's to keep me from writing."

"Because you're a spellscribe?" It made sense, she supposed. He could barely move his fingers.

Kev nodded.

He had grabbed and threatened her in a fight aboard his ship, after Cly had already skewered his buddies. Kev let her go as soon as her birth father came at him. Cly would have jammed a sword through his heart without a second thought if Sophie hadn't intervened.

He was harmless, not scary. What distressed her, as she searched his face and her nose caught a familiar waft of fear sweat, was the memory of Cly. Her birth father not quite smiling, leaving bloody footprints as he advanced on them, sword raised.

"Sit down," she said to Kev.

"I can't sit if you don't."

"Fine," she said, dropping into a cushy chair that seemed to have been brought just for her. "You and your pals were raiding ships."

"I won't deny it." He perched on a wooden stool.

"You killed the crews, too. I'm no booster for the death penalty, but I don't see why I should go out of my way to help a multiple murderer."

"There's more to it."

"You're gonna tell me you had an excuse?"

"Uh . . ." He swallowed.

"Maybe you were compelled?" Sophie threw this out as bait, to see how dumb he thought she was. And he paused, weighing it—weighing her—before shaking his head.

By now she'd noticed that they'd pulled the rotten tooth he'd had when they captured him, and had stitched up a cut on his neck. The nails of his hands had been cleaned recently; he couldn't have done that himself, not in those restraints. The Fleet cared for its prisoners.

Kev said, "Our captain—Eame, the one His Honor shot first . . ." His hand drifted past his throat, where the crossbow bolt had struck. "He wrote to me a year ago about stealing *Incannis*. We were old friends. I'm Haver, but I studied magic on Tug Island."

"You're college buddies, so what? Why'd you take it into your heads to steal the ship in the first place?"

"You saw the sloop—she was a terrible thing. She used human corpses to make salt frights."

"It wasn't you who wrote the original spell into the boat?"

"No! My specialty is compulsions for troubled children."

Sophie leaned forward. "You cut the heart out of a dead body and used it to make the monsters that attacked *Sawtooth*."

"Any of us could have raised them. *Incannis* herself bore the frightmaking intention."

Frightmaking, Sophie thought. The wooden creature that had sunk *Kitesharp* was a fright too. Two sets of sinkings, tied to a type of magic that had supposedly been eradicated. Annela had suggested that wasn't coincidence.

"Tug's slave hunters were going to launch *Incannis* and go looking for escapees," Kev went on. "Eame said why not make off with her, change the quarry?"

"Quarry. You were hunting smugglers, right? Amber shippers, drug guys." She groped for the name of the opiate-producing plant. "Maddenflur. You were sinking maddenflur smugglers."

He looked puzzled. "The hard cargo provided funds to buy food. But what we were after was . . . All the ships came from portside nations. They weren't just shipping goods. They were trafficking in soft cargo."

"Soft what?"

"People."

Sophie felt a jolt. "You were sinking slavers?"

"Didn't you—truly, did you not know? The home ports of the ships we attacked were Isle of Gold, Ualtar, Sylvanna, Tug itself—"

Sophie put up a hand, interrupting. "If that's true, where'd the slaves go?"

"I—" He faltered. "We met a ship."

"What ship?"

"Allies. Friends of Eame's."

There was a stink of lie coming off him now. Sophie opened her mouth to say so, but he rushed in to fill the silence. "If you knew where they were, you'd be honor-bound to report it to the Watch. The people we freed would be captured and returned to bondage."

She flashed briefly on Annela, her smug certainty that Sophie couldn't go a week without oathbreaking. Still . . .

"Kev," she said. "You're hiding something."

He bonked his hands together, probably meaning to wring them. "We liberated far more bonded people than we—"

"Than you slaughtered slavers?"

"Rescuing slaves at sea is one of the few ways to truly free them. They're shipped with the scrolls that hold their will in thrall."

He meant intentions that forced them to obey their owners. Sophie thought of the scrips Beatrice had written. Of their essential fragility, and of Bram demanding that she hide them.

"We sent them away, my word on it. And whenever the ships' crews surrendered, we sent them along with their former cargo, as prisoners. We only killed those who resisted."

"But you won't tell me where to find anyone who can vouch for you."

He shook his head. "If you don't take me on, I'll have to opt to be beheaded, lest I'm claimed for bondage by Tug Island or Ualtar. They'll wring the truth out of me; they'll force me to expose the people we liberated. Sylvanners, you're more humane."

"I'm not . . . Oh, forget it."

"You're kind, Kir Sophie. You saved me once . . ."

"So could I please do it again?"

He gave her a weak smile. "It's a thin wind, but it's all my sails can catch."

"I have to think about this," she said, getting up.

He shot to his feet. "My execution's scheduled for high sun, in a threeday."

Sophie closed her eyes. Then she made herself walk out without looking back.

They didn't give her any time to pull herself together. The guard escorted her to an office, where they laid out the procedure for claiming Lidman, if she chose. It looked about as complicated as buying a car. Finally, they patted her down, checking again for weapons or contraband, before letting her onto a ferry bound for the residential quarter.

Exhausted to the point of numbness, she let herself deflate into a seat on the rail of the upper deck, staring across the Fleet as the crews of the government ships embarked on their afternoon shift change. Trios of uniformed cadets from the dawn shift stood just to starboard of each ship's bow, unrolling three flags: the Fleet flag first, the ship's national flag next, and a third designating its purpose—military, governance, or justice. On the hour, a shrill whistle blast sounded from each ship.

"Chi hurrah, hurrah achi yeh!" The ceremonial cheer echoed faintly from each deck. Sophie had heard it was a Verdanii peace cry.

The ferry captain tapped the last few grains out of his hourglass, then flipped it. The trio of cadets on each ship passed their flags to cadets on the evening shift, who held them in place over the port side and cheered again before rolling them up and marching off to work.

"Another bright day in the century of peace, *neh*?" said the ferryman, apparently to himself.

Sophie got comfortable in her seat, paged through her book of questions, made a couple notes, and then opened another of her letters, which turned out to be from Xianlu of *Shepherd*. It began:

> *Kir Hansa,*
>
> *Your man Krispos asked that I write to update you on the investigation of recent sinking of* Kitesharp *(and, by extension, the earlier victims).*

The sailor you identified as having a missing finger is named Darel Lest of Ascro Island. He is not thirty, and was a fisher until an accident six years ago which resulted in his disfigurement. His injuries would have been fatal, but two spellscribes restored him. Afterward, having lost his nerve for sailfishing, he trained as a mechanic.

He claims to have no involvement in or memory of an action against his ship. However, his medical history shows signs of recent magical loading.

It seems probable that Lest may have had his name stolen by an unscrupulous scribe, and that he was used as a template, to use your term, for the wood fright. The Watch is even now tracing the scribe who cured him after the accident. They seem to believe there are some name-stealing crime rings proliferating in the western isles and on the more populous nations.

We have recommended that ships to the rear of the Fleet perform regular inspections, seeking the mark you saw on the day of the sinking—the outline of a hand, in wax.

If the raiders strike again, as seems likely, you would be very welcome to rejoin us aboard Shepherd. *We have commended your efforts thus far to the Watch.*

She felt a bit of a glow at that. She'd been useful; she'd helped.

"Your stop, Kir." The ferryman handed her into a makeshift elevator, a crude platform dangling from simple pulleys, hauled up by workmen on the deck of the ship above.

Sophie was an old hand at this now. She let them hoist her aboard, then went to check in with the ship's purser.

Bram had moved them into adjoining cabins across the corridor from Krispos, two narrow slots with bunks at shoulder height and small lounging areas—a chair and a half-desk, essentially—contained below. There was a vanity between them for washing up, and a sliding panel for privacy.

He'd obviously had time to swing through one of the market ships that acted as seagoing shopping malls. A pair of ram skulls jostled together in a net bag near his pillow, and he was paging through a thick book called *Compendium of Starter Spells, Fleet-Approved and Fit for Children Ages 9–16.* Small satchels and paper bundles scattered near the book were probably spell components.

"It looks like there may indeed be a ward against burglars I can work on our house," he said.

"Did you get food?"

"Forgot."

Classic. She felt a wave of mixed affection and exasperation.

"More mail for you." He pointed out a crate filled with stiff brown file cards. "Oh, and Krispos dragged home a bag of spores."

"Club moss," she said. "Early version of fingerprint powder."

"Whom are we printing?"

"Once we've built a fingerprint database and identified those found bodies, we'll practice lifting latent prints from surfaces. The folks in the Watch are basically federal cops. If we can lay out a procedure for identifying prints and convince them it's useful, they'll be thrilled to do the heavy lifting on developing a proper bureau."

"Okay, but this place is superstition central. What's to keep some competing expert from saying a certain whorl pattern proves a criminal is guilty, or something?"

"We lay out the procedure, claim proprietary rights, do a few cases, and then license it to the Watch . . . with a rule that they can't testify unless we approve the work."

"Sounds like a lot of report reading and rubber-stamping."

"Easy enough to do that at sea, while we're on our way to somewhere cool for a dive," she said, hoping this would eventually prove true. So far, Stormwrack had yielded far more procedure and paperwork than time in the field. "Once we have an expert or two who buys into the whole procedure, we can set them on the rubber-stamping."

"Works in theory."

She opened his duffel, pulling out Beatrice's scrolls. Good luck, good looks, silver tongue, intellect, grace, and—she sent up a mental flare of thanks for her birth control implant—fertility. Last came the mystery scroll, lettered in green, on birch bark.

"You okay?"

"No, Bram," she said. "Five out of five no."

"What can I do?"

She shook her head.

"Want to tell me about Prison Man?"

"Kev?" She recounted their interview.

"You gonna take him on? You don't owe the guy anything, Sofe."

She rocked back on her bed. Both options pretty much sucked. She didn't want to let Kev get beheaded, but owning him, even temporarily, was a horrific prospect. And there was something about Kev—his smell, perhaps?—that unsettled her in some deep but hard to articulate way. She felt off balance, almost seasick. "He says Ualtar will snatch him up and torture the location of liberated slaves out of him."

Bram bit his lip. "You think that's true?"

"Well. . . . Obviously, he wants to live. I don't know that I believe he's telling me the whole story."

"Why?"

"Just a feeling. I mean, slave escapes must be a thing, right? They must happen? Must have been happening all along? The portside nations must have put resources into stopping them. Do they really not know where the escapees go?" She thought about what Kev had told her: slaves being transported with spells that forced them to behave. They'd need some kind of legally binding name change, wouldn't they, to be truly free of bondage? That meant government involvement. Birth certificates, citizenship papers. "The free nations have got to be helping them. But I bet that's one of the thousands of things they never talk about openly in Fleet."

Bram rubbed the pearl in his thumb. "You're saying *Where are the slaves going?* isn't an interesting enough question to make it worth torturing the guy—"

"Kev," she said again.

"Was it okay?" he asked. "Seeing him?"

She experienced a surge of feeling. A sob threatened, powered by the sick feeling and leftover emotional fragility from her storm of tears the night before. Her memory served up footage of Cly, skewering Kev's crewmates one by one.

Instead of answering, she leaned against him, taking comfort from the heat of his shoulder against hers. "Did anything come of searching Bettona's quarters?"

"Yeah, actually. Parrish and your constables found two books in Bettona's room, in a plastic bag from home. I left them in the bag, in case you want to do prints, but you can see the covers." He waved something, at the edge of her peripheral vision, but she kept staring at the scrolls.

"What are the titles?" she said eventually.

"*Things That Go Boom!* and *Domestic Terrorism for Young Patriots.*"

"Teeth," she said. "That can't be good."

"Nope. So my point is, you've got plenty on your plate. You don't need to take this guy Kev on."

"I just keep thinking: beheaded. Whatever else is going on, I don't have it in me to sit on my hands and—"

"Sofe, put the scrolls away."

She opened his duffel, pulling out Beatrice's scrolls and laying them on the bunk.

"That seventh spell is about bonding," she said. "Beatrice thought it'd bond me to the parents so hard I wouldn't ever even think to look for her. Instead, look at me. I'm not a committer, Bram—I've never been."

"Sofe—"

Whatever brotherly advice he might have offered was interrupted by a knock at their cabin hatch. Sophie leaped up. Bram hurriedly tucked the scrolls away in a lockable cupboard under his lounge.

It was Garland, and he had Septer Xianlu with him.

"What's wrong?"

"*Shepherd* is bleeding."

CHAPTER 12

Sophie imagined she could feel fear knotting through the people of the Fleet, stitching them together in crowds. Abovedecks on a hundred ships, worried citizens lined the rails, turned to watch the great rescue vessel, now at the rear and surrounded by smaller helper ships.

Shepherd might not be the symbol that *Temperance* or *Breadbasket* were, but she was official. This was no kite shop or glazier.

This was the ship that kept other ships from sinking.

"Nobody's downed a rep ship since the Cessation," Garland murmured. He'd washed, at some point between the goat wrangling and getting the Mayday from *Shepherd*; his still-damp hair gleamed in the sun, and he exuded a faint scent that Sophie had come to associate with Fleet soaps, an oil that was neither clove nor citrus, though similar enough to evoke memories of mulled wine.

"Nobody's sinking one today," snapped Xianlu.

Their transport cleared the Fleet followers—what Sophie thought of as the suburbs of the seagoing city—and sailed into the muddle of ships. *Shepherd,* by far the largest, was encircled by sailing vessels big enough to hold her crew if it came to the worst.

She wasn't conceding to an evacuation yet.

The transport deployed a ladder and they climbed aboard, one after another.

"Have we found an outline of a hand?" Xianlu asked as soon as she came aboard.

The cadet she'd spoken to shook her head. "Still searching."

"Maybe we can pinpoint it from outside?" Sophie asked.

"Sollo Mykander's mermaids are looking."

"I'll get below and help."

"Is there a plan?" Garland asked.

Xianlu nodded. "The first two ships were sunk before we knew about the wood frights. The creatures formed on the outer hull, creating a hole, causing the ships to take water. Kir Sophie disturbed the third, on *Kitesharp*, and it tore itself free."

"Yeah, I'm sorry about that—"

"It was a crucial discovery," Xianlu said, doggedly on task. Her expression was that of a fighter expecting to take a blow. "The three ships were tiny; they couldn't survive a hole as big as a person. *Shepherd* can, especially if the thing simply separates itself from her hull after it has taken whatever it needs to grow."

"So the plan is to let it be . . . born?"

"Yes. Separate it from the hull, capture it, patch the leak, and pump out the water. We'll be repaired within a week."

"Kir?" A shout from the waterline. A swimmer—female, dark-skinned, bald, and nude, with heavily muscled shoulders—was treading water about three yards out. The nine-foot-long expanse of her tail, a silver cord of muscle, was visible in the water below, undulating from side to side.

"Report, Torren."

"It's near the rudder, Septer. Starboard side."

"Mermaid," Bram murmured. "Holy crap! Mermaid."

His astonishment lightened Sophie's mood. "I know, right? I should get down there."

She already had her wetsuit on; now she checked her breathing rig and lowered herself into the water. The ocean was warm; its surface choppy. She turned automatically to avoid a slap of water over her face, then submerged. Once under, she took a few careful breaths, checked her watch, and turned on her light. Her mermaid escort, Torren, waited. The boy Sophie had seen transformed a few weeks earlier was with her, a flaxen-haired, quicksilver shadow.

When she gestured that she was ready, they swam toward the rear of the vessel.

Shepherd was a massive boat, almost two hundred feet long. Her hull was fouled, covered in barnacles and seaweed, a spongy biomass seeping redness.

The sea was full of merpeople.

As with the previous victims, the blood seeping from *Shepherd* had attracted sharks. A squad of long-tailed soldiers with tridents was keeping an eye on them, making themselves seen. The merpeople seemed practiced at it, alert and cautious, but calm, too. The sharks were keeping their distance.

A second crew of mers waited starboard and to the fore of the ship; they held sacks of tools.

Military engineers, waiting to patch the leak, Sophie surmised.

Heavily muscled individuals with nets were waiting near the rudder.

All the mers' eyes reflected her light back at her, as if they were cats.

Sophie turned her light and camera on the fouled hull. Torren pointed, and she spotted the fright—a crimson growth the size of a one-man rubber dingy. A translucent and bloody balloon, it wobbled in time with the press of the water around it, emitting enough blood to create a haze of red around itself.

They had picked away enough of the seaweed and covering encrustations to reveal the amniotic sac. It was low on the hull and just to starboard of the rudder.

Sophie shone her light on it. The sac was sufficiently translucent that she could see the figure within the amniotic fluid. It had formed a twiggy skeleton in there, and muscles were growing, fiber by ropy plant fiber, on its frame. It had a vitality that suggested life, rather than the cold-meat inertia of death.

As she watched, a clot of red tissue was disgorged from the sac. It drifted beyond the protective line of mermaids and got snapped up by one of the sharks.

Wait and watch. Adjusting her dive vest, Sophie lost herself in observation as the thing developed.

She'd often found she did her best thinking underwater, waiting for animals to show up, or timing out her safety stops. Now, as the fright grew—and grew, and grew some more, muscling up like a bodybuilder—she wondered, *Was* Shepherd *the target all along?*

The other ships might have been test runs. Tests for what, though?

Terrorism, she thought, remembering the books Bram had found at Bettona's. *Sowing fear.*

If so, what could matter was that the next ship wouldn't have *Shepherd* there to save it. Maybe *Shepherd* was the means to an end, a penultimate target.

Who would they be after? The Piracy had gone after the Fleet's flagship, *Temperance,* before. Then again, if they sank *Constitution,* they'd take out the government, at least symbolically.

If Bettona was in league with terrorists, then the sinkings and Annela's poisoning—*Alleged poisoning,* Sophie amended—were related.

The creature was almost complete. Bark was forming on its muscular back and legs—skin with birchy spots—and it was beginning to move. It wiggled and fidgeted, breaking its connection to the hull of the ship. The amniotic sac shivered but showed no sign of sucking inward.

The wood fright gave one long head-to-toe stretch, pulling itself free of *Shepherd*'s hull, leaving a gigantic hole as it broke away. Pieces of wood splintered in every direction. Twisting, it stuck its head in the hole it had made, kicking hard and clumsily, like a kid trying to make progress with a flutterboard.

As its hand touched the hull, it rooted and stuck. When it pulled it away, its body language all but shouting surprise, it made the hole bigger.

Then two brawny mers surged forward, grabbing the wooden legs. With one coordinated yank, they tore the fright clear of the ship. Two of their comrades clamped on, drawing it away.

Sophie turned, filming the struggle. The fright was obviously strong, but it was outnumbered and out of its element. They had it bound and netted quickly enough. Its roots grew and knotted into the strands of the net, twining in fast, increasing the bulk of the tangle in which it was caught.

Once the fright was separated from *Shepherd,* the engineers swam in, efficiently wadding something that looked like putty into the gap in the hull, working it around a long pipe with a sealed opening—for a pump, Sophie guessed.

Mission accomplished. Ship saved, Sophie thought. They all ascended to the surface. *Shepherd* lowered a ladder, allowing Sophie to climb aboard and shed her tanks.

The wooden figure—it was female—stopped struggling as it was borne into the open air. It swiveled its head from side to side, as though it was seeking something.

Xianlu said, "Have it brought aboard. Don't let it touch the deck."

The crew hauled the fright up on a pulley, dangling in its bonds and net of rope.

Xianlu gave it a careful glance.

"Niner Rills, step forward."

One of the cadets, a young woman with the Bluto build of a Fleet cannoneer, stepped up.

The creature's reaction was instantaneous: its skin grew thorns all over, slicing into the net that held it. It opened its mouth, exhaling a green-yellow cloud of pollen as it tore free of the net. It rushed the bug-eyed woman—the bone structure of their faces was identical, Sophie realized.

The crew rushed to intercede. The thing swept one of them up and around, slamming him to the deck and puncturing his forearm with thorns before rounding, once again, on the cadet.

Garland Parrish slipped like oil between the fright and its target, catching its outstretched wrist easily, right where it had scraped away its own thorns, and giving it a light, almost effortless-looking flip. It rolled, its backside sending roots into the deck and then tearing the wood as it jerked itself free. Regaining its balance, still intent on the cadet, it moved again.

Garland circled, intercepted. This time, when the thing rounded on him, he planted his feet, caught it again, and added to its momentum sufficiently to throw the wood fright overboard.

The cadet was gasping at his feet. "Me? It was me? My name's in the wild?"

Xianlu gestured to a couple of uniformed cadets. "Come on, Rills. We'll sort it out."

They led her away as the fright surfaced, clearly intent on swimming its way back to the ship and its target.

"Catch it again," Xianlu ordered to the mer leader. "We'll have to find a dead rope to bind it."

"*Nightjar* has a length of iron chain," Garland said.

Xianlu grimaced. Wrackers, among their other peculiarities, had some beef against iron or anything they suspected of having been tainted by petrochemicals. Even so, she nodded.

"It looks like you're arresting that cannoneer," Sophie said.

"We have to be cautious until we know she's not at fault. It's likely we'll find she had her name stolen, just like the fellow from *Kitesharp*. If so, we'll order her home for a name change."

"The bottom of the ship is badly fouled," Sophie said. "Seaweed, barnacles, you name it. Can the mermaids patrol the Fleet? Would they see that developing on a new target?"

"Possibly." Xianlu shook her head. "It's a big Fleet and they're a small detachment."

"The frightmaker isn't choosing random targets," Sophie said. "Focus the patrols on ships more important than *Shepherd*."

"Agreed." Xianlu broke into a smile, suddenly, looking around the ship. "Still afloat, crew *Shepherd*!"

Cheers broke out from bow to stern as she shouted it again—"Still afloat!"—and pounded Sophie genially on the back.

Sophie gave a hearty two thumbs up, managing not to say what she was thinking: maybe they'd saved the ship, but they were no closer to preventing the next incident.

CHAPTER 13

By the time she had disentangled herself from the situation aboard *Shepherd,* caught an hour or two of much-needed sleep, and ferried herself out to the legal quarter to ask her lawyer about the finer points of hauling an *OMG prisoner slash slave* back to Sylvanna, it was late afternoon and she was ravenous.

The Fleet was approaching Mensalohm's home island, Tiladene, and he had eschewed his usual tunic and trousers for a long, loose-fitting cloak in sunflower-yellow silk. The traditional garb reminded Sophie more than a little of a bathrobe. He offered her a pressed cake of fried salted cod. She ate it, glad of the protein but thinking wistfully of hamburgers. Then he produced a -long platter of skewers—grilled peaches and dates, mostly, alternating with biscuitlike slices of chewy baked eggplant.

"Paperwork's in order," he said. "You need a couple signatures and an exceptional circumstances waiver permitting you to transport a bonded individual. Also, written support from a captain willing to sail with you and Lidman."

"Captain Parrish of *Nightjar* has offered . . . well, insisted."

"The man Lidman is a violent criminal. I'd want to keep an eye on you too. The more so if I were . . . fond."

She nodded, not wanting to get diverted into the subject of Garland and his protective instincts. "My question is, what then? Having a slave for a month at sea is bad enough. I'm certainly not hanging on to him."

"Sell him?" Mensalohm's expression was too innocent.

"Yeah, that's totally the answer."

"Sophie, the man seeks to avoid having *Docket* separate his head from his shoulders. He's thrown himself at your feet to save his life. You're doing him a kindness, even if you do sell him or ask your father's estate to take him on."

"Theoretically, once he's—" She choked on the word "mine." "Once he's bonded to me, I can do what I want?"

Mensalohm, who had until then seemed unflappable, nearly spat out half a roasted peach. "You can't be proposing to free him? He participated in banditry. He murdered those ship crews."

"Seas, I know. But . . ."

"But what?"

"What if he was kind of a freedom fighter?"

The lawyer blinked. "Explain."

"The ships they sank were smugglers. Lidman says the crews were smuggling more than amber and maddenflur. 'Soft cargo,' was the euphemism."

"Slaves."

"What if they were freeing people?"

"I can claim to have ridden the great stud Tamulay in a world-famed horse race and then bedded her owner," Mensalohm said. "That doesn't make it true."

Sophie felt tears threaten. "This is a dream come true for Cly. To stick me with a Sylvanner passport and a slave I can't get rid of and then to go all *Ha-ha. Get off the moral high ground, daughter.* Screw that. I'm not owning Lidman for one minute more than I have to."

Mensalohm handed her a handkerchief. "There are regulations with criminal enslavement. His will must be shackled."

"Shackled?"

"Magically. You might not have to entirely break him to service—total obedience is a hard inscription to pull off, even if the subject has no previous intentional load. But if you were to free Lidman, I think the very least the law requires is that he be inscribed so he's incapable of killing . . . anything. He'd never eat animal flesh again. If someone attacked him, he'd not fight back. It's called a pacification spell."

"He'd have to give me his name, wouldn't he?"

"The bonded are renamed."

"By their owners?"

"They *are* slaves, after all."

"Pacification, huh?" Stripping someone's free will didn't sit well with her.

But if the alternative was giving Lidman to Low Bann—to Cly—she wasn't sure she had a choice.

"There's something else you haven't considered."

"What's that?" Sophie said.

Mensalohm gave her a sympathetic pat. "You're unmarried, aren't you?"

Yeah, so what? died on her lips. "Teeth."

"On Sylvanna, being single makes you a child. Decisions about Lidman, once you're there, would fall to the head of your family."

"To Cly."

Cursing in Fleet wouldn't do, now. She switched to English and let go with every foul word she knew. Maybe this had been Cly's plan all along. To get his hands on Lidman.

Which led her back to: What did everyone want with him?

She leaned back in the chair, letting her eyes unfocus, and tried to breathe.

"What are you doing?"

"I read somewhere that if you let yourself feel something for two minutes, the emotion changes."

"Is it working?"

"It's been, like, ten seconds."

"So you're . . . angry?"

She waved her book of questions. "All the things I want to do here. I keep getting dragged away from learning about . . . well, about the world."

"I'd have thought this whole process offered a certain amount of education."

She said, "You're a legal wizard, right? Am I stuck in this or is there a way out?"

"Send the execution forward."

"Yeah, let's have a guy beheaded for freeing a bunch of the bonded. Cly would love that."

"Sophie," Mensalohm said. "You need to detach yourself from this concern about your father's wants."

"Could you let the guy get beheaded?"

"I regret to say I could. I might not sleep well afterward, but a pirate's a pirate."

And pirates did just try to help your near neighbor invade your homeland, didn't they?

"Yeah," she said, "but if Lidman's on the block for trying to help people escape bondage . . ."

"Hmm." Mensalohm slid a peach off the skewer, contemplating the orange flesh and the caramelized edges of its outer skin. "There's one way."

"Tell me."

CHAPTER 14

After her meeting with Mensalohm, Sophie found she wasn't quite ready to face either Bram or Garland. She caught a ferry to the courthouse, instead, showing the receptionist her bundle of papers from the Watch. She felt a little like she'd gotten away with something when they assigned her a clerk who was only too happy to fetch her the trial minutes—as they called them—of Kev's case. The document only came to twenty or so pages.

She was about to photograph them, page by page, when it occurred to her to ask, "Can you copy this to my assistant?"

"Of course," the clerk said.

She took a quick flip-through before handing it back.

They didn't do word-for-word transcripts here, settling instead for written summaries of trial evidence. Kev's prosecution consisted of an account of the sinkings and an inventory of hard cargo found on *Incannis,* stolen things from the missing ships—amber beads, various kinds of narcotic, spell ingredients, and, from Sylvanna, "contraband medical records." There was no mention whatsoever of smuggled slaves. The listing was followed by Cly's statement about the fight between *Incannis* and his ship, *Sawtooth*.

She wasn't about to read that. She asked, "This says the cargo samples are in . . . Exhibits?"

"That's in the hold. Do you wish to see them, Kir?"

"Is that okay?"

"You've taken the Oath?"

She nodded, wondering why anyone would take her word for it. Still, the clerk happily took her below, descending four decks to a massive locked hatch.

"Sign in here, Kir."

"Okay." A first glance reminded Sophie of movie renderings of top secret government warehouses—a vast hold filled with crates. Then it occurred to her that, big or not, this couldn't possibly be everything. "This can't cover all the backlogged cases."

"No, Kir. We store materials for cases likely to see adjudication or the dueling court within a tenmonth."

"Where's the rest?"

She started pointing at sections of shelving. "Homicide cases are held by Issle Morta, because they serve the dead. Matters of commerce go to Sparta, for they eschew profit. Paperwork for petty criminal matters is on Drake's Shoal."

"They eschew pettiness?"

It was a small joke, and it failed to gain any traction with the clerk. "The Shoal has little natural wealth. The government contract to store state records is crucial to their economy."

Sophie looked at the last section of shelves—the biggest. "And all your resource fights? Ownership of plants and animals? Biodiversity feuds?"

"The natural history case archive is on Murdocco. I'll come back, shall I?" With that, the clerk left her, closing her in and noisily throwing the latch.

Sophie went looking for her case. At home, each of these caches would be stored in a cardboard file box. The same idea held here, but these were wicker baskets, handmade, one for each case. Each basket was covered, labeled, lashed shut, and tied to its shelf, lest the rocking of the ship dislodge crucial evidence.

She found the basket matching Kev's case number, examining the samples of Incannis's plunder—beads, drug samples, and a description of a Sylvanner kid with symptoms reminiscent, at least to Sophie, of ADHD. The boy's name had been burned from the page. The notes indicated an unproved suspicion that the file had been acquired by a name-stealing ring.

There was nothing to either support or refute Kev's story.

The clerk wasn't back yet.

She roamed the shelves, reading labels, until one caught her eye: "Counterclaim Year 57—Marine Bats, 2 Species."

She opened it up, remembering the bats she'd encountered during her accidental first visit to Stormwrack. The crate held two pickled samples and two skins. Each sample had a distinctive set of tufted ears.

She riffled through the case notes. The two islands in dispute had agreed that both species inhabited each nation's forests . . . but both claimed rights to profits from spells using the animals' larynxes.

She looked at a bat in its jar of brine. The biodiversity shelf held perhaps two hundred such baskets, a small fraction of the total pending cases. What if most of them contained samples, items like these, all tagged with data about the animal species involved—where they were captured, habitat info?

After the cases wrapped up, the samples might be up for grabs.

She felt a burst of greed, as if she'd fallen into a treasure hoard. Samples, information, details on animal behavior, all of it here for the—well, not plundering, exactly.

Who knew what she might find?

She kept browsing.

Snail collection, island of Erinth.
Shrews of Zingoasis.
Lesser chindrella, dispute between Tiladene and Ualtar.
Peacocks, 6 species, latterly rumored unnatural.
Fright ingredients. Pouched lion.

"Pouched?" she said aloud. "Poached?"

The basket wasn't any bigger than the others.

Pouched . . . marsupial?

"I'm investigating frights," she said, justifying herself, even though nobody was there to tell her not to rifle through other people's case evidence. She hefted the basket down, tipping the lid.

Painted wooden eyes glared out at her.

"Lion-skin rug," Sophie muttered. "Marsupial by-the-Seas lion-skin rug. OMG."

She pulled it out, marveling at everything—the silky, koala-dense fur, the huge forepaws with their strange, cleaverlike thumb claw. The rug only encompassed the top of the marsupial lion, so there was no chance to look at the pouch.

Extinct at home. Alive and well here. She photographed it and clipped a hair sample, labeling it carefully.

The rest of the basket contained a selection of samples tagged as ingredients for the frightmaking spells that, according to treaty, had been outlawed. The inventory had gaps: she found a listing for a jar of salamander eggs but not the container itself. There were twenty labeled acorns, two catkins, a lungfish, three kinds of dog, tree bark samples, braids of horse and cat hair (both half as long as the notes said they should be), sealing wax, and an unlabeled box of what looked like bits of fingernail.

She was about to pack it all back up when she found one last sample in the bottom of the basket: a lizard, the length of her hand, with thin, iridescent glider wings.

Sitting cross-legged in the hold atop the lion, she examined the lizard—the blue scaling on its belly, the mottled green on top. She imagined it slithering its way to some high point, wings pulled tight against its back, then dropping off, or possibly springing into the air.

To catch what prey? Flying insects, perhaps?

She tipped her head to take in the shelves. Box upon box of potential treasure, and a total-access card to visit.

Strangely comforted, she took the basket out, advised the clerk that there was material missing from the collection of fright-related exhibits, and—in a last quick burst of footwork—hit the hospital ship to see if there was any chance of seeing Annela Gracechild.

She found Beatrice, instead, sitting vigil with three separate guards. A forbidding, seven-foot Amazon type with a headdress made of pheasant feathers stood in front of the door, next to a uniformed Fleet officer and a young towheaded woman wearing what looked like black pajamas.

"Triple guarded," Beatrice said, indicating the trio. "One from Verdanii, one from the Convene, a third from the Watch."

"How's Annela doing?" Sophie asked.

"Still unconscious."

"Do they know what's wrong?"

"The doctors here call it salt-and-sugar tilt," Beatrice said. She fiddled with the straps of an enormous leather purse, red in color, that looked to Sophie like a Coach knockoff.

"Meaning what? Sugars . . . diabetic coma?"

Her birth mother nodded. "I'm guessing nonketotic hyperosmolar coma. But if I say that to them, it'll be gibberish."

"It's gibberish to me, too. I don't know anything about diabetes."

"They're rehydrating her and administering sugars; she'll probably come out of it."

"Was she getting insulin shots?"

"No. Fasting wasn't the best idea she ever had, but she's managed it before all right." Beatrice gnawed at her thumbnail. "If someone sabotaged her, it might have been by swapping out her pills. Very hard to prove."

"Bettona's still AWOL?"

"Yes. But she has an ironclad alibi for the other thing, remember? She didn't bring Gale's assassins you-know-where."

"She has accomplices. Helpers. We found how-to books about terrorism in her cabin."

"Helpers who can eraglide," Beatrice said, sourly.

"Speaking of blood sugar, you look like you could use some food. Are you on guard here, or . . ."

"'Nella's safe enough with all this at her door." To Sophie's surprise, Beatrice smiled. "Come on. You'll enjoy this."

She led Sophie out of what seemed to be a VIP wing and into a patient ward—a double-row of injured and sick sailors in wide flat hammocks. They were tended by nurses and orderlies of both genders.

The hospital ward was clean. Wrackers might not understand germ theory, but they seemed to believe that cleanliness prevented contagion: the smell of ammonia was all it took to confirm that.

Typical of Fleet, the patients were a racially mixed group. Some wore crisply ironed pajamas emblazoned with a stylized version of *Constitution*'s paddle wheel. The Fleet sick bay uniform, Sophie supposed. Others, presumably civilians, were in a mix of robes and smocks. One seemed to be deep in prayer. Another was embroidering. A third was browsing through a book titled *Veterinary Inscription: Magical Loads and Domesticated Animals.*

A young man moved among them, followed closely by an elderly nurse.

The man was what the Wrackers called an oddity, someone altered by magic so that his or her physical appearance was no longer entirely human. The man's arms, from the elbow down, had the dull sheen of fish scale, and instead of terminating in fingers, his hands had the blunt, dangerous faces of eels. His female attendant—whose knuckles, wrists, and elbows all had a lumpy, arthritic look to them—was rolling a trolley. It had two levels: there was a tub of water, above, and a bowl of fish roe—bright red salmon eggs and white globes the color of cataracts—below.

After soaking his arms in the water, the man laid his eel-head stumps on a young sailor who had an enormous leg cast. The patient had been watching intently as he approached. Her hands were clenched and her breathing was tightly controlled—signs she was struggling against significant pain?

As the nurse's flesh met the patient's, there was a low crackling, and an ozone smell. . . .

"Electric eels," Sophie murmured, and Beatrice nodded.

The sailor relaxed back against her pillows with an audible sigh of relief.

The nurse turned, holding up both arms, as his attendant produced the bowl of roe. Eel tongues extended slowly into the bowl, and this time Sophie could see the current, little flicks of lightning traveling from nurse to eggs, leaving the roe flickering like banked coals.

"What gives?"

"The nurse draws the pain out of the patient and transfers it to the eggs," Beatrice said.

"Where it . . . what?"

"Ha. Good question. It waits, basically, for the egg membranes to break. Then it makes for the nearest warm body."

"Literally warm? Mammalian?"

"Yes."

It was the first time Sophie had seen her birth mother looking comfortable, at home with herself or her surroundings.

Her birth mother beckoned, and nurse and attendant approached. Beatrice took a flat wooden probe and extracted two of the tiniest specks of roe. She set one on Sophie's palm and took the other herself, between index finger and thumb. "Go ahead," she said. "It won't hurt much."

By way of demonstration, she popped her own between finger and thumb.

Sophie followed suit. There was a shock at first, the sort of jolt one got from static on a cold winter day. Then, just for a second, aches bloomed in her femur and the back of her rib cage, quick jabs in both places.

She looked around the room, past the woman with the broken leg, and saw a patient lying on her stomach with a huge bandage on her back, behind the heart.

She took a sniff at her fingers: fish, nothing more.

"Believe it or not, there's a trade in these," Beatrice said. "There are cultures that use them in religious ordeals, as tests of strength or, in one case, a mode of penance. Hail Mary and *pop!* And there's at least one exotic dish, isn't there?"

"Yes," said the nurse. "There's a chef who uses herring roe laced with pain from burns. I can't say it's something I'd want to taste, but . . ." With a shrug, the young man reached for his attendant. The movement looked both habitual and almost unconscious. Energy crackled between them.

Those arthritic joints, Sophie thought.

The old woman relaxed within her uniform and held up the eggs for the transfer. Then she straightened the eel man's shirt.

"Isn't that terribly inconvenient?" Sophie asked.

"I was born without hands, Kir. I could write with my feet before I was ever inscribed. Jamla and I take excellent care of each other."

Repurposing the disabled, as they did with the kids they're turning into the mermaids. She hoped her discomfort with the idea didn't show in her face. Somehow, Beatrice's presence at her side, the consciousness of the spells she had worked on Sophie, made the whole conversation feel incredibly loaded. "This ability . . . You're somehow reconfiguring the patient's nervous system with a dose of low voltage. . . . But why are the eggs necessary?"

That *Don't know, don't care* shrug. "I was trained as an auramancer, Kir. I align their auras out of the pain and move it into the roe."

"And are there side effects?"

"Fewer than with maddenflur," he said, with an expression of distaste as he referenced the opiate. "No dependence. Patients do sometimes mistake the absence of suffering for recovery."

"We have surgery in fifteen," Jamla said softly.

"Kirs, thank you for the demonstration," Beatrice said.

The two of them bowed and withdrew.

"That was interesting," Sophie said. "Thank you."

Beatrice led her in the other direction, out of the ward and belowdecks, past a dispensary—there were guards on the portal that led to the drugs, which seemed pleasingly sensible to Sophie—and through an ordinary-looking physio clinic equipped with weights, bars for people relearning to walk, and a swim tank.

Here, Beatrice paused again, watching as a uniformed therapist did range-of-motion tests with a patient whose arm bore deep scars.

The patient was unusually tall and muscled, in her fifties, and marked with a grayscale tattoo Sophie had seen on other Verdanii women around her birth mother's age. The tattoo depicted a hawk in midflight—the line of scar tissue had just nicked one of its outstretched talons.

The therapist finished testing the patient, then strapped her into a brace that immobilized both shoulder and upper arm before setting a dexterity puzzle beneath her dangling hand and wrist. Moving clumsily, the patient began to assemble the puzzle one-handed.

"Is this just a tour, or is there a point?" Sophie asked.

"You're getting a reputation," Beatrice said. "You look at people, you learn things about them—or know things. The jury's out on your possibly being uncanny."

"You know that's not true."

"I thought I'd waft you past a few of my people. Let them see you looking."

"Us."

"What?"

"Let them see *us* looking," Sophie said. "In a couple days I'm going to be off sailing. I don't mind you using me as a magnet for trouble. Though, come to think of it, maybe I should."

Beatrice let out a snort.

"But if you draw anyone out, it's you they might come after."

"My sister's murder is unsolved. My cousin may yet die." The skin around Beatrice's eyes pinkened. "Let 'em come."

"Then what? You have an M16 in there?" The purse was almost big enough.

Her mother cracked the bag. Inside was an ordinary plastic sandwich bag from home, half filled with fish eggs. "Our young nurse friend wouldn't say anything so barbaric to a stranger, but these pain roe would drop a raging moose."

"Ah . . ."

"Come on," Beatrice said. "You're right about me being hungry. And there's a Gracechild tenner working in the cafeteria."

Their next stop was a strangely low-ceilinged galley with a buffet: ceviche and pickled fish, several variations of coleslaw, sliced pears in citrus juice, protein jelly, and a range of vegetable purees arranged by spice. Everything was easy to chew, pastel colored, and just above lukewarm.

"Hospital food," Beatrice said, helping herself to something broccoli colored, with a scent of coriander and turmeric. "See, the two worlds aren't that different."

Sophie took a sampling of the ceviche and a turnip dish, thinking again of hamburgers, and chose a table that afforded her a view of the servers. "Is that the guy we're interested in?"

Beatrice followed her gaze to a young man in a stiffly starched cadet's uniform. "How'd you work it out?"

"You said he'd just joined Fleet, and he's the newest one here. He's making an effort not to look at us," she said. "Skin color's that same coppery shade as Annela's. And Verena's got a pair of boots with that same design."

"You didn't strike me as a shoe hound."

"People keep stealing my boots."

"Rubber soles are like gold here."

"I'd have thought the general prejudice against—What do they call them? Atomism and mummer handicrafts?—would keep the larceny at bay."

"People can be hypocritical about their superstitions. One of the things I love about Americans, actually, is that they're so often up-front about what they want."

American. An identity that meant nothing here. Sophie felt an odd thrum of dislocation. "Tacking back to the point . . . I've been taking notice of where and how people can vary up the Fleet uniform while still wearing a marker of nationality. So is he? Verdanii?"

Beatrice nodded.

"What is he . . . fourteen? Is he really a good candidate for a conspiracy?"

"He doesn't have a timepiece and he's not a Feliachild, so he shouldn't be able to eraglide." Beatrice seemed to reach a decision. She opened her voluminous purse and withdrew a wooden box with a stonewood latch. "This was in Annela's office. It contains, for lack of a better term, priestess stuff. All the physical materials used in the rituals to make eragliders of me, Gale, and Verena."

"It's empty."

"Yes. Mumma'd have my hide if I shared the mysteries with you."

Then why bring it up? Sophie waited.

Beatrice opened it, revealing a box within a box—a cigarette case, made of tin and fronted by an ivory panel. She opened it, revealing nine ordinary cigarettes from home, and one butt.

"Forgot about those." Her birth mother's voice was falsely casual. "One's been smoked. Not by you, I take it?"

Sophie shook her head.

"Taking tobacco with the Allmother is the final stage of the ceremony."

"No fear of me getting converted, then." Unless the ceremonies were just so much hoo-ha. "So. One person, at least, Bettona's definitely tried to initiate. Her accomplice?"

"That's my theory."

"Why do me on the sly?"

"So the blame will fall on you, of course," Beatrice said.

Sophie leaned back, fiddling with her turnip mash, and took in her birth mother. Beatrice was watching the tenner, exuding a sense of having a lot going on, mentally. It was that same quality Bram had when he was multitasking.

Let her think, then. Sophie opened her book of questions and paged through it. She had made a few notes on Bram's proposed experiment—leaving his magically hardened time capsule at home, possibly somewhere near Mount Rainier, and then seeing if they could find it here.

He'd gotten to this same page, adding notes about the items he planned to leave in the box: a bone, a zircon, and a piece of lava whose age had been verified by one of his geologist roommates. TAKE IT BACK TO CE AND TEST ITS AGE.

Inspiration struck. Sophie added: INCLUDE A SHEET OF MESSAGEPLY.

As for leaving it near Mount Rainier . . .

Garland hates Issle Morta, she thought.

There was a sanded-down version of Clingmans Dome, in Tennessee, that still existed on the map of Sylvanna. She had a friend who lived near there, a caver.

ALUM CAVE IS NEAR CLY'S ESTATE, she wrote.

Did Garland have any favorite mountaintops?

The question took her back to a whole set of things she hadn't written down—questions about Garland and whether he thought he was in love with her, questions about whether it could possibly be real for him. The prophecy about his falling for someone just before Gale's death, on the one hand. Beatrice's spells, on the other.

Pretty and graceful and fertile, oh my. She flipped the page. It should've been blank, but Bram had drawn a cartoon portrait of Mr. Spock, with a beard.

A snort. Beatrice had come out of her reverie and was smirking at the drawing.

Sophie cleared her throat and spoke in English. "He'd have been thinking about . . . We're trying to determine if this is a future of our . . . you know, home."

"Believe it or not, I have seen *Star Trek*. So what?"

"Either Stormwrack is a far-future version of you-know-where, or it's a parallel. If the latter, there may be an infinite number of each of us: you, me, Bram—"

"Yeah, yeah. Good ones, evil ones, Spock with a beard. You don't think one of us has an evil twin, do you?"

"No." Though it did open the field to an even bigger number of suspects. "If Stormwrack is literally the future, then something catastrophic is going to happen to home."

"Soon?"

"Within ten thousand years."

Beatrice laughed.

"Yeah, sounds trivial, but—" Sophie objected.

"You need to learn to prioritize."

"My *parents* are in San Francisco."

"Honey, the Big One's more likely to hit. Ten thousand years is a long time."

It was true. Sophie felt deflated and then relieved. Chances were, there was no disaster on the way. "It's still an important question."

"I'm all for science. Until it keeps you up at night, anyway, worrying about remote, unlikely doom," Beatrice said.

The Verdanii guard approached, bowing. "The convenor is awake, Kir Feliachild. She's asking for you."

Before Sophie could ask, the guard added, "Just her."

Beatrice closed her knockoff purse and slung it over her shoulder. "You have another sheet of that messageply?"

"I can make do," Sophie said, writing HANDING THIS TO BEATRICE on the half-full page she'd been using to swap texts with Bram. "Here."

"I'll let you know if I get anything from 'Nella." Before she turned to go, Beatrice frowned a little, half reached for Sophie with one hand, and then turned the gesture into a clumsy fist bump. "'Kay, 'bye."

She bustled off, drawing the guard with her, and leaving Sophie, who hadn't so much as touched her birth mother yet, openmouthed and a little at a loss.

CHAPTER 15

Lovely Kir Sophie:

How thoroughly delicious to hear from you!

You are quite right—the chindrella you saw in the exhibits archive are mine, and the dispute between my family and the Ualtarites over my attempt to breed their spiders may come to court soon. We have cross-charged them with trying to kill me. Mensalohm is representing my collective. He says that, since everyone's equally guilty, it's anyone's guess as to which side will win.

There's been no talk of dueling it out, in case you're wondering.

You ask if I have any sense of Ualtar remaining on a war footing—if I think they are still looking to invade Tiladene. I have asked some of our trader cooperatives who do business with the Ualtarites, and they say the general consensus seems to be that their government feels it overstepped . . . that the Piracy, by using Ualtar as a game piece, exposed and embarrassed them. That Ualtar supports a war is in no doubt, but the chitchat on the racetrack has it that there will need to be some kind of public outrage, the sort of thing that can trigger full-scale hostilities on a grand scale.

One example that comes up repeatedly is a long-running myth about an island of escaped slaves, oddities, and giants, a place called Nysa. The story currently going around has it that Nysa is working up to invade the portside nations. The assumption made by those telling this tale is that the abolitionist nations might be tempted to let an attack stand unopposed, and thereby break the mutual defense compact on which the Cessation is based.

If any other gossip comes my way, I shall gladly share it. I will be taking horses to Stilence, Verdanii, and several other islands for the racing season, and I will keep my ears tuned to the chatter.

With all due warmth and affection,
Lais Dariach

Garland's ship, *Nightjar,* was a seventy-foot cutter with a crew of twenty. Her sails had a pearly sheen to them and her rigging was shot through with silver threads—some of it the hair of her former owner, Sophie's aunt Gale. An enchantment on Gale had made her hard to remember, harder still to take seriously. She had moved among ports like an unwanted and unruly cousin-by-marriage, playing the dotty old lady as she ferreted out conspiracies and state secrets. The threads of her hair, woven into the rigging of the ship, allegedly made *Nightjar* easier to overlook.

Stepping aboard *Nightjar* was like coming home.

The ship's first mate, Antonio Cappodocio, was waiting to greet Sophie as she climbed aboard via a net thrown down to the ferry.

"No Garland?"

Tonio shook his head. He was a compact and clever-looking man in his early twenties, from a volcanic island nation, Erinth, that was located where the Mediterranean should be. Today he was clad in dark breeches and a cable-knit sweater that suggested he was expecting cool weather.

"I have to talk to Garland as soon as . . . practically yesterday."

"He's overseeing your property transfer."

She almost gagged.

"Forgive me," Tonio said. "I assumed you wouldn't want to say . . ."

Slave. "No, don't say that, either."

"We could call him a prisoner, I suppose. Yes, prisoner."

"Tonio, if there was any way I could've let this guy . . . The last thing I ever wanted was . . ."

She searched his face. What did they think of her?

If he was disappointed in her, he was far too suave to show it. "*Ginagina,* we've been in stranger situations."

"Apparently nobody disapproves of my being Sylvanner except me."

"You can't help your parentage," he said, but he was bowing now to the rest of her . . . did three people qualify as an entourage?

Krispos was looking, to Sophie's eye, a little like he'd come from a performance of *The Importance of Being Earnest.* He'd gotten himself a chocolate-colored frock coat, new boots, and a white shirt, along with a heavy leather valise for his papers. He had hired someone to embroider a patch depicting the Forensic Institute insignia—a more formal version of something Bram had sketched on their initial proposal to Annela. The patch was pinned to his valise; he hadn't gotten around to sewing it on yet.

Sophie and Bram had encouraged him to memorize every resource on inscription and spellscribing Annela would let them open, and now he was reading everything he could find about the fright spells that had been used to attack *Kitesharp* and *Shepherd*.

Krispos was flanked by two uniformed police constables from the Watch—the officers who would be learning fingerprinting and building the database.

"This is Cinco Mel Humbrey, from Ylle," Sophie told Tonio, speaking clearly and distinctly, triggering a bow from the elder of the two men, which Tonio returned. "And his partner, Sixer Ragan Selwig, of Cardesh."

She was watching Tonio closely again, because Cardesh was a slaver nation. Apparently, it was policy, within the service, to partner portside officers with starboard ones. "They're here to work on some Institute stuff and to make sure Kev Lidman doesn't escape."

"Welcome to *Nightjar,* Kirs," Tonio said, with every evidence of cordiality.

Sophie said, "Did a guy show up? From my lawyer?"

"Achi, Nightjar!" This came from a small sailboat—privately chartered, from the look of it—that was whisking close to *Nightjar.* Its passenger was waving vigorously. He was lanky, blue-eyed, and had the peaches-and-cream complexion you'd expect of a lute player in a pre-Raphaelite painting. The effect wasn't hurt by the fact that he was clad in an open peasant shirt—so white it practically shone in the sun, winter be damned—and leather breeches.

I didn't think he'd be cute, she thought, dismayed.

"You're Daimon?" Sophie called.

"Yes, Kir, of Tiladene."

Tonio gave her an inquiring look as one of the crew, Beal, threw Daimon a rope ladder. "Gift for me?"

She punched his arm. "This is Mensalohm's new clerk, Daimon. He's . . . When did you say Garland would be aboard?"

"When he's got Lidman, I expect."

"What about Bram?"

"Kir Bram is coming?" Tonio lit up. "Better and better. Ship full of blossoms, and me the bee."

Before she could answer, Daimon had climbed aboard. Close up, he was just short of picture perfect.

"I'll get everyone settled, Kir." Beal, one of the crew, gave her a wide grin, followed by a kiss on the cheek, and swept up a double handful of traveling bags.

Sweet, the bosun, climbed down from the rigging, where she'd been inspecting the mainmast. Sophie decided to delay the explanations a moment longer, in favor of collecting a hug.

"Welcome home," Sweet whispered.

That lifted her spirits, and Sweet seemed to sense it. "Come on. You're forward, in Kir Gale's old cabin."

"Isn't that Verena's?"

"Verena's still asea. We don't have space to keep a room for someone who isn't here, not when the main guest cabin will be in use and you've brought all these people."

This was a polite way of reminding Sophie that Lidman would be in the cabin with a door that locked from the outside.

"Lead the way."

She whisked Sophie off to the cabin. "Maybe you're thinking to start bunking with someone else?"

Sophie felt herself blushing. "Fat chance of that." Garland was an old-fashioned guy, with ideas about extended courtship. And when he found out what she was up to . . .

Sweet scratched her head. "Want to talk? It's just us."

Did she?

"I'd rather talk about Verena's detachment ritual and why Annela was fasting. If you know enough about Verdanii customs to tell me."

Sweet nodded. "I know enough."

Sophie eased herself onto the bunk. She'd never stayed in this particular berth. By shipboard standards, it was an opulent room, three times as big as the berths Bram had rented aboard the apartment block. Verena had never properly moved in. A framed sketch on one bulkhead depicted a horse running on a beach, hooves churning the foam. There was a big lighthouse in the background of the image.

A clock was fixed to a low shelf, and Verena's practice dummy for sword fighting lay under the sack of sand she used as a free weight, along with a leather jump rope and a bated fencing foil.

Verena had a book half read—*Fleet-Approved Spells Pertaining to Mem-*

ory, Mental Acuity, and Madness—and a pair of others in languages Sophie couldn't decipher.

Sweet had been gathering her thoughts. "The Verdanii are coy about their bloodlines and the abilities of the Allmother, but I do know—everyone does—that she is only the fifth to hold that position, and the longest lived. She was in power well before the Cessation."

"That was a century ago!"

Sweet nodded. "Magic. She should have picked her heir-designate by now, but it's never happened. It has to be someone from the ruling families. Rumor has it there's a quest, or a vision. At this point, we're well into gossip, but Convenor Gracechild was attempting to qualify. According to the wags, she tried once before."

"And failed?"

Sweet nodded.

"What about Verena?"

"Her passion for the captain wasn't good for her; you saw how deep it ran, and what it cost her when you two . . ."

"Didn't quite start dating," Sophie finished wearily.

"The detachment quest is supposed to help."

"I suppose I should be glad she's not home fasting herself into a coma, too." It was hard not to feel guilty about having gotten involved with her half sister's crush object. She could remind herself a thousand times that Garland had never cared, romantically, for Verena. It still felt oddly like betrayal.

"I doubt anyone would accept Verena as an Allmother candidate. Too young, and she's nearly as much a foreigner as you are. Everyone wanted it to be Convenor Gracechild. They sent her into government to build up her international experience. Now that she's failed again, Verdanii is vulnerable."

Sophie perched on the bed. There were four or five bundles sitting on it, traditional pouches of wayfaring gifts, meant as wishes for a good journey. One smelled of apricots and anise.

Garland's bunk was on the other side of the bulkhead, she realized.

"The Verdanii sent *Fecund* to collect Verena," Sweet said. "She asked Captain to deliver the goat—"

"And he did, and here we are. I wonder if she's feeling better."

"I think she was glad to go. It's been awkward aboardship."

Sophie thought, *Does he like me because I'm magically pretty or because*

I'm magically charming or because I'm magically smart or because he thinks it was fate that we met . . . ?

"I need to be up on deck," she said, even though the thought of moving was entirely unappealing. She was weighed down by the thought of Beatrice and her seven scrolls; they were like boulders, rolling around in her belly. "I have to talk to him as soon as he's on board."

"Haul away, then," Sweet said.

She got herself upright and they made their way upward, only to run headlong into Beal, making his way down the ladder in a rush.

"Messenger for you, Kir," he said, a little wide-eyed. "From the Golders."

Sophie climbed up. Was it Convenor Brawn again? But the young woman on the deck was the big-eyed Fleet cadet who'd accompanied Brawn to their previous meeting. She had long auburn hair, tinted black at the tips. High boots added four inches to her height. Her extended, clawlike fingernails had been clipped short since Sophie saw her last.

"From His Honor Convenor Brawn from Isle of Gold, with all good wishes for peace," she said, holding out an envelope. Her accent was an exaggerated version of Brawn's, full of drawn-out vowels. "I'm to wait for your reply."

Sophie took the envelope and bowed for good measure. She looked around for Garland before she opened the envelope. Inside were three pages.

> *Kir Hansa,*
>
> *I write for it seems that you may be asail soon, and I wish to discharge the favor I have lately come to owe you.*
>
> *You see before you as much answer as I might offer to your question about the individual who conveyed the agent John Coine to the outland my people name as Powderkeg.*

It was a neat bit of doublespeak, Sophie thought. He wasn't quite admitting that John Coine had been his agent.

> *Coine might have told you more about how his journey was accomplished, but as he lies dead in Issle Morta, you shall have to resurrect him if you wish to ask.*
>
> *What I will say, from Coine's accounting, was that Powderkeg was what we call a bakoo marvelous place, jammed with more*

people than the great city Moscasipay, with much to overwhelm the senses. Once there, he was escorted to two places where you may continue your investigation. One was a dining establishment in a province or ville called Tenderloin. The place was called Sunny Side Jim, and enclosed, as proof, is one of their price sheets, written I believe in your native Anglay.

Sophie glanced at the diner menu. Eggs, bacon, hash browns, all at rock-bottom prices.

She had Coine's picture. If she could get home, she could see if the waitstaff at the diner remembered him.

The other locale was the munitions supplier who provided the grenades, muskets, and other oddments of war which Coine and his coconspirators employed in their ill-fated attempt to stir trouble. I know that the supplier was a short distance from Sunny Side Jim and that the name of the place was Freedom TwoFourSeven GunsGunsGuns.

It is possible the shopkeepers in one or the other establishment will have seen your agent with Coine. I hope you will acquit me of any obligation to you in this regard.

Sophie couldn't quite keep back a laugh.

"What is it?" Sweet said.

"Oh. The guy comes to me. He offers me a favor. And now he's all huffy about having discharged it."

"It's our way," the messenger said, visibly offended.

"Sorry," Sophie said. The letter went on, rather at length. She turned the page.

I approach as well with another point of business, one which would naut tout la cause for you to journey through the Stringent Sea and Northwater to Sylvanna. My people are prepared to make a generous purchase offer for the murderer, Kev Lidman.

As I am sure you know, one of the ships sunk by Incannis *was Golder. The families of the ship's crew would be much comforted by material compensation, in the form of a guilty bonded man, for their loss.*

I suspect I comprenne the forces that have motivated you to accept the burden of responsibility for Lidman, and I am prepared to offer an ironwood surety that his life would not be endangered, should you accept. He would live, and I would not see him molested for all his days going forward; you have my word on it.

This will be, I assure you, the only way to truly save him.

I would consider it a favor if you would oblige me in this matter. The price, and other terms that may quiet your antislaver sensibilities, are negotiable, but I suggest a starting point here.

"Sophie?" That was Sweet, who'd declined to leave her alone with the messenger.

Sophie swallowed and showed her the number at the bottom of the sheet. "Is that a lot? I have the idea it's a lot."

Sweet's jaw dropped. "'*Bakoo* shine o' coin,' as the Golders say. A fortune."

Sophie turned to the final page of the letter. Beneath Brawn's signature was an agreement to negotiate—multiple choice: accept, decline, or amend—and a space for a signature.

Sweet was still staring at the number.

Sophie said, "Rustle up Mensalohm's law clerk—his name's Daimon—and have him check that, when I say no to this, I'm not breaking my oath or agreeing to anything else."

"Kir!" The messenger's tone was sharp. "It's unwise to deny a man like Brawn, especially as he's shown you so much patience."

"How much would a killer usually go for?" Sophie said. "Does Isle of Gold routinely pay . . . *bakoo* shine, was it? . . . for condemned criminals?"

"I wouldn't know, Kir."

"Lidman has some value beyond mere revenge. Brawn wants him for a reason."

And I'm bringing him to Cly . . .

No, I'm not. One way or another, I'm gonna wiggle out of it, if that luck spell Beatrice worked on me is good for anything. . . .

"Sounds as though you might have something to discuss with His Honor after all."

"I'm *not* selling."

The girl wasn't ready to give up. "There are ways, I am sure, to convert value here to currency . . . elsewhere. You are short of funds in a certain outland nation, are you not?"

"That's none of your business!"

Daimon appeared, Krispos bustling in his wake, and took the pages, murmuring over the fine print. Sophie felt that bit of angst again. If she'd been able to learn the Fleet code of law, she wouldn't need people to do all these things for her.

Knowing it didn't mean understanding it, she told herself. *And I don't want to be a lawyer.*

He handed each page, as he read it, to Krispos so that the memorician could absorb it.

"You're selling?" The clerk's eyes widened. "Does this mean we're not going to Sylvanna?"

"I'm not selling," she said. "Of course I'm not selling. You're just reading it for—" The messenger pulled herself up, stiff, and Sophie bit back the word she'd meant to use: "traps." "Anything I should know?"

Daimon's brow creased, making him look comically like a *sad* pre-Raphaelite lute player. Was he disappointed?

Sophie tried to pull herself together. "You're doing me a huge favor here, I know that—"

"Kir, you should reconsider," the courier interrupted. "The funds would free you to do whatever you wished. You could give up chasing after government work and simply explore the Nine Seas."

These people sure know a lot about me. "That would be so incredibly superfantastic, except for the part where I buy that freedom with someone else's."

"He's not free," the girl said with contempt. Her accent got less extravagant when she was angry. "It would be *bakoo* grave error to even try to change that."

Sophie said: "You want to worry about something, ask yourself what happens when I figure out why Lidman's so damned important to you."

The girl appeared to realize she had overstepped. "I'm just the messenger."

"Yeah, tell me that again."

"I'm—"

"You're not!" Now Sophie was the one losing her temper, and she couldn't even have said why. This was just another minor functionary, dispatched by a government official, and why it was that all of these high-ranking Fleet people had made it their hobby to jerk Sophie around was beyond her. "I can see the family resemblance."

The girl sucked wind through clenched teeth. She might almost have been afraid.

"You and Brawn have the same earlobes, and your jaw . . . Plus, your nails may be short now, but they have the same crosshatched fingernail polish. That's like a clan tartan, isn't it?"

The messenger relaxed. "You've been studying Golder customs."

"What are you, Brawn's granddaughter? His niece?"

"The curious come to no good end, Kir," she said.

"I'm not selling Lidman. Not to the Golders or Ualtar or anyone else, for that matter. And I'm not going to take him back to Sylvanna and chain him to a plow. And, let's see, what else am I not going to do?"

"Behead him?" she suggested.

"No! And I'm definitely not turning him over to His Honor the duelist bleeping adjudicator—"

"If you think the Sylvanners are going to permit you to loose a murderer in the Autumn District like some kind of wild stoat—"

"I thought you were just the messenger."

"Are you accusing me of dishonesty?"

"Sophie. Kir." Sweet put a hand on her arm and whispered, "This verges on blood feud."

Sophie turned to the rail, unfisting her hands, making herself breathe. "Daimon, can I sign that form?"

He had been waiting, watchful and silent. Now he nodded. "Do you have a pen?"

Right. Stop arguing with the pirate king's fourth cousin twice removed, get her off the ship, and deal with what actually mattered. Sophie put an *X* in the No box, in duplicate, wrote her name with shaking hands, and handed it back. "Are we done? Can the nice and exceedingly honorable courier who's in no way offended by me leave now?"

"*Oui,* I'll go," the girl said.

"Fantastic." Sophie handed over a copy of the signed pages. "Thank the convenor for the information he sent, and tell him, you know . . . no to the rest."

"Give Lidman a message from Crew Brawn: there's nothing ahead for him but sorrow and torment unless he cedes himself to us." The girl raised her voice, addressing everyone on deck. "Anyone who tries to intervene in this doom will sup woe with the murderer."

"Okay, now your welcome's totally worn out," Sophie said.

"Let me see you to your ship," Daimon said, all politeness, whisking the messenger aft and handing her up to the rails so she could scamper down a rope ladder to a waiting taxi.

Teeth, teeth, teeth! Sophie opened her notebook, jotting a few quick lines about the encounter.

"Are you all right?" Sweet said.

"Brawn's people know I'm broke," Sophie said. "At home, I mean. You heard her say that, right?"

"About converting their gold to outland money? I heard. So?"

"It's evidence. That they're involved in some break-ins back at my parents'. Evidence, as opposed to supposition, see? And you witnessed it."

"I'll log my having overheard it." Sweet nodded. "There's the captain."

Garland was perched in a skiff from *Docket,* a black-clad speedboat propelled by something dark and squidlike below the surface. Across from him was Lidman, whose hands were encased in their red carapaces.

They pulled up alongside *Nightjar,* and Tonio directed a crew to lower a boat, the better to raise them to the rail without Lidman having to climb.

Garland assisted him, expression unreadable.

He thinks I'm a terrible person for taking this on, and he doesn't even know the worst of it.

"Captain Parrish," she said, voice raised and a little formal, as he stepped onto the main deck, taking in the crowd.

She searched his face. Was he repelled? Proud? Angry?

"There are rather a lot of people aboard."

"Yes, and we so have to talk about that." Privately, Sophie tried thinking, *So come with me, will you?*

Maybe Beatrice's final spell had made her telepathic.

Garland seemed to get the idea . . . or perhaps he read her not-too-subtle expression. "Beal, show Kir Lidman to the guest cabin."

Kev held up his goo-encased hands. "Might someone break me out of these?"

Garland winced, and looked to Sophie. "It is, of course, your decision. But Kir Lidman should, perhaps, remain cuffed."

Oh, this was going to be a nightmare, wasn't it?

She said, "I'm not that comfortable with, you know, keeping some guy in chains in the hold."

"The accident of your contractual relationship aside," Garland said, "Kir Lidman is a convicted murderer. You're doing him a kindness, but we oughtn't to take unnecessary risks."

His tone was gentle.

He doesn't! He doesn't think I'm a terrible person, oh thank the Seas. . . .

"I killed slave smugglers," Lidman said. "Terrible people. And I'm standing right here."

His voice was a little strangled, and he was sweating. Sophie frowned. He looked afraid. Had he believed she might sell him?

"Okay, rule one: we won't talk about you as if you aren't present. But the captain is right," Sophie said. "You're not exactly some helpless bunny. You cut the heart out of one of those corpses to do that spell against *Sawtooth*. It was only luck the salt frights didn't kill any of the cadets aboard—and they weren't finished with puberty, let alone smuggling anything."

"The crew of a Sylvanner ship—" he said.

"Fleet cadets," she corrected.

"And you attacked Kir Sophie," Garland said softly.

The vibe on deck changed in that instant. She could feel Sweet, Beal, and the others reassessing the tubby, ill-shaven spellscribe.

"You will be treated gently and with respect," Garland said. "But make no mistake—you're not among friends here."

Frights, she thought. *Salt frights at sea. Wood frights sinking ships in the Fleet. The trial minutes from the salt fright cases, stolen from the exhibits locker . . .*

Kev hung his head. "The carapaces come to hurt, after a while. As they harden—I think one of my fingers might be dislocated."

"What?" Sophie said. "Garland, if his hand's broken—"

Garland put a hand on Sophie's arm. "Tonio, find Watts and ask him to have a look at the prisoner, will you?"

She tried to draw him farther away from Lidman, toward the bow. It wouldn't do to get Kev's hopes up . . . Even if it were possible to free him, should she?

How can I not? I can't just own him.

Her teeth came together in a click. She would find her way through this, she *would.* At core it was just another snarl of red tape; all she needed was the patience to detangle it.

Garland followed her willingly enough, but their path took them past Krispos, who took the opportunity to wiggle in with a bow. "Pleasure to see you again, Captain."

Garland nodded gravely.

They were just about out of earshot. Watts had sat Lidman down on a low bench and was bent over his hands, the two of them conversing in low voices.

Just tell him.

"You remember when we were on Sylvanna before . . . it was the end of summer?"

"Of course," Garland said.

"I had that sash and papers that said I was a foreign adult."

"Yes."

"Thanks to Cly, I'm not a foreigner anymore, and—"

"Watch your heads, Kirs!" A taxikite swooped overhead. Folding its immense wings with a practiced jerk, the kite's pilot dropped down onto the deck about a yard from the two of them. She bowed. "Captain!"

. . . And opened the passenger basket to let out Bram.

Okay, this was good—it meant she'd only have to explain herself once. Sophie gestured urgently. *Come here, come here!* But Bram turned to pay the taxikite pilot, and his gaze was traveling down *Nightjar*'s main deck, where something Watts was doing had elicited an indignant "Ouch!" from Lidman.

"Bram! Over here!"

Bram shook Tonio's hand and exchanged hugs with Beal. His eye lit on Daimon, with his glorious red-gold hair and tight breeches. Standing straighter, Bram smoothed his shirt. "New crewman?"

"Bram—"

"Oh. He's not the guy you own, is he?"

"What?"

"*That* individual would be the prisoner," Garland said, pointing at Kev and using his prissy voice. "The one who threatened your sister."

"Oh." Slight deflation in Bram. "Have you figured out what you're going to do with him?"

"Yes. Maybe." Bram's voice had carried—she could see Lidman's posture change. He was straining to listen. "Look, we three should talk about it in the galley or something. Can we go down?"

Lidman leaped to his feet. "I'd like to hear this. I think I have—"

"A right?" Sweet's voice had a razor edge.

Kev kept his gaze locked on Sophie's. "This is how it'll be, is it? Whispered conferences about what to do with the slave?"

"We're using the word 'murderer,'" she said. "Or 'prisoner.' I like 'prisoner.' All in favor of 'prisoner,' say . . ." She foundered; they didn't say "Aye" here.

"Lock me up, bind my hands, use me to bait the butterfish nets—"

"Don't you even try to guilt trip her," Bram said. "She's saving your life, remember?"

"Attempting to manipulate Kir Sophie's abhorrence for the Sylvanner custom of bondage . . ." Garland agreed.

"Guys, I can stick up for myself here. And don't pile on him. It makes me . . ."

"Feel guilty?" Tonio said. "Sophie, you mustn't let this man manipulate you."

"Seas! Don't pile on *me* either, okay?"

"If he's this much trouble, perhaps you should sell him after all," Daimon said.

"Sell?" Bram said.

Daimon said, "Isle of Gold offered—"

"I'm sorry, Kir," Garland interrupted. "And you are . . . ?"

"Wait," Sophie said. "Everybody wait."

But it was too late. Daimon had drawn himself up and said, in his smooth-as-Scotch manly tenor, "I'm Kir Sophie's fiancé."

CHAPTER 16

The legal issue was simple enough. Sophie wasn't an adult, on Sylvanna, unless she was married. And she couldn't free Lidman if she was legally a child.

"Being engaged is a transitional state," she explained. "Two engaged 'kids' make one adult. As long as Daimon and I both sign off on the paperwork, we can, between us, let Lidman go."

To her vast relief, Bram didn't look as though he thought she was in need of an MRI or a room filled with soft objects and pastel-clad caregivers. "So you're not actually going to—"

Daimon interrupted. "If either Kir Sophie or I said we *didn't* mean to marry, we'd be publicly stating intent to commit fraud. Any of you could be called into court to say the engagement was . . ."

"A sham?"

"We're definitely not saying we won't get married," Sophie said. "That's our story. Nudge nudge, wink wink."

"Gee, congratulations," said Bram.

Garland hadn't come out with a word since Daimon introduced himself. He stood, rooted to the deck, looking as if someone had belted him one across the face.

"Parrish? Garland . . ."

She must have looked like she was going to reach for him; he drew back a hair. "We can't go to Sylvanna without a citizen adult," he said. "You're skirting the edge of oath breaking, but it is a feasible plan."

She bit her lip. "I'd meant to tell you—"

"Feasible, yes." He walked past her to the captive spellscribe, Lidman. "How are his hands, Watts?"

"No broken bones here, Captain."

Lidman, obviously, had heard the whole exchange. He gave her a dazzled-looking smile. "Kir Sophie, your generosity of spirit—"

"Don't thank me," she said. "You've put me in a rotten position, and getting us out of it will require strings. Big, sticky ones."

"I understand."

"Watts, can you take those things off him?" Sophie said.

The doctor glanced at the captain, confirming that it was okay.

Garland nodded.

Humbrey, the elder of the two Watch guards, coughed. "Where will he be kept?"

It was a chance to get out of everyone's sight, however briefly. Sophie led Humbrey aft and then down a ladder. The smaller guest cabins were at the rear of the ship, nestled behind the crew quarters and galley, opposite Garland's and Verena's larger cabins, up at the fore.

The guest cabin had been stripped of every possible amenity—writing materials, artwork. Nothing but bare walls, a few blankets, and a wooden bowl of water. It was the only cabin in which the bulkheads couldn't be shifted, the only one that could be locked from outside. It therefore did double duty as a brig, when need arose.

"Corsetta kept getting out of there, didn't she?" Bram and Garland had followed them below, creating a crush in the narrow corridor.

It was true. On their last voyage together they'd picked up a scam artist, a teenage girl who'd had something of a gift for escapes.

"I believe Corsetta may have been inscribed . . . slippery, they call it," Garland said. "It's a common intention on certain nations where there's a large class of people in service. The intention can be laid on adolescents who work as cleaners or tutors in the homes of powerful people. Living in a stranger's home creates vulnerabilities . . ."

"Slipperiness keeps the lord of the manor from meddling with the help?" Bram said.

Garland nodded. "By making them hard to trap."

"Lidman will be secure enough," Humbrey said. He'd been watching the two men closely—reading their lips, Sophie realized.

"I'll be spending time with him," Bram said. "Learning about inscription. Is that okay?"

"Everything to do with Lidman is up to your sister," Garland said. "We'll be under way within an hour."

With that he turned, moving forward toward the galley, and away.

"Give him time," Bram murmured, before Sophie could follow.

Sophie returned to their cabin. Bram had made copies—without her name on them—of the texts of the seven Beatrice inscriptions. As they eased out to the edge of Fleet, turning into the wind, she brooded over that last one.

Beatrice meant to bond me with my adopted family. To keep me away. But it didn't work; she doesn't know what the spell does.

Bram had circled one of the letters within that scroll, noting it with a question mark.

She was, momentarily, so weary that her eyes crossed. The past few days had been a whirl. Meeting Beatrice at the hospital, exploring the exhibits archive, all the paperwork . . .

It would slow down now.

She made herself sit, closed her eyes, started to breathe on a four count. Inhale, two, three, four. Exhale, two, three, four. In time, her mind stilled. Everything would start coming together now. Sailing meant long days with nowhere to go; it was like a retreat of sorts. The Watch and the courts couldn't throw new things at her from here. The bandwidth for communications in and out would narrow. She'd start knocking some questions off the list in her book.

She kept up the count—in, out, in—until she was calm. Then she lay in her bunk, letting the sea rock her into a catnap.

When she resurfaced, she started by sorting her papers and notes: pieces of messagepl y, the letter from Brawn. One by one, she pinned them to the bulkhead.

"Of course," Bram said, when he appeared. "If we're going to play at being cops, we might as well have a crime board."

"Never call it playing," she told him. "This is real-time, grown-up work, Bram. No more ivory tower."

"Aye, aye, Boss."

They don't say "Aye, aye" here, she thought, but he handed her a pin, along with the list of things that had gone missing from that basket of fright spell ingredients.

As the masts of the Fleet shrank into the distance, the two of them settled into a rhythm, gathering, sorting, and displaying their artifacts and clues, working in a way that reminded her of fall nights spent doing homework at the kitchen table. It was a feeling at once companionable and tinged with the faintest hint of homesickness.

CHAPTER 17

Traveling within the Fleet was less like sailing than being in an especially tricky-to-navigate city. After *Nightjar* broke away, setting sail westward in what would be at least a three-week journey, the ocean stretched once more in every direction. There was nowhere to go, nobody to call, nobody to see. A powerful sense of isolation set in.

The ship was small. Garland was remote. Tonio had taken a quiet dislike to Daimon—on the grounds, Sophie suspected, that Bram found her fake fiancé cute.

As for Bram, he gave every appearance of being supremely pleased to be asea again. When he wasn't busy chatting Daimon up—on the pretext of practicing his Fleet, usually—he was trying to learn more about inscription from Krispos, from the books Verena had left, and from Kev himself.

Sweet's time was taken up with ship repairs and being ridiculously in the throes of newfound love with Watts. As for Daimon, Humbrey, and Selwig, they were strangers.

On the third day out, a note appeared on the sheet of messageply whose other half Sophie had left with Beatrice.

ANNELA IS STABLE. THERE WAS SOME BRAIN DAMAGE, WHICH WE'VE HAD CURED. IT WAS A HEAVY INTENTION, BUT SHE NO LONGER NEEDS TO PRESERVE HER MAGICAL LOAD FOR A MORE EXALTED CAREER.

In other words, she had officially failed in her quest to become Allmother.

SHE SAYS BETTONA AND A GIRL WERE SPEAKING ANGLAY AND SEARCHING HER OFFICES AS SHE FIRST FELL INTO THE HYPEROSMOLAR

COMA. THE GIRL REFERRED TO BETTONA AS "SIR," A COUPLE TIMES. AN ERSTWHILE MILITARY CONNECTION?

MOVING ON TO GOVERNMENT GOSSIP, THE SLAVE NATIONS HAVE BEEN TRYING TO GET THE CONVENOR OF SYLVANNA TO REBUKE CLYDON PUBLICLY FOR TAKING ANNELA TO HAVERSHAM ABOARD *SAWTOOTH* DURING THE DIPLOMATIC INCIDENT EARLIER THIS YEAR. IT'S PART OF A BIGGER BROUHAHA OVER THE SYLVANNER ELECTION—THERE ARE SOME HOTLY CONTESTED RACES BETWEEN ISOLATIONIST AND PRO-FLEET FACTIONS, AND SOME ABOLITIONIST PAL OF CLYDON'S IS RUNNING FOR GOVERNOR.

VERDANII AND SYLVANNA HAVE ALWAYS HAD MUCH IN COMMON DESPITE THEIR DIFFERENCES OVER SLAVERY. IF PEOPLE ARE TRYING TO CHIP AWAY AT THAT ALLIANCE WHILE VERDANII IS PERCEIVED TO BE VULNERABLE, IT SEEMS LIKELY THAT THERE'S HOPE IN SOME QUARTERS THAT A FLEETWIDE WAR CAN BE TRIGGERED SOONER RATHER THAN LATER.

The note ended abruptly, as Beatrice filled the last of the magical page.

Working from the books she'd loaded into her phone, Sophie reinvented a wheel, working up basic how-to-procedures for the beginnings of a fingerprint process.

The Fleet had begun taking prints from new cadets about fifteen years ago—as fallout from some kind of lawsuit, naturally. The cards were in with the rest of the personnel records, which were filed according to an arcane system based on country of origin and term of service. They sometimes used the prints when a body turned up in the ocean without its tags or its face. It only really worked when they had a good guess as to who the body was.

What Sophie had done was to request all the prints of people who'd gone AWOL or otherwise missing from Fleet in the past five years, along with a thousand randomly chosen from the archive, and all of the unidentified corpse prints.

Identification was first a matter of classifying the prints—basically, indexing them in a way that made it possible to look them up again. Two guys named Azizul Haque and Edward Henry had come up with one such system in the nineteenth century, for use in British India. The technology proliferated as police around the world taught themselves to do it, using written manuals. Now Sophie was doing the same, figuring out how to turn ten finger impressions into a code: once you determined the dominant pattern on each finger, you gave it an *A* if it mostly had arches, a *W* if it was whorls, and an *L* if it had loops. This gave you something that looked like AWALLW-LALL, which let you order your print cards into one of thirty-two piles.

The next order of classification was finer grained, but it got you into the right drawer before you started looking for what fingerprint techs called "points of similarity."

The idea was that she, Humbrey, and Selwig would examine and file all the print cards, without knowing which ones belonged to the missing sailors. Then they'd do searches on the corpse prints. If the matches they produced did indeed come from people who'd vanished—and if all three of them came up with similar results—the Watch would concede that the classification system worked and would expand the scope of the project.

It was a big task, suited to long days. Luckily, both men were good at pattern recognition. Humbrey was especially keen—he relished the prospect of carving out a new direction for his career, now that his hearing was shot. Selwig was younger, a burly giant of a soldier who looked like he'd be happier loading hay bales, working as a club bouncer, or playing football. He was less interested in desk work and his disposition leaned toward surliness, but he learned well enough . . . as long as he was praised almost constantly.

Since their duties included guarding Kev, Sophie moved the entire dactyloscopy operation right to Kev's cabin. "You have options," she told him. "Sit on the fringes, help Bram learn inscription, or help out with the fingerprint stuff."

Rather than lie around being bored to death, Kev settled into drinking endless cups of sweetened tea while answering Bram's magic-related questions.

When she found herself wanting a break from the group, Sophie would leave them with the pile of prints and practice the next step: record keeping, comparisons, and lifting latent prints.

Printing a subject was easy enough. A sponge laced with locally made dyes made a perfectly respectable ink pad. Capturing latent prints was another matter. It was harder, but also more fun.

At home, a lot of fingerprint powders were made of synthetic materials or graphite. Here, Sophie would need to rely on powder recipes from the nineteenth century. Over the first week, with slow and meticulous work, she experimented with powder mixes and dusted much of the ship for latent prints, exploring ways to lift them off wood, silver, ceramics, and the Erinthian obsidian that served as window glass.

The hardest thing, technologically, proved to be transferring powdered latent prints to cards for use as permanent records. Stormwrack had no plastic, and thus no clear lifting tape to deploy. Bram took a day off from studying inscription and got Daimon to help him with applying a thin layer of glue to cards, lifting the prints, and then shellacking the resulting image to fix it to the page.

As they nailed down each stage of the process, Sophie wrote out a procedures manual in Fleet, translating existing English documents and adapting them to Stormwrack's technology and resource base.

This was where Krispos came in. As Sophie made translations of the procedures manuals she was using as sources, she wrote them out in Fleet and then had him memorize the texts.

She was putting her cabin back to rights one afternoon, after a serious print-gathering binge, when Garland passed by.

"Garland," she said. "Can I speak to you?"

He stepped inside, taking in the dust patches and the fingerprint cards drying in the weak winter sunlight. "More practice for the Watch cadets?"

"For me, too," she said, handing him a pair of dried, shellacked cards.

"What's this?"

"One's Verena. I don't know which. The other, probably . . ."

"Would be Gale." His features softened a little as he compared them.

She attempted a change of subject. "So—Kev."

He raised his eyebrows.

"The law says he can't just be freed," she said.

"Given his crimes, that's unsurprising."

"But if he's harmless, it's allowed."

"A pacification spell? He would have to give you his full name."

"Mensalohm told me that, once we get to Sylvanna, they strip a slave's previous identity. I have to rename him."

Garland frowned. "You've told him this?"

"Not yet."

"Once the pacification spell's done, he's defenseless?"

"Yeah."

"But you can free him. Will you?"

"I want to. But something's wrong with this picture. The pirates want him. Cly, too, maybe. But he doesn't seem especially scared."

"No. Which is strange. Even if you free him, his enemies could presumably chase him down."

"Exactly." *He always knows just where I'm going with these things.* "So does he think we can protect him indefinitely?"

"He'd have to be quite the optimist." Garland considered it. "There's no bottom to these depths."

"Kev claims the thing the Golders want from him is the location where the slaves went. The ones he supposedly freed."

"They're more likely to want his coconspirators."

"Cly killed everyone aboard *Incannis.*"

"Their sponsors, then."

"Sponsors?"

He fiddled with one of the print brushes as he explained. A good proportion of the bonded had light intentions laid on them at birth, spells to make them tractable or obedient. Even if those intentions hadn't been laid, or got destroyed, a slave who ran had to know that his or her owner could lay another inscription on them after the fact.

"There is a tiny window of opportunity," Garland said. "A person's name must be changed before they're found to be missing. Otherwise, their owner can kill them from afar or compel them to return."

Sophie swallowed. Her own name was in the wild; the only way to change it would be to do so legally, in the United States, or perhaps now in Sylvanna, where she was—on paper, anyway—a citizen.

"You mean some free nation is making escapees citizens, and then renaming them," she said.

"If Kev knows who, and how, it would give him significant political value."

"If we get him to tell us who his contacts are, maybe we can warn them—"

"Sophie, as a Sylvanner yourself, and a sworn official of the Fleet, it's better that you don't know."

Suspicion bloomed. That made it sound like Garland knew something. "Fair enough. But if there was a hidden slave colony on one island or another, couldn't Kev go there after he's pacified? To be safe from the Isle of Gold types and their happy torture fun?"

He considered it, dipping the edge of the brush in the club moss dust and lightly buffing the corner of Verena's clock. A print—Sophie's own thumb—started to take shape. His hands were as nicely proportioned as the rest of him, and they moved with increasing assurance as he familiarized himself with the brush. "It might be," he said at last, "that there's a place where he'd be welcomed."

"You know where the people he rescued ended up." She couldn't help beaming at him. "You're *totally* in with the abolitionists."

"I can no more allow to having an idea of an escapee's whereabouts than you can admit to a lack of commitment to your present romantic relationship," he said, in the extra-prissy voice.

She tried not to be stung. She had brought a fiancé, however fake, aboard. If their positions were reversed, she'd be hurt.

"Fine, let's change the subject." She indicated the cards with Aunt Gale's and Verena's prints on them. "I've compared both of these cards with that print the police in San Francisco bagged from my parents' house."

"You thought Verena ransacked your room? I could have told you—"

"She isn't here, is she? She's on Verdanii. Intelligence types there could totally have ordered her to go see if she could find Gale's pocket watch."

"I know things were awkward between you, because of—" He barely paused. "Because of me. But you can't believe Verena would violate your privacy."

"I'm supposed to be the proof squad, not the take-people-at-their-word patrol," she said.

"Ah, yes. Indisputable facts. No trust without proof. Did you suspect her of transporting John Coine, as well?"

"Of course she didn't help kill Gale!"

"But you'd like to prove that, too?"

The only enclosed space on *Nightjar* that was bigger than this cabin was the galley, and yet it seemed too close, suddenly. She fought an urge to pace, which would have brought her, in one step, right up to his nose. "Brawn told me John Coine went to a Tenderloin diner, Sunny Side Jim. And a gun store. We'll assemble pictures of all the Feliachild suspects, me and her included, and find someone to show them to the restaurant staff and gun store folks."

"Someone?"

"Would your Anglay be up to it?"

"Possibly." His tone was still guarded.

"Seas, Garland! I'm not trying to lock up the family. I have to eliminate Beatrice and Verena as suspects."

"Your sister would never have helped John Coine and his cronies kill Gale. If you think—"

"I don't think that! Not even a little."

That got a genuine smile from him. "And Bettona Feliachild?"

"Her? She's in this somehow, up to her knobby neck."

"Beatrice believes she trained someone to eraglide."

"Yeah. We have to figure out who . . . and whether they are indeed genetically related to the Verdanii nobility. If not, Annela and the gang at the Watch can move on to being unhappy about foreign eragliders instead of suspecting Feliachilds of treason."

"I suppose that might be an improvement." He handed the fingerprint brush back.

When he turned to leave, she said, "Don't go."

His brows rose in question.

Don't start babbling, don't start babbling. "Let me print you."

"Why?"

"To eliminate you from the mix here." She pulled out a fresh page, wrote Captain G. Parrish of Issle Morta on it, and the date. "Give me your hand."

With the barest of pauses, he did. His skin was warm.

She rolled his left thumb over the sponge, laid it on the table, and then rolled it on the card. "What does that look like to you?"

"Truth," he said.

What did you do with that? She kept going. "Index, middle, fourth, pinky. Now your left."

He consented with a faint smile.

Thawing, she thought. *I'm just a little irresistible, then.*

Hard on the heels of that thought came the memory of the scrolls Beatrice had given her. Charm. He was just succumbing to the magic.

"Sophie?"

She finished printing him and tried to sound cheerful. "All done!"

"Whatever's wrong?"

"Nothing. Thanks for helping." She kept busy with the cards and brushes until he went.

There had been half a dozen weird things about her protorelationship with Garland, even before she'd found out she was some kind of magically jumped-up Mary Sue Supergirl. He had been told Gale would live until he found true love, for one thing. And ten minutes after the two of them had first met, Gale had been murdered.

How could she buy into the idea of fate? Not to mention love at first sight?

The rational argument went this way: they met, Gale died, and, in a state of grief heightened by guilt and superstition, Garland had latched on to the first new woman in his life. Obviously Sophie was the author of his fate, the fulfillment of the prophecy.

But how could she even broach the topic without being insulting?

Add to that the awfulness with Verena, the crush her half sister had had on Garland, practically since birth.

They came from different worlds.

Beatrice had . . . bewitched her.

She was fake-engaged.

She flung herself onto her narrow bunk. “Let it go,” she muttered. “Let it go, let it go, let him go.”

She’d never had trouble walking away from a guy before.

It’s the close quarters, she told herself. *Nowhere to walk. If only I could* swim *to Sylvanna.*

The sword-fighting practice dummy stared at her, glass-eyed, from across the cabin. The clock ticked ponderously, seeming to tap a steady cadence against her skin. She should let it run down.

Instead, she got up, opened it, and stilled its pendulum outright. Verena could call ahead if she wanted to eraglide in for a visit. With the clock quieted, her head cleared a little. She gathered up her notes on the sinkings in Fleet and the forbidden art of the fright—marsupial lions, salamander eggs, tree people, and all. Where was Krispos?

If she couldn’t forget about Garland, she’d just busy herself with making connections and closing cases until her libido punched out for the night.

CHAPTER 18

The late watch on Northwater. *Nightjar* rose and fell in an easy, slow-dance rhythm, knifing through inky waves. The black sky unfurled, smothering the last orange gleaming of the sun. Their course was due south, and the days seemed longer with every day's journey farther from the north pole. In fact, they were shortening; solstice was coming and daylight was scarce.

The green-and-silver dance of the aurora borealis had tempted most of the crew up to the main deck hours earlier, including Sophie and Krispos, who'd been sifting through their trove of knowns about frightmaking and the sinkings in Fleet.

The blackness of a sky entirely untouched by light pollution, velvet sprayed with glittering whorls and clusters of stars, was a stark backdrop to the flashier aurora display of undulating green and white. Sophie had sailed north once, back home, on an expedition to film narwhals in the Arctic. Even then, the remote setting had made the nighttime displays spectacular.

This was better. Even Bram was, gratifyingly, openmouthed.

Garland steered the ship. Watts and Sweet were high in the rigging, cozied up against each other and murmuring in unfamiliar tongues.

The show outlasted its audience. Krispos retreated first. It was cold on deck and, Sophie had noticed, he was a delicate man, easily bruised, prone to chills, with those scarred feet and a corresponding totter to his gait.

His departure triggered others; the daytime watch had been about ready to turn in before the aurora burst forth. As they called out their goodnights, she realized Kev and his guards had missed it entirely.

Next time, Sophie thought, *we'll have to bring him up on deck.*

She took the amidships ladder down to the galley, brewed a pot of coffee using beans Bram had brought from home, and brought it to their cabin. Krispos was wrapped in a blanket as he nosed through one of the sets of court minutes. Bram had set up his calligraphy pens in the uncluttered corner he'd reserved for himself.

"Fact one," Sophie said, passing out cups. The cold air had revived her. "Someone's using fright spells to sink ships in Fleet."

That much was indisputable. She took four slates and wrote the names of the ships, one atop each board.

"The attack on *Shepherd* suggests an escalation," Bram said. "Destroying a rescue vessel makes it harder to save the next target." He dipped a brush in ink, practicing the spellscrip lettering for a spell to ward would-be thieves away from their parents' home. It was an exercise that left him with plenty of surplus brainpower for participating in a little victimology exercise.

"That's not a fact," Sophie said. "You've jumped to supposition."

"Each ship was bigger than the next," he amended. "More crew, better location within the Fleet. The first ship was an unlicensed merchant, right? But *Shepherd* has official status. People were more upset by the attack."

"More upset" wasn't easily quantifiable, but she wrote the ships' sizes and crew complements on the slates. "Krispos, did you say you'd memorized all those stats on Fleet ships?"

"It's a standard accuracy test for memoricians."

"Can you make a list of official ships that are physically larger and have bigger crews than *Shepherd*?"

Krispos practically purred as he unrolled a sheet of paper, pinned it to the ever-diminishing space on their bulkheads, and started writing, producing beautifully formed letters at a speed that almost rivaled that of a laser printer. "What benefit is there in attacking a higher-status vessel?"

Bettona had had texts on terrorism in her quarters, info imported from San Francisco. Sophie picked up *Things That Go Boom!*, rubbed the last traces of fingerprint powder off its cover, and opened it to a marked page. She translated the original English to Fleet, for Krispos: "The ultimate goal of terrorism is to introduce people to fear, and thereby change their behavior."

He nodded, absorbing that, as he finished the list of ships larger than *Shepherd*.

"Start at the top," she said. "The Piracy went after *Temperance* once. Could they be trying to sink her outright?"

"Frights make holes the size of a person. That wouldn't sink a ship as big as *Temperance,*" Bram objected, without looking up.

"Good point. But . . . !" She turned over her list of facts gleaned from the material she and Krispos had assembled about frightmaking. "Some wood frights can get bigger than their templates, giant-sized even, if they're left to grow long enough."

"It takes a long time to gestate those things. The ship filths up and bleeds. If *Temperance* was growing a giant on her hull, the mermaids would see it."

She flipped *Things That Go Boom!* over in her hands. "If I was building up to a bigger target, I'd have foreseen an increase in security."

Bram nodded absently, returning to his calligraphy.

Back to facts. Opening her phone, she poked through the e-books on profiling. "What do the targets have in common? Port of call?"

Krispos took this as a request to jot down the names of the different island nations for the four ships in question. No commonality there. He put a little star next to the three civilian ships. "Registered at portside nations, except for *Shepherd,* with portside captains," he explained.

"So three slavers—"

"Kev's ship, *Incannis,* was sinking human traffickers," Bram noted.

Both rounds of sinkings had been a source of international tension. The story going around Fleet was that the portside nations were under attack by abolitionists, and that the starboard nations had decided such ships were less worthy of protection and justice than those from freeholding lands.

"Three slave nations, but *Shepherd* breaks the pattern. Where were they built, Krispos?"

A clattering of chalk: TALLON, MOSSMA, CARDESH, EHRENMORD.

No commonality there.

She eyed the list of potential targets. "Can you put an *X* in front of *every* ship that represents a starboard nation? We'll call that strike one."

He did it.

What else? "Can we eliminate ships that have had magic worked on them?"

"Most vessels bear at least one or two intentions," Krispos said. "*Shepherd* turns naturally to face oncoming waves. She's hard to swamp. All the important ships will have been inscribed."

"Important" sparked something. Sophie asked, "That thing you Wrackers say—'We're no great nation' . . . Is that a subject for debate or a matter of fact? Do people agree on the great nations and the not so great?"

"There are perhaps twenty nations in the middle whose influence is contentious," Krispos said.

"Okay," Sophie said. "Give another strike to all the indisputably *not* great nations. Leave the middle powers on the list for now."

Krispos began working his way down the bottom two-thirds of the list. *X, X, X.*

"What else would make something less attractive as a target? Bram?"

"Um," he said. "Troublemakers, unpopular countries, seacraft earmarked for replacement, and ships that should be scuttled?"

Krispos pondered that for a second and added a half dozen marks. Two of the ships on the list had accumulated three strikes—Sophie had him cross those right out. That left forty ships with no strikes at all.

"Redundancy," she said. "There are three refitters, right? Taking out one repair shop or clarionhouse or food storage ship doesn't materially threaten the Fleet. But get rid of the mermaid training center, Fleet cadet school, or the dueling court and you've created a big hole, both functionally and symbolically."

"Nice reasoning," Bram murmured, as Krispos began *X*-ing. Quite a few ships got third strikes in that round. The top prospects, those with no strikes at all, dwindled to eleven.

Now what?

She kept at it, raising possible points of commonality and mostly finding they didn't apply. Were the ships attacked all from northern or southern hemisphere nations? No. Three were civilian, one military. Two were owned by their captains, as *Nightjar* was owned by Garland. One was held by a corporation, and *Shepherd* by its home nation.

She heard a hatch open on the other side of the bulkhead, where Garland's cabin was, and the sound of his steps on the deck, barely a yard away. A creak of weight on his bunk. It was easy to imagine him taking his boots off, preparing to turn in.

Focus, she told herself.

Temperance, the flagship of the Fleet, was at the top of the list, high in influence, with only one strike—the one indicating that it represented a starboard nation, Tallon. Sophie was itching to declare it the obvious victim. "We know Isle of Gold wants *Temperance* out of the equation before war breaks out."

"Would it even be possible to sink it using a wood fright?" Bram said. "*Temperance* has a stonewood and sharkskin hull."

"You're the one learning inscription; you tell us. Does the target's hull have to be wood?"

Bram waved an arm in a random-looking helicopter motion, roughly indicating the pile of information on frights. Krispos took this—correctly, as it happened—as a request for information. "Forest guardians do require nurse trees."

"This is a repurposed murder spell," Sophie said. "Someone's compelled to draw the image of their hand on the ship's boards. The fright growing and then putting a hole in the ship is a side effect—as far as it knows, it's just trying to kill the person who created it."

"In year eighty-two of the Cessation, a murder committed in this fashion was tied to a spellscribe on Mossma," Krispos said. "The trial minutes say the spellscribe admitted to revising the theme of the original spell. That killing, and a massive fright outbreak on Tug Island, led to the international ban on frightmaking."

"Stonewood is magically treated wood, right? They make it super hard?"

She spread the materials on frightmaking across the table, looking for information. Bram, meanwhile, stopped lettering and opened one of the magical texts he'd acquired.

"Kev might know," Sophie said.

Krispos scratched his beard. "It's the middle of the night. Shall I wake him?"

"No need," Bram said. "Here's a passage about material substitutions. It says stonewood lacks the original enchantable properties of the source material. Being magically treated itself, it is neither perfectly wood nor perfectly stone and lacks the purity required to be treated as either."

"Stonewood is eliminated, then," Krispos said. "And we can also put a. . . . was the word 'strike'?"

"Strike, yeah."

"A strike on everything that doesn't have a wood hull." Krispos took up his pen, clearly delighted with the process, and began *X*-ing.

Sophie was relieved when the latest round of strikes earned the Verdanii ship *Breadbasket* its third X. The prison ship, *Docket,* with its carapace hull, was eliminated too. Then again, so was *Temperance.*

She tapped the nearest slate. "How specific is this thing about the wood? Do we know what the hulls of these victim ships were made of?"

Krispos switched from pen to chalk and wrote across the four slates: WHITE SPRUCE, GASPER SPRUCE, SIKKA SPRUCE, GASPER SPRUCE.

"Spruce, spruce, and spruce. Coincidence, Bram, or significant?"

"Um . . ." Now it was his turn to flip. "Best I can do for you without the original spell is give it a rating of *likely significant*."

"Okay. Add strikes to the ships that aren't made of spruce, Krispos, if you can, just to see."

She began fine-combing through the notes about the sinkings, turning up a list of the things that were supposed to be in that basket of evidence about the frightmaking case. There were amphibian eggs missing, some cat hair and horsehair, plus the paperwork.

"We need more information about the text of the frightmaking spell," she said. "I'll write to the head of the Spellscrip Institute in the Autumn District."

"Why her?"

"She's an expert, she was nice, and she and Cly are tight." She left out the part where she'd embarrassed herself at a party Autumn Spell was hosting. "She can only say no, right?"

"I think you'd better write the Watch first," Krispos said. He had finished marking up the target list.

Constitution, the head of the government, was the only ship with no strikes at all.

Sophie's flesh crawled. Practically everyone she knew within Fleet worked aboard *Constitution*. Annela, and Erefin Salk, of the Watch, even lived there. All the librarians and messengers who'd helped her find resources when she first stayed in Fleet, the convenors who'd been kind, the woman who ran the tea cart . . .

Bram said, "*Constitution* is a portside ship?"

"She's the rep ship from Cardesh," Krispos said. "Same country as our strapping young Watchman, Selwig."

"Seas," she said. "Wait, okay, calm down. This isn't conclusive. Krispos, can you write something explaining how we arrived at this? The process?"

"Immediately, Kir. Do we have a way to get a message to the Fleet?"

"Beatrice filled that messageply page I gave her. Maybe Verena can run a message to the government?"

"If not, we may have to divert to a clarionhouse," Krispos said.

"Divert? In the North Atlantic?"

"I don't know 'Atlantic,' but we're near Ylle."

"Before you hyperventilate yourselves into a faint," Bram said, "remember that what I said about *Temperance* applies to *Constitution*, too. A human-sized hole isn't a gimme to sink a big ship. Plus, there's the mermaid patrols."

"Good point," said Krispos.

"No! Bad point!" Sophie objected. "An attack, by itself, would be plenty upsetting."

Bram made a raspberry noise to show what he thought of that. "The ship sinkers look ineffectual if they attack ships and fail to sink them. They want to be scary."

"If it's placed just right—"

"No. I'm not trying to be a pain, Sofe. But if they do want to sink *Constitution,* they'll need to power-up their plan. And if you go crying wolf and nothing happens, it undermines everything you've achieved so far."

He was right, as usual.

Maybe it was a matter of giving a massive fright time to gestate? She grabbed for *Things That Go Boom!* again.

"New sheet, Krispos. Things about *Constitution.*" She started listing everything she could think of about the government vessel: the weird, enormous, magical paddle wheel that propelled it through the Nine Seas; the three landing pads for the flying taxi service; the two elevators that connected with the ferries. Libraries, restaurants, lots of public art. Did the ship have any kind of Achilles' heel?

Bram asked, "Do they restrict access to the wheel? Would it have to be someone with . . . I dunno . . . a security pass?"

"Not that I know of. Once you're oathed up, you're pretty much free. Free to roam." She remembered the ceremony, Cly showing up, all the young cadets, all their relations and friends.

Krispos started to speak, but Bram made a *Shut up* motion, mouthing something at him.

She shut her eyes. "Lots of people," she said. "The flow of people on and off *Constitution* is massive."

"Indeed. *Constitution* is the most frequently visited ship in the Fleet," Krispos said, in his quoting voice.

"Tourists, diplomats, people attending ceremonies, witnesses, people coming to watch the government hash through something related to their island. They have an art museum and a Fleet history museum aboard. People come to see the original Compact for the Cessation," Sophie said. "They come to lodge complaints with their convenors and fill out paperwork."

"Meaning what?" Bram said. "You don't need to steal a crew member's name; you can put an inscribed person aboard?"

"Or ten inscribed people," Sophie said. "Or twenty."

Bram pursed his lips, thinking. "Yeah. That'd do it. That'd work. Write the letter."

CHAPTER 19

SOPHIE,

I PASSED YOUR CONCERN ABOUT *CONSTITUTION* MAYBE BEING THE TARGET FOR THE SHIP-SINKERS ON TO THE WATCH, AND TOLD THEM YOU'RE WORRIED ABOUT PEOPLE BRINGING MULTIPLE FRIGHTS ABOARD. YOU'RE ORDERED TO SEND A FULL, DETAILED REPORT ASAP, PREFERABLY WITH ONE OF YOUR PEOPLE, DIRECTLY TO EREFIN SALK.

VERENA

Days passed. Bram successfully inscribed the followbox, for good or ill, so that it fit into the skull of a dead ram named Mellur. They closed it up with a steak bone, a zircon, a piece of Hawaiian lava from home, and a sheet of messageply. The plan was to take it back to San Francisco, next time one of them went, and mail it to one of Sophie's spelunker friends in Tennessee.

"You know this probably won't work," said Bram.

"Nothing ventured, nothing gained," she said. "If it gets us more information, hooray. If not, you learned to do another inscription. Hooray also. Speaking of which, how've you made out on enchanting Mom and Dad's place against break-ins?"

"If the legal description of the property will serve as its proper name, it should be doable," he said. "The inscription has to be lettered on the skin of a specific type of badger, and the brush has to be topped by the fang of a guard dog. Sylvanna will have the supplies."

The evenings grew cooler, chilly enough to drive them below to the galley after sunset, but the afternoons were clear and mellow, with soft lemon-colored sunshine. Cook's nets yielded butterfish, cod, herring, and snailfish, along with random marine samples for Sophie: bits of seaweed, jellies, even the occasional crab.

They were sitting out on the quarterdeck one such afternoon, everyone relaxing after a day of print identification, self-taught magical practice, and ship maintenance. Daimon was pretending to study for his law exams. Humbrey and Selwig were murmuring over a long report they'd written for the Watch about the fingerprinting as they kept the mandated eye on Kev, whom Sophie had invited to join them.

Kev gave every appearance of enjoying the sun. He ate his way through a bowl of leftover stew, watching the sea roll and foam, apparently without a care in the world.

His calm troubled her. At the least, shouldn't he feel guilty about his victims? But, whatever his feelings, having him around had been something of a benefit. The mere thought of him no longer raised her hackles or brought up the image of Cly striding toward them with empty eyes and upraised sword.

"Maze ahead," Beal called.

Sophie hauled herself up for her first look at Ylle.

They were in what would, at home, have been the North Atlantic. Garland had taken them west, skirting the storms they would apparently hit as they turned south toward Sylvanna. Bram, with his predilection for expecting natural disasters to break out everywhere, had already muttered about whether they were going to experience death by iceberg.

This wasn't a berg.

Nightjar was sailing toward a mammoth formation of ice, perhaps five hundred feet tall above the surface, a stunning blue-white pyramid with a glimmering, glassine shine. It was the first of many; they cragged ahead like mountains, steaming faintly, reflecting back sunlight in blinding flashes.

"Why am I reminded of *Titanic*?" Bram muttered.

"That's a kids' tale," Tonio scoffed.

Sophie met her brother's eyes, then opened her book of questions and made a note: *TITANIC* IS A KIDS' TALE?

As they neared, the light within the floe turned amber, the whole thing taking on the appearance of a gigantic crystal lamp.

Excitement burned off her worries about Kev. "What gives?"

"The floe riders come from the nation of Ylle. Their island territory is very small. Many of them, therefore, live here." Daimon was staring, goggle-eyed, at the enormous glowing iceberg. "They are skilled ice-scribers. Their homeland grooms many lichens used in ice spells."

"Are they slavers?"

"No, Kir," said Selwig, looming over her. He spoke in a bland tone that he'd perfected—specifically, she thought—to remind her that civilized people didn't constantly bring up the slaver/nonslaver divide.

"Why are we sailing toward them?" Bram said. "I don't care if it's populated; that is a big old ship-sinking iceberg."

"It's perfectly safe," Garland said. "A maze pilot will take us through the field. They'll have news and mail and information about the weather ahead of us."

By nightfall they could see more of the bergs, lit in a range of golds, blues, and greens, luminous pointy blocks laid across their path.

They tied up on a floe of low-hanging ice, shaped like a buoy. The harbormaster caught the rope from the crew and tied it to an ice hook jutting from the side of the berg. As they watched, a pad of spongy moss grew in the space between the iceberg and *Nightjar,* creating a bumper between them and serving as a more sturdy tether.

A ramp formed, a flat plate of ice with icicles dripping from its bottom, stretching out like a finger and thickening into a bridge. Garland left Tonio in charge and made his way across to talk to the authorities about the pilot.

Sophie had her camera out, capturing everything she could in the waning light of sunset. An outcropping on the floe's side formed a bathtub-size chamber of clear ice above the waterline, through which a bed of rocks and pebbles was visible. The rocks were covered by a layer of moss, maybe nine inches deep, and a pair of snow geese slumbered atop it, their long necks curving around their bodies, their beaks issuing a hint of condensed breath.

The floe riders lived on fish and seal, not surprisingly, as well as on eggs from the seabirds and several species of fungi they were able to cultivate within caverns carved into the bigger icebergs. They kept pools of various sizes and temperatures. In some, they kept algae and plankton, and crabs kept alive on a mix of table scraps, blubber, and algae.

It was a spare existence, with a lot of hard labor, but Sophie had seen at least one culture so impoverished that it made the floe riders seem positively wealthy. They looked as though they might be mostly self-sufficient, but Garland nevertheless asked for twenty of Sophie's protein bars as a trade offering.

With *Nightjar* under Tonio's care, Lidman was locked up, still under the eye of Selwig. The senior officer, Humbrey, had been tasked with packing up half of the fingerprint cards, the procedures manual, and, most importantly, their victimology work on the sinkings and the possible threat to *Constitution*. He'd send a more detailed report ahead using the Ylle clarionhouse, then make his way back to the Fleet on the first westbound ship. He'd present their results on the bodies they'd identified so far.

Sophie was heartily sorry to be losing him. He had a good sense of humor and worked diligently. Selwig, by contrast, was an adolescent mastiff: big, too serious, and a little clumsy. Not to mention defensive about being one of the few portside citizens aboard *Nightjar*.

Watts was bringing up the rear; he was apparently looking to trade for medicinal lichens.

It was a cold day but the seas were calm, and it was possible to hike across the floes as easily as if they were snow-covered mountain crags. The trails were sanded and there were people working everywhere. A duo of teen girls was building up beds of pebbles and moss to attract nesting birds, on a floe obviously set aside for that purpose. This floe was connected, by a springy woven bridge of vegetable fiber, to a hunk of ice so mammoth it could have gone toe to toe with an aircraft carrier.

The bridge took them over the open sea to a carved-ice staircase that led up, up, perhaps five hundred feet, to the landing deck.

"Welcome to *Sledge*," their guide said. "Weather office, clarionhouse, and outlying post of the Fleet of Nations."

"This is Ylle's rep ship?" Sophie said.

"We keep our place in the Fleet." Which meant yes.

Their guide made them pause several times as they climbed upward. "Get warm, good. Get too warm, sweat. Breeze up top'll freeze you solid if you're wet. You know." Sophie couldn't tell whether the guide was just brusque or she couldn't speak the language properly.

"How do you survive up here when it storms?"

The guide gave her a gap-toothed grin. "Is fine. Winds are fair."

"I'm just curious."

The guide considered this—curiosity—with that expression that suggested it was something akin to an open wound, something Sophie should have a medic look at. Finally she said, "There is a chamber inside. We gather and sleep it out."

"You hibernate? For how long?"

She shrugged. "Months, once or twice. Weeks, most often. The birds die, now and then, but otherwise it's safe."

"Couldn't this all break up?" Bram indicated the floe with a wave. "While you're unconscious?"

"This berg's good five or six more seasons before she goes pocky." Peering at Sophie's gear, she said, "This is . . . Is this a light?"

Sophie handed over her flashlight, waiting to see if the woman would figure it out. She didn't even try, just held it until Sophie clicked the button. Then the guide pressed the bright end against the floe.

The glow penetrated into the ice, just a few inches, but enough to reveal, within it, another colony of lichens in orderly, radial patterns, apparently stretched through the ice.

"We tend the outer bergs," their guide said. "Lichens create give. Harder to shatter. Ready? Let's climb again."

They came out on a mammoth plain of ice, and Sophie was again reminded of an immense aircraft carrier. The port and starboard sides of *Sledge* were built up, scraped like the plowed edges of a road. To the fore and aft were immense sculptures. At the front was a pack of wolves, leaping into the space before the floe, like a ship's figurehead or a dog pack pulling a sled. To the rear, a polar bear—white, glimmering, and more than sixty feet in length—gave chase. Its outstretched forepaw was the only thing connected to the floe, as though it was running after the sled and had just caught its rear.

All two hundred and fifty flags of the Fleet of Nations were strung on a wooden pole fifty feet high, planted deep in the snow.

Between the bear and the dogs was a village's worth of people, some out on the exposed surface of *Sledge,* others occupying a permanent-looking settlement within a deep trough dug into its center, a canyon of glacier-blue ice partially roofed by sealskin and lichen netting. The temperature below had to be warmer; a dozen kids were running around on its floor, lightly dressed, under the care of a couple elders.

Above, adults were tending cauldrons formed out of ice blocks—they looked a little like roofless igloos, lined with leather and other insulating substances. One was apparently a desalinizing operation: two teenage girls were stirring it with ornately worked paddles and were drawing out salt, which they dumped into another sealed tank.

There were algae pools and a tub of heated water. A line of villagers visited both the potable water and the hot, filling skins and hauling them down into the trench.

Aft, near the floe and the dog sculpture, Sophie saw a single man—so smooth of face he might have been a baby, but for his size—looking into a pool that cast dazzling light back onto him.

Their guide was heading that way.

His pool's surface was remarkably black. It was contained within a tank made of bones—ribs?—that had been woven like wicker. Spellscrip notes edged its upper lip, and Sophie saw Bram taking it in, reading the words, memorizing them.

"Weather office," said their guide, bowing to the baby-faced man.

Baby Face smiled at Garland. "Welcome back, Captain. Where are you bound?"

"Sylvanna, Autumn District."

The man crumbled a powder into the fluid, and little winks of white light settled on the surface, forming constellations.

"Stars," Bram whispered.

Sophie nodded. A puff of flour next, making clouds. Beneath them, they could suddenly see landmasses, the northwestern hemisphere of Stormwrack.

A weather map, by any other name.

Sprays of color, green and red, purple, gold, and white, an aurora borealis in miniature, shivered through the tank.

"Here," the operator said to Garland, pointing. "A vortex of cold air—it meets the warm. Keep east of that, though, and all is calm."

"What about the approach to Autumn?"

"Perhaps a bit of chop. The seas will be calming as you approach. You won't be alone out there, Kir."

"The cod fleet?" Garland said.

The man sprinkled a minuscule something and the picture shifted. "They're here," he said. "But also *Sawtooth,* of the judiciary."

Cly's ship. Sophie felt a stone dropping into her belly.

"She came through?"

He nodded. "Three days ago. His Honor took an Erinthian swindler off our hands, turned over the mail, left a nice crate of dried peaches."

"He's bound for Sylvanna?"

"Where else?"

Garland didn't react, instead asking, "How are things to the far south?"

"Stormy, as always. Summer. How far south do you mean?"

"Well into the emptiness," Garland said.

Emptiness. Sophie supposed that meant the refuge for the escaped slaves was somewhere in the south, off the charts.

"I wouldn't recommend that, Captain. Stormy down there."

"Always," Garland said. He handed over the box of protein bars and a satchel of savory cakes, a sort of bread with curry that *Nightjar*'s cook seemed to believe was obligatory after every single meal.

"You will stay the night, yes? The pilot will bear you out of the maze at dawn."

"We are grateful for your hospitality," Garland said, which apparently meant yes.

Their guide shook herself back to her feet. She led them into the trench, setting them up with a hot water bottle and communal sealskin blankets, bringing them each a bowl made of a skull—seal, Sophie thought—filled with a dense brown powder. Pouring boiling water into each skull, she thereby made a soup. "Seal meat, lichens, and mushrooms."

Sitting down to eat was apparently a signal that the visitors were socially available, because kids came to investigate them, mobbing the bunch, joining them under the blanket. Sophie felt tiny hands roaming over her, respectfully enough—they didn't grab anything she wouldn't want grabbed. They, at least, were curious enough to work out how the light worked.

Perhaps Wrackers aren't innately lacking in curiosity. The cultural taboo against it takes hold as they age.

Their guide cast a covetous eye over the light.

"It dies after about three hours," Sophie told her. "Hard to recharge in the winter. I have one with a crank on *Nightjar*, though, that you could have."

"Crank . . ."

"You feed it, basically." She mimed the motion. "It's a fair amount of work."

"Our nights are long and we have many hands," the guide said. "I will take this crank light, with thanks."

By now the kids had snuggled in, along with a half-bear, half-human child who was only too happy to be photographed, and a husky dog.

"So," Bram said. "Cly's going to Sylvanna."

She groaned.

"That's gonna make it harder for you to glide in, crack the shackle off Kev, and get out, don't you think?" Watts said.

She could feel awkwardness ratcheting up as they all contemplated but didn't speak about her fake engagement. But she'd been needing this: a chance to talk to Bram and Garland about what to do, without Selwig overhearing or Daimon offering opinions. "First, I have to tell Kev about this pacification spell that's required if I'm to release him."

Garland said, "Will he even agree to regaining his liberty, when you've shown you're resolved to protect him?"

"It's his *freedom*."

He extricated one of his curls from the fist of a toddler who had taken over his lap. "He may prefer to oblige you to continue in perpetual ownership, knowing you won't be on Sylvanna, you won't mistreat him, and you won't allow anyone else to do so. It might be preferable to having his capacity for violence curbed and then to be set free where all the people he's angered can hunt and hurt him."

"I'm not owning him indefinitely."

"If he possesses information about freedom activists, and if people are after it, what then?"

Sophie sucked on her lip. "Maybe his memory will have to go, too?"

"What?" Bram said.

"If he agrees, obviously."

"Is that even possible?"

She nodded. "Annela shook the prospect at me like a club . . . Oh."

"What?"

"It was her big threat for a while. Then she stopped bringing it up. And I just realized why: Beatrice told her about those damned scrolls. Told her I was too loaded for an amnesia spell." She opened up her book of questions, found a note about Annela and the threat, and crossed it out. "One mystery down, four hundred to go."

"She does this," Garland murmured to Watts.

"Watching the woods for an unwary bird, we call it."

Bram was glaring at her.

"What?" she said. "Do you think I *want* to amnesia Kev? What would you do, superdork?"

He stuck his tongue out, then began to roll the problem over in his mind. She knew he'd bounce against the same walls of the trap that Cly—if it was Cly—had set for her: she lacked the hard-heartedness to let Kev go to his execution, but now she'd stuck herself with a ship-sinking, crew-killing, possible freedom fighter.

That sense of certainty rose again: *I will puzzle this one out. I'm up to this.*

"You believe your *father* was the one who told Kev he could ask you to take him on?" Watts asked. His incredulity was endearing. He was, in some ways, easily shocked.

"Kev killed human smugglers. Cly kills criminals. 'How is this any different, daughter?' In other words, it could be a bit of an object lesson."

"Among other things," Garland agreed.

It occurred to her that the Feliachild side of the family had warned her, repeatedly, that Cly was a jerk. "Also, I think Cly's one of the people who's so keen to interrogate Kev."

It was cozy there, under the sealskin blankets. The night was wearing on, though the sky had already been dark for some time. The lamps were going out, here and there, making it even dimmer.

The little kids showed no interest in moving on. Unlike the adults, they were interested in the unfamiliar. They fiddled with the zippers on Bram's jacket until they got them to open and close, and one of the boys found a spring-loaded ballpoint pen and got ink on both hands in an effort to mark up the leather mat they all lay on.

Watching them was reassuring. There were times when she thought all of Stormwrack had taken a vow against intellectual curiosity.

Garland hasn't, she thought. He was whispering back and forth with a four-year-old, the two of them exchanging words in yet another language she didn't know, the child erupting into giggles at Garland's utterances. The kid had a hand laid flat on Garland's cheek, dark fingers and pale, white nails, and she remembered Garland kissing her, up in the mountains of Issle Morta, and felt an ache, like muscles pulling deep within, a sensation that felt almost like desperation.

The silence lengthened and the kids burrowed closer. Watts held them rapt with a long, almost tuneless song in his native language. It had lots of repetitions, meowing, too, and gestures and spitting that made it apparent, to Sophie at least, that the hero of the story was a cat. A toddler small enough to still be nursing tottered off into another circle, where his mother welcomed him with open arms.

Within an hour it was so dark she couldn't see the others anymore—just their shapes in the dark. Up above, the portion of the village trench that wasn't covered in netting revealed a vivid strip of jeweled blackness, stars clear and brilliant, a sickle of moon so bright and slender it looked like a break in the sky itself.

Sleep was a long time coming. Sophie lay among the others, warm but not drowsy, and mentally paged through the various things she had going on. If Humbrey could demonstrate dactyloscopy to a couple more Watch clerks while she and Selwig made more progress on identifying the remaining found bodies . . .

When she'd opened her book of questions, she'd seen a note on the messagepy, in English, from Verena. Now she read it by the fading light from her flash.

> SORRY I HAVEN'T WRITTEN. THE FELIACHILD MATRIARCH BANNED ME CONTACTING OUTLANDERS, BUT NOW YOU'RE OATHED, SYLVANNER, AND ARGUABLY THE SAVIOR OF *CONSTITUTION,* SHE CAN'T STOP ME.
>
> I AM WORKING WITH THE VERDANII EQUIVALENT OF HOMELAND SECURITY, FOLLOWING UP ON STUFF YOU AND MOM LEARNED ABOUT BETTONA, LIKE THIS THEORY SHE MAY'VE TRAINED AN OUTSIDER TO ERAGLIDE.
>
> ANNELA HAD GIVEN BETTONA AN ALIBI, AND IT CHECKS OUT—THEY WERE WORKING WITH HALF A DOZEN CONVENORS ON SOME LEGISLATION WHEN GALE WAS ATTACKED. BUT IF SHE'S GOT AN ACCOMPLICE AND THAT ACCOMPLICE IS VERDANII . . . WELL, THEN WE HAVE TWO OR MORE TRAITORS ON OUR HANDS. (IF THEY'RE NOT FROM HERE, SOMEONE FROM ANOTHER NATION CAN ERAGLIDE. EITHER WAY, IT'S A POLITICAL CAN OF WORMS.)
>
> ON THE UPSIDE, THEY'RE NOW SATISFIED IT'S NOT ME OR MOM.
>
> THE GENETIC BOTTLENECK, AS YOU CALL IT, ISN'T THE ONLY QUESTION. THERE'S THE CLOCKS, TOO. THE BELIEF WAS THAT YOU NEEDED A FELIACHILD *AND* A BLESSED TIMEPIECE TO ERAGLIDE. WHEN I COME TO *NIGHTJAR,* FOR EXAMPLE, I HOME IN ON THE SOUND OF GALE'S CLOCK.

Sophie thought about this for a minute, then wrote a reply: HAS ANYONE CHECKED ON THE ACTUAL ARTIFACTS: PHARMANN'S CLOCK, YOURS, ENNATRICE, LIKE THAT? ATTEMPTS TO STEAL GALE'S WATCH HINT THEY DO NEED THE CLOCKS.

She added the times of the two break-ins at her parents' house, and the information she'd gotten from Brawn about the diner in San Francisco and the gun shop.

Thinking about Beatrice reminded her about the scrolls.

There had been a time when she'd thought finding her birth family would offer an answer, a nice neat something that would connect her with an ordinary mother and a father. She'd imagined coming away with a firm idea: this is who I am.

Instead, she seemed to have created an endless pattern of bifurcation. Every discovery led to more questions, new doubts. She felt further from knowing herself—whatever *that* meant—not closer.

The whirl of thought brushed against one topic, then another, until—sometime after the moon had vanished from the narrow view of the sky—she finally slept.

She opened her eyes the next morning, still in darkness, to see that an empty corral she had spotted the night before was full of a species of penguin, each about as big as a nine-month-old child and clearly drowsing. They had come in through a vent in the ice and were generating enough heat, as they slept, to steam up the curved ceiling of their chamber.

She took a long look around the village, failing to see any penguin skins in evidence, or any obvious bones or beaks. *What are they using them for?*

As she scanned, she saw that she and Garland had rolled closer in the night.

The kids had chosen to clump on the two of them. Maybe he was the warmest? Whatever the attraction, Garland had a toddler on his chest, and the eldest boy snugged against his farther shoulder. A little girl lay in the narrow groove between Garland and Sophie. Her tiny hand was atop theirs; they had found each other in the night.

Holding hands. She felt a silly, pointless thrill of something that ran deeper than lust.

There was no extricating herself without waking both man and child. She fumbled out her camera with her free hand and took a picture. His looks were ridiculous, breathtaking.

Pull it together, she told herself. *You need to stay on task. Get Humbrey back to Fleet and work out what you're going to say to Lidman.*

In time, *Sledge* and the village came to life, the penguins erupting into noisy chattering. Garland's eyes opened. He took in Sophie and the pile of kids and broke out his best smile.

"We appear to be trapped." His lips moved, the words reaching her ear. Yet his voice was so soft the kids didn't even twitch.

"Nothing you can do," she agreed.

"Helpless," he said. Then he sprang to his feet, holding one of the kids out and away from him. She yawned and kicked—*Put me down,* she meant. Then she walked away.

"Diaper," he said, by way of explaining why he'd suddenly decided to move her.

An elder bustled up, pulling the other kids out of the puppy pile. Bram sat, instantly awake, as always. Watts burrowed under the remaining blankets, muttering what sounded like a protest.

"Specter people," an Yller muttered. "Lazy."

Over at the penguin corral, a teenager was lifting the birds up to the vent in the ice, setting them on a slide, presumably to the open ocean. Two, though, she first held to a vessel shaped more or less like a chick. The birds calmly regurgitated half-digested fish into the vessel.

"Ugh. If that's breakfast, I'm going vegan."

"I believe they use it for an inscription," Garland said.

As they packed up, their guide returned.

"Crank light," she reminded Sophie as they climbed out of the trench, and from there to the edge of *Sledge*.

Nightjar had been frozen into an ice floe from the rails down.

It was a pristine chunk of ice, glass-clear, ship shaped, and several feet thick, and the cutter was trapped within it. Above the rails, the deck, rigging, and sails, even the wheel, were an inch thick in frost crystals, dense and sharp as pine needles. Glimmering crystals winked, throwing reflections of the scarce light of Ylle's illuminated ice floes.

Sophie cried out—she'd felt a little as if someone had jabbed her with something sharp.

Garland put a hand on her arm. "It's a cleansing technique. The ice kills the growths on the ship's outer hull—parasites, shellfish, weeds. When it breaks away, the floe riders salvage anything of use within it. See there? We'd picked up a few barnacles. They'll go. The scouring lessens how much life we carry from one sea to the other."

"Where's the crew?"

"Below, I imagine."

As if summoned, Tonio lifted a hatch, coming up on deck and placing his feet carefully. Sweet followed, eyes searching the party. She lit up when she spotted Watts. The doctor waved at her with full-bore, bandy-armed enthusiasm.

I wonder if I look like that? Sophie forced herself not to glance at Garland. Instead, she looked to Tonio, who was busy not looking at Bram. Her brother was, as often happened these days, admiring Daimon the fake fiancé and his pre-Raphaelite hair.

Sorry, Tonio, she thought. *I was pulling for you.*

She'd seen this happen before, on sails on research vessels, everyone pairing up and getting besotted. It had never been more than a casual hookup for her.

Emotions churned: desire, confusion, a sense of nostalgia for those earlier relationships whose complications were lost to time and memory.

Disembarking was no less a muddle than usual. Sophie had to get the crank light for their guide, and teach her to use it, and accept a bag of husky dog teeth—for Bram's home protection spell—in turn. After a dozen similar exchanges, they were finally under way.

The pilot from *Sledge* stood on the hollow deck of the ship of ice that had swallowed *Nightjar,* miming with his arms a swimming motion reminiscent of the butterfly stroke. Suddenly they were moving at quite a solid clip, gliding between the icebergs that were the floe riders' fields, villages, and outlying outposts, their bird nesting areas and seal rests and the like. It was a tight fit, and *Nightjar*'s ice sleeve rasped as they squeezed through, scraping away and lowering them ever closer to the sea. Ice melted from the rigging, pattering down in a surprisingly warm rain. Everything smelled clean and a little like thunderstorm.

With a last turn to port, the pilot made a parting-the-Red-Sea motion atop the prow of ice. It split down the middle, each side cleaving away and then sticking to a smaller nearby floe. The pieces floated, glistening with recoverable bits of shellfish, seaweed, and other flotsam as *Nightjar,* freed of the ice maze and all its encrustations, glided, clean and steaming, into the open seas and a late dawn.

CHAPTER 20

Gracious Kir Sophie thank you for your message. I think you are very kind to ask after me and my beloved Rashad. His family keeps us at a distance, so far as they can. We will marry tho, soon as we get the means. Love blow down the walls, we say.

You sent word asking if I can tell somewhat of the bandits who sailed Retrograd Incannis *when I slipped aboard to free the cat. How is the cat anyway? But I have to tell you I did not see anyone. If I've seen them, they've seen me, you understand? Bad for business!*

I did hear a woman and man speaking, in the language of the Golders.

Also you ask what our captain, my beloved's brother Montaro, wanted of the Incannis *crew and they of him. They helped us in our quest for a snow vulture as you know, and Montaro I think gave them spellscribing materials; we had beeswax, spruce needles, and sealing wax from Mossma aboard and after that I saw them no more.*

If you find use for one such as me in your service of forensic truth-making, I would be happy to serve. Or could you try to get me into Fleet? It would help us marry, me and Rashad.

Yours,

Corsetta di Gatto, Tibbon's Wash

The next morning, Garland asked the cook to lay out an extra-massive breakfast: shrimp and eggs, small bread rolls, pan-fried green mangoes, and fried shredded potatoes. The last was a new dish for the cook, something he was learning from Bram.

Sophie had fetched Lidman, along with his now one-man escort of a Watch clerk, Sixer Selwig.

"Oh!" Lidman had eyes only for the food. He began piling a plate high.

"There'll be time to go for seconds," Selwig told him. He looked tired; with Humbrey gone, he'd been bunking outside Kev's door. Tedious, lonely duty. Sophie had taken a few watches for the big soldier, out of a sense of duty. He couldn't be on watch night and day, after all. Part of her felt, though, that it sort of served him right. He was a slaver; who else should watch Kev?

Of course, the obvious answer to that was *His owner, duh!*

"Making up for lost meals. I've been hungry ever since we put to sea in *Incannis,*" Kev said. He had continued to put on weight, at least around the belly, since they'd taken him off *Docket.*

"Didn't the ships you raided have food stores?" asked Selwig.

"We gave everything to the people we liberated."

That much was probably true. He had been a rack of bones when he grabbed Sophie.

"Sit," Selwig ordered, taking a more modest portion of the fare.

"Sit, *please,*" Sophie amended, and the young sixer flushed red.

Before that could turn into any kind of discussion about the care and feeding of her personal pet convicted murderer, Garland turned up. "Shall we begin?"

"Begin what?" Kev asked.

Sophie grabbed a serving of the mango and one of the egg and shrimp, taking a seat. "Kev, I need to decide what to do with you."

Kev shrugged. "Your false engagement means you mean to free me."

The smart thing to do would be to play it cool—dangle the possibility of freedom without making promises. Bram—where was Bram?—had told her to do just that. But no. "I'm not selling you or turning you over to the duelist adjudicator's family. And I won't own you for a second longer than I have to."

He was infuriatingly placid. "What remains to be said?"

Daimon hadn't turned up yet, so she looked to Garland. "Do you remember the relevant statute?"

He nodded. "As a citizen who committed heinous crimes asea, you can never be entirely at liberty. Sophie's options are to sell you, carry out the execution, or lay a behavior compulsion on you."

Kev choked on a bit of egg.

"It means—"

"I'm a scribe, remember?" He looked at Sophie accusingly. "You'd leash my will?"

"Kev, come on. Nobody's going to let me turn you loose if you're just going to run back to sinking ships and making more homicidal frights."

"I'm not the frightmaker!" If he was faking the outrage, he deserved an Oscar. He wiped his chin. "I helped people. I curbed naughty children."

"So when you talk about stripping people of free will, you know all about it," Sophie said.

"They're *children*."

"As opposed to what, animals?"

He was spitting mad now. "You can forget about me giving you my name if you're going to break—"

Garland interrupted. "Once we reach Sylvanna and you are ceremonially bound, you will have no name besides that which Sophie gives you."

Sidelong glance. For the first time since he'd heard of her fake engagement to Daimon, Kev looked uneasy.

"She could compel you to reveal everything: where the escapees went, who you're conspiring with, how the ships you and your friends attacked may be tied to the recent sinkings in Fleet."

Sophie tried to interrupt, but Garland had apparently decided to run with playing bad cop. "You escaped the ax by imposing on Kir Sophie's kindness, but you cannot continue to take advantage."

"Stop it!" Sophie said. "You're being a bully! Kev, if I want to release you, there's a thing called pacification."

"Pacification?" His eyebrows rose. "A mosquito could bite me, or a dog, and I'd not raise a hand to defend myself? That sort of spell?"

"Exactly."

"Pacified." He looked, to her surprise, almost awestruck. "Whatever happened, I could do no harm."

"No *further* harm," Selwig corrected.

Kev picked up a bun, slathered it with butter, and took a healthy bite, considering as he chewed. By the time he'd swallowed, he was nodding. "I freely give you leave to do this."

"Swell!" She felt a wash of gratitude and saw Garland trying to give her a warning look. What was he trying to tell her? *Don't hug him; he's the villain*?

Right. Interrogation. She cleared her throat. "While you're cooperating, you want to tell me why the Golders offered to buy you? Are they after your friends?"

"They're all dead at your father's hand," he said.

"You mean the rest of the *Incannis* crew? Who were they?"

"Abolitionist friends of Eame's. Six of us had been spiriting people away from Tug for years."

"Spiriting how?" Garland asked.

"We used the names of children I'd worked with in the past. I'd redrafted a compulsion spell." He swelled a little, with obvious professional pride. "The variation compelled the children to seek out and burn scrolls that imprisoned their family slaves."

"Obedience inscriptions," Garland said.

"Yes." Kev nodded. "Once their will was restored, Eame could approach them about escaping. Else they'd have turned him in."

Sophie found herself wishing she knew more about economics. Slavery in America, back in the day, must have required a lot of infrastructure—safeguards, basically, against escapes and revolts. Being able to limit a slave's capacity for rebellion was a disturbing game changer.

"The logistics are very delicate," Kev said. "Once the compulsion spell is destroyed, there's a tiny window of opportunity. Eame had to approach the person, secure their agreement, and get them away."

"And from there you'd have to make them citizens of some allied nation and rename them," Garland said. "Otherwise, their owners could inscribe them again—to obedience, even to death."

"There's nothing I can tell you about that," Kev said.

"Indeed. It's probably better if you don't."

Dangerous and difficult. Sophie's mind turned to the notes on Kev's trial. Medical records from Sylvanna, with kids' names, had been seized from *Incannis*. "There was a list of Sylvanner kids aboard the ship when it was taken."

Kev picked at a slice of mango. "That would have been our next project. Swing 'round there, get the children to burn their slaves' inhibit scrips, and get as many as we could across the Butcher's Baste."

This rang true. *Sawtooth* had been on her way to Sylvanna when they ran into the bandit ship. *Incannis* could have been bound for Autumn, same as them.

"Would the Havers shelter them?" said Garland.

"Two of the crew, Pree and Smitt, seemed to think they could be convinced."

Sophie gave Kev what she hoped was an easy smile. "You and Eame and your four college buddies were liberating people for years?"

He nodded.

"And Pree and Smitt were *new* friends?"

He had been about to take a sip of water, but instead he snorted it, coughing hard, turning red.

"Were there six people aboard *Incannis* when we encountered you, or eight?"

Kev continued to choke, less convincingly as time went on. Sitting next to him, Selwig was wearing an expression of surprise that was almost insulting.

"Cly killed one woman," Sophie said. "We should be able to find out if she was called Pree."

"None of us used our real—"

Kev was interrupted by the arrival of Bram and the law clerk Daimon.

She'd thought the shine Bram had taken to her fake fiancé was one-sided, visible only to her and—sadly—to Tonio. Now she wondered: were they arriving together, or were they *together*?

"Just getting to know my future brother-in-law," Bram said, answering her unspoken question with a smirk. She nudged his ankle with her boot, not quite kicking.

Garland had tightened up upon Daimon's arrival, becoming more rigid and proper. He said, "Might the Golders be hoping you'll expose these crewmates?"

"What crewmates?" Daimon asked.

But the pendulum of Kev's mood was on the backswing to panic. "I don't know! I don't! An oath on it!"

"It's not me you have to convince, Kir Lidman." Bad cop was back. "Where will you go once Sophie pacifies and releases you? Your enemies may yet track you down."

"Pacifies?" Daimon said.

"Keep me on Sylvanna. Protect me!"

Sophie shook her head. "I can't, Kev, if you're lying."

For a moment his masks dropped and he looked hopeless and terribly afraid. "Until such time as you do in fact strip me of my will and pour my secrets out like water from a cup, you'll have to wonder." He gathered a few more buns and a spoonful of the potatoes. "May I go back to my cell?"

Selwig looked to Sophie, who nodded. He took him out.

"Little hard on him, were we?" Bram asked.

"He is endangering the slaves he supposedly freed." Garland, clearly, wasn't in a mood to coddle. "His allies, too, if Pree and . . . what was it?"

"Smitt. Pree and Smitt." She was jotting it down. *Buddies of the Sainted Eame, but not from the original cell of abolitionists. Recent additions to the crew. This is promising!*

"I understand Kev's reluctance to take the blade, but why not give us a chance to protect his allies?"

"Reluctance?" Bram said. "Did you say reluctance to be beheaded?"

"Shush, all of you," Sophie said. She could feel an idea coming together. "They stole a magical ship with creepy attack spells on it, and they attacked portside ships smuggling . . ."

"People," Bram said.

"And spell components. Amber, and maddenflur," Daimon said.

"And the names of Sylvanner children. That was Kev's role. He was meant to compel the children to burn the family inscriptions," Garland said.

"I thought he created salt frights," Daimon said.

"Shush, dear," Bram said.

Sophie shook her head. "The ship, *Incannis,* had been enchanted so that *it* made frights when it got human hearts to eat. When they attacked *Sawtooth,* Kev's buddy Eame had to hit him to get him to actually cut up a corpse. He looked revolted when I accused him of being the . . . what was the word?"

"Frightmaker," Garland agreed. "He did, didn't he?"

"I believed that," she said to him.

"Yes. Yes, so did I."

This shouldn't be sexy. Don't think about kissing him—

"Revulsion proves nothing," Daimon said.

Sophie paced away from Garland, over to the coffeepot. "Why invite Kev at all?"

"What do you mean?" Garland said.

"She's right," Bram said. "They could have mailed him the stolen kids' names and left him to do the compulsion spells at a prearranged time, from the comfort of his living room in Haversham."

Daimon said, "He told you so much of their plan?"

"Sophie's very persuasive," Bram said.

Magically persuasive. An accompanying roil of confused emotion derailed her thoughts. Had she cheated somehow—*forced* Kev to offer up the information? She must have looked stricken; she could see Bram was sorry he'd brought it up.

"He's started to talk," he said, his tone just a hair too hearty. "Good start, guys. You'll get more out of him next time."

She nodded, clapping the book shut and heading forward, toward her cabin.

Daimon rushed to follow. "Kir Sophie?"

"Yeah?" She was, suddenly, drained. Did magically persuading people to do things take more energy than normal persuading?

"I wonder: must we truly render Kir Lidman helpless?"

"It's the only legal option if I want to free him. Unless you know of another?"

"Ah." His peaches-and-cream complexion pinkened.

"I'm guessing you haven't been planning to specialize in slaving law," she said drily.

"I hope to study mercantile regulations," he apologized.

"Well, feel free to read up on any useful loopholes that might apply here," she said. "But Kev's a criminal. Just because I don't think he deserves beheading doesn't mean he gets a Get out of Jail Free card."

Daimon's cupid-bow mouth dropped open. "Where does one find such a thing?"

"Ask Bram to explain the expression," she said, giving him a little arm squeeze to indicate the conversation was over, and heading into her cabin.

Solitude was impossible to come by, as usual. Krispos was installed at her desk, scratching out paperwork at high speed. "I had to come in here," he said. "Bram and Daimon were . . ."

"I gathered." She kicked off her boots, flopping on her bunk. "Should I write Mensalohm a note telling him his boy apprentice is no big study nerd?"

"If you're actively disappointed in Daimon . . ."

"No. I mean, all he has to do for me is come along for the ride and claim to want to marry me, right? He doesn't need to graduate summa cum laude for that."

"No," Krispos agreed.

She flipped open her book of questions and wrote, KRISPOS UNDERSTANDS LATIN???

"If he makes Bram happy . . ." She closed her eyes. If Bram was into Daimon, she should try to like him better. Make more of an effort.

Poor Tonio, she thought. *I'll totally have to stop shipping them.*

The *scritch-scritch* of Krispos's pen on paper was soothing. She let her mind wander, turning over the conversation with Kev, getting nowhere.

After about fifteen minutes, Krispos said, "I almost forgot. Tonio said they'd found one of those purple crabs in a net. Dead, so it's inedible. If you want to . . ." She could almost hear him shudder.

Imagine how he'll react when I manage to get people doing autopsies for the courts. It was a good idea, though; a little dissection, a change of pace. She took the fore ladder up to the deck.

A half dozen crew were working on the Sisyphean task of ship maintenance: checking ropes and sails for faults, polishing the wood, oiling the stonewood hinges on the hatches that led belowdecks. Watts was splayed in a hammock chair with the cat, Banana, in his lap and a mortar and pestle, for making drugs, abandoned just out of reach. He wouldn't move until the cat found business elsewhere, even if it meant risking sunstroke. Sophie paused to carefully arrange a scrap of sail over him and got a loud, quite convincing purr in response. Bram was alternating between reading up on magical inscription and staring off into space.

She interrupted long enough to throw an arm around him, offering up a quick squeeze. "Your birthday's coming," she murmured.

"Buy me a pony." Half smile; he was far away.

Sophie found the crab in a bucket and claimed a space on a waist-high equipment locker, laying a cotton sheet over the surface and then setting her camera to record video as she examined the animal's exoskeleton, eyestalks, and swimming legs. Except for its color, a royal purple with black mottling, it didn't seem very different from a blue crab. It had the wide abdomen of an adult female, and a few hundred roe clung to it, a sight she found a little forlorn.

Tonio peered over her shoulder whenever he passed by, moving between the crews he and Sweet were supervising, but he didn't speak as she opened the crab's shell, revealing muscle and brain, gills and heart. There were no organs she didn't recognize, nothing but its largish size and unusual color to suggest it might be a creature that didn't exist on Earth.

When she had done and her mind was calm once more, she checked the video file, plugged the camera into her solar charger, and then flung the remains of the crab overboard to the waiting, eager gulls.

CHAPTER 21

My dearest Kir Sophie:

Does Garland know you've contacted me? I suppose he would have to say he didn't mind: quailing at the thought of having his current amita corresponding with his former lover is exactly the sort of undisciplined emotional behavior he doesn't brush into his mind's self-portrait. Do give him my love, if you dare.

I should say I feel a strange kinship with you, with your strange predilection for asking questions. Fleet folk are so averse to questioners, a reporter has a rough go of it. I am often threatened with arrest for spying, and was once dumped overboard from a bar ship.

I shall start by answering your query about whether I know much about what will happen with the Verdanii succession, now that Annela Gracechild is out of the running. I am not surprised you seek outside counsel on the matter; anything your family tells you is sure to be laced with half-truths and bloody barbs.

The general wisdom runs that a Verdanii matriarch from the Gorsedotter line, one with nine children and a good deal of influence, will be the next Allmother. But she's got great-grandchildren, and the Gorse, though they are of the Nine Families, have never been considered either wise or emotionally stable. Their gift is prophecy, and some consider the Gorsedotters out-and-out frauds. (Though they did predict Gale Feliachild's murder, in the end, did they not?)

For my part, I have laid bakoo *shine with a reputable bookmaker on Beatrice Feliachild. She will protest and rail, but despite her notable reputation for histrionics, what I see in her is pure stonewood. She took the reins of Convenor Gracechild's office, while she was poisoned, and never seemed to notice the weight of responsibility. Now she has whipped one of the hospital ships out of a lamentable habit of uncleanliness and drug theft. I believe she did it merely for the fun of seeing the rats scatter. This is the sort of thing the Verdanii consider presidential.*

Finally, Beatrice has daughters by two different men. The Verdanii can talk about holy fasts and horse-race winners and virtuous self-denial until the skies turn green, but there has never in their history been an Allmother who hasn't displayed the particular type of strength that is showcased by powering, more than once, through that horrific experience (I am blessed that I may merely imagine it horrific) known as childbirth.

Write again and ask me other things, dear Sophie. I will be of so much use to you that we shall become great friends, and Garland will be maddened by it, in all the best ways.

Langda Pike

The corridor outside Kev's cabin was a narrow dead end, a stub of a space at the aft of the ship, directly across from Watts's infirmary and—except when she had the hatch open and the fingerprinting operation in full swing—crowded by the chair set outside it for whoever was guarding the prisoner at any given time.

Sophie had sent Selwig off to get some sleep and was working her way through the mountains of correspondence—despite her many adjustments to Fleetspeak, she still thought of letters as snail mail—generated by her barely nascent Forensic Institute.

She had sent out about thirty notes when they were aboard *Sledge*, requests for information, drafted by Krispos and shipped to just about everyone she knew, both in and out of Fleet. She didn't understand the postal system at sea at all: *Nightjar* had met up with a mail ship this morning, barely ten days after their stop at Ylle, and half a dozen responses to her queries had been in the bag. Given their distance from Fleet, this seemed incredibly fast.

She folded the pages from the reporter. Beatrice as Allmother was an idea she could barely encompass. It would mean she'd have to move back here. With her husband and stepson from San Francisco? She'd also have to live on Verdanii, presumably, and Sophie was persona non grata there. It would make seeing each other difficult. Which might suit Beatrice.

How it would affect Verena, Sophie couldn't even imagine.

Putting the pages away, she opened her book of questions. A few things, finally, were starting to be crossed off the list, though she was adding mysteries to the book at a rate of three per day.

She looked at the newest notes on Kev. WHAT IS HIS VALUE? IS HE A PARTICULARLY GOOD SPELLSCRIBE? was circled.

To find out, they'd have to test him. Which was definitely Bram's department.

Bram himself chose that moment to appear. "What are you doing?"

Kev was, of course, just a hatch away. Rather than speaking aloud, she showed Bram the question.

He switched to English. "He's okay as a teacher. And if he did create a brand-new spell . . . that's supposed to be a rare gift."

"Where did you put my Beatrice scrolls?"

"You threatened to destroy them."

"So? I'm fine now."

"Yeah, Sofe, your identity crisis is totally over."

"I want you to show them to Kev. Assess his expertise."

He nodded. "I'll show him the copies that don't have your name on them."

This made sense, but the refusal nonetheless irked her. "I have your middle name, too, buster."

"Don't even fake threaten that, Ducks." He seemed untroubled by the threat, or by much of anything. Was it the euphoria of his new relationship with Daimon?

"What?" he said as she scrutinized him.

"Sylvanner expression. You're thriving like throttlevine."

"We're unlocking the mysteries of the universe," he said, with unmistakable satisfaction. "That's a birthday gift you'll never top."

"Where are my scrolls, Bram?"

"I'll get the copies and jaw them over with Kev."

Selwig returned shortly after that, leaving her free to huff off to the main deck. When that, too, seemed to offer little in the way of space or privacy, she adopted a trick from Verena's playbook and climbed the rigging behind the mainsail.

Two hundred and fifty nations to see, and I'm going to Sylvanna again.

They were days from port. A fishing fleet was visible to the east; big ships, with flags from about two dozen nations, all working in tandem in an area roughly where the Grand Banks of Newfoundland should be. The charts placed a couple island nations there, but Garland showed no inclination to stop. They all wanted to be free of the obligation represented by Kev, even if they weren't quite sure how to pull it off.

Headache, she thought, meaning both the thrum in her temples and the problem of their prisoner. "If I can't convince him that I'll revert to Sylvanner type and treat him like property, he'll walk all over me."

Her musings were interrupted by the appearance on the western horizon of a mirage shimmer, at water level, with an emanating trail of steam.

"Thing," she called. "Unknown thing to starboard."

"It's a Jocelynchild courier," Garland said, from his position almost directly beneath her, at the base of the mainmast. "Verdanii steamhorse. Very expensive."

"Steamhorse" conjured something out of a fan convention—brass goggles and clockworks—but when she had climbed down, retrieved her camera, and zoomed in, what she saw had more of a look of the pony express, on water. A horse and rider were coming straight at them, bathed in an intense steam that rose from the horse's hooves. The ocean frothed and bubbled at every contact as if it were boiling. Together they trotted over the waves, as sure-footed as if they were crossing rolling prairie hills.

"Correct course to intercept," Garland ordered, and *Nightjar* swung round, spilling wind from her mainsail.

Sophie paged through her book, checking her various sheets of messageply. The page she'd left with Verena was all but full, but her half sister had crammed in two words: SENDING PHONE.

As they came around, the rider coaxed her mount into a full gallop. A sound of hot pans being plunged into cold water intensified, and every hoofbeat kicked up salt crystals. The horse's progress was leaving a wake, a furrow of twenty-foot waves spreading backwards to the edge of sight, widening foam lines that marked her speedy progress.

When they were maybe eighty feet away, it gathered itself to jump, bunching, flying through the air and over *Nightjar*'s prow. The horse dispersed into steam, leaving the courier, a woman made of cloud, standing on the deck. She removed a leather satchel from her hip, lowered it to the boards, and, with a bow, misted away to nothing.

Garland bent to open the valise. Nestled within was a medium-size blue egg, spattered with dark-gray spots.

"Phone," Sophie said. "Verena says phone."

Garland looked to Tonio. "We'll need a cage."

"You'd cage it, Garland? *Verro?*"

"To keep the cat and ferret off it, yes." He raised it, cradling it to his ear. "Once we feed it up, you can talk to Verena."

"Pairs of birds," Sophie said. A market vendor had told her about this. "Connected, like the messageply."

"Yes," Tonio said.

"Quantum entanglements," murmured Bram.

"Verena must have something important to say."

"Yes." Garland frowned. "Are you all right?"

She nodded, though in fact the headache was worse and she felt a little dull. "I'll grab some aspirin."

"Whatever that means." He reached out, then checked himself and almost bowed.

She headed back to the cabin, leaving them to take care of the magic egg, and dug in her stash of over-the-counter meds. A couple of acetaminophen, and some ibuprofen, too. What the hell.

Then, picking up all the fingerprinting materials, she headed back to the aft cabins and Kev's quarters. After sending Humbrey back to the Fleet with the report on the sinkings and the first half of the fingerprint index, she and Selwig—with occasional help from Daimon, who seemed more fascinated by its possibilities than he was with the law books he was supposedly memorizing—had continued to code the rest of the prints, using the Henry system. They had a couple hundred prints whose codes they agreed on; the remainder they had to look over together.

Selwig happily claimed the box from her, working through their card index to find the remaining prints from the corpses they hoped to identify by counting ridges, measuring distances between features, and identifying points of similarity.

Sophie coached him for a while, coaxing him over a couple hurdles. Between watching Kev and learning dactyloscopy, he was working diligently. Still, she missed his partner, Humbrey. Was it just because Selwig was a slaver? If so, did that make her some kind of a racist?

I'm one, too, remember.

Her mind wandered again to the inscriptions Beatrice had written for her.

Bright, charming, persuasive. She didn't feel anything of the kind, not right now. She had a fleeting memory: Bram once telling her that the only time she had a poker face was when she was sick.

If there was any chance she might be harder to read right now, she might as well put it to good use.

"Bram in there?" She indicated Kev's door.

Selwig shook his head, unlocking the hatch, and went back to his prints.

She found Kev hunched in his hammock, staring at one of the spell copies—it was the seventh spell, the one whose purpose Beatrice didn't understand.

"Give me something to work with," she said. "Have you thought about what happens once we free you?"

A perplexed frown. "I . . . go home."

"You forfeited your Haversham citizenship when you committed banditry. They can't welcome you with open arms."

"If not Haver, who am I?"

"You'll be a sort of citizen of Sylvanna, after."

"I can't stay on Sylvanna."

"No," she said. "You haven't even considered this?"

He shrugged. "Something will resolve itself."

"Something like your fellow bandits? Pree and Smitt?"

His face froze.

"Come on, Kev. Two other crew members. Strangers to you, friends of your leader, Eame. They weren't aboard when Cly captured you. You honestly believe they're gonna sail into Autumn and carry you away?"

He turned bright red and refused to meet her eyes.

"OMG, you do! You totally think they're coming for you."

"I did a good thing. I freed people. Why should you mind if someone helps me find shelter?" He fished out a red citrus fruit, from Tonio's homeland, and began peeling it. "I won't be able to harm anyone . . . you'll see to that."

"What if *they* harm someone? A guy and a woman, right? Were they Havers?"

He shook his head. "The man was one of Eame's countrymen. Of Tug."

Another portside abolitionist, in other words.

"Where'd they disembark?"

He looked startled. "What do you mean?"

"They weren't aboard when we captured you."

"Eame ordered us to make for an islet, to see if we could abandon ship," he said. "We knew *Sawtooth* would sink us. We weren't close enough, I hadn't thought, but they must have swum."

"Must have?"

"It was like they vanished."

Now that *was* interesting. "Any chance the woman was Verdanii?"

He gaped at her, flabbergasted. "Verdanii?"

She showed him phone photos of all her Feliachild suspects. "You said 'vanished.' I'm looking for a Verdanii who can vanish."

"Teeth—you're inscribed persuasive," he said suddenly, brandishing one of Bram's spell transcripts. "I won't tell you anything!"

"If she wasn't Tug, was she Golder?"

"I can't say . . ." But, involuntarily, he nodded.

"Gotcha." He had an uneasy look—maybe the headache *was* making her hard to read. "Let's not pretend, Kev. You raided those ships. Those crews are gone. I saw you cut the heart out of one of the bodies. You're not a good guy. At best you're an idealistic but ruthless terrorist."

"Then you shouldn't let me trouble your conscience."

"Are you trying to save your skin?" she said. "Or are you acting with purpose?"

"What purpose could I possibly serve now?"

What purpose indeed? A Haver and a spellscribe, on a ship full of bandits. Kev was notorious, now, because of his trial. Haversham and Sylvanna had been enemies for centuries.

Kev thought the two strangers sailing *Incannis* with him had been abolitionists. But if one of them was Bettona's eragliding accomplice . . .

She rubbed her temples. "You claim *Incannis* met a ship that took liberated slaves away," she said. "But Golder Girl just vanished with them, didn't she?"

"I'm not helping you!"

"And you aren't laboring under some demented fantasy that she's going to sail into Autumn in a big old three-masted rescue vessel. She's going to magically appear, grab you, and spirit you off to freedom."

She'd magically appear here, where there's a clock for eragliders to use as a focus, she thought. *Maybe she would have already, if I hadn't stopped Gale's clock.*

Kev turned in his bunk, putting his face to the wall and covering his ears. He pulled a blanket over his whole head. "Not helping!"

The realization, when it came, was like having floodlights come on. The cabin almost seemed to brighten. The jolt of it made her head throb harder.

You were infiltrated.

Sophie barely managed to keep herself from ripping the blanket off and shouting it in Kev's face. Golder Girl—Pree—and her ally on *Incannis* were the bad guys.

All for one and one for war and terrorism. Things That Go Boom! *indeed.*

So she had played Kev and his friends. Were still playing him, if Kev's belief that they were coming to rescue him was more than empty hope.

She had to talk to Bram and Garland.

"What'd he say?" Daimon was settling in next to Selwig as she locked the hatch to Kev's cell.

"He said nothing."

"No progress, then?"

"It was surprisingly informative." The painkillers hadn't touched the throbbing in her head. Maybe she was hungry? She dragged herself to the galley, found the cook's basket of spiced buns, and made herself eat two. Even with water, it was like eating sand.

After, she was feeling wretched enough to just sit, leaning against the wall, eyes closed. *Tick, tick, tick. I stopped that clock in Verena's room. Which one is this? Beatrice's, in San Francisco?*

She'd heard that watch of Gale's, like an earworm, until they got a mile or two from the safe-deposit box. She heard the clock at Annela's when she was in Fleet, and Bettona's watch.

You can hear the Worldclock, Beatrice had said.

"What's wrong with you?"

The words shattered her train of thought. Tonio was staring down at her, concerned.

"Where to start?" she said. "All these things I thought were central to who I am . . . they're just spells. How I look, how I think. People kneading me, like dough. Tick tick earworms from eragliding—"

"You're sick," Tonio said. He coaxed her to her feet.

"Just a migraine."

"I don't know 'migraine,' Sophie."

"Don't make me move. Hurts."

"We're going twenty paces, to Watts."

"Migraine," she repeated. "I'm migraine woman now. There are people who build whole identities around being sick, aren't there? Sophie, the invalid."

"*Dottore,*" Tonio called. The raised voice made her flinch.

"Cute, cheery, full of vim. Fertile to boot. Without all the prenatal tweaks, I'd probably be a juvenile delinquent." The spiced buns weren't sitting so well.

Buns, she thought. *Bettona gave me anise biscuits.*

She concentrated on not throwing up on Tonio's boots.

"Yes, yes." That was Watts. "Just keep your eyes shut, Sophie. That's fine. Over here."

Biscuits, and then ticking. If it was Golder Girl who was aboard Incannis, *how did she learn to eraglide? Did she take John Coine to San Francisco? An athletic woman ransacked Mom and Dad's house.*

The men guided her down to a bunk.

"Take Banana," Watts added, putting the fuzzy anvil that was the ship's cat on her chest. He'd fattened up. Like Kev. To Tonio he added, "Get her brother."

As cures went, there were worse things than "Pet the cat." Sophie focused on rubbing Banana's much-abused ears and listening to his noisy freight-train purr. Tears etched hot paths down her cheeks. Her teeth hurt—her cheekbones were ringing, resonating to an unheard high note, vibrating as hard as the pipe in a church organ.

Watts rubbed something on her temples. It had a eucalyptus smell. She wasn't sure the pain decreased, but it was a bit of a relief.

The cat was kneading at her chest, pressing her breast uncomfortably, offering distraction. "When Mom's cat, Muffins, does this, it's puncture, puncture, puncture."

"Someone's been clipping his claws," Watts said, in a tone of disapproval. His people worshipped cats; as far as Sophie could tell, he thought *Nightjar*'s only real mission was to serve as palace and transport for the beast. "Front and back. Sophie, what have you eaten today?"

"Get a bucket and I'll show you," she said.

"Nauseated?"

"Big-time."

"Have you eaten or drunk anything the rest of us haven't had?"

"Anise and apricot biscuits. No, that was weeks ago."

"Smoked anything?"

"What? No."

"Open your mouth." She did, and he laid something warm on her tongue. "Don't swallow."

It felt like a tea bag, fresh from a cup of boiled water, and it tasted of herbs.

A clatter of feet and the sound of the hatch. Suddenly, Bram's hand was folded in hers. She tried cracking her eyes open but it hurt too much, and she couldn't talk around the tea bag, so she just squeezed.

"It'll be a bad few hours."

"Poison?" Bram demanded.

No audible answer from Watts. Maybe he'd shrugged. "She's strong."

Truth, or bravado?

The sound of them speaking was beginning to hurt, too. She focused on the cat, feet kneading back and forth, the pressure of his weight on her chest, the silk of the fur and the thrum against her flesh. The men had lowered their voices. Watts was asking about migraines—what the word meant, did Bram know the symptoms.

Bram was dismissive. "Sophie doesn't get migraines."

It all had a smeary, faraway quality.

It was the tea bag, she decided. The tea bag held an anesthetic of some kind, or a sedative. Since, by now, every beat of her heart was smashing out her temples like a hammer blow, she decided a sedative was a great idea.

Tick, tick, tick. That rhythm again.

To eraglide, you had to be a Feliachild. You had to break bread with the Allmother. *Bettona fed me anise biscuits, and that's when I started to tick, tick, tick . . . So she did Golder Girl, Pree, too, right? Annela heard her talking to someone who called her Sir.*

"Conk me out," she started to say, but the tea bag was still in her mouth, an obstruction she couldn't speak around, and there were eucalyptus fumes and she was a little afraid to breathe deeply lest her head explode.

"Turn on your side, honey," Bram said, and she didn't fight as they rolled her. *Am I gonna barf after all?*

Something was pressed against her upper lip and she found herself thinking, *Oh, part of the ache is the burn of blood in the upper sinuses. I remember that from the time I was climbing in Arizona,* and now there was more eucalyptus or whatever on the back of her neck, soothing and cool, and a new tea bag to replace the old, which tasted of blood.

My gums are bleeding, too? They must have been, because Bram had just let loose with a string of whispered profanity, undertone—*Cut it out. I need to cut this out. I'm scaring the crap out of him. It's not fair, ow, ow*—and then there was one piercing, lucid moment where she thought, *It wasn't Sir,* and it was the most important thing in the world, even more important than *Cat claws,* before she lost consciousness entirely.

CHAPTER 22

Kir Sophie:

Constitution *has instituted a shipwide ban on the sealing wax used in the final stage of the frightmaking spell, and has been searching everyone who comes aboard and detaining those who have any on their person.*

Of those detained, seven have been found to be under compulsion, and were subsequently induced to create frights on decoy hulls made of spruce. These individuals have been moved to Docket *and are being examined by the Watch, to determine whether they are innocent victims or willing coconspirators.*

With such proofs at hand, it has been accepted by the Convene that the target of the ship sinkers is indeed Constitution. *The matter has not been made public, but Erefin Salk suggests that the government and courts may be inclined to view our work with an even more friendly eye.*

Yours,
Cinco Mel Humbrey, fingerprint technician
of the Forensic Institute

When Sophie opened her eyes, the infirmary cabin was dark and full of men, all awake, all looking at her. Bram had her hand. Watts, the cat on his lap now, was within easy reach of two pots of steaming fluid. Garland was at the foot of the bunk, looking pensive.

He'd make a good portrait, looking like that. He could pass for a Romantic poet midway through a serious brood.

She enjoyed the view a moment longer before finally moving her tongue.

Finding no obstruction in her mouth, she swallowed—taste of blood—and counted her teeth. All present and accounted for. "How long I been out?"

"About three hours," Bram said.

"That's anticlimactic. Am I better?"

Watts nodded. "There was some blood loss."

"Contagious?"

"No."

She looked at the trio of grim faces. "So it's Twenty Questions time? Come on, what happened?"

"Doctor," said Garland. His voice was steely.

Seas, it's bad. She felt a bright stab of fear.

Watts was checking her pulse. "This migraine you mentioned? You've never had one before?"

"Migraines don't make your gums bleed, as far as I know." The thought of altitude sickness flitted through her mind. But that was ridiculous for half a dozen reasons. Among them, the fact that they were at sea level.

"It is possible you just got a bad seed in something, or reacted to the *Sledge* food."

"But?"

"The most likely explanation is inscription. Someone worked a magical intention on you."

She realized that she wasn't surprised.

"Lidman?"

"Too carefully guarded," Bram said. "He has nothing to write with, and no components. Selwig searched his cabin, top to bottom, while you were out."

She said, "It could be anyone, aboardship or off."

"Your name is known," Watts agreed.

"We don't know what they did? I could grow a second head, or—"

"If you'd been transformed, we'd know by now."

"Perhaps Bettona did something else. Another eragliding ritual?"

"That's very likely," Garland agreed.

"Chances are it's quite a light intention," Watts said.

"Why?"

"With the load you're already carrying, a heavy one . . ."

Would have killed me, she thought.

"What about next time?" Bram demanded.

"Danger increases with every inscription," Watts said. "The suffering, too."

"There's no relief if we tear up the other spells?" Bram said. "Beatrice's?"

"You already know she's borne that load," Watts said.

"Reversion is its own form of unpleasantness," Garland added.

"Unpleasantness." *What would you know about that? Nobody's ever scribed you.*

"Sophie." He tried smiling, but it came out false, almost ghastly. "You must write your father immediately. As a Sylvanner parent, he should be able to change your name."

"When a spell bites, it chews and swallows," Watts said. "Changing her name won't alter whatever's been done to her."

"No, but we must shield her from further mischief," Garland insisted.

Her throat was scratchy. "Can I get up?"

"Tomorrow," Watts said. "But only if you're truly abed all day."

Something in his tone made Bram stand up, as if he had been shooed. He ruffled her hair, said, "Holler if you need me," and vanished.

She caught Garland's hand as he, too, tried to make it past her.

"You should rest," he said.

"Garland. I'm not gonna be fake-engaged for much longer."

She thought he would give her a lecture about admitting the thing with Daimon was a sham—don't ask, don't tell and all that—but instead he gave her a look that positively smoldered, and kissed her forehead before heading out of the cabin.

"Ah, so that's how you get forgiven for coming aboard engaged to marry," Watts said drily. "Bleed from the gums."

"Who asked you?" She could feel a sappy grin spreading across her face. "I'm not gonna feel rested if you don't give me something to do."

He uncovered the window. "Is the light all right?"

"Yes, the eyestrain or whatever is gone."

"Watch the sea. And this." He brought out a wicker cage the size of a milk jug. The egg Verena had sent was nestled within, in a nest of wool. A hairline crack ran across its surface.

"There's a bowl of grubs and one of berries around here somewhere—I'll find them." With that, he, too, made himself scarce.

"I want to film this," she called after him. He returned with her camera and a bowl of mealworms, then collected the cat, who yowled in protest.

"Is there any way to know what the spell on me will do?"

He shook his head. "Not until the intention reveals itself."

"This whole headache and bleeding thing. Next time I die, or what?" She meant to sound offhand. Instead, her voice quavered.

"Once you're into the pain, as we say, each spell's effect is worse. The tolerance for suffering and damage varies. Some people survive an appalling magical load. Others . . ." He made a gesture, like a twig snapping. "Rest, *neh*? Captain will get your identity changed."

"It's not as though I had much of one to begin with," she grumbled.

"Your birth inscriptions didn't change your essential nature."

"Is that a scientific fact, Doc, or something you hope is true?"

"Oh, be a good patient," Watts told her.

"Meaning . . . ?"

"Meaning shut up."

"That's not rhetoric," she yelled as he let himself out.

Why hadn't the intention manifested yet? The pirates wanted Lidman. Could it be a compulsion? She imagined selling him, giving him away. Neither thought triggered any overwhelming urges.

Maybe it would only kick in if Brawn showed up.

If it was even the pirates. Anyone could've done it.

What about the eragliding? Could she hear the Worldclock more clearly?

"Tick, tick, tick," she muttered. Nothing.

Cly, she thought. *Maybe it's an obedient daughter spell. It'd only be fair. Beatrice had her shot at enchanting me.*

Bettona and the Golders were the likeliest suspects. The whole point of Brawn doing her the favor was to honorably clear the decks before moving against her. It was part of the whole Isle of Gold feud tradition: where possible, lay eyes on your enemy before taking them on. John Coine had confronted her in an Erinthian market, months ago, for the same reason.

"Sir, Sir, Sir," she muttered, turning on her camera screen. She had taken a shot of her bulkhead, once she'd covered it in clippings. Now she zoomed in on her note from Beatrice. Two women, Bettona and a stranger, had searched Annela's things as she slipped into a coma. The stranger had called Bettona Sir.

Or *soeur.* Wasn't that French, for "sister"?

Brawn said *bakoo,* too. It meant "lots" . . . *beaucoup*? "*Bakoo* gold," that was the saying. Maybe he'd said *oui,* too, or was she misremembering?

A snap, from the egg. The crack was pulsing slowly, the chick within pushing on it. Up, down, up down.

Sophie set her camera to take a shot every thirty seconds and waited, sometimes gazing out to sea, sometimes watching the egg breathe. She heard the faint ping of a second crack running through the shell, and thirty minutes after that a taloned foot shoved itself two-thirds of the way out into the air.

Cat claws, she thought, watching the baby bird toes wave. *Banana's getting clipped.*

They had picked up the cat on a sail in the summer. It had been starving aboard the wreck of one of the ships Kev and his pals had attacked. And before that, it had been on Kev's ship. That teenage con artist, Corsetta, had made off with it.

ASK THE AUTUMN SPELLSCRIBE ABOUT FRIGHT SPELLS REQUIRING CATS' CLAWS. She jotted it in her book of questions. WHAT IF KEV WORKED HIS WAY INTO THIS SITUATION JUST TO GET ABOARD *NIGHTJAR* TO HARVEST BANANA'S SCYTHES?

Selwig had searched his cabin. He was under guard. Kev couldn't be clipping Banana.

Yet, so much of this was tied to Kev. "Slave rights activist by night, magic Ritalin dispenser by day," she told the egg. "He writes spells to make kids behave. Then he forces those same kids to destroy their families' slave inscriptions."

The egg wobbled and rolled, revealing a dime-size hole opposite the foot. Sophie saw a tiny eye and a hint of lemon plumage within.

Over the course of another hour, the chick worked free, kicking its sticky way out of the shell and heaving itself to the side of the wicker cage. Sophie lit the candle on the heat lamp, as Watts had shown her. The chick rolled into the flow of warm air, quivering as it dried, becoming ever fluffier.

After it worked out how to sit upright, it consented to eat first a mealworm and then a berry. It quickly graduated to standing and pecking its own meal out of the bowls. By afternoon, it was molting, transitioning from gawky, wide-eyed adolescence as it came rapidly into its adult plumage.

It wasn't any species Sophie was familiar with. It had a distinctly corvid shape, though it was smaller, and the butter-yellow on lemon-yellow markings, subtle though they were, had the pattern of a magpie's black and white markings.

"Canola crow." Watts had turned up with a tray of soup and bread. "How's your stomach?"

"Sore," she said.

"Fire or cavern?"

"What?"

"Acid sore or empty sore?"

"Empty, I think."

"Start with the bread. If it sits, drink a little of the soup."

She nibbled a mouse-size corner off of a bun, thinking about anise biscuits.

The bird shifted and muttered at Watts. "I smell of cat," he apologized.

"I think it's Kev clipping Banana's claws," she said. "For spells, maybe?"

He frowned. "I'm missing a sweater."

"Made of cat hair?"

"Of course. But Selwig looked for it."

"They were collecting cat hair on *Incannis*." And there'd been a braid somewhere . . . She searched her memory. In the basket of frightmaker evidence, back at the courts. It and the horsehair had been cut to half their length. There had also been a small box . . . Could those have been cats' claws?

It was another connection to the frightmaker and the sinkings. Bettona's accomplice had been on *Incannis*. And if Kev was right, she was a Golder.

"We'll have to search the ship. Maybe there'll be a stash of claws we can fingerprint. Would you tell Garland?"

"Of course."

"Are you staying here? I could go back to my cabin for the night."

"I want you here tonight, near all this. . . ." He gestured at his vials and pots. "I'll bunk with Sweet."

"Go you," she said, feeling something of a pang. Being sick and abed had given her a faint craving for female company.

He sat, feeling her forehead, taking her pulse. "You'll have to name that bird, when it's bigger. Don't let it steal your bread."

"Okay." She nibbled her way through the roll, then sampled the contents of the bowl, which contained a light chowder, mingled fish and roasted corn. The heat of it and the rocking of the ship lulled her into a doze.

She woke slowly, to find the bird fidgeting on its perch, looking at her as if it expected something.

Names. Polly?

"Uhura," she said aloud. "What do you think, little guy? Want to be Uhura? 'Hailing frequencies open,' all that?"

The bird dipped its head and let out a guttural croak. The feathers at the tips of its wings and tail changed color, brightening into a hint of crimson. Full adult plumage.

"Uhura it is," Sophie said.

It flapped twice and then said, in a thin approximation of her half sister's voice, "I knew you'd give it some nerd name."

She felt herself misting up a bit—whether it was the bizarre miracle of it or just hearing from someone new, after all this time asea, she wasn't sure—and fought to keep her voice steady. "'Uhura' means 'peace,' Verena. Or 'freedom.' Or something. Everyone loves *Star Trek*. What'd you name yours?"

"Speakerphone."

"Seriously?"

There was a pause. "Well. PeekyPo for short."

"Okay, wouldn't have guessed that. Have you seen Annela?"

"Mom says she's sharper than ever. Now they've inscribed her, I mean. Super memory, even more charisma."

"Any sign of Bettona?"

"Her watch is silent and nobody's seen her. Where are you guys? Your clock's silent, too."

"Did you try to come through?"

"No. I'm still knee-deep in Verdanii politics. Nobody will give me any dirt on *Nightjar*."

Sophie filled her in on everything: Lidman, the fake engagement, the trip to Sylvanna, and her recent migraine-by-inscription.

"You're into the pain? After two inscriptions?"

"Beatrice gave me a bunch of going-away magic before she adopted me off to the Hansas. Smarts and good luck and fertility."

"All the hits." And then, slightly pleased, "Oh."

Sophie knew what was going on there. Verena had been nursing something of an inferiority complex ever since they'd met. Knowing that Sophie's best qualities all had a magical source must have felt pretty sweet.

"What about you?" Sophie asked.

"Your tip about the clocks bore fruit. Great-Uncle Pharmann's clock has been tampered with. Its second hand is missing. The hands are the key element in the watches. They're slivers of the Worldclock, and they help us eraglide to specific locales."

"So there's an eragliding timepiece out there that doesn't belong to the

Feliachilds. And the pieces came from . . ." She squinted, remembering what she'd picked up. "Bettona's father?"

"Yes," Verena said.

"Did your mom tell you about Bettona talking to a woman who called her Sir?"

"Yeah. As in, 'Yes, Sir, Cap'n, Sir!' "

"What if it was more French? *Soeur*?"

"So?"

"Could Pharmann have had a fling with a Golder?"

Quick, shocked laughter. "If so, he's lucky he's dead."

"What if Bettona's got a Feliachild sister whose mother was Golder? They got a kid with the right genes, they got the Worldclock slivers from Pharmann's clock, and they convinced Bettona to figure out how to prime and train a rogue eraglider?"

"Prime how?"

With a sigh, Sophie told Verena about the ticking noise, about how it had begun a day after her meeting with Annela, about the anise and apricot biscuits. "It's Beatrice's idea. What if the whole 'break bread with the Allmother' thing is, I dunno—"

"Blessed flour," Verena said. "Important Verdanii who live away from home will sometimes have a sack of sacred flour for ceremonial baking. I wouldn't have thought that would do it, but—"

"But nobody's ever done any serious experimentation on how eragliders are made."

"Why would Bettona want you to eraglide?"

"So I can be the fall guy, and thereby obscure the fact that she's got a sibling? If I can do it, there are people who won't look any further."

"True. So our spy is, in a sense, a Feliachild."

"Feliachild and yet foreign, same as me. At least it suggests the Piracy isn't making teleporters left, right, and center and sending them home to buy bazookas."

"Yeah, that's an upside," Verena said. "Anything else?"

"One thing. Pree—the eraglider, I mean—was aboard *Incannis* and escaped with the frightmaker."

"Okay, I'll follow up and call when I know what's happening."

"If you go to San Francisco, can you discreetly check on my parents?"

"Of course."

"It's nice to sort of—you know . . . to hear your voice."

"Yeah. Hey, Sophie."

"Yeah?"

"You'll do it, won't you? Swallow your pride and suck up to Cly to change your name?"

"Why wouldn't I?"

"Because you're all outraged about him. But you have no choice."

"Yeah," Sophie agreed. "I know. I will."

"Okay. I'll call as soon as I get back."

She was getting drowsy again. Setting Uhura's cage on the windowsill, she let herself drift off to sleep.

CHAPTER 23

To: Sophie Hansa Banning, Institute of Forensics
From: Autumn y Spell, Sylvanna Spellscrip Institute
Further to your request for information on homicidal doppelgangers, vengeance sprites, forest guardians, and salt avatars (hereafter collectively known as frights) and the attempt to eradicate the creation and misuse of same, the Institute can confirm the existence of documentation regarding the practice, constituent materials, and philosophy of frightmaking. These have been kept on behalf of the Fleet of Nations by the Institute. These materials are classified government documents and reside within the great vault at the Autumn Institute campus. Properly certified Forensic Institute staff who have taken the Fleet Oath of Service will permitted to access the vault on-site.

Eradication Treaty 1712.4 forbids shipping, transport, or copying of these materials. You or your representative will have to come to Sylvanna; if you do, everything we have will be available to you.

Two days—six long watches—passed. Everyone on *Nightjar* held their breath, waiting for Sophie to grow a second head or to come after them in the night with an ax. Garland and Tonio debated turning into the storm front, to see whether they could make more direct progress to Sylvanna, but playing with a hurricane would put them at more risk than continuing to go around.

Bram holed up with Kev and Krispos, trying to work out the nuances of the Beatrice scrolls and, simultaneously, to discover whether their prisoner was any great shakes as a scribe.

According to Kev, the luck spell was the strongest of the intentions. It tipped random events in Sophie's favor, made her less likely to suffer what he called "mistakes of inattention" or to miss opportunities. The looks, fertility, intelligence, and charm intentions he referred to as natal polishing inscriptions. These, he claimed, merely maximized what was already there—they hadn't changed her much more than would optimal prenatal nutrition and superb childhood care.

He meant to be comforting, but to Sophie it seemed a little hairsplitty.

As for the bonding spell, the one that was supposed to have kept her from looking for her birth family, he claimed the two misshapen sigils within its text—a paw-print shape and an ivy leaf—had him stumped.

All Kev could say was that the mystery spell's phrasing reminded him of inscriptions used to curb wildly disobedient children, to force them into a state of unswerving love and loyalty, which sounded a little like a variation on slavery.

They all knew spells with mistakes in them didn't take. But the text of this spell, sigils included, glowed, indicating active magic.

To pass the time, she kept working. She and Selwig—along with Daimon, whenever he felt like volunteering—had identified another batch of "found sailors." Sophie also began showing Selwig how to lift latent fingerprints from crime scenes. The active work interested him more than the laborious process of comparison, and despite his size—she was always tempted to think of him as someone who lumbered—he was proving adept at finding and lifting usable latents.

Verena called, using the canola crow, three days after what everyone was calling "Sophie's migraine," catching the group in the forward cabin that had belonged to Gale. "You want the good news first, or the bad?" she asked.

"Bad," Sophie said, even as Bram said, "Good."

"I brought a couple Verdanii intelligence operatives to Erstwhile. We went to the café and the gun shop. The waitstaff and the store owner identified John Coine from Sophie's pictures. I had Fedona go in and show them pictures of me, Mom, Sophie, and Bettona, mixed in with a few others, as you suggested. All they'd say was the woman who'd been with John Coine might have resembled Bettona but was more like me physically."

More athletic, in other words, Sophie thought.

"They'd been to a bookstore, too. The gun store guy saw the bag."

"Really? Weird that Convenor Brawn would leave that out."

"It's sort of a survivalist bookstore. It must be where *Things That Go Boom!* and the other book we found at Bettona's came from."

"And they didn't expect us to find those. Okay, mystery solved."

"There was a young guy with them who did most of the talking."

"Did he have an accent?" Bram asked.

"Nope. American."

"Dead end there," Sophie said. "I hope that was the bad news."

"Yes, it was," Verena said, and there was no mistaking the satisfaction—smugness, almost—in her voice.

"We're on the edge of our seats," Bram promised. "What'd you do?"

"I was setting up to pull us home," Verena said. "I mean, back to the Worldclock. I had tuned in, and the angles were good, and suddenly I could hear Bettona's watch."

"Yeah?"

"I grabbed Fedona and her partner, and instead of making for Verdanii, I glided there."

Sophie sat upright. "There where?"

"A bandit vessel somewhere in the northern hemisphere. I have a phone pic of the stars, so you can try to narrow it down, but it's pretty crummy resolution."

"Whoa. A bandit?" Sophie said.

"Serious pirate warship: a ship burner. Immolators, they call them. Its common name was *Hawkwasp*."

"You boarded a pirate ship?" Bram sounded appalled.

"Pretty Gale of me, huh?"

Sophie couldn't help smiling. "Very Gale. Did you find her? Bettona?"

"Yep. Fedona grabbed her before she could screech or jerk away and we glided back to Verdanii, neat as paint."

"So . . . you have her?"

"We have her. She's lawyered up, as we'd say at home. But she's under arrest and, sooner or later, we'll get her to tell us about the rogue eraglider and the other coconspirators."

"This local person, from Erstwhile—how does he fit in?" Bram asked.

"Someone who speaks the language would be handy," Sophie said. "I mean, how does John Coine buy a gun? You have to give a driver's license—and a thumbprint, I think."

"I see what you mean," Verena said. "Someone with ID."

Bram frowned. "Can you even buy grenades, legally, as a civilian?"

"Seas, I hope not." Sophie thought this over. She had wondered if someone from Earth was in on not only the existence of Stormwrack but also the conspiracy to murder Gale. Now she rearranged the papers pinned to their bulkhead, clustering the players. A mystery man from San Francisco. Convenor Brawn from Isle of Gold, orchestrating Gale's homicide and working with Ualtar. The two Golders, Smitt and Pree, who'd infiltrated Kev's crew. "This smells like a big operation. Lots of people, from a bunch of different countries, all working to break the Cessation."

"How are we supposed to run down some huge conspiracy?" Verena said. "You and I barely have investigative powers here in Stormwrack. What are we back home? A kid who can't even drink yet and a camerawoman."

"Videographer," Sophie corrected. "Anyway, Verena, you just scored big-time by catching one of the traitors. That should light a fire under the investigation."

"Speaking of lighting a fire, you contact Cly yet?"

"She totally hasn't," Bram said.

Sophie looked at the half-written letter to her birth father, waiting under a ballpoint pen and a stick of half-melted sealing wax. "We're almost to Sylvanna. Three, maybe four days."

"So close? Is he even—"

"*Sawtooth*'s supposedly in the area."

"You don't know what kind of intention was laid on you?"

"Not yet," Sophie said.

The bird tootled. "Fedona's here. Maybe we can get more out of Bettona. 'Bye."

"Garland should hear about this," Bram said.

"He's on deck. Would you go fill him in?" Sophie asked.

As soon as Bram was gone, she beelined next door, into Garland's cabin.

She had been searching the ship for the hidden Beatrice scrolls, under the pretext of looking for the clipped cat claws and Watts's sweater. The search had proved more challenging than she'd imagined. Of the crew, only Garland, Tonio, Watts, and Sweet had their own cabins; Beal and the cook shared a semiprivate compartment, and the others slept below, in a room strung with hammocks, a compartment that did double duty as mess and crew lounge.

Garland wasn't the sort to leave his hatches unbattened. Even in the accessible corners and crannies of the ship, things were stowed carefully and in many cases locked up.

Sophie couldn't pick locks, though she was beginning to think she should learn. But the real barrier was turning out to be her conscience. The better she knew the crew, the harder it was to go through their small scraps of personal space. Especially when, half the time, she'd get a compartment to herself and start prowling, only to have someone turn up and ask what she needed.

At first glance, Garland's cabin looked as it always did. She had seen his collection of shells and leaves, the globe that he had painted with the islands he had visited. A wooden turtle had been added to one wall—a memento of their blind run through the Butcher's Baste in search of the clockwork turtles used to sabotage Sylvanna's ecosystem? Or was a turtle just a turtle?

She glanced at his leather jump rope and felt a thrill of desire.

A fingerprint card was tucked into the corner of a shelf, near his bunk.

Sophie glanced at it—professional curiosity—and realized that it was her thumbprint.

There were a couple crumpled pages in a bucket in the corner.

We're here to look for scrolls, not to snoop, she told herself as she lifted them out of the trash.

The first pages were a draft of the letter he had sent her, so many weeks ago, about courting. "I can't wait to begin," she murmured.

There was one page that was just a line drawing, and not a bad one, of Kev Lidman's face. The thing wasn't written in text but in pictograms: there was a stick figure with a captain's hat, and arrows from Kev to his head. A four-legged something was pouring things into an upturned bicorne hat. Parrish's captain's hat?

Requesting information? About Kev? From someone who didn't read? She tucked it away.

The other page was a draft of a letter to Cly: *I would urge you to act quickly to legitimize Sophie and engage in renaming—*

He went behind my back?

It wasn't enough that Beatrice had decided who she was going to be, that Cly had stuck her with a slave and a passport, that even Bram had confiscated the scrolls, as if she were a petulant, untrustworthy child. Now—

He was standing behind her.

She wasn't sure if she was going to cry or yell, so she just stared at him, wide-eyed, and waited for him to explain himself.

Garland stepped fully inside, closing the hatch, and she saw a hint of his dimple.

"You think this is funny?" she said.

He shook his head.

She waved the letter. "'I write Your Honor in the hope of finding that our thoughts will blow in a common direction as regards Sophie Hansa and the matter of her name having fallen into the wild. . . .' Garland, you know how I feel about Cly."

"Do *you* know how you feel about Cly?" he said.

She tossed a stick of sealing wax at him. "Don't muddy the waters. I can understand, me falling sick was . . . oh, a bit of a stressor for everyone."

"You understate—"

"And we don't know what they did to me. I know I should just cave and contact him myself. But Garland, it's up to me, and I'm just not ready."

"No."

"You had no right!"

The ghost of a dimple again. Laughing?

Maybe because I'm standing in his cabin with my hand in his wastebasket, lecturing him about right and wrong . . .

"I'm really mad at you," she said. "Like, five mad. Seven, even."

"Understood."

"Stop that!"

He tilted his head, waiting. For her to say what he should stop?

"I didn't send the letter to your father," he said.

She felt a rush of both relief and disappointment. "Where did Bram hide my scrolls?"

The change of direction didn't, as she'd hoped, catch him off guard. "They are safe."

So much for my elite interrogation skills. "Aha! So you admit you know where they are?"

"They're aboard my ship. Of course I know."

She dropped the drafts on his writing desk. "Where are my scrolls, Garland?"

"Bram says you're not to have them."

"So you flirted with writing Cly, decided in the end to respect my wishes, but—"

"I came to an agreement with your brother about the scrolls. Yes."

She balled her fists, trying to stare him down. *Damn it, now I'm the one who wants to laugh. . . .*

Nothing for it but to try to flounce past him.

He caught her by the arm.

"Sophie."

"What, Garland? What?" She turned, closing the space between them. *Gonna pause? Gonna chicken out or back off?*

No. He kissed her.

His arm circled her shoulders, and her knees came within a hair of buckling as she kissed him back, letting a happy little growl work its way up through her throat. She gave his full, plummy, ridiculously gorgeous bottom lip a bite, and then he was crushing her against the bulkhead, and she felt all the reasons why she shouldn't, they shouldn't, all blow away in a gust, straw in the wind. She put a hand in his hair, sinking her fingers deep into the lambswool curls, crazy thick hair and heat baking off him.

Don't think, not thinking, too damn much thinking going on. She started to work on the button of his shirt with her free hand. That made *him* growl, which made her giggle a little. They were breathless, and she let go of his hair and gave his cheek a stroke.

Something tugged there, a residual stickiness on her skin, wax from his papers adhering to a curl, not quite strong enough to pull his hair. She arched her back a little, making room for that wandering hand of his as it navigated ever closer to her breast.

Red splodge, wax in hair. Just a bit of sealing wax on the side of her hand. But the wax on his desk was blue, wasn't it?

Who cares? She tugged open the button at the top of his shirt and put her lips on the hollow between his collarbones as his hands closed over her breast and she groaned.

Red splodge. Wax. Hand.

"Sophie?"

It was a jolt, a flash of nightmare, a half-remembered sense of kneeling at dawn this morning on cold decking. One hand out, the other tracing around it.

"What is it? What's wrong? Are we—" He swallowed. "If I've presumed—"

She felt the first tear working its way down her cheek. "I know what the spell did."

CHAPTER 24

Sophie,

I appreciate the good wishes you sent with your Institute apprentice, Humbrey. Thank you. I am much recovered and have returned to work.

Given that I now no longer have an assistant, I have had little time to devote to the fifty or so questions you sent about the implications of a conspiracy, operating between Erstwhile and Stormwrack, to undermine the stability of the government. You've asked about ways and means of identifying Erstwhilers involved in buying musketry and insinuated (none too subtly, I might add) that any such individuals must have some tie to Beatrice's Erstwhile family.

(I should have referred your questions to Beatrice, if not for that, if only to get her out from underfoot.)

A Verdanii intelligence officer, Fedona Robinsdotter, has been conducting that portion of the investigation. Her Anglay is all right and improving but she doesn't know your home nation well. Verena is assisting her, but I need Verena here. Is there any chance you might send Bram to help?

It is only natural that you would want to know what we of the Fleet might do with an Erstwhiler who was interfering in our political affairs. There is no current legislation that blows on such matters. The Watch would, therefore, do as it judged necessary. You may ask Erefin Salk for more information, but I imagine that in some cases a person might be brought here, marooned and set to fend in our society, with no permission to return to the outlands. Or, had we their full name, they might be inscribed to forget.

Maintaining secrecy about the existence of Erstwhile and limiting unnecessary transit between the worlds remains a significant government priority . . . and it is obvious our seals are not tight. Do not hesitate to ask for resources if you can turn this inquiry in useful directions.

Convenor Annela Gracechild

The outline of Sophie's hand was in the aft hold, near the ship's rudder, five fingers spread like a sea star. The ship wasn't leaking yet, but the wood was beaded with tiny drops of condensation—evidence that it was colder than the rest of the boards.

"Crap." She was still crying. She had known what they would find, but seeing it made her flesh crawl. "I'm so sorry. I'm so—"

"Sofe, this isn't your fault."

She ignored Bram.

Garland looked like someone had kneecapped him with a sledgehammer.

"Garland," she said.

Two sledgehammers. Both kneecaps.

"Bram's correct. You aren't to blame." His voice was controlled and faintly hushed, the tone she'd expect to hear at a deathbed.

Tonio, at his side, was ashen. "This will be an attempt to abduct Kev, no?"

What can I do? Nightjar*'s gonna sink. Sink! It's all he's got and it's my fault.*

"The first thing is to not touch it," Sophie said. "The one I poked tore *Kitesharp* in half."

Garland nodded. "It needs time to mature. It was about a day? After the ships started to—to bleed? And take water?"

"Twenty-four to twenty-eight hours."

"We're not bleeding yet."

There were five of them in the compartment: Sophie, Bram, Garland, Tonio, and Sweet.

"Could we seal off this part of the hold?" Bram murmured to Sweet.

"It's a big compartment," she replied. "If she floods, we'll take a lot of water. Staying afloat at that point . . ."

"Difficult, yeah," Bram said, but they looked thoughtful.

If the ship could be saved, the two of them would do it. Sophie turned to Garland and Tonio. "Do we tell the crew?"

"We must," Garland said. "Our best chance is to make for a Sylvanner shipping lane at top speed. The lifeboats will have an excellent prospect of rescue."

"It won't come to that," Sophie said. "We've got a lot of information on frights now. Maybe we missed something. Perhaps we can slow its growth."

They left Bram and Sweet in the hold, strategizing, and climbed to the galley.

"Tonio, get the crew on deck," Garland said. "Sophie, talk to your people, will you?"

Her people: Daimon, Krispos, and Kev. He probably didn't want her front and center when he told his crew she'd destroyed their livelihood.

Wrestling guilt, she splashed icy water from the galley basin onto her face, then groped for a towel to dry herself. "Be the boss," she said, twice, gripping the counter. The second time, she almost sounded normal.

She headed aft, through the galley, to Kev's cell. Selwig was bent over the fingerprinting cards; Daimon was in the cabin, once again ignoring his law books in favor of keeping the prisoner company. She felt a sting of gratitude for this guy who'd come along to playact Kev out of his predicament.

Selwig took one look at her and reached for the hatch to Kev's cabin, clearly intending to shut it. "What's wrong?"

She caught the hatch before he could lock it, leading him into the cabin. Kev immediately pulled the blanket from his bunk up in front of him, hiding his face.

Drama queen, she thought, irritated, and then became even more irritated when Selwig gave her a look that clearly meant *You don't have to put up with this kind of insubordination.*

She spelled out the situation as fast as she could. Above them, on deck, they could hear the crew reacting as Parrish broke the news. Beal's voice rose above the babble, talking a mile a minute.

Sophie said, "There's no *Shepherd* to bail us out of this mess, so we need to figure out what we can do about the fright before it holes our hull."

"There's little I can add to what we know," Krispos said. "The Spellscrip Institute said we can't read their archive on frightmaking until we arrive on Sylvanna."

"Kev? Any thoughts?"

"No." His voice, behind the blanket, was small.

"Maybe you still think your chums from *Incannis* are going to come get you," Sophie said.

"Chums?" Daimon said.

"Turns out two of the *Incannis* crew got away from Cly," Sophie said. "A guy from Tug Island and a woman from Isle of Gold."

"Kev told you this?"

Selwig snorted. "Why do you think he's hiding his face? He thinks Kir Sophie witched the information from him."

Sophie gave the foot of the blanket a yank. "You paying attention back there, Kev? I've got some bad news for you: Tug Boy and Golder Girl, they weren't on your side. You sank those human smugglers, but wherever Pree took your escapees when she vanished with them, it wasn't to a land of peace and freedom. They probably went straight back into shackles."

"Oh!" Daimon said. "Surely not—"

"They were running some big spy con on you, Kev, to figure out who your allies were. Now they've set a fright on the ship, and when they get their hands on you—"

"Hold a moment," Selwig said. Kev was clutching his gut, emitting little gasps of anxiety.

Oops. Went too far.

"Lie down," Selwig said, putting his enormous hand behind Kev's head and lowering him to the bunk, then applying gentle, steady pressure to his forehead and upper chest.

"Listen to me, Lidman. *Accouteh!*" Selwig boomed the last word, and Kev's half-closed eyes sprang open. "We are engaged to transport and protect you. We will not see you come to harm. Now. Draw breath. Count to five as you let it out." His voice was loud but not cruel; it brooked no disobedience. "Again."

"One, two, three . . ." Tears were running down Kev's face, and his arms were jammed straight down by his sides, fleshy posts terminating in white-knuckled fists. After a dozen or so five counts, his fingers loosened.

"Do you need the doctor?" Selwig asked.

He shook his head. "May I be alone, please?"

Daimon threaded himself around Selwig, laying a hand on Kev's shoulder. "Sophie and I do mean to free you," he said. "Try to stay calm."

Kev jerked away as if burned. "I said alone!"

"I'll be on the other side of that door," Selwig said, gesturing to the others, *Get!* "Breathe. Two, three, four, five."

"Five," Kev mumbled, snuffling. "One . . ."

Sophie and Daimon cleared out.

"That poor man," Daimon said, seeming preoccupied. Sophie nodded.

"Can you pack up the fingerprint stuff?"

"I'll do it." Selwig stepped out of the guest cabin, ducking low to avoid hitting his head on the hatch.

"He any better?"

"Anxious," Selwig said. "The revelation was clearly a shock."

"Thank you for . . . you know, helping him through it," Sophie said.

He nodded. "He'll cooperate now. Once it sinks in that these supposed friends aren't coming to save him."

Krispos coughed. "Speaking of sinking . . ."

Right. Fending off a wood fright. Keeping *Nightjar* afloat. Sophie said, "Did you go through our notes?"

"There are a few dozen variations on a wood fright. Originally they were used to create benevolent spirits aboard ship—His Honor's ship, *Sawtooth,* has a talking masthead named Eugenia, remember?"

"Yes. And they guard forests."

"We believe this spell is an embroidery on a forest guardian spell from Mossma," Krispos told Daimon.

"It's not originally meant to sink ships—it's a murder spell." Sophie shuddered. Even now, a copy of her was feeding off of *Nightjar.* Whoever had inscribed her meant for it to sink them all, but as far as the thing on their hull knew, it simply needed her dead.

"Heave, heave, heave!" The ship's timbers creaked slightly and the deck tilted in a course correction. Sails up. They were running for the Sylvanner shipping lanes.

"Let me know if you come up with anything," she told them, turning on her heel and making her way back to the forward cabin.

Garland and Bram were climbing down as she arrived. Bram was saying, "The guys who got copied aboard the first two ships . . . were they killed?"

"*Shepherd* rescued the crews and the ships sank. Nobody knew the frights were there, and they couldn't have kept pace with the Fleet, swimming."

"So there are doppelgangers of those early victims floating around in the open ocean? Bobbing around, wanting to kill their templates?"

"Hypothetically," Garland said. "Some frights continue to grow in size until they find their targets."

"Grow . . . as in, giant-sized?"

"I doubt they'd last long in salt water."

"Could one catch up with Sophie if she were in a lifeboat?"

"It's not coming to lifeboats," Sophie said, startling them both.

Garland gave her a bleak look.

"Seriously. What are our options?"

"Find and tear up the scroll, obviously, before the fright separates from our hull."

"Any chance Kev knows something?" Bram asked.

She shook her head. "He practically had a stroke when I told him his so-called pals were conning him. Could we send an SOS to your abolitionist friends, Garland? You have contact with them, don't you?"

"He does?" Bram said.

"Sophie found a note I sent them, asking about Kev."

"We're sure it's not them?" Bram asked.

"The liberated wouldn't bother with subterfuge or magic. They count several stunningly powerful oddities among their number." Garland shook his head. "They could sink us and take Kev without effort."

"Could they help us now?"

"They wouldn't come this close to Sylvanna unless they were ready for a real fight." Garland reached for her hand. "Sophie, will you write your father? *Sawtooth* might be near enough to assist."

"I'm on it. I just need our position and heading."

He recited the numbers calmly.

She went into her cabin. She had one last sheet of messageply, the other half of which belonged to Cly. It was blank and pristine. As if by mutual agreement, neither had touched it.

Now she didn't hesitate.

> CLY,
>
> *NIGHTJAR'S* IN TROUBLE. SOMEONE CAST AN INTENTION ON ME AND I'VE SABOTAGED THE SHIP WITH A WOOD FRIGHT. WE'RE GOING TO SINK WITHIN, AT MOST, FORTY-EIGHT HOURS.

Here she paused to check the time and write it in, along with their location, heading, and speed.

> THE WEATHER OFFICE SAID YOU'RE IN THE AREA. CAN YOU ASSIST?

She hesitated a mere second before signing it SOPHIE.

Not "Sincerely." Not "Love." Argh.

There was no immediate reply. She turned her attention to the bird, Uhura. "Verena. You there?"

Silence.

"Strike two," she muttered.

Okay. They were going to save the ship. They were. But somehow that didn't keep her from bagging her camera and other electronics and leaving them out on the bed where she could get to them quickly. Then, folding the messageply into her book, she took it up on deck.

The crew had raised every sail and was making for Sylvanna at top speed. Everyone not actively engaged in sailing was involved in a complex stuff-shifting operation, moving barrels, crates, you name it.

"What's happening?" Sophie demanded.

"Sweet and Bram have a plan to keep *Nightjar* afloat," Tonio said.

"Tell me how to help."

She didn't bother to ask what the plan was, but as she joined the crew in lifting and toting, the general outline of the scheme became obvious.

The compartment Sophie had chosen for the wood fright was big. Big enough that, were it to flood, the ship would take on too much water to stay afloat.

Bram's scheme was to simply reduce the size of the compartment by packing it with empty, watertight vessels—basically, reducing the volume of space available to be flooded. If it was sealed and they pumped like mad—and if the fright didn't rip the ship in half, as it had *Kitesharp*—they should be able to stay above the waterline.

The difficulty was that watertight barrels tended to be full of useful stuff—potable water, wine, food—even the weird combustible sand the cannoneer, Krezzo, used to make fireballs.

The crew was draining the water supply into as many canteens, cups, and bowls as they could free up, drinking as much as they could stand, and pouring out the rest.

They poured out barrels of water and wine, and a cask of live butterfish. The cook was madly baking dry rations, packaging them in linen sacks, and loading them into the lifeboats.

"None of this will make any difference if that thing rips its way out of the compartment and into the rest of the ship," Sophie pointed out.

"We have to separate it from the ship," Bram agreed. "Make sure it goes out to the ocean, not into the hold."

"How do we make it do that? It took six mermaids to peel it off *Shepherd*."

Bram grimaced. "We use you as bait."

"Of course!" A rush of relief. She'd caused this, but now she could *do* something. "Me. In the diving rig. Outside the ship."

"Then we have to catch it and destroy it."

"We can't risk Sophie," Garland objected.

"It's me or all of us," Sophie said.

He didn't argue with that.

By nightfall they had stacked thirty barrels, sealed with a hot rubbery something, and had bound them to the compartment bulkheads so they couldn't bob around when the water came in. Bram was looking over the remaining area, calculating.

"Is it enough?"

"I'd be happier if we could force another forty cubic feet of air into the compartment. Isn't there anything else?"

Garland shook his head.

"Wasn't there a big black trunk in the hold?" Bram said.

"Watchboxes are a variation on followbox enchantments—an embroidery of that child's spell you've mastered, Bram," Parrish said. "They go to the bottom when we sink, and can only be retrieved by Watch officers who hold their keys. It would drag us down, or hole the hull itself."

"Are we bleeding yet?"

"No."

"Trailing sharks?"

Garland shook his head. "Not in these waters, not in winter."

"Those spongy flotation devices don't absorb water, do they?" Sophie asked.

"Not quickly."

"Can I have a look?" Bram asked. Garland nodded, and Tonio headed off to get them.

"What if we made balloons? Salvage floats, out of sail? If we sealed the seams with that rubbery goo. . . ."

"They wouldn't dry soon enough be watertight."

"We have time, we have time." They gazed around the empty space within the compartment. Thinking, wishing it smaller.

I picked the worst possible spot, she thought glumly.

The bird, one deck above them, suddenly said in Verena's voice, "So, I'm back."

"OMG!" Sophie lunged for the ladder, stumbling in her climb and almost smashing her chin against one of the rungs. "Stay on the line, stay on the line! Can you hear me?"

"Yeah, I hear you. As they say at home, chill!"

"Verena, *Nightjar*'s sinking. Can you get to a kayaking store? And then back here?"

"You absolutely cannot ask Verena to join us," Garland said.

"Don't be an idiot, Garland," the bird said. "Sophie, it'll take maybe two or three hours. Tell me what you need, exactly."

"They're floats—urethane balloons. You put them in a boat to take up space that'll otherwise fill up with water." She gave Verena the name and address of a kayaking store in San Francisco.

"I'd rather have industrial salvage balloons," Bram said.

"We'd need a pressure pump to fill them," Sophie told him. "And I have no idea where to buy them or what they cost. Verena, if they don't have . . . say . . . ten sets of the floats, just buy a bunch of self-inflating lifeboats, okay?"

"Okay. Hang on guys. Help's on the way. And Sophie—"

"Yeah?"

"I can't get there unless you wind, set, and start Gale's clock." Uhura whistled then, indicating that Verena had signed off.

Up top, the crew continued to load lifeboats. The cook's cakes had come out of the oven, and there were supplies of water and dried fish aboard each craft, as well as blankets for sun protection. Watts was kitting out a boat for Banana. Cats had to be aboard a seagoing vessel at all times; there was a spell, or curse, that kept them from invading other island ecosystems.

Sophie opened the book of questions again. The sheet of messageply had a one-word reply from Cly: COMING.

"*Sawtooth*'s on its way," she said. "Hopefully, we won't have to do this."

Tonio had been allocating lifeboats. "We need one for your diving tanks," he said. "And whatever we're going to use to catch the wood fright after it tears away—after it comes after you. We gave Xianlu our steel Erstwhile chain."

Garland winced delicately at the word "tears."

"You have to have Kev with you, and Selwig says that means you have to have him, too."

"Prisoner security is my duty," Selwig said. "But who's going to help catch the creature?"

"Me," Garland said.

"Your lifeboat's full then," Tonio said.

"Bram . . ." She paused. *If Verena comes, she can evacuate him to San Francisco.*

Hours passed. The moon rose, and water began coming in through the compartment. They took turns cranking the pump, keeping the hold empty. They couldn't put in the floats unless there was room for them.

They were staying ahead of it.

We just need one lucky break, Sophie thought, and she was suddenly grateful for Beatrice, for the luck inscription she'd worked on her at birth. Was that hypocritical?

Who cares? she answered her own question. Then she begged the forces of magical fortune, *Scrolls, or whatever, don't fail me now.*

CHAPTER 25

They worked feverishly through the night, pumping out the chamber as it filled and refilled, waiting on Verena, tying down everything that could be tied.

"You should put the fingerprint files in the Watchbox," Garland said, late, as they were feverishly packing. He jerked open a large black trunk. It was lined with cream-colored leather that had been inscribed with light amber letters. The writing was raised and looked a little like dried maple syrup. It had a glint to it, almost like embers.

Within the trunk were a few sets of notes—and Sophie's scrolls.

She couldn't help herself. She took them out, unfurling them one by one.

"Leave them," Garland said. "They'll be safer there than anywhere else."

She fingered them, feeling that deep-seated heartache, the loss of something. Her own sense of self? Sentimental, unscientific nonsense. Almost as stupid as the idea of true love.

I wonder if Garland will cling to the idea of true love always, once his ship's gone down.

"He's right. Don't take the scrolls anywhere near Cly," Bram said. Even as he spoke, he was multitasking, memorizing the spellscrip letters covering the interior of the Watchbox.

"Anything could happen to the scrolls on a lifeboat," Garland said.

Sophie tried to summon the anger from earlier, that willingness to tear into the inscriptions and scatter the shreds to the winds. But who gives up good luck when they're on a sinking boat?

Who gives up good looks and brainy superpowers?

"Such as they are," she said to herself. Rolling the scrolls together, she tucked them back into the Watchbox, then turned to the others. "We're planning to not sink anyway, right?"

Bram nodded. Garland gave her a faint, bleak smile that meant, she suspected, that he was waiting for another shoe to drop.

Before she could interrogate him, Uhura stopped preening her wings and said, "Coming through."

They had left the clock in Gale's old cabin, under guard. Now Garland locked the Watchbox and led the three of them there.

Verena was clad in jeans and a blue jacket. She had cut her hair, to Sophie's surprise: she had always kept it cinched in a super tight ponytail that pulled her eyes open wider. Now it was shaved to a half inch. She had bulked up a little, too.

She had two duffels with her.

"Here," she said. "Twenty canoe floats and a steel air pump. Who wants 'em?"

"Me," Bram said, hefting the sack and calling for Sweet as he headed below.

Verena straightened up, giving Garland a steady smile. "Hello, Garland."

"Verena," he said gravely.

They held each other's gaze—she perhaps showing that she'd come to her senses; he simply acknowledging. He reached past her, stilling the clock again, and nodded to the crewman who had been guarding it.

"I brought two inflatable life rafts as well as the floats," Verena said. She looked at Sophie, managed a grin, and then gave her an awkward hug.

"You're not on the lam?" Sophie asked.

"Nope. I am free and in the clear, and so is Mom. I left PeekyPo with her."

"Hey, you captured Bettona!" Sophie put her hand up for a high five, and Verena clapped it happily.

"I totally want to hear details, and follow up, but . . ."

"But the ship's sinking. Yeah. What can I do?"

"Take Bram home?"

"Not you?"

Sophie shook her head. "The wood fright might freak out. Break away from the ship early, and then—"

"Tear *Nightjar* apart."

"What about the crew, Garland? Can we evacuate them to San Francisco?"

"No. We're sworn to—"

It was as far as he got before a cry from the main deck brought them all outside. "Sail!"

Cly?

Sophie felt a mix of relief and dread as she led the charge up to the main deck to see.

It wasn't Cly. It was a cutter, longer than *Nightjar,* with one more mast. Her sails were red and leathery and her hull appeared to be smoking. She was moving fast, against the wind.

"Immolator," Garland said.

"Pirates?"

"Unofficially." He nodded, looking numb.

"That's *Hawkwasp,*" Verena said. "The ship Bettona was hiding on."

"I should've guessed." Sophie sighed. "Did you, Garland?"

He nodded. "There would be little point in sinking us if they didn't have a pickup planned."

"Pickup?" Verena asked.

Sophie nodded. "Theory is they're after Kev. Garland, how long until they're here?"

"Twenty? Twenty-five minutes? We'll have to abandon ship and scatter."

"They'll pick the lifeboats off, one by one," Verena said.

"*Nightjar* can't hope to fight them, and taking water as we are, we can't outrun them." Garland shook his head. "The ship's lost, Verena."

He turned to Tonio. "Get the doctor's boat into the water first. Watts, keep *Nightjar* between you and that immolator."

Watts said, "I'm not going anywhere without Sweet."

"I'll get her."

They bolted down to the hold, where the drawn outline of the hand had expanded into an outline of all of Sophie's body, with her facial features. Its eyes were closed.

Creepy!

Bram, Tonio, and Sweet were pumping up the inflatable floats, working to fit them into the spaces and cracks within the compartment,

"Stop working," Garland said. "Sweet, up top. We're abandoning ship."

"What the hell?" Bram said.

"It's an immolator."

Bram blinked. "Verena. Hi."

Sophie bulled in. "Bram, you and Verena have to go to San Francisco."

"Without you?"

"I'm wood fright bait, remember?"

"Not anymore."

"We are saving the damned ship," she said, furious. "I don't care if everyone on the planet attacks us."

"Sophie, we're grossly outnumbered."

She wasn't leaving *Nightjar* to burn or get ripped in half and everyone to get picked off. "Not in IQ points. Shut up and help."

Bram looked around. "How?"

"You're the engineer. We need to keep them from incinerating the ship, right? Immolator. That's not just a pretty name, is it?"

"No," Garland said. He laid a hand on the hull. "They'll burn her."

"Stop mourning, right now. You're not losing anything else because of me."

"Sophie—"

"You're not damn well losing her! Come on, Bram. Do that thing of yours."

He thought it over. "We sink *Nightjar*."

"What?"

"Excuse me?" Verena said.

Bram was already deflating the floats. "If she's underwater, she won't burn. Everything's packed up and battened down and ready to evacuate, right? We scuttle her now and . . ."

"And salvage her later?" Sophie said.

"Nice in theory, but—" Verena began.

"You can do that?" Garland said. "Raise a ship?"

Yes. Yes, this would work. Sophie swallowed. "I promise, Garland. We'll get her back up."

"Okay, water's already coming in at the bow. We want to open the other forward compartment. Get those barrels open—we need to offset the buoyancy."

"Aunt Gale's ship—" Verena said, her voice breaking.

"It's the only choice, Verena," Tonio said. "If we try to fight an immolator, we will burn."

Verena started opening barrels.

"Garland?" Sophie said.

His eyes were very wide, but at last he nodded. "Give the order, Tonio."

"What about the wood fright? If it tears the ship in half, there's nothing to salvage," Bram said.

"Same plan as before," Sophie said. "I put on my rig and lead it away from *Nightjar.* Just, now, I lead it back to the source. It sticks to wood, remember?"

"Cap'n!" Beal shouted, voice muffled as he pounded down the ladder from the main deck. "The caravel's coming! *Sawtooth.*"

"Is she near?"

"Immolator's going to get to us first. Assumin' that's what you're asking."

They passed around a grim look. "Right," Sophie said. "Sinking the ship. Temporarily."

"For the record, I hate this plan." Bram said.

"It's *your* plan," Sophie said, and left him to execute it, while she ran up the ladder, yet again, to get her wetsuit on.

CHAPTER 26

Sinking a ship in twenty minutes was as much work as trying to save it.

With the locks open, *Nightjar* took water quickly. The crew brought down and reefed the sails and then lowered the rest of the lifeboats, evacuating as the bow sank and the stern rose. Arranging themselves five to a boat, they rowed madly in the direction of *Sawtooth*.

Cly's caravel had every sail unfurled, every cannoneer on deck. She was too far away, and the fiery ship, preceded by a sulfur smell, continued to close the distance between them.

The last of the lifeboats held the cannoneer, Krezzo, and the cook. The two of them were turning loose floating smudge pots filled with combustible powder and some kind of moss, filling the air with a pall of thick, white smoke.

"Looks desperate," Sophie observed.

"We are desperate," Garland said. "We're sinking the ship."

"Temporarily," she insisted. He nodded without conviction.

There were just seven of them still aboard: she and Garland, Bram and Verena, and Kev, Daimon, and Selwig.

"You next," Sophie said to her brother and half sister, ushering them to the cabin they'd been sharing. The tilt of the ship was severe here; the fore cabins would be underwater in another ten minutes at most.

Verena unfastened Gale's heavy clock—it was about the size of a breadbox—from the wall, stopped its gears, and wrapped it in a heavy rug. Reaching inside, she wrapped it in a heavy rug.

"How do you plan to get aboard the immolator with a homicidal wood fright chasing you?" Bram asked.

"Garland says he's got an idea."

"He didn't share?"

"Maybe we're hoping to get lucky."

"Sofe," he said.

"Bram, go. I will lose what's left of my mind if you end up in pirate hands again. Anyway, you and Verena need to be home if you're to find out who Coine's Erstwhile accomplice is."

"She's right. Come on, Bram."

Sophie stepped back; Verena took Bram's hand. She heard two distinct sets of clockworks—the ticking of Verena's clock, about ten feet away, and the one in Beatrice's house, in San Francisco.

"How do you keep them straight?" Sophie asked.

"I concentrate," Verena said, but she didn't sound unduly stressed.

Sophie's vision swam. Her eyes flooded and she blinked fiercely. Verena and Bram were gone.

The residue of ticking remained, little *plinks,* as if there was one more clock, far away and barely audible.

"We have to go," Garland said.

She took a last look around the cabin. "Where's my camera?" She'd left her electronics in a bag on her bunk.

"Someone must have packed it."

There was no time to search it out. Swallowing once, she marched back up to the stern, using the rail to keep from slipping on the ever-steeper incline.

Garland had packed one last wooden lifeboat with one of the flattened inflatable rafts Verena had brought. Now he turned it upside down and lowered it into the water. "The lifeboat will drift, as if it were a spare that came off the ship," he said. "Kev, Daimon, and Selwig can shelter under it until we've taken care of the fright."

"That's the plan?" Kev demanded. "Pretend to be wreckage?"

Before Garland could answer, *Nightjar*'s stern lurched upward, fast enough that Sophie's stomach did an elevator-lunge, and they swiftly found themselves fifteen feet higher than they had been a moment before. The fore cabins sank underwater. Air bubbled madly from the open obsidian portals.

Garland put a hand on *Nightjar*'s deck.

"She'll be submerged before they're close enough to burn her," Sophie said. "She won't burn, you hear me?"

"What matters now is keeping everyone alive."

That, and retaining custody of Kev. And getting him pacified. And protecting him from torture. . . .

"We'll raise *Nightjar*."

"Let's see if we can turn that fright on the immolator," he said.

"Garland, we'll raise her."

His smile was a bit forced, but at least it was a smile. "One thing at a time."

They slid the overturned lifeboat into the water, hiding it from view by keeping *Nightjar*'s upturned stern between themselves and the immolator. Selwig arranged himself in the bow, treading water. Gesturing to Kev, he produced a length of white ribbon, lettered with a single line of glowing silver spellscrip, and bound Kev's hands together.

"Um . . ." she said.

"It's symbolic," Selwig said. "A leash. Shows he's yours. Not an escapee, and therefore not subject to immediate execution."

"Fine," she said, though it was far from it.

"Why not shackle me right to *Nightjar*'s anchor?" Kev said. "That would solve the problem, won't it?"

"Why are you mad at *me* all of a sudden?" Sophie said. "I'm not the one who infiltrated your cell and betrayed your friends."

"No," he said, flinching as Selwig tugged the knot, testing. "That wasn't you. . . ."

It's ribbon, it's ribbon. It's not hurting him.

"The boat won't pass for wreckage if we turn it into the amphitheater for a shouting match," Selwig said.

"Selwig's right," Daimon said. He had tied his curly red hair back and skinned down to a peasant shirt and short breeches. "If we don't row together now, we're sunk. There is still a chance, Lidman. You must trust—"

Whatever he had meant to say was interrupted as Garland surfaced in their midst, making the space even more crowded.

"You three, kick gently for *Sawtooth*," he said. "Selwig has a compass, I believe? Excellent. Here's your bearing. They should close the distance soon. Sophie, it's time to go."

"Go?" Kev yelped. "You're leaving me?"

She ignored him. "How are we getting aboard the pirate ship?"

"You worry about leading the wood fright." To her surprise, Garland grinned. "Remember, it'll tear its way through anything to get to you. And it will bind with wood, wood fibers, anything from a forest."

"Are you okay?"

Garland's eyes brimmed, and his expression became almost as cold as Cly's. "Sophie, this will be a real clash, with a sincerely violent enemy."

"Commit," she murmured. "Commit, commit."

With that, she kissed him, hard. Then, taking a few deep breaths, she put her mouthpiece in and her mask on, dropping below the surface.

Nightjar's stern was just dropping below the waterline. Streaming bubbles from every portal, she glided in slow motion, setting a slow course for the bottom of the ocean.

They'd had the ship cleaned at the ice city, Ylle, but the spell had created fresh layers of contamination, weird fusions of mammalian reproductive tissue and forest floor: chips of wood, beetles burrowing in moss studded with oxygen-rich, bloody bubbles, dirt, humus. Earthworms twisted in agony as their bodies met the salt water. Lichens turned black and dropped into the deeps.

Sophie descended slowly, looking for sharks, shining her light ahead of her, and taking as little depth as she could. She wouldn't have time for a safety stop, and she didn't want to get close to the fright, in any case. As she descended, looking over the filth-encrusted starboard side of the ship, she suddenly saw a jagged-edged hole the size of a department store mannequin.

It's already inside, she thought.

Now what? She couldn't enter the ship from outside and hope to outmaneuver the fright—it would just start ripping the ship to pieces.

So lure it out. She shined the light on the hole and began clinking a metal clip against her air tank—*plink, plink, plink*—in time with the ticking rhythm still echoing at the back of her mind.

Was that movement within the chamber?

She took another second to get her bearings, shining her light back at the upturned lifeboat, barely making out the chaotic whirl of Kev's, Daimon's, and Selwig's legs as they kicked frantically, blind and vulnerable, making negligible progress, caught in a streamer of the ship's blood.

Teeth, guys! Row together.

Over at her three o'clock, Garland's part of the plan had made itself obvious. He had swum for the surface and tangled himself into a net. Floating, he probably looked as though he'd gone down with *Nightjar,* lost consciousness, and surfaced. Now he lay faceup, just waiting for a pickup. The net spooled in the water beneath him.

Handy and ready for the grabbing, she guessed. *Will they want him?*

Who wouldn't want him?

The bandit ship was getting closer. Its boards, below the surface of the water, cast an intermittent orange glow, flickering like banked coals in a campfire. *Nightjar* had sunk well beneath her, though; she was safe.

When did sunk become the new safe?

Movement inside *Nightjar*. Maybe the fright could hear her. She kept flashing the light and clinking the clip against the tank.

Yes—there it was: a human-shaped shadow moving inside the hold.

Clink. Clink.

What about my voice? She let a low tone burr through her throat, articulating around the mouthpiece. "*Rr-r-r.*"

The fright burst back through the hole it had already made in *Nightjar*'s hull, enlarging it.

Holy crap! It was an inhuman thing, entirely bent on killing her, equal parts repulsive and fascinating. It was, after all, a naked, animated mannequin with her own face. Sophie began to swim for that strip of net dangling below Garland. She moved slowly, until she was sure the wood fright had seen her, then kicked for all she was worth.

It wasn't clumsy in the water. Why would it be? *That must be what I look like swimming. Skinny-dipping.*

Garland blew a few bubbles, then gestured with one hand, opening the fingers then closing them, repeatedly.

Shut off the light? She doused it, kicking blindly in sudden blackness, hoping for the best.

There was a splash. A pirate, diving down to secure a rope to Garland?

Did you think they'd just use a robo-magnet to grab him? Which movie was that from? The Matrix?

She reached the bottom edge of the net.

How long before the wood fright caught up to her? She kept one hand twisted in the net; with the other, she checked to make sure her air tanks and hoses were clear.

She didn't climb—she didn't want whoever was stringing up Garland to feel her scrambling around down here.

If, if, if.

If they took him aboard without killing him first.

If they lifted her up without noticing.

If the fright didn't catch up with her before they boarded.

She felt a little convulsion in the net, above, a thrashing that stopped abruptly. Then they were moving, drawn upward and toward the immolator.

The urge to turn her light back on was all but irresistible.

She kicked gently, raising herself at the speed of whatever winch was hauling them.

Weighing you down, weighing you down like an anvil. Got your ship sunk, got Gale killed. Can't imagine what you see in me, Garland.

Magic, she thought glumly. *Charming-pretty-smart-persuasive-fertile, remember?*

And lucky.

She needed to be lucky now.

She was ten feet below the surface, close enough to see Garland dangling above her, streaming the length of the fishing net beneath him, and the murk of the sea below. Where was the fright?

Come on. Don't you even want to kill me anymore?

She started handing herself down the net, staying below, letting it pay out, looking, looking.

There. And, oh—it was close!

She reversed direction, climbing fast. As the net broke the surface, taking her weight, it stretched downward.

A shout. Someone on *Hawkwasp* had spotted her.

Her feet, in flippers, couldn't get purchase within the net, so she paused, pulling one off. The fright was close; she didn't dare do the other. Instead, she climbed up toward Garland, using arm strength and her left toes to grip the net.

Calm descended, as it so often did in an emergency. Lifting one hand at a time, spinning, she looked around. The fright was doing the same thing, a sight that raised the hairs on her neck. It scanned past her, up to the net, to Garland, to the pirates hauling them up.

Don't kill him, don't kill him. Sophie sent a desperate thought upward.

The fright gave her an eager, hungry smile. Then it turned its gaze on Cly's caravel, *Sawtooth,* bearing on their position but out of cannon range.

It didn't so much as glance at the turned-turtle lifeboat sheltering Kev, Selwig, and Daimon.

Why would it? All this thing wanted was her.

Having worked out to its satisfaction that there was nobody close enough to save her, her doppelganger began to climb in earnest.

Sophie skinned off the second flipper, tossing it into the sea and ascending higher, toward Garland and *Hawkwasp*. The fright was strong, but it kept growing roots that bound themselves into the net's strands, forcing it to jerk itself free of the threads each time it tried to lift itself higher.

What's your plan, Garland? They haul you aboard and I get up there unseen and the fright follows? No chance. They've already seen me.

She imagined herself scrambling around the lower decks, chased by a deck-shredding wood fright.

And the pirates doing nothing? Again, not likely.

At least we got Bram to minimum safe distance.

As the *Hawkwasp* crew pulled him the last few yards to their rail, Garland burst into motion, swinging out of their reach, leaping to grab the rope, and bounding aboard. Sophie felt the increased lift of the net dragging upward as his weight came off it, jerking her upward a foot, or even two.

The fright froze.

Little roots and suckers started running up and down the net, extending toward the hull—where they smoked heavily, even as they penetrated the boards.

She changed direction, crawling down toward the fright. The net was thickening up, its weight dragging it against the side of the ship as the fright kept growing.

She shifted, reaching down for a loose frill of net and flinging its edge around and down, catching the thing on the elbow. More tendrils grew, tangling the fright's arm.

Its hand met the side of the hull with a snap and grew into the wood. It tore itself free with a splintering crack.

Now Garland was leaping over the side, trailing a rope and rappelling down toward her.

"Sophie!" He reached out, caught her hand, and swung her away from the net, running against the deck, supported by the rope.

"It didn't work, I take it? Whatever it was?" she said.

"No."

The fright had both hands pressed to the hull now, sticking like Spider-Man. Its pose put her in mind of a small lizard, an anole or chameleon. Humps of moss and little plant runners were spreading out from it, and when it crabbed closer, in single-minded pursuit of Sophie, it had to rip its hands free, sending a rain of wood chips down to the water. They sizzled when they hit.

Garland said, "They aren't going to let us dangle here for long."

She glanced east, past the *Nightjar* crew in their lifeboats. *Sawtooth* was almost in the game now, closing to cannon range.

"The fright'll stick to *Hawkwasp*'s hull—let's rush her. A good push and she'll do some real damage when she busts free."

He nodded. "Ready?"

She pressed her feet against the ship. "Go!"

They swung back, forward, then back again. The fright paused, evaluating, thoughtfully moving its hands and feet to avoid getting too tightly bound into the deck.

"She's so like me," Sophie said.

Garland looked at the fright, coughed, and nodded.

Oh, teeth. She's naked. "I meant she *thinks* like me."

"Oh. Yes. That follows."

They swung forward, and Garland got a hand on the fright's bicep, looping the line of rope around its arm and thereby binding them to her. Roots obligingly burst out of its elbow, entangling it, but it only had eyes for Sophie. It grabbed for her throat.

Sophie caught it with both hands, wrestling the wooden version of herself, trying to brace her feet against the roots growing outward from the thing's body as she worked to force its elbow against the outer hull of the ship.

It was *much* stronger than she was.

"Commit, commit," she grunted. "Commit!"

The elbow bounced off the hull, stuck, and made a small dent as the fright jerked free, once again reaching for Sophie's throat. Simultaneously, it kicked out at Garland, almost catching him in the hip. The roots in its other foot were making serious inroads on *Hawkwasp*'s hull. Boards lumped and separated, like a sidewalk breaking under the onslaught of underground oak roots.

Hawkwasp was buckling, cracking. The fright would make a big hole, albeit one above the immolator's waterline.

Maybe I can get past it and run inside, Sophie thought, finding the strength to heave, once, and drive the wooden elbow back against the dented hull. *Lure it amidships and—*

And then everything changed.

The figure shocked in her grip, then turned into boards. These fell, silently, even as Sophie and Garland, disconnected from rope and the fright's tangle of roots, dropped off the side of the immolator.

The slick of amniotic by-products and detritus on the surface of the water swirled and disappeared, drawn down by a vortex of water. The net from *Nightjar* was suddenly pristine, no longer entangled with vine and flower.

Wood chips flew out of the ocean and reassembled themselves on the outer hull of the pirate ship. A splinter in Sophie's hand ripped itself free, likewise making for the hull, managing to hurt without leaving a mark on her skin.

"The hell?" She felt sore, winded, as if someone had punched her in the diaphragm. Her nose was bleeding again.

"Reversion," Garland said. "They tore up the inscription to keep the fright from damaging the ship too badly."

"Why?"

"*Sawtooth*. She's almost in cannon range. Come, we have to get to Kev."

The lifeboat with Kev in it had been puttering along, getting steadily—if none too subtly—away from the scene of the fight. Now, though, it was dead in the water, adrift in a puddle of blood.

They swam hard to catch it, ducking up under the lifeboat. Kev was beneath, his hands still bound in white ribbon. His fingers, crabbed together, were wound into Selwig's collar, holding his head above water.

The Watch officer was gasping up little sprays of blood.

"Sophie, your light."

Sophie fumbled with the switch as Garland unbuttoned the young officer's coat. Crimson diffused into the seawater from two wounds in his abdomen: one in the left side, just under his ribs, the other a little lower down and closer to the center of his belly.

"He's hit his head," she said. Bruising was spreading from his left eye to his ear. "Kev, what happened?"

"There was an oddity," Kev gasped. Keeping Selwig afloat had exhausted him. "Big, black, reptilian."

"Where's Daimon?"

"Oddity bit him," he huffed. "Dragged him down."

"Daimon's dead?" She remembered the reptile oddity she had encountered on a previous dive. It had tried to twist her leg off.

"They wanted you?" Garland demanded, in the same instant. He pressed a handful of white fabric to the higher of the two wounds.

"*Neht,*" groaned Selwig, opening his eyes.

Did that mean no? "Daimon's not dead?" Sophie asked. "Or they didn't want Kev?"

Of course they wanted Kev. What else could they want?

In the lambent blue light cast by her LED lamp, Selwig looked gray-green. He fish-gasped a few times, letting out intermittent nonsense words—in Cardeshi, she assumed.

"Wait. Was that 'fingerprint'?" she asked. "Print who?"

"*Battoh,*" he rasped. "Daimon *gref sareen*—latents, *yeh battoh.*"

"Daimon? Is Daimon dead?"

"Kev, Kev *senna*—"

"Kev's fine," Sophie said. "And *Sawtooth*'s here. You can tell us everything once we get you to the infirmary."

She tried to ignore the look on Garland's face, the one that hinted that Selwig wasn't going to make it that far, even if a reptilian oddity didn't show up to *Jaws* them into snack food.

The big Watchman's voice dropped to a whisper. "You should behead him now. For everyone's sake."

Sophie felt a rush of relief. If he was speaking Fleet again, maybe he wasn't so badly hurt. "Come on," she said, trying to keep her tone light. "If you believed that, why not let them take Kev?"

"Same oath. As you." With that, Selwig's eyes rolled back and he lost consciousness.

Garland had been about to tear off one of his shirtsleeves to make a compress for the second stab wound, but now he pressed two fingers to Selwig's throat, checking his pulse. "I'm sorry. He's died."

I was responsible for him, Sophie thought. *I taught him dactyloscopy and treated him badly and left him sleeping in the corridor outside Kev's cabin.*

After a minute, Kev asked, meekly, "Did you sink the immolator?"

"Sinking a ship is no small thing," Garland said, tone sharp. With his hair wet and slicked against his head, he had an uncharacteristically vulnerable appearance. He was treading water in an armored, focused way that spoke of great fatigue or pain.

Grief. For *Nightjar.* Selwig dead and the ship sunk.

"Do you know our position?" she said. "I mean, do you know where the ship went down?"

"Yes." If there was a spark of hope in Garland, she couldn't see it. He unfolded Selwig's massive hand, untangling the white spellscrip-marked ribbon from his grasp, and passed Sophie the makeshift leash.

"I'll check *Sawtooth*'s position," he said, ducking under the boat, leaving them in suffocating silence with the corpse. He was only gone a minute. "It's all right. The immolator is in retreat. His Honor's crew is picking up our lifeboats."

They swam clear of the wooden lifeboat and Sophie yanked the painter cord that triggered the inflatable raft Garland had packed. Two gas canisters triggered with a loud hiss, and Kev shrieked.

Poor guy. His nerves must be shot. "It's okay, Kev. It's just a balloon. You can climb in in a second."

They helped Kev into the inflatable first. Garland winced as he climbed in.

"Are you hurt?" she asked.

"*Hawkwasp* had magical countermeasures on her main deck," he said. "My feet are burnt, through my boots. It's why I jumped so quickly."

"Oh, Garland. I'm so sorry. Is it bad?" Her stash of antibiotics was . . . She wasn't sure what had happened to her things.

It was probably all underwater. Her cameras. Her clothes. Bram's equipment. The enormity of it hit her again. It wasn't just the ship, or even the stuff within. *Nightjar* had been home to two dozen people.

"There's Blue," Garland said. The ship's half-snake, half-ferret oddity floated past in a mixing bowl.

"Stay," she ordered, skinning off her tanks, handing over Kev's leash, and diving into the ocean. It felt good to save something.

She pushed the bowl back to the inflatable.

Garland took the transformed ferret in his arms, stroking both of its heads at once.

Treading water, Sophie took a look around. The wooden lifeboat was drifting away. She dove out again, towed it to the inflatable, and had Garland fix a line to it. Then the three of them wrestled Selwig's massive body onto the life raft. It was slow work; he was a blocky guy, and the sea seemed determined to suck him down.

"I don't think there's anything else to save," Garland said, offering her a hand into the boat.

"No."

It would be a while before *Sawtooth* rescued them. She turned her attention to the body.

"What are you doing?" Kev said.

"External exam." She had Selwig's left hand spread in front of her. There were three cuts: one that had cleft the pad of his middle finger, another in the web between thumb and index finger, and a third on the side, about where hand became wrist. "Tell me about this lizard, Kev."

A long pause as his mouth worked open and shut. "Big. Black."

"Teeth?"

He looked down at Selwig's hand. Swallowed. "It had a knife."

"What is it?" Garland said.

She'd thought she might catch Kev in a lie there. She'd have to double check, but the cuts were, she was pretty sure, defensive wounds, more fitting a blade than a mouthful of teeth.

"Knife cuts," she said.

Garland nodded, indicating the bloodied jacket, now shut but not rebuttoned, over Selwig's stab wounds. "Those too, I think."

"He kept me behind him as he fought," Kev said before curling up like a kid, arms wrapped loosely around knees, in an apparent sulk.

Same oath as you, Selwig had said.

An open boat was no place to perform an autopsy, even if she'd been qualified. She and Garland sat alongside the body, with Kev as far from them as he could get. They all waited in a silent funk of their own thoughts until *Sawtooth* came to haul them out of the water.

Last time Sophie had been aboard her father's sailing vessel, it had been crewed by cadets—tenners and niners still learning to sail, some as young as fourteen. Now the people who came to load them aboard were adults—duelists, presumably—muscled, fit, and serious. They lashed the inflatable to the side of their wooden rescue craft and transferred Sophie, with Kev. She barely managed to grab her tanks in time.

It was perhaps two hours since *Nightjar* had sunk.

They came aboard without fanfare, brought up on deck, where the rest of the crew, and the canola crow, Uhura, were waiting.

She turned a slow circle, switching Kev's ribbon from hand to hand as she looked around the deck. Where was Cly?

They had been running flat out for sixteen hours, maybe more, scrambling first to save the ship and then to scuttle her. Sending messages, moving loads . . .

. . . Getting Bram back to civilization. Losing Selwig. And . . .

She looked, without much hope, in case Daimon had been found, brought aboard.

No. So much for avoiding misfortune.

Beatrice only protected me against casual misfortune.

This was usually the point where she started bawling, wasn't it? She didn't feel like crying. She felt burned and tired, shakily furious at Kev and, most of all, terribly in the wrong. Tainted.

She was a *calamity.* A charming, magically prettified calamity who destroyed everything in her path.

"No sign of Daimon?" Garland said. He was perched on a deck stool, sliding off his burned boots under Watts's eye. The bottoms of his wool socks were stained with red and wet with fluid, presumably from broken blisters.

Behind him, Krispos had already found himself a book and was turning its pages as he shivered in a blanket. He had his body half turned, avoiding the sight of three *Sawtooth* deckhands as they hefted Selwig aboard, wrapped in a bloody shroud.

"*Hawkwasp* is making herself scarce, I see."

Cly's voice made her startle. He'd come right up behind Kev.

Garland would have stood, if Watts hadn't right then all but grabbed his foot.

"Your Honor. We're in your debt."

"Yes," Cly agreed. He was looking at Sophie.

Okay, what do you do now? She pulled herself upright and saw him take in her wetsuit with a frown. "Cly," she said.

"The proper form of address in these cases would be 'Father.'"

Great. He's determined to make this difficult. "Propriety's not my strong suit."

"True. Quarters, what are you doing? Help Captain Garland and the other wounded down to the infirmary."

There was a flurry of activity as Watts established his credentials and directed the sailors, who transferred Garland into an improvised sling made of sail.

Sophie used the time to try to pull herself together. She'd messed up, before, by failing to fully listen to Cly. By attending to the wrong things. The whole of *Nightjar*'s crew could be in trouble if she dropped her guard now.

Calamity, she thought again. She tightened her grip on the ribbon—the symbolic leash—that bound Kev's hands.

Cly was waiting, patiently, no doubt reading every flicker of emotion on her too-open face.

Start with gratitude. "We appreciate the assistance."

"Do you?" He broke into a smile. "You'll have an opportunity to enjoy our hospitality. Where are you bound?"

"Sylvanna," she said. "As you know."

He affected mock surprise. "I've not been made privy to your plans, child. Unless some letter of yours has gone astray—"

"Don't call me child." She didn't have energy for cat and mouse right now.

"I think having our relationship on a traditional parent-child footing for a time might be for the best," he said. "All the customs and proprieties. Speaking of which . . ." He turned, taking a close look at Kev, who scooched back to the rail. "I'll be taking custody of—"

"Oh, you will not! He's . . ." She shuddered and made herself say it: "Mine."

"This is a Sylvanner ship, Sophie, and you are a dependent minor of Sylvanna, Sophie. Our law is clear."

"I'm not a dependent anything," she snapped. "I'm . . ."

"Yes?"

Daimon the fake fiancé was gone. Dragged under by the knife-wielding monster, Kev had said. She'd gotten him killed, just like Selwig. And Bram had liked him.

"Yes?" Cly repeated. He had Kev's symbolic leash between two of his fingers. His expression was thoroughly predatory.

She didn't owe Kev anything. He'd gone into terrorism on his own. He was hiding something.

Behead him now, Selwig had said.

"It's all right," Kev said. "You did the best you could. There was never any—"

To stall, she said to Cly, "You wanted this all along, didn't you? You engineered this situation so you could maneuver Kev back to Low Bann, I guess, and compel him to tell you all his secrets. . . ."

"You are *what,* daughter?" He tugged the ribbon—a light tug, like someone teasing a cat.

Can't free Kev without a fiancé handy. Two engaged kids make one adult. Nothing else I can do, just have to hope. Can I claim the pirates have Daimon, but we're still . . .

"Engaged," she said. "I'm engaged."

"Indeed? Congratulations. To whom, pray?"

She swallowed. "To Captain Parrish."

CHAPTER 27

SOFE,

MADE IT HOME. SWINGING BY THE PARENTS' HOUSE TO CHECK SECURITY CAMERAS, SEE HOW IT'S GOING WITH THE NEW PUPPY, AND ATTEMPT HOME PROTECTION INSCRIPTION. THEN VERENA AND I ARE MEETING THIS VERDANII COP/SPY/WHATEVER, FEDONA. LET ME KNOW YOU'RE NOT DEAD OR I'M COMING RIGHT BACK. CAN'T BELIEVE I LEFT YOU ON A SINKING SHIP. WHAT WAS I THINKING? WORRIED.

BRAM

Sophie was saved from an immediate, awkward interrogation when Sweet interposed herself between them. "Actually, Your Honor, our doctor has asked for Sophie to join Parrish in the infirmary."

"The man's a little scorched. He hardly requires a bedside vigil."

"We're sentimental aboard *Nightjar,*" the bosun insisted. "Cap'n just lost his ship. Kir Sophie would be a definite comfort."

A narrowing of eyes, and then Cly conceded the point. "Let's all go, shall we?"

"Not all," Sophie said, gesturing madly at Krispos and handing over the white ribbon, along with temporary responsibility for Kev. "Don't let anyone . . . you know . . . clap him in irons."

The memorician gave her a pat that was probably meant to be reassuring. "Coming, child?"

She swallowed. Why had she lied? What if Garland didn't play along?

"Sophie?"

"Coming." She had been aboard *Sawtooth* before. Now, with Cly right behind her, she headed down to the infirmary, following the same route through the ship that she'd taken just after she rescued Kev, so many months earlier. The infirmary was a cramped box, three beds and little in the way of floor space. The air was dense with a nostril-tingling mixture of herbs and poultices. An extraordinary array of interlocking boxes was fixed to the walls, repository for remedies for everything from infectious cuts to whooping cough. Cly's doctor managed to give her a bow as he looked over Garland's feet, clucking. The socks were off; his soles were raw and seeping.

"How bad is it?" Sophie asked.

"Superficial," Watts said. "Looks worse than it is."

"No magic required," the ship's doctor agreed. He began spreading a yellowish goo that looked like mustard over the blisters.

"We're making more fuss than is required, I'm sure," Garland said. His voice was distant. He was almost certainly feeling the loss of *Nightjar* more keenly than anything that was happening to his body.

Sophie hunched next to him, on a low stool, guilt cascading from of every pore, wondering if she dared look him in the face.

"Will *Sawtooth* go after *Hawkwasp*?" she asked, trying to buy time. How could she tell Garland what was up?

Garland shook his head. "We're on course for Sylvanna, I believe. Your Honor?"

"Indeed we are," Cly said. "Sophie needs a new name, and quickly."

One of his aides had turned up, carrying a folded bundle of clothes that Sophie recognized as a sports suit for women—the Sylvanner equivalent of jeans and a shirt.

Cly continued, "My captain, Beck, has messaged the South Sylvan navy. They'll catch your immolator, if they can."

Garland nodded.

"I suppose congratulations are in order," Cly added.

"Congratulations?" Garland said.

"I told him we're engaged!" Sophie blurted, in a completely upbeat, perky, not-at-all-a-calamity voice.

Teeth, I sound like I'm on a reality show.

She had picked the one person on Stormwrack who was crappier at lying than she was.

Garland held her gaze for what seemed like twenty years. Her face heated—her whole body heated, the embarrassment so intense that she might have dried off through her wetsuit.

Finally, Garland inclined his head in an approximation of the Fleet bow. "Your Honor. This wasn't quite how I imagined . . . But. We would be grateful for your blessing."

"Seas! You're asking his permission?"

"I should be glad you chose someone who'll take the trouble to be polite, given your significant deficits in this area," Cly said.

"Thanks very much, Cly." She was weak with relief.

"Sadly, I must decline to approve of your choice." Cly held the clothing out. "Would you kindly go change? That . . . thing . . . is indecent." He gestured at her wetsuit, and then a hatch.

"You should've seen the wood fright," she muttered. But what the hell. The room was a broom closet for medical stuff. She'd be able to hear them.

Of course, Cly knew that. He said something in a low voice to Garland in . . . was it Sylvanner? Did Garland speak Sylvanner?

No, she decided, as Garland replied in kind. *It's Verdanii. Of course Cly speaks Verdanii; he married one. Why couldn't I end up in Narnia? Or some other nice, Eurocentric world where even the animals speak English?*

She wriggled out of the wetsuit, fumbling for something she could use as a towel, and slid into the sports jacket, fighting to get it over her damp skin.

Dottar. Garland had said "daughter."

"Done," she said, bursting out on them, but whatever sneaky agreement they'd been coming to, it seemed to be done.

I'm just gonna ask him what you wanted as soon as your back is turned.

But Cly said, "We ought to leave Captain Parrish to recover, Sophie."

It was all sort of equally unbearable. She swept around Cly, back to the empty spot beside Garland, and took his hand, bending close. "Can I come back later?"

"Come in the morning," he said.

A pang of hurt. *But I deserve it. I do.*

He surprised her then with a quick kiss. "Good night."

Cly ushered her into the corridor. "He certainly acts as though he means to marry you."

"He's not the one with commitment issues," Sophie said. "Where am I staying?"

"As before," he said, leading her to the same cabin she'd occupied on her earlier visit. To his evident surprise, Kev and Krispos were within, sitting across from each other, one on the bunk and the other at the small desk.

The yellow bird, Uhura, was pecking at a bowl of seeds between them. Rounding out the crowd was a *Sawtooth* fiver, big of muscle and of scowl, who was obviously there to protect Krispos from Kev's murderous machinations.

Which was almost as laughable as the fact that her tottery, fragile assistant was keeping himself positioned, ever so protectively, between the soldier and Kev himself.

"Renly, move Kir Sophie's memorician into the berth next door," Cly said. "And take the—"

"Prisoner," Sophie said. "And if you're about to say 'Lock him in the brig'—"

"Lock him in the brig, indeed. But Renly, see that everyone knows he's Kir Sophie's property and she means him to be treated with excessive gentility. Three square meals and a kind word whenever he wants it."

"It's all right, Kir Sophie," Kev said in his best Eeyore voice. The sangfroid he had displayed through most of their voyage was utterly gone. He was wide-eyed with shock; the skin under his eyes was blue.

"I'll come check on you later, okay?" Sophie said.

Kev nodded.

"I'll see him properly settled," Krispos offered. They trooped out, leaving a second sports suit and a bulky-looking gift-wrapped box behind them on the bunk.

"What's that?"

"An index of moth wing diagrams," Cly said. "I had ordered it before we . . ."

Bickered? Fought? Imploded? "Before we disagreed?"

He nodded. "Your laboratory is across the hall. I left the space untouched."

"Can I get the lifeboat, the wooden one, sent there? It's Institute business."

"I doubt there's room, unless we cut it into pieces. Can you examine it on deck?"

"Sure, if it can go under a tarp or something. . . ."

"Easily. Now then, we'll bestow an additional name on you as soon as we reach Hoarfrost."

She nodded. Part of her wanted to reject his help, even now. Taking anything from Cly—especially something as personal as a name—seemed wrong.

But if I'd done it a month ago, Nightjar *would still be afloat. Daimon and Selwig would be alive.*

Would they? The immolator had presumably been out there, hunting them, all along. Hunting Kev.

She sat on her bunk, at a loss for words.

"It will come out all right, child," Cly said, closing the hatch as he left, leaving her to dissolve into tears.

CHAPTER 28

Dear Mensalohm:

I am writing today with bad news. Your clerk, Daimon Tern of Tiladene, was killed yesterday in a ~~battle~~ . . . ~~skirmish~~ . . . ~~scrap~~ . . .

"I have no idea how to do this," Sophie said.

She was in the infirmary with Garland, who was drafting letters of reference for *Nightjar*'s six newest crew members. They were leaving his employ, seeking berths elsewhere.

Garland glanced at her page. "The usual form is to say 'altercation with a ship meaning to sink *Nightjar*.'"

"Thanks."

. . . killed yesterday in an altercation with a ship meaning to sink Nightjar. *Daimon was ~~a great guy~~ . . . ~~nice~~ . . . a smart and pleasant man who was popular with our crew. He took up the study of fingerprinting when he was with us, and seemed to enjoy it. He was kind to Kev Lidman, the man we've been trying to help. . . .*

Garland nudged her, then handed over a handkerchief.

She wiped her streaming eyes. "I suck at this."

"It's an area where it's hard to excel. Just don't mention that he wasn't studying very hard for his exams. Did he sleep with Bram?"

"What?"

"Tiladenes value sexual prowess. If the two of them formed a connection, Mensalohm might like to pass that along to his parents."

"Um. . . ." She wrote:

> *At the time that we were attacked, I think he'd been having a very satisfying fling with someone on board.*

"Excellent," Garland said approvingly.

> *Mensalohm, I am so, so sorry this happened. We are all saddened by his death. Can you send me his family contact information, so I can write to them, too?*

She set the draft aside. "I'll rewrite it after I do Selwig's letter. And I have to tell Bram about Daimon, too. I guess that'll give Tonio another shot."

Garland bit down on a chuckle. "I'm not sure that's funny."

"None of this is funny," she said. "What are you up to?"

"Sweet and Watts have asked to remain aboard *Sawtooth*, with the cat, until the spring. They'll take the opportunity to train up—she's a much bigger vessel, and His Honor's doctor is a combat physician. I am writing Captain Lena Beck to document the loan of personnel."

"They'll come back to *Nightjar* when we raise it?"

His jaw clenched slightly, but he nodded. "Tonio and the rest I'm sending to Erinth, to see if we can hire a ship from the Conto's merchant fleet. Our cook intends to sail home until I reestablish myself."

Someone rapped on the door. "Coming into port, Kirs."

She left Garland, climbing up to the quarterdeck as they came into dock in the Winter District.

Nightjar's initial course would have brought them into the city of Autumn. But, in their flight from the immolator, they'd caught a fast wind around the tip of Haversham, Sylvanna's closest neighbor and bitter enemy. Cly had opted to take them around Haversham and into the nation's capital.

Her birth father's nation was divided into four administrative districts—provinces, essentially—each named for a season. Sophie had seen the Autumn capital and Cly's estate there.

The city of Hoarfrost was not the winter wonderland its name implied. Autumn had been decorated in red leaves and harvest motifs; it looked a bit as though it had rolled wholesale off some set designer's drafting table. Hoarfrost was older and looked more like a city that had grown normally, in bits and pieces, over centuries.

Its predominant color was the blue-green of spruce needles; the wood, along with slate and blue marble, was the primary building material of its biggest structures. The buildings were stark, windburned. There was little adornment of any kind.

Sylvanna lay at about thirty-six degrees north, as it would have been reckoned on Earth, near Tennessee. Sophie hadn't expected much in the way of winter cold. But this side of the island was more much mountainous than the swampland on its eastern shore. Hoarfrost's port was at sea level, but much of the city climbed up into higher elevations.

With the winter solstice about a week away, it was cool enough that people were wearing wool coats and even, in a few cases, fur stoles. Many of the coats were colored like blue spruce too, and all of them were tailored to leave space for the identity blazers worn by everyone—beauty-queen sashes covered in brooches that spelled out the social pecking order in incredible detail. Landholder, Fleet personnel, single, married, professional, clerk, private employee, civil servant . . . A glance at someone's chest took all the guesswork out of social interaction.

Cly wafted up beside her. "I've taken rooms at a hotel called the Mancellor, in the city. There will be room for the two of us, Parrish, and your memorician."

Sophie had other plans for Krispos, but first she wanted to discuss them with him. "What kind of hotel?"

"It caters to foreigners from the starboard side." He held out a small wrapped parcel. Cly seemed constitutionally unable to keep from giving her gifts.

"Does that mean the staff are paid employees?"

"I remember well the hunger strike you threw to protest the labor practices on Low Bann." That was a dare: *Go ahead; upbraid me about slavery.* "There's room for Bram and Verena, should they turn up."

"What about Kev?"

"There's a secure lockup at the Institute."

"Oh no. I don't want him jailed where I can't protect him."

He conceded so quickly, she thought perhaps he had expected the objection. "You'll need rooms at a second hotel, in that case. One that will accommodate your slave."

"Prisoner."

"There's a place directly beside the Mancellor. I'll get you a room. What are those papers?"

She showed him the drafts of the letters—to Mensalohm, about Daimon; to the Watch commander and Humbrey, about Selwig.

"Condolence letters are a bane. I'm very sorry you've had to . . . Well, may I make some suggestions?"

She nodded gratefully and he jotted a few notes.

Once they were docked, Cly sent Kev ahead, under guard, with instructions: "Check him in with the staff manager at the Black Fox Inn, and book Kir Sophie a room. Then confirm our family suite at the Mancellor."

"I'll come see you as soon as I can, Kev," Sophie said.

He nodded, expression locked, breathing slowly and steadily in a way that made her think of Selwig, when he was coaching him through that earlier panic attack.

Poor Selwig.

They spent an hour in thank-yous, farewells, and good-byes with the *Nightjar* and *Sawtooth* crews before Cly ushered her to an empty carriage hung with Fleet and judiciary flags.

She scanned the dock. "Where's Garland?"

"Sending dispatches. He'll meet us at the Mancellor as soon as he's disposed of his crew and been to the clarionhouse," Cly said, climbing in across from her.

The ride to the hotel was oppressively quiet. She looked out the windows, searching for new wildlife species and feeling the loss of her camera like a missing limb. When the urban development got dense enough to make nature studies impossible, she opened the latest gift box. It contained a supply of messageply.

Her breath caught. It was a costly gift.

He was watching her over his case file.

"Thank you," she said.

"Practical gifts show thin affection, we say here. I'd rather traffic in luxuries. But you need it. Ah!" They wheeled into a long carriageway, circling a grand lawn and ending up in front of four majestic columns. Uniformed porters trotted out; a moment later, Sophie felt the weight of the carriage shift as their bags—Cly's luggage, mostly, as she'd been reduced to a mere handful of things—were unloaded.

She followed her birth father upstairs.

Cly's idea of a cozy family suite was typically palatial. A young man was busily engaged in the dining room, laying out cold meats and fruit for a self-serve lunch. Beyond him, she spied what looked suspiciously like a real bathroom.

"Does that have running water?"

"Of course, Kir. Cold and hot," the young man said.

"Sold!" She all but ran inside, taking advantage of the shower to freshen up—and to get a little distance from Cly.

Once she was clean, dry, and again dressed in the sport suit, she shook away the urge to hide. "Bull by the horns, face the music, run into the guns . . . whatever it is they say in these situations," she muttered to a steam-hazed mirror reflection that reminded her a little of the wood fright.

Emerging, she found her birth father in a small parlor, ramrod-straight in a chair and thumbing through a thick hardcover with an unreadable title. He had a small contraption arranged between his right hand and the reading table and was pressing it up and down in a complicated series of slow motions. The device offered resistance, stretching one finger after another and kneading the muscles of his hand. Some kind of physiotherapy gadget, Sophie deduced.

He switched it to the other hand. "Feeling refreshed?"

Sophie nodded, casting about for a neutral topic. "This place must have ten bedrooms."

"I will be obliged to invite my awful cousin Fenn and her family," he said.

"Why?"

He glimmered at her.

"For the wedding, I imagine." Garland appeared at the door, back on his feet, trailing a porter clutching an anemic-looking carpet bag.

Sophie blushed and discovered a sudden need to serve herself a plate of peaches. "Are your feet all right?"

"Scorched," he said. "Sore."

"Get off them, Parrish," Cly said. "As for my family, I doubt the Fenns will come to your bonding, but social niceties require that I'm waiting with open arms."

Of course. Cly would march them right up to the altar—assuming there was an altar—just for the pleasure of seeing her admit the engagement had been a bluff.

She had to get Kev freed and get them out of here.

She looked across the table at Garland. He gave the porter a coin, closing the door behind him. Then he walked—his gait was off, almost mincing—to the lunch table and sat. Helping himself to a slice of smoked fish, he ate with every appearance of serenity. Was he angry about this situation? There was no sign.

"We have a good deal to accomplish in a short space of days," Cly said. "Your renaming—"

"Kev's too," she said.

Cly looked surprised.

"I need to talk to some spellscribes," she said. "Beatrice cast a whole bunch of spells on me at birth, and she doesn't even know what one of them does."

"Sophie is already into the pain," Garland added.

"Damn Beatrice and her impulsive heart," Cly said, sliding his physiotherapy gadget into a velvet bag. "It's a full day's work, then. Will you dine?"

She shook her head.

"We'll leave once you've eaten, Parrish."

"First things first. I have to go bully Kev," Sophie said.

"I'll enjoy witnessing that," Cly said.

"You're not invited."

"You don't know where he is," Cly said, bowing and opening the door for her.

"You won't tell me?"

He made for the stairwell. "Washing dishes in the hotel across the yard."

"At . . . you said the Black Fox?"

"This, the Mancellor, is a hotel for foreigners and abolitionists. It excludes the bonded and derives no benefit from free labor," he said. "You're not permitted to keep Lidman at the Mancellor, so you also have rooms, and quarters for your *property,* across the courtyard."

It was a short walk around a keyhole-shaped courtyard, but Sophie was brought up short by the sign, which had a black fox and a familiar-looking symbol—the paw print from her mystery scroll.

"Is that a fox paw?" she said, trying to be casual.

"Black foxes," he said. "Unusual creatures. The mothers will sometimes feed or even suckle an orphaned raccoon or, more commonly, a weasel. The creature thus sheltered becomes a member of their family group. Raccoons, you know—those hands."

"They take slaves," she said, her mind chasing this in four directions at once.

Cly shrugged and continued toward the hotel.

They found Kev scrubbing floors under the supervision of a female staffer who seemed to be specifically designated as a sort of domestic overseer. Seeing Sophie, Kev stood and attempted a brave smile. "It's not so bad, Kir."

There was something in his attitude, a shift, that brought the hairs up on her arms. He'd been afraid, before she took custody of him—desperate to avoid execution. Aboard *Nightjar,* when he'd believed his pals would free him, he'd seemed relaxed, almost happy. When she told him they'd been ringers, he'd freaked out.

Now . . . what was this?

"You said a big lizard man attacked you, Kev, when you were all hiding under the lifeboat?"

"It had a blade," he said. "It pulled Daimon away, down—fast. Then it came for me, but Selwig . . . Selwig wouldn't let it."

"Tell me about the blade."

"Metal. Silver in color, or near it." He shuddered. "Horribly sharp. Like nothing I've seen."

She changed direction, watching him closely. "I'm filing papers or whatever to rename you today." *Here we are, stuck between the train and Superman,* she thought. "You want to suggest a new name, you better do it now."

"What was it you suggested? Bambi McThumper? It doesn't matter."

"I've got to have you pacified," she said. "It's the only way to legally release you."

"It's all right." The desperation she'd seen before seemed to be gone. "I don't want to hurt . . ."

"Kev?"

"Hurt anyone. Anyone *else,* Selwig would have said."

A definite note of guilt there, and one she did believe. But he was hiding something, too. . . .

She rocked back on her heels, taking him in. There was little to see. In his smock and the horrible pewter-colored bangle that marked him as property, *her* property, he was stripped of all context.

What did she know? He'd come from Haversham, Sylvanna's big rival, but had gone to study on Tug Island. He'd been the magical equivalent of a child psychologist, someone who'd written spells to amend the behavior of disturbed kids.

He and his buddies had forced some of his patients to find and destroy shackling scrolls, and then helped the slaves thus freed.

He'd put to sea in that ship, *Incannis,* that made salt frights. He'd done it for friendship as much as idealism.

He wasn't a fighter by nature.

Stress made him hungry.

Her scrutiny was making him nervous.

"It's fatalism," she said. "Suddenly it's like you don't want to live. You could've stayed in Fleet and gotten beheaded, if that was where this was going to take you."

"I thought my friends would rescue me, remember?"

"Yeah, and they were the bad guys. Sucks to be you. My offer still stands. I'll pacify you so I can free you. And if I can protect you, I will."

"And in exchange?"

"The truth would be nice. Do you have info they want? Or did they have some other reason for grabbing you?"

He fiddled with the scrub brush. "My friend Eame, he knew things. Knew people. I don't know where Nysa is or anyone who does, and nobody's coming for me. You say Pree and Smitt were spies for Isle of Gold, looking to destroy us. Well, we're destroyed now. All dead."

"Why did Selwig tell us to behead you?"

"I'd got him killed—reason enough."

Liar, she thought. "Clearly, they still want something. Why won't you let me help you?"

"Mistress, nobody can."

"*Incannis* got caught. The attempt to sink *Constitution* failed. What's next?"

He shook his head.

"Fine. Tell me about Pree and Smitt."

He shook his head.

"I could make you."

He looked her up and down. "You won't, Kir. You haven't got it in you to subjugate a man, however depraved you may think him."

"No," Cly's voice made them both jump. "Sophie is a generous and uncommonly forgiving individual." Kev began to bow, but Cly caught him under the chin, just with a finger. "The bonded don't bow."

Kev straightened. His eyes fell on Cly's sword.

"As long as Sophie is here on Sylvanna, she will obey the law to the letter," Cly said. "Perhaps reluctantly, perhaps in a fury."

"Cly, don't terrorize him."

He ignored her. "You've endangered her twice. It would please me to wring every drop of blood that she shed when they inscribed her, every drop, *slave,* from your still-beating heart."

"Cly."

"Whatever scheme she hopes to engage in on your behalf, to salve her conscience, it depends on her not putting a foot out of place. If she does misstep—when—I shall swoop in, accuse her of fraud, and assume custody of you."

There was that assumption again, that she'd break the law or that damned oath the first chance she got.

"Your Honor, I beg—"

"The law requires Sophie to register you," Cly said, in a pleasant tone. "I'm taking her to the office now, where she will do precisely that. You will be licensed and, apparently, pacified."

"And then?"

"Then you may enjoy her gentle semblance of ownership for as long as it takes me to find a legal pretext for wresting custody of you from her unwilling grip." He gave Kev a smile that would have frozen the sun. "Unless, perhaps, you'd like to give us the particulars of your colleagues' scheme against Sylvanna?"

Kev was visibly terrified. Yet, with an effort, he shook his head.

"So be it." With that, Cly summoned the hotel supervisor to once again take charge of Kev, before escorting Sophie back through the opulent lobby of the Black Fox and into the courtyard. The paving stones had been heavily salted against ice, creating a pocked expanse of stone, salt, and meltwater.

"You're right about him. I have seen men with that same look," he remarked. "They believe they will die, that there's no way out."

"Where to now?" she asked.

"Over there . . ." A carriage draped in Fleet and judiciary livery was waiting for them. Its driver was a cheery-looking woman, ample-bottomed and dressed in a sports jacket and top hat. The horses were bays, tall geldings whose manes had been artificially dyed with a single streak of spruce blue.

Garland was waiting in the carriage.

Sophie looked at Cly in surprise.

"Two affianced make one adult, remember? Your betrothed must also sign Lidman's various papers."

Oh, crap. Now I've really gotten Garland into slave ownership.

They rode in suffocating silence through the blue marble streets.

There's no getting out of this, Sophie told herself. *I don't do the paperwork, Cly will just take over. Kev's a convicted criminal, and he chose this sentence. It's just a prisoner transfer . . . just a transfer.*

What does Garland think of all this, of me?

The carriage paused at the edge of the city, waiting on a uniformed gatekeeper, who opened ornately carved wooden panels that hid the entrance to a hundred-foot archway of stone. Within, Sophie saw an enormous cylindrical compound, cut like a giant core sample from the stone of the mountain. Its rim was limned in icicles, huge stalactites that dripped water down the edges of the cylinder and fed a series of lakes and streams about five hundred feet below.

Buildings rose from the ground, some of them more than a dozen stories high. Clad in blue-white wood—more spruce, she assumed—they tapered to points at the top, like icicles.

"This is the heart of the Winter capital, Hoarfrost," Cly said.

"And, I'm guessing, the Spellscrip Institute?" Sophie asked.

Cly nodded.

Their driver left them near the top, at a walkway that yawned over the chasm, connecting the outer rim of the cut-stone cylinder to the tallest of the buildings. An ordinary-enough elevator carried them down and Cly led them into the compound, threading his way over bridges and paths to a comparatively nondescript building—the bondage registry.

Even at home, the registry's decor would have screamed government office—blue spruce shakes on its walls, plain waiting room within. As was his way, Cly sashayed past twenty or so Sylvanners waiting to transact their business and demanded an immediate audience with a registration clerk. He got it, too. Within a minute they were in a private office, with a bureaucrat at their beck and call.

"It is traditional to name convicts after their victims," Cly said, proffering a page.

Sophie took the pen and wrote KEV EAME LIDMAN.

The clerk whipped through the rest of the document. Then, to her surprise, he slid an entirely different page under her nose.

"The Spellscrip Institute would like to purchase the aforementioned bonded individual."

It was another big number; she was familiar enough with the Sylvanner currency, the akro, that she didn't have to ask anyone to confirm it. She pushed it away with a shake of her head and a smile that she hoped was polite.

The clerk did not react. "Will you scrip him fully compliant?"

"Fully what? Like, my every wish is his command?"

"He has been withholding information from you," Cly pointed out.

"Forget it," she said. "Except for the violence thing, we're leaving him with free will."

"Very well," the clerk said. "A pacification spell?"

She looked to Garland and spoke in English. "Can you see any other way?"

If he minded being rude by excluding Cly, it didn't show. "He gave permission, did he not?"

"Twice."

"If he is incapable of provoking violence, it might actually make him safer. A landholder might attack him here, then claim he started the fight."

"Seriously?"

"Sophie, we are responsible for him," he said. "He may yet hurt someone. There's a chance he killed Daimon and Selwig. There's no legal possibility of release if he's not rendered harmless, and whether he's an idealist or not, Kev's predicament is of his own making. You and I cannot continue in perpetual ownership over a murderer."

"Agreed." She nodded at the clerk. "Okay, do it."

Once the notes were made for that, she asked, "Is there a form to fill out for freeing someone?"

The clerk looked as though he was prepared for this, and handed over a big envelope. She glanced inside: six pages of dense handwriting in Sylvanner.

"Is there a version written in Fleet?"

"No," Cly purred.

"I don't suppose you're going to help translate."

"Would you trust me to steer you aright?"

"I might."

"It would please me to think so, daughter."

More games. Annoyed, she pocketed the pages.

Cly gave the hotel address to the clerk, demanded a big carved key of blue-tinged stonewood, and led them out across another walkway, through a tunnel to the surface of the mountain. He unlocked a gate, using the key, and led them into a gated park.

"There's a bit of a walk here, Captain," he said. "How are your feet?"

"The medics' salves are effective, Your Honor," Garland said. "I can walk on flat terrain without much discomfort."

Cly's estate on the southeast coast of Sylvanna had been a mixture of orchard and swamp: lowlands, apiaries, peaches, crocodiles, and a particularly toxic species of leech. Here, the microclimate was alpine forest: drier, with abundant evergreen trees, hardy stock adapted to lower temperatures and a bit of altitude.

At home, these would be the Great Smoky Mountains, Sophie thought. There should be lungless salamanders in these forests . . . But no; the air seemed too dry.

The trees were busy as a preschool. She saw young adult owls in a number of the trees, sleeping off the night's hunt while lazily watching the forest floor for rodents. Songbirds squabbled in the understory.

They passed the picked-over carcass of an elk and a limestone stalagmite that had been embedded just off the path, in the shade of a pair of spruce. It was covered in sluggish blue butterflies. Sophie reached automatically for her camera, remembered it had sunk with *Nightjar,* and felt a stab of grief.

The butterflies were dying. The spruce above were dotted with eggs, and the butterflies, their laying finished, were waiting for the cold to finish them off. A woven basket below hinted at the purpose for the stalagmite that had lured them—the Spellscrip Institute was collecting the bodies.

Farther up the trail was another collector of sorts: a massive wooden platform, towering skyward.

"Bat roost?" Garland asked.

"They migrate," Cly confirmed. "And pause here. Some few are too weak to continue the journey. Those, we capture and tame."

One of Sylvanna's major industries was writing and discovering spells . . . and, when they could, acquiring species that weren't quite native to their microclimate.

"We're being sued over the platforms," Cly said. "The people of Murdocco say the bats wouldn't pause here if they weren't encouraged. They'd have us tear the platforms down and pretend the bats aren't perfectly capable of roosting in the trees and caves."

Sophie didn't take the bait. It might be possible to prove whether the bats were or weren't behaving naturally, but she wasn't going to get involved in another Sylvanner lawsuit.

"Captain, the ground becomes difficult here, but there's a bench ahead," Cly said.

"Thank you, Your Honor."

The trail forked back on itself, revealing the base of a cut-stone staircase so steep it would have daunted Frodo and Sam. A wrought-iron bench was set in place to offer a view of the core-sample layout of the Institute, with its icicle-shaped buildings.

"Parrish?" Cly gestured to the bench.

Garland sat without arguing.

"Cly, why are we here?"

"For the renaming."

She had assumed that would require another government office.

He produced a wrinkled page. "Some old family names."

She scanned it. "Eugenia. Pels. Kalotte, Merina, Stayz, Clyonna, Ammonna, Harlot—Harlot?"

"It means 'nurturer.' Why?"

"No reason. Do I have to choose one of these?"

He shook his head. "Of course not. Choose anything you like. It's who you are, after all."

Who I am. The thought felt heavy and cold, like a wet towel after a chilly swim. *Lucky-fertile-cute. Clever-persuasive and . . . and something to do with a fox that adopts raccoons.* "I threatened to name Kev Bambi. Maybe I should call myself Thumper."

"Don't martyr yourself to that odious man."

"You don't know him."

"I know he threatened you and seeks to start a war."

You stuck me with him. Cly would just play innocent if she accused him. "What's this name—Melia?"

"It means 'contrary,'" he said.

"Contrary." That at least captured their relationship. "Melia it is."

Cly inclined his head, handing the page to Garland. "We will be an hour or more."

"Understood." Garland caught Sophie's hand, looking straight into her eyes in that way that made her weak at the knees. Keeping up the pretense that they were engaged?

No, he wasn't that kind of a person.

"We will sail through this storm," he said. She felt a rush of heat to her face. Here he was, consoling her, when she was the one who got his ship sunk and his feet burned.

Contrary, she thought. *Calamity.*

"Daughter?" Cly said. "After you?"

They began to climb.

The vertical climb was about two hundred feet, and just steep enough to excuse her from trying to converse. It required concentration, but the stone was dry and the steps well maintained; in good weather, they weren't truly dangerous.

They came out on bare blue stone. Sophie glanced around, hoping to sample a loose fragment of the shale, but saw nothing nearby. They were on the edge of a cliff overlooking the city and, beyond and below, the sea. The cylindrical bore of the Spellscrip Institute was invisible from here, folded into the crags.

The rocks were smooth and had a scrubbed look. There was no moss in the cracks, no little profusions of wildflowers, no discarded insect casings or spruce needles. The distance between the cliff's drop-off and the beginning of the trees was about ten feet—a generous stretch of path. The trees themselves were close-planted into a hedge; spruce branches matted together into a solid wall of needles, an impenetrable barrier. Their trunks were wound around with a thorny vine studded with white berries and pale yellow flowers.

"Are you going to tell me where we're going?"

"It's a temple. Children are named here."

"Temple. There's a religious element to it?"

He showed his teeth, forcing his face into an approximation of his usual, open expression, and nodded.

Religion, she thought. Another Stormwrack thing that varied from nation to nation. Another interesting line of inquiry she hadn't been able to dig into. If your people could work magic, what did you worship?

What constitutes a miracle on a world where you make mermaids out of broken-backed children?

They ran out of cliff, and the stone trail curved inland, the wall of trees clearing into a corridor, the trunks rising up soldier-straight to a height of about thirty feet, then bending to meet in a peak like a cathedral window. About every ten feet there was one tree that didn't bend; it left a gap in the roof, a skylight through which she could see a glimpse of blue.

It got colder as they walked. By the time they came out of the corridor, they were leaving prints in a three-inch fall of powdery snow.

They were descending now, Sophie noted, through an ever-frostier corridor of trees. The forest was unusually quiet, but for their steps and breath and one steady, pulsing—

Oh.

Cly's hair-trigger senses went off as the recognition gelled within her. "What's wrong?"

"Nothing," she said. *At least, I hope it's nothing.*

"Lying is beneath you," he said, and the strain in his voice was obvious.

"It's just . . . I've been having this weird symptom. Sounds, or like having someone tap me behind the ear. Tap, tap, tap. Or . . . like shocks in the air, very faint, that I'm feeling on my skin." She stopped there. Everything she'd said was true, and she didn't want to get into eragliding and her newfound ability to hear the Worldclock.

"Since when?"

Since Bettona fed me those anise biscuits. "It's a long story, Cly. But it might mean someone—this woman Pree, possibly—is nearby. She's involved with Gale's murder, and everything that's happened since."

His face grew serious. "Let's hurry."

They picked up the pace, stepping out, ten minutes later, into a bowl of moss and pine needles, and soft furze, developing, over time, into a carpet of soil laid over the unyielding stone. The cleared circle was walled with trees, but these were divided into four quadrants, with corridors between them, and two streams—one steaming, one filled with chunks of ice—flowing to the bottom and vanishing into the leaf litter.

There was a stand of willows just breaking into spring leaves to the right of the ice-limned spruce, and then, moving clockwise from that, an orchard whose trees were laden with fruit at peak season, peaches so ripe she could smell them. Last was a stand of maples in full, glorious autumn red and yellow.

Winter, spring, summer, and autumn, she thought.

Four people came out of the trees to meet them. A naked, knobby-kneed boy of about eleven years slipped between two willows, pushing them aside like curtains as a woman Sophie's age ambled out of the peach orchard. A man in his forties or fifties, just going to gray and resembling Cly himself, stepped around the autumn maples. Crossing the ice of the stream, meanwhile, was a crone in black, so aged she looked like a mummy.

"*Calle Izt*?" the crone rasped.

Of course. They wouldn't speak Fleet.

Cly, to her surprise, dropped to his knees. He uttered a short phrase, the only word of which she caught was *patter.*

Father.

Should she kneel? He didn't seem to think so.

Tick, tick, tick. She shuddered. How far had she been from the pocket watch in San Francisco when the ticking stopped? Two miles?

The crone made her bone-clicky way to Cly, letting her skeletal fingers trickle through his hair and then over his face. Her expression was haughty, disdainful. She made a sepulchral clicking noise—*tsk, tsk*—and began to shake her head.

Cly let out a rush of words, and she backhanded him with shocking force. The blow brought him off his knees and tumbled him halfway down the bowl.

"Hey!" Sophie protested.

"Don't interfere," Cly ordered. He was fixed on the old lady. "We must do as they ask."

Not liking the looks of this, suddenly.

The crone gestured to the child, who came and took Sophie's hand. He pressed it to his ear.

"*Teck, teck, teck,*" he whispered, in time to the shock rhythm on her skin. "*Est vere. Verdanii metchen.*"

Sophie tried to memorize the words.

The four strangers looked at one another, consulting silently. Cly rolled up onto his seat and dabbed at his mouth with a handkerchief.

Consensus seemed to sweep through the quartet. The peach woman came and put an arm around Sophie. She smelled of freshly mown hay and flowers. Sophie found herself thinking of Garland, and not in a chaste way, as the woman drew her toward the orchard.

"*Resteh,*" she said, urging Sophie to sit. She didn't relinquish her grip . . . and Sophie didn't delude herself that she'd let her go.

She met the woman's eyes, and the ill-timed lust got worse.

What was the word for "dad" again? She whispered, "*Patter?*"

The woman patted Sophie's hair. "Shh."

At a gesture from the autumn man, Cly got to his feet and descended to the bottom of the bowl, coming to stand in the pool, his feet disappearing into a scrim of fallen needles, maple leaves, flowers, and chunks of ice. He brushed at the litter on the pond's edge, revealing a quartet of statue hands, reaching up from underground.

Like zombies digging their way out of the grave, Sophie thought. One of the hands was made of supple-looking greenwood. Another was thorny and dry, like blackberry cane, and a third was stone. The fourth was skeletal.

Cly examined them all before choosing the stone hand. He took it as though he was shaking hands. It moved, clasping him in return. The summer woman chose that moment to tuck her hand into Sophie's, making it eerily as though she was involved in all of this, somehow.

Cly straightened, drawing the hand with him. Its stone wrist tapered to a point, and a slender stem bound it to the ground.

The old woman muttered a few words.

Cly looked at Sophie. "I'm directed to tell you now how I've failed you, as a parent."

His words cut through her growing sense of drowsiness and arousal. "Failed?"

"Shh!" Peach girl's arms tightened around her.

Cly continued. "I failed by marrying in contravention of our beliefs, by accepting a union that could end in divorce. I failed to pursue Beatrice after she left me, and failed by letting you go to the outlands to be fostered by strangers like a raccoon in a fox den. I failed by allowing you to come to this world unprepared—"

This all had an air of confession—confession and penance—that Sophie wasn't liking. She tried to shake free of Summer's iron grip. "What are you guys gonna do?"

"Your lost name, your disconnection from your people, your lamentable beliefs—" Here, a quirk of a smile. Was he teasing?

The old woman growled.

"If you guys are gonna hurt him, I'd just as soon—"

"You are into the pain, Sophie, and entirely exposed. This, too, I take upon myself," Cly said.

"Stop!" she said.

The pool at his feet erupted into a geyser, a vertical thrust of water that engulfed Cly, ripping him off his feet, hurling him into the air. The only thing anchoring him to the ground was his grip on the stone hand, with its thin stem acting as a tether. *Steam and ice, and the rock hand must be slippery,* Sophie thought, as the tears came. She tried again to get out of the peach woman's grip and failed.

Her birth father was completely upside down, now, Superman in a dive, pointed down fist-first and struggling to bring his other arm down to protect his head as chunks of ice within the geyser pelted him.

All he could do was hang on. Was that it? How long would they expect him to endure?

The ice had given way to hunks of mud, spattering fists pounding against Cly's body, and then, after an eternity, the water clarified and began to steam.

Cly bared his teeth and clenched his eyes shut, turning away from the heat.

"Stop! You're scalding him! Stop!"

Then it was slush, creeping up around his hand, which was still impossibly clenched—

Clenched in hers, and ice cold. She felt ice crystallizing around her wrist and lower palm, and the grip of his fingers around hers, warm and impossibly strong. She closed her eyes, breathing, imagining being on a rock face and holding a rope, just keeping her grip.

She closed out everything but that sense of hanging on. Her hand and arm ached; her shoulder felt as though it might pull out of its socket.

Words thrummed through the clearing: "Zophie Opal Meliadottar Hansa—"

The crone's voice filled her ears, and then, impossibly, she was kneeling at the edge of the pool and Cly was within, sputtering. Drowning?

They were holding hands.

She got to her feet, braced, and pulled him up and out. He was soaked to the skin, shivering. A bruise was coming out on his cheek.

"Don't fret, child," he said, in a voice far too thready to allay her distress.

"You didn't say there'd be an ordeal!"

"What difference would it have made?" he asked. "But that I should have had to drag you up that incline by force?"

She had no answer for that.

He sat heavily on the leaf litter and peeled off his shirt, rolling the fabric tight to wring it out.

"Where's that handkerchief?" He handed her the sodden square of fabric. "I've broken some stitches on my shoulder. Would you?"

"Sure." She found the water feeding from the hot spring, cleared the floating refuse, and soaked and heated the handkerchief. Then she pressed it to the gash. "Dueling wound?"

He nodded, rolling the shirt out and beginning to pick bits of spruce off of it. "Next time we do this, I shall bring a change of clothes."

"Let's not have a next time."

"Agreed. How's the ticking? Gone?"

"Uh . . ." She stretched out her free hand. "Fainter. Further away. Maybe we left whoever-it-is behind, or maybe they weren't following us."

"Perhaps your betrothed turned them back."

Garland. She swallowed. It was odd and overwhelming, Cly half-clothed and all his many scars on display.

"How's the bleeding?"

Right. Stay on task. She glanced under the handkerchief. "Not much. It was mostly healed."

"Tsk," he said, looking regretfully at the shirt before shrugging free of her and working his way into the garment.

He did look a mess, there was no denying it.

"I didn't know you'd have to go through that."

"It might have been worse," he said, cheerfully. "I'd heard rumors of an ordeal involving open flame."

"You're pyrophobic?"

"*Psychoanalysis. Pyrophobic.*" A weary grin. "These atomist words of yours."

"It just means afraid of fire."

"I'm going to regret telling you that, one day," he predicted.

She found herself smiling, and then froze up, remembering the reasons why relaxing around Cly was a bad idea.

"Why did you? Tell me?"

"Why should you not know?" he said. "You're a good person, Sophie. I have no reason to fear you."

She rolled that over, thinking she shouldn't have mixed feelings about it. "Is it tied to the spell your parents had worked on you? The one to stop you setting fires?"

"Create the fear, stop the behavior." His lip curled. "Same type of magic your Kev used to practice. Caging the mind, limiting one's ability to choose . . ."

As I just did with Kev himself, she thought uncomfortably. "Are you ready to go?"

"Not quite now; I'm yet a little shaken." Cly flexed his knees. Then he added, "I wish you would explain what it is that has so marred your trust in me."

"Cly—" She felt a stronger than usual compulsion to answer him.

"On my oath, Sophie, I will answer any question you put to me. This is a holy place. Nobody would dare lie here."

"Really? Anything?"

He would get her talking, and then he'd ask her something . . . and she had secrets, too.

"I got myself soaked and encrusted in filth for you," he said. "What's an interrogation to that?"

"You are such a fashion victim," she said.

He gave her a faint grin as he tried to comb out his hair.

Manipulative. He knows you feel bad about the ordeal and he's trying to work his way into your good graces.

Wise or not, the temptation to know overcame her, as it always did. "Was it you who told Kev he could ask me to claim him?"

"Clever girl. I arranged for someone on *Docket* to tell him."

"Why?"

"Buying him at auction would have been prohibitive, even if he hadn't opted to take the blade."

"Seriously."

"I believe as you do. The voyage of the *Incannis* was part of some greater scheme against the Cessation. Kev is a piece in a political gambit whose endgame is the breaking of the Fleet. If we can hold him for a time, and truly see his nature, we can bring this plan to light."

"Why not ask me to help, instead of being all Machiavellian?"

"Ah. That brings us back nicely to the issue of the discord between us."

Us. And maybe there was a spell in play here, or his suggesting it had some kind of psychosomatic effect, but it felt wrong not to clear the air. "Okay, here it is. Do you fuck your slaves?"

Cly froze, with his fingers in his hair. It was the move of a stalking cat who'd heard a noise and stopped to threat-assess. He turned to face her squarely, swallowed, and said, softly, dangerously, "I hadn't thought your opinion of me was quite that bad."

She stood her ground. He'd gone out late one night, she knew that, and one of the kitchen slaves had been in hysterics the next day. And there had to be owners—her stomach turned as she remembered that category included herself now—who did it. "You're saying no?"

"Part of me is tempted to reply as you did when I learned about your sordid liaison with that Tiladene: 'Who I sleep with is none of your business.'"

"Not the same thing. Are you raping your slaves, Cly? Yes or no?"

If he was faking his hurt, someone should put him onstage. "No. I find the idea repugnant."

She believed him. There was no great reason to, sacred grove or not, but a surge of relief overtook her. "Okay. So, no then. Um, thank you."

"I have nothing to hide."

But she did, didn't she? And she was bad enough at lying as it was.

Fortunately, Cly still had father-daughter relations on his mind. "You'd cooled to me before we got to Low Bann. When did you take to wondering—" His face twisted in disgust. "There's something else."

She thought for a second. "There's no question I can ask about the other thing."

"There is 'another thing,' though?"

"I can try to explain, but it'll take a while," she said. "How about on the walk back? You're getting cold, and we have to get down those steps."

"Agreed." He opened and closed his hand around the pommel of his sword, checking his grip. "After you."

She looked at the snow and ice. "We can't take one of the other ways down?"

"They lead to the other Spellscrip Institutes," he said. "Far from Winter."

Wow. Teleportation? You go in there and come out near Low Bann?

Why not? Verena can travel in time, or between dimensions. All those timepieces containing slivers of the Worldclock; she just bops between them.

"Okay," she said. They crunched through the snow—Cly actually picked up a handful and let his hand cool in it. "So, pyrophobia—"

"Fear of fire."

"It's an example of a kind of . . . mental disorder. Very minor."

"Yes," he agreed. And then, doing the math: "You fear I'm *mad*?"

She gave him a sideways glance. "There's a condition. At home, we call it sociopathy. People with it are disconnected from a lot of their emotions. They aren't good at empathy. Do you know what empathy is?"

"Understanding and sharing the feelings of others."

"Sociopaths take advantage of people, and often they're quite charming . . ."

"Social grace as a sign of madness." He rolled that over. "You're saying I playact some of my feelings?"

Seas, he was quick! "A lot of sociopaths are scam artists. Some make out all right in corporate environments, where ruthlessness pays."

"I'm not sure I appreciate being lumped in with criminals and devious pencil pushers."

She drew a big breath. In a way, it was harder to say because he seemed so incredibly unconcerned. "Some are homicidal. Some are . . . you'd say monstrous."

He burst out laughing. "Ah, I see. I kill a few bandits on *Incannis* and you decide I'm not only unbalanced but intractably wicked."

"That's just it. You're laughing off killing."

"They endangered my ship, my cadets, and my only child." He shrugged. "Does defending my ground make me a . . . sociopath?"

"There are . . . signs." It sounded ridiculous. It sounded like pseudoscience. "Those fires you set as a kid—"

"Oh, Sophie," he said. "This is an outlander superstition, and you'll have to look past it. I am a warrior born. It's my nature. I use it for the good of my nation and the Fleet. I keep the peace, child!"

"You're not taking me seriously."

"No," he agreed. "Frankly, I'm relieved. And speaking of manipulative, you've managed to get us out of the sacred grove before I could ask if you truly mean to marry that man Parrish."

"We've had enough truth for one afternoon."

"Perhaps," he agreed, in infuriating good humor now.

Their progress down the stone steps was slow; Cly was bruised, moving slowly. Sophie glanced at the angle of the sun. They'd kept Garland waiting for over two hours.

He seemed content enough, breaking into a dazzling smile as they descended, and she saw he had been collecting what he could—he had a little pile of insect casings, yellow flower petals, and one small black pebble for her.

"It's not much," he said, holding it out. "But this wing is interesting."

She kissed him. For Cly, she told herself. For show. Seas, it felt good. "You see anyone while you waited?"

"I heard someone further down," he said. "Light-footed and nimble, from the sound of their steps. They took another path."

"Come, children," Cly said airily. "Let's get you home. Lots of figures to dance before your big day."

They hiked back into the Winter Spellscrip Institute, this time coming out within a structure whose interior walls were plated in white stone—quartz?—worked to resemble ice crystals, snowflakes, and blooms of frost. There, Sophie left a query about fright inscriptions and anything employing cats' claws.

"If you'll both wait here," Cly said, vanishing down a corridor.

"It ended up being Meliadottar," she murmured in Garland's ear, while they were waiting.

He nodded. "Understood."

His own middle name had been lost at birth. Sophie had yet to get the whole story on that, but Tonio had unearthed the name recently and had shared it with Sophie. Burdened her, was how he had put it, and he'd sworn her to secrecy.

Garland hadn't had so much as a tooth-straightening spell.

"What is it?"

"Just thinking—you're all you. You're untouched."

He shook his head. "Our elders lay intentions on us in all sorts of ways. What we make of their gifts, whether we can cut ourselves free of their wishes and intentions . . . some say it depends entirely on circumstance, nature, and our own choices."

"Some?"

"I fear, in some ways, it's an impossible task."

How can I know my nature when I've been molded from the start? He'd have an answer to that, too, but it wouldn't help, and she was too emotionally exhausted to put the question to him.

She felt herself droop a little, and then, before he could be concerned or comforting, she turned it into a stretch, bending, taking a couple of deep breaths. It was calming . . . for all of a second. Then the earworm started up again: *tick, tick, tick*.

"Sophie?"

"Someone's here," she said. "The other eraglider."

"Pree?"

She nodded. "The clock sounds tiny, like a wristwatch. Someone made off with a few slivers of the Worldclock."

"This person is nearby?"

"Within a couple miles."

Garland looked around. "There must be thousands of people in this complex."

Cly turned up then, in a cloak that somewhat concealed his bedraggled state. "The carriage is here," he said. "The scribes will contact us when they've looked over the papers and completed the work."

They passed through a corridor lit by spectacular chandeliers of quartz and candlelight, coming out into a lane where the carriage, with its blue-maned bay horses, was indeed waiting.

A twenty-minute ride took them into the city. Sophie looked over the series of samples Garland had given her. He was right about the patch of wing. There was also a scale—from a reptile, she assumed, but the scale was large. If it was a snake, it was a big one.

Did they have dragons here on Stormwrack? They had harpies of sorts, altered humans with wings long enough to carry them aloft. And those mermaids . . .

As she considered the possibilities, she continued to scan the streets and pathways, looking for Verdanii eragliders. Instead, she saw someone familiar disembarking from a carriage ahead of them.

Cly, as usual, sensed her reaction. "Rees Erminne and his mother," he said. They were with a woman clad in white, her face covered with a wafting assortment of veils. Rees and the veiled woman wore the crimson sash of the engaged, just as Sophie and Garland did. "Fralienne found someone to marry her boy at last. Foreigner, from the look of her. Perhaps from Gellada?"

Sophie found herself blushing. She'd gotten the idea, a few months ago, that Cly was trying to marry her to Rees. She'd tried put a pin in that by declaring, during a full-bore society event, that she was promiscuous.

Garland saw that, she remembered.

She said, "So it's not on, you and Rees's mother?"

"Politics sailed beyond us. *Sawtooth* playing host to Annela Gracechild . . . We may have kept the Havers from firing upon *Nightjar,* but the forces against continued union of the Fleet have been making much of the event. I cannot afford to flout society's conventions again—not too obviously, in any case. Fralienne and her abolitionist allies have, therefore, evolved a new strategy."

"She's running for governor of Autumn, isn't she?"

He nodded. "And so Rees needs must marry."

"Politics and business," Sophie murmured.

"It's past time," Cly said. "He's long been too old to remain childish."

Rees and his mother had freed all their slaves, and were land rich and cash poor as a result. Cly had been considering an alliance with them, much to his family's distress. The Banning estate was run by unpaid laborers, slaves who maintained apiaries and picked orchards, and a dozen household servants. If he had divested . . .

Cly had let Sophie think it was all for her—that he'd hook up with Fralienne and throw all his family retainers to the wind, just because Sophie was dead set against slavery.

But was that likely?

Before she could ask, they'd reached the hotel.

"I need to have my stitches seen to," Cly said. "You've got time to change and eat."

"Eat before what?"

But he'd gone on ahead, striding through the lobby and bounding up the staircase.

Garland helped her out of the carriage. "I'm sure he's dying to get out of those wet breeches."

"Would you promise me something?"

"Anything," he said, without a second's hesitation.

She felt a little flutter. "I was just going to say that, if you're ever facing an ordeal, don't hide it from me."

"I promise." He nodded. "You too."

"What would I go through? Renewing my driver's license?"

"Nevertheless . . ."

"I promise," she said, and the words felt weighty, more momentous than the Fleet oath. They were holding hands.

Whatever might have happened next was interrupted by a discreet cough. Krispos was waiting at the gate to greet them.

"Were you with Kev?" Sophie asked.

"Yes. The pacification took hold about an hour ago. I'd got him some ostrich from the Mancellor . . . He nearly choked, spitting it up."

"He's ill?" Garland said.

"He can't eat flesh anymore," Sophie reminded him.

"No, he's ill," Krispos said. "I think that Kev may be well into the pain."

Sophie flashed on the coppery flavor of her gums bleeding. "Has a doctor seen him?"

"Yes, I sent for one," Krispos said. "He may be abed a few days. It'll get him out of scrubbing floors."

"I should go—" *And do what? Apologize?*

"I left him sleeping," Krispos said. "The concierge will send a messenger when he wakes."

Sophie sagged against the gate, letting her head fall into her hands. "He's no better off than he was a month ago. We're just dragging out the suffering."

Garland said, "We may yet find a way, once he's free, to get Kev to refuge."

She shook her head, trying to extricate herself from the turmoil of guilt. Failing that, she turned back to Krispos. "Listen, I want you to go to Low Bann. The observer in the turtle case sent copies of our data there, thinking we'd be going to Cly's. And there's other mail. Get it, then go to the Spellscrip Institute and read the stuff Autumn Spell said she'd show us on frightmaking."

"Is that important now?"

"You know, I think it is. I think the frightmaker's . . . crucial to what's happening in Fleet *and* what's happening to Kev. Oh, see how that young cousin of Cly's, Merelda, is doing as a spellscribe apprentice, too. If she's not working out, we might scoop her for the Forensic Institute."

Krispos gave a brisk nod, noting all of it without writing it down. Then, turning pink even before he moved, he put his arms around her in a sudden, tight, and terribly awkward hug. "There's nobody to help Kev, nobody else willing. What you are doing . . . You can't even guess what the Golders might do to him. Even if he has done bad things, terrible, *terrible* things, he doesn't deserve . . ."

Sophie's mouth fell open.

Krispos's words dried up. He pulled away, scarlet-faced, and almost tottered into Garland before fleeing in the direction of the gardens.

"Should I go after him, do you think?"

Garland shook his head. "Let the poor man recover his composure."

They arrived upstairs only steps ahead of a hot dinner—goat stew, heavy with bay leaf, with a juniper chutney on the side, and a barely fermented peach cider to drink. Cly had ordered Garland a white shirt, slacks, and a coat with tails. It was faintly like a tuxedo and went well with the crimson sash. Sophie headed into her room and found a similar outfit, fitted by Cly's tailor, no doubt.

She came out wearing it. "Check out the lady suit. All I need is a top hat."

"Mine fits quite well. His Honor has an eye for clothes."

"I was just calling him a fashion whore. Question is, what's it for?"

"Cohabitation class." Cly appeared, washed and dressed and presumably newly restitched. He was toweling his salt-and-pepper hair briskly.

"Excuse me?"

"I can't fling you into marriage unprepared, can I? Custom requires that you be taught certain realities."

"OMG. Is this sex ed?"

"Among other things."

"Cly, you already know I'm—" She ran aground on his amused expression, but bulled on. "You already know I'm sexually active. Half the damned Autumn District knows."

"The better half, to be sure. Marriage is about more than physical intimacy, child. But . . ." He leaned back in a leather chair, not quite hiding a wince. "If you're telling me you aren't serious about this relationship, it's not too late to dissolve it."

"And be not engaged, and not an adult, and let you scoop up Kev."

"Whereupon I should no doubt do something terrifically *sociopathic*—was that the word?—to him."

"That is not funny."

"I am determined to ascertain how Kev fits into the greater scheme against the peace. To put my hand on a moving piece in this game and thereby sweep the board."

"I'm all for winning, but you still don't get to torture him!"

"You shall have to rely on your deductive faculties to stop me."

A glimmer of hope. "If we work it out, you'll let me do as I please with him?"

"Why not?"

"Would you help us get him somewhere safe?"

"You'd need to work something of a wonder for the Cessation if you want me to go that far."

She found herself grinning. "Fair enough. We'll reassemble the crime wall here on this nice big stretch of plaster. Consider the suspects, go through their moves: murdering Gale, trying to disarm *Temperance,* the bandits on *Incannis,* this new scheme. All the stuff."

"No time for that now," Cly said. "The carriage awaits. Here's a tip for the driver."

"Fine." Premarital counseling; putting pressure on. *This is a big game of chicken.* She looked apologetically at Garland, who shrugged.

"Okay, down we go."

The same carriage, with the voluptuous woman and the bays with their streaked manes, was waiting.

"I am sorry about this, Garland."

"No, no. It's possible I'll learn something."

Was he joking?

She leaned forward and called up to the driver. "Do you speak Fleet?"

"Little, Kir."

"We need to go back to that registration office in the Institute tomorrow."

"Must to ask His Honor."

"I thought you were at our disposal."

"His Honor pays me."

"How much for a ride to the registration office?"

"Twenty-two akro, or nine Fleet dollars."

She glanced at Garland.

"My signing privileges would have been put on hold when our Watchbox sank," he said.

"So I not only destroyed your ship, I've reduced you to poverty."

"You mustn't trouble yourself," he said.

"We could walk it, I suppose." She remembered his feet. "No, we can't."

"I could manage, Sophie. We'd want to go early—the line."

"No barging the line without help from the big Fleet judge." That would take a big chunk of time. An hour for the walk, then the waiting, and paper pushing.

An ugly thought occurred to her. She tapped on the driver's window again. "Does it cost anything to free a slave?"

The driver's attitude softened noticeably. "Six years on since I was freed, and it was three hundred akro I had to pay. Average gone up since then."

She fell back in her seat. "Teeth."

The carriage pulled up at a walled park, and an interminable stop-and-start took hold as they edged through a bottleneck at the gate. Uniformed guards were letting crimson-sashed young people, some as many as ten years younger than Sophie, out of the carriages. Beyond them, in a lantern-lit copse of birch trees, silk tents stretched along a promenade strewn with tiny white flowers.

"What is it?"

"It's a conjugal traffic jam. They're registering—I see a registration table. It's like a convention of . . ."

"Of the engaged," Garland said.

They shared an uneasy glance.

Sophie tapped the window again. "Driver?"

"*Hes,* Kir?"

"Everyone in Sylvanna gets engaged in the summer, is that right?"

"*Hes.*"

"So . . ." She swallowed, and heard that ticking in her ears. In her current state of mind, it made her think of a time bomb. "How long are they engaged for?"

"Until solstice, Kir."

"Everyone marries on the solstice?" Garland asked.

"You didn't know?" the driver asked.

Garland shook his head. "Sophie . . ."

"I know. I know. Oh—" A mild Fleet epithet wouldn't cover this. "Shit."

Solstice was three days away.

CHAPTER 29

Three days. Three days to free Kev and get him off Sylvanna without a ship. Three days to come up with hundreds of akro for the fee.

She and Garland registered for marriage counseling in a shared state of shock and were directed to a tent near the rear of the assembly, designated for foreigners and abolitionists—troublemakers, in other words. Inside was a table set with steaming teacups and a circle of low love seats, each big enough for a couple. Two other pairs of young people dressed in suits were drinking tea and sitting across from each other. One was two women, which left Sophie to wonder whether, despite Cly having assured her that gay people had equal rights here, the same-sex couples automatically ended up in the outsider tent. The other couple was straight, a Sylvanner boy of sixteen and a girl with mint-green spots on her face and a Fleet uniform.

Is that chlorophyll? Sophie wondered, once again reaching for the camera that had sunk with *Nightjar,* and finding instead a satchel crammed with things she hoped might prove useful: the book of questions and some other papers, pens, a few envelopes for biosamples, and—for no good reason except that she couldn't make herself leave it behind—her latent fingerprinting kit.

Their classmates had the bored air of kids in detention. They didn't mingle but murmured quietly, just waiting.

As Sophie poured herself a cup of the steaming, lemon-scented tea, the tent flap opened again and Rees Erminne stepped inside with the veiled woman. The pins on her sash seemed to indicate she had been retired from service within the Fleet.

"Rees!" Sophie was half delighted and half horrified.

Rees had tried his utmost to keep her from bellowing "I'm a slut!" at the top of her lungs at the Highsummer Festival. But—

Embarrassment be damned. This was an opportunity.

He bowed. "Kir Sophie."

"Hi. Can we talk a sec?"

"I'm here with Cleste, my betrothed." Rees was more than usually kempt. When she'd met him, he'd reminded her of a good-natured giant koala bear. Now his beard had been trimmed and the suit, though patched in spots, was impeccably turned out.

"Hi . . . Cleste? And congrats. Rees, it doesn't have to be a private convo." *Come on, persuasive spell.*

Maybe it was the magic, or just the fact that he was trapped, but his shoulders slumped.

The fiancée patted his shoulder. "All's well, Rees."

Before anyone had a chance to rethink, Sophie yanked Kev's emancipation papers out of her satchel. "I'm trying to free a guy. I can't explain how I ended up with him—"

"All of Winter knows about your murderer." His voice was neutral. "That he's a Haver spellscribe. Who it was he killed. The reason *Incannis* targeted the ships it sank."

"He agreed to a pacification spell," Sophie explained. "But this paperwork, to free him . . . I don't read Sylvanner and Cly won't help. Do you see anything about a fee?"

He scanned down. "Ten thousand akro."

She sucked wind for the second time that night.

"Ten thousand?" Garland said incredulously.

"Fees are at the discretion of the bonding office," Rees said.

"I don't suppose you have ten grand lying around that I could borrow?"

That got a glimmer of warmth from him. "I'm poor, remember?"

She turned to Garland. "They don't have credit cards here, do they?"

"There is another way," Rees's fiancée said.

"Yeah?" Sophie perked up.

"I've been rude, haven't I?" Rees said. "Cleste, meet Sophie Banning and Captain Garland Parrish."

Cleste bowed, sidestepped a couple who'd taken the opportunity to try to dive between them—when the group huddled around the slavery paperwork, they had inadvertently blocked the tea table—and made a *Come here* gesture to regroup them off to the side.

Rees added, "We've— You might guess that our political inclinations are aligned."

Meaning Cleste was opposed to slavery. As usual, nobody was supposed to say so aloud.

"Avoiding the fee?" Garland prompted.

"*Oui,*" Cleste said. "The fee is a barrier to the bonded. They have to reimburse their owners and the government to buy their freedom . . . They are, in effect, double charged. It's not meant to penalize landowners. You can free anyone with a simple declaration, on a holiday. It's what Rees's father did."

Sophie said, "That sounds too good to be true."

"When's the next eligible holiday?" Garland asked.

"Solstice, at the feast before the wedding."

"Does the feast happen long before the ceremony?"

"We eat. The toasts and declarations of liberation are then made. After that, we wed."

Garland winced, ever so slightly.

"In the morning, having been made adults," Rees added, "new married couples go to vote for the first time."

"Teeth," Sophie said. "So if we want to free Kev, we have to show up for the wedding?"

"Why wouldn't you show up—" Rees was interrupted by a pair of drill sergeant types, one male, one female, marching through the tent flap, pushing one last couple before them, and barking out orders.

"Sit, children, sit!"

Garland chose a blue love seat across from the entrance, drawing Sophie after him. It was a snug squeeze.

"This is marriage!" the woman bellowed. "Two beings crammed in the same boat, rowing to common purpose."

Their instructors were a married pair of retired Fleet officers—she from Sylvanna, he from Tonio's home nation, Erinth. They opened with some patter about the glories of the Fleet in bringing together diverse peoples. Then the woman broke into a fire-and-brimstone speech about the sanctity of Sylvanner marriage and their total ban on divorce.

I bet they don't have annulment, either, Sophie thought. Cly had to have himself declared dead to legally detangle himself from Beatrice.

The woman went on in mind-numbing detail: marriage was a partnership, building a life together a sacred duty. Across the circle of cushions, Rees wore a pained expression.

Garland listened to every word as though it was at least as interesting as the time Sophie had told him about insect pheromones.

So we stay right up to the last minute, free Kev, and make a dash for it . . . to where? And with what ship?

The earworm lay beneath it all. *Tick, tick, tick.* Somewhere in this dense Sylvanner city, fairly close, there was a sliver of the Worldclock, a timepiece. An eraglider. The sister Bettona had primed with those apricot and anise biscuits.

The sensation faded as Sophie focused on it.

"Kir Hansa!" The drill sergeant gave her a warning glower, and Sophie tried to look engaged.

After the lecture on the sanctity of marriage, the instructors went around the circle, directing the foreigners to talk briefly about customs in their homelands.

"Where I was raised, we have divorce," was Sophie's contribution.

Garland's was "Marriage does not serve the dead."

Then they were required to look each other in the eyes, sitting nose to nose in the too-small love seats, and talk about their hopes for the future.

"How many children do you want? How soon do you want to have them? How will you allocate and manage your shared property? Do you follow the same faith? What are your parents settling on you?"

The last made her laugh. "I think I'm probably dowry free."

Garland smiled. "I have a claim on a grave in the capital of Issle Morta."

"Don't be frivolous." Their instructor loomed over Sophie. "Say something of import. Now."

Be honest on command. Great. She looked into Garland's eyes. "I want to raise *Nightjar.* I want to make up for some of the damage I've done since—"

His hand closed around hers. "Don't, Sophie."

The sergeant smiled. "And you, flailer? What do you expect from this woman?"

Right. This is exactly how to conduct an intimate conversation.

"I want to set your mind at ease," Garland said, as if baring his soul in front of strangers was the easiest thing in the universe. "About the question of destiny that bothers you so, about the intentions laid upon you."

Now she was almost in tears. "Beatrice made me charming. And my looks—"

"Do you think it's the gloss that matters?"

She opened her mouth. What came out was a small, choked sound.

"I know who you are, Sophie Hansa," he said. "I know your need to understand everything you encounter. I know you're determined to shield Kev from abuse, despite his crimes. Your courage is no work of outside magic—"

"Stop," she said.

The drill sergeant said, "Reply, child!"

She fought the urge to snap back at the facilitator, kept her eyes locked on Garland's, groped for words . . . and suddenly felt something settle, within, with the solidity of good boots on bedrock. For just an instant, she was hammered by jaw-dropping, bolt-from-the-blue surprise. "Of course. Of course I know you."

Their instructor grunted. "Love matches," she muttered in a weary drawl before moving on.

It went on like that for another hour: trapped nose to nose on the cushion, interrogated about their hopes and dreams, obliged to share, while their instructors circled and eavesdropped and intervened whenever they got too shallow.

By the time they got to stretch and eat a sandwich, Sophie was wrung out, almost physically shaky. Then their wranglers drew a curtain across the tent. "I'll want the ladies here on this side," said the woman. "My husband will take the gentlemen."

This made it six to four, since the lesbians came together.

"What's going on?" Sophie said.

"I'm going to acquaint you with the basics of physical intimacy." The woman opened a large hardbound book. The left page was an illustration of a nude woman; the right was a diagram that might have been at home in a California sex education class. "There's no need to feel awkward, Kir Sophie."

"I'm not," she said. "But your drawing's wrong."

"Wrong?"

"Well, incomplete. Her ovaries and fallopian tubes are missing, and if we're going to talk about sex, the real organ we need in the mix is the brain."

The entire tent, both sides, had fallen silent.

"Your outland notions about marital congress—"

"They're not notions, and I don't need a bunch of half-baked information on sex. I've *had* sex," she said.

The women, but for Cleste, ootched two steps farther from her.

"Kir!" The instructor remonstrated. "Your betrothed is mere steps away!"

"Oh, he knows. Believe me, everyone knows."

"It's true," Garland's voice sounded, from the other side of the curtain. "And, actually, we've both been—"

"*Stop!*" The instructor glowered at Sophie. "We are not interested in the lewd customs of your adopted nation. You're here as a Sylvanner. Conduct yourself accordingly."

"Or what? Is this class a pass/fail proposition? If we don't pass this unit, do we get forbidden to marry?"

The woman sputtered.

"It is an excellent question," Garland said. He was right on the other side of the sheet of fabric.

I know you. At the thought, a shiver went through her.

He added, "We're likely to be disruptive as well as scandalous."

The instructor glowered. "Go, then! Take your indecent selves out and be back in ninety for dance lessons."

Sophie was feeling reckless and rebellious both. She took Garland's arm and, cuddling up, attempted to flounce as they left the tent.

"Everything you need to know about sex in ninety minutes," she muttered. "Raging Seas."

It was cold out. The tents, with their warming stones, had trapped a lot of heat. But the stars above were clear, cut white diamonds set in a black marble sky. Light snowflakes were falling.

She began to giggle as soon as they were clear of the tent. "Talk about dodging a bullet. Sorry if that embarrassed you."

"I didn't wish to sit through a description of intimacy mechanics."

"Was getting away worth the risk of hypothermia?"

"Let's see if we can avoid that, too."

"And get you off those burnt feet."

"They're much better." Garland led her to the rear corner of the park, to a darkened tent. Peering inside, they found staging materials for the seminar—more tea on trays, cushions, and llama skin blankets.

"Over here," he said, nudging three of the cushions together and pulling her close.

His lips met hers, and it was as if they hadn't been interrupted, all those weeks ago, in his cabin. His hands gently tugged her shirt out of the lady suit trousers and his fingers ran up her rib cage, pausing at the foreign structure of her bra.

"There's a fastener on the back," she said, sliding her hands down to his pants buttons. Then, rather than rushing things, she laid her head against his chest for a moment. "What are we going to do?"

"Free Kev and flee before the wedding."

"Cly's gonna be expecting that."

"He did essentially say that, if we can expose the conspiracy, he'll release us from this deception."

"If not?"

"We outmaneuver him."

"What if we fail?"

He brought his nose close to hers again. "If we were force-marched to the altar, Sophie, and they asked if I wanted to marry you—"

"Don't say it."

"I would never trap you in an alliance you didn't want. I merely wish . . ."

"What?"

"Perhaps . . . that we'd known each other longer."

She ran her hands down his hips, marveling at the statue smoothness of him, the welcome warmth of his skin. She wasn't sure she'd ever waited this long, with anyone, but she wasn't about to say so. She wasn't going to say anything that might change his mind, or even slow him down.

Soon there was nothing between them—no fabric, no belts. They kicked off their boots at the same moment.

"I wish I could see you," she said.

"Me too." He kissed her, lips eager and edging to roughness, and she thought about the things they should talk about, all the unresolved stuff. But he'd been right, all those months ago, when he wrote to her. They could work it out.

He knows me. A flood of relief. She'd been swimming against the current of something that, unscientific as it was, nevertheless had to be.

"I'm eager to begin," she whispered, quoting that letter, and he got it. He laughed breathlessly and eased the whole of his body against hers, forehead to toes, and all that heat in the middle. It was a jolt. She curled her hand into his hair and met him, reaching, kissing, trying to hold all of him at once.

Then they were joined, moving together, the waves of sensation so intense she found tears running down her face even as she laughed. The two of them were like a live wire, voltage boiling through a cable, and it was all she could do to hold in the sound, to keep from shouting or sobbing or laughing this whole sleepy park full of virgins awake.

She shuddered to a final, electric, head-to-toes jolt, pressing her head against his shoulder, and as they relaxed, breathing shallowly, he ran a finger down her cheek, wiping the tears there.

"It's you," she whispered in the dark, before she could rethink it, before he could get the wrong idea.

"You're crying." She couldn't tell what was in his voice.

She caught his face in his hands, kissed him long and hard, and said it properly. "I love you."

"My heart is yours," he replied. And then, a shift. "We should—I hear people. Someone's coming. We might be missed."

"Oop!" So much for holding on to the moment. She wriggled back into her bra, grabbed a shirt, felt for the top collar and the inner seams, and began buttoning.

They scrambled to get dressed in the pitch blackness, occasionally pausing to kiss again.

She had never felt this before, this particular sense of happiness, of having eaten so much of a meal that she was bursting; it almost hurt.

They muddled through the darkness, fumbling their way to the tent flap and snaking out, straightening each other's tuxedos in the dim lantern light of the park.

"Sophie," Garland said. "Does . . . is romantic love not much valued on Erstwhile?"

She broke into a smile. "Ha! I'm gonna read you *Pride and Prejudice*."

He seemed to understand her meaning. "We should seek our classmates."

"Guess we passed the intimacy exam, huh?"

"I'm sure if we consulted them, they'd find fault with our technique."

"Well, we can practice."

"Indeed we can." He offered her his arm and they went back to the troublemaker version of the couples class, their skin cooling in the winter air.

CHAPTER 30

SOFE,

YES, I'M OKAY. I LIKED DAIMON A LOT, AND OBVIOUSLY I'M SHOCKED AND UPSET THAT HE'S DEAD. BUT I'M NOT INCAPACITATED, SO TRY NOT TO WORRY.

I THINK I HAVE ID'D THE ERSTWHILER WHO HELPED JOHN COINE. HE'S A FRIEND OF BEATRICE'S STEPSON . . . HE CAME THROUGH HER HOSPICE WITH MENINGIOMA WHEN HE WAS 12 AND HAD A MIRACULOUS TURNAROUND—MAGIC, I'M THINKING. THEN HE POPPED UP A COUPLE YEARS LATER AND BEFRIENDED SHAD.

DO WE TELL VERENA'S COP FRIEND, FEDONA? IT MIGHT BE BAD FOR BEATRICE, IF SHE'S BEEN CURING HOSPICE KIDS MAGICALLY. AND WE DON'T KNOW WHAT THE WRACKERS WILL DO TO HIM.

PS—GOT FEDONA'S FINGERPRINT, AS REQUESTED. 80% SURE SHE WASN'T THE ONE WHO BROKE INTO MOM AND DAD'S.

PSS—SPELL ON PARENTS' PLACE USING LEGAL DESCRIPTION DID, IN FACT, WORK.

PSSS—THAT POLICE DETECTIVE, BETTEL, CALLED AGAIN AND ASKED ME WHERE YOU'D GOT TO NOW.

BTW MISS YOU 5

BRAM

They returned to class and discovered that after sex ed had come dance lessons, a welcome shift to physical activity, conducted in a large communal tent with all the other couples. They crept in, hoping to avoid notice, and found their peers mincing to the music of a quintet of flute players and percussionists. Everyone was clad in white suits the same as those Cly had procured for Sophie and Garland—snow-white slacks, vests, and dress shirts adorned with the crimson beauty queen sashes that proclaimed them engaged.

The uniformity of the outfits gave the dance a military feel, and although Sophie's shirt kept bunching distractingly at the back, the steps weren't hard to pick up. They were happy to let Garland take lots of breaks, for his feet. It was a definite improvement over being hectored into sharing by the drill sergeant and her mate.

Cly met them afterward and gave them a single hair-raising look.

He can't know, Sophie thought, but all he said was, "I've heard from your half sister, via that bird. She's sailing here with your first mate, the fellow from Erinth. They met a vessel. *Capo.* It's possible she'll make the wedding, if winds are fair."

"Heading here?" Garland raised his eyebrows. "Perhaps Bettona confessed—exposed her coconspirators."

"If so, why not tell us?"

Cly nodded. "Garland, you're a man of the Fleet, in your heart if not in name—"

"I'll marry him," Sophie blurted. "If you march us to the altar, I will totally vow—"

"While that's a lovely sentiment," Cly said, "I was not about to appeal to your lover to break your engagement."

Lover? Seas, he does know. How *does he know?*

Garland, far from being chagrined, lit up.

"I truly despair of you both." Cly strode up to a driver with a team of tubby and tired-looking palomino mares and a sagging carriage that bore, Sophie saw, the Fleet judiciary drapes. "Where is my driver? Where's Latasha?"

"Family emergency, Your Honor."

"This is the best you can muster?"

The coachman waved at the crush of coach-and-fours. "Short supply tonight."

"We're bound for Innobel."

"Kir? Did you say—"

"Get on with it! Take the civil access lane and turn left at the park exit; I expect you to bypass the usual impromptu parade." With a huff, Cly yanked open the door.

They piled inside. Garland took the rear-facing seat and Sophie moved to follow, but Cly caught her arm, directing her to the seat across. She resisted, as a matter of course, and so he outmaneuvered her, planting himself next to Garland and leaving her across from them both.

It was a position that combined the worst aspects of a job interview, a visit to the principal's office, and a blind date.

"So!" she blurted, before anyone else could introduce some fun topic of conversation, like premarital sex. "We uncover Kev's scheme and Cly gives up the project of claiming him for torture. That's the deal, right?"

Cly nodded curtly. "Parrish, you understand the politics in play here. The frightmaker and his cronies are involved with Lidman, yes? What might they be trying to accomplish here on Sylvanna?"

"Causing trouble internationally," Sophie said. "Causing incidents that will lead to conflict."

"There are those who believe the Cessation is doomed," Garland said, running a finger inside his shirt collar to settle it, stretching his neck. "That sooner or later the port and starboard sides of the government will break, probably over slavery, and there will be a resumption of hostilities over the question of bondage."

The tension eased as they once again ran through the *pas de deux* of international incidents so far. Kev and his friends raiding and sinking slaver ships in an apparent strike against the bonded nations. Aunt Gale's murder, before that—a blow to the Verdanii, intensified now that the All-mother was ill.

None of that seemed sufficiently incendiary.

Sophie said. "It takes drama to start a war. Theater."

"Agreed. And so they moved on to sinking *Constitution*." Cly gave her a pleased look, almost as though he'd invented her. "Several times now, the parties who desire war have been balked by your intervention in their intrigues. You solved the murder of your aunt, then disrupted the attempt to disarm *Temperance* and spark conflict between Ualtar and Tiladene."

"Bully for me, but now they're on to plan C. How does Kev figure in?"

"He murdered slavers and is now himself a slave. I suppose one might make of him . . . something in the way of a martyr," Cly said.

"He knows his so-called allies were undercover spies. Why is he still cooperating with them?"

"He's under threat," Garland said promptly. "He is demonstrably more afraid of what they can do to him than he is of you . . . either of you, Your Honor."

"Well, if they've got the stick," Sophie said, "we'll have to be the carrot."

Cly looked baffled.

"In order to get Kev to tell us what's up, we have to convince him we can protect him. Not only free him, you see? We have to get him somewhere beyond the conspirators' reach."

Cly said, "Where could a man like that go?"

"You're the locals. You tell me."

"Parrish?" Cly said. "Perhaps a certain island locale . . ."

Garland looked wary. "It would be entirely wrong to claim such a place existed, particularly in the presence of someone such as Your Honor."

"Sophie's taken the Oath as well, remember. But if Lidman is to disappear beyond the reach of the conspirators, I fear we must speak of Nysa."

"Nysa is a myth," Garland said.

Sophie added this up. "You're telling me there's an island inhabited by escaped slaves."

"There's a story of such a place," Cly corrected.

"Right, right. Because it would be wrong for us oathy types to admit to knowing of its existence." It had been a long night, but the doublethink didn't seem as onerous as it usually did. Brimming as she was with happiness, it almost felt like play.

The men kept fencing, Garland making noises about how hard it might be to get someone like Kev to the fabled haven—the challenge of finding a ship willing to bear him, the risk to that ship and its crew from the immolator.

"But surely, you, Parrish— Ah. Forgive me. I forgot momentarily that your *Nightjar* was lost."

Sophie squeezed Garland's hand. "I'm guessing the islanders, if they did in fact exist, wouldn't want anyone following Kev to their location anyway."

"Good point," said Cly. "Simply discovering Nysa might bring us closer to war, unless . . ."

"Unless?"

"Unless something convinces the portside that it cannot prevail in a battle."

Sophie blinked. "Did I hear that right?"

"If the nations of the Fleet remain on the edge of war for long enough," Cly said, "some pretext for hostilities will inevitably be found."

"True," Garland agreed. "If the Cessation does break, we will return to an age of raiding and small alliances. The seas won't be safe, and the little nations . . . it's not exaggerating to say many would be annihilated. It's why Gale dedicated her life to the peace."

"Dumping water on sparks," Cly said. "As Sophie has been, since she arrived."

"You want to build a firebreak? You, Cly? Why?"

"Imagine the Cessation breaking tomorrow," Cly said. "I would be called home. I would be tasked, probably, with leading the invasion of Haversham."

"But what? You'd rather not?"

"I do not believe the portside can survive, no matter how much damage it inflicts in a war."

"Don't pick fights you can't win, in other words?"

"You'd rather I was an idealist than a pragmatist." It wasn't a question.

I'd settle for trustworthy. If any part of it could be believed . . . but before she could speak, the coach jerked to a halt.

They had been traveling through ever-scabbier neighborhoods, and now they were parked before a low hut on the edge of what was clearly a poverty-stricken little village.

"Innobel, Kirs," the driver called.

"Why are we here?" Sophie asked.

"I want you to meet someone."

"Who?" She stepped down, letting Cly walk her to the house.

He knocked quietly. *"Pinna, sella Cly."*

A rustle, and the door creaked open.

Inside was a woman of about fifty years, fair-haired and blue-eyed, bearing the scar of a bangle that had been burned off. Beaming, she hugged Cly, letting out a flood of Sylvanner.

He replied, *"Fas Sophie, ella dottar per ne Beatrice."*

The woman cried out in delight, seizing Sophie's hands.

"Who's this?"

"Sophie," Cly said, "this is your aunt, Pinna."

Sophie let out a long rush of air, goggling from one to the other. "Aunt? Aunt?"

The woman urged her to sit.

An aunt who'd been a slave. Sophie had accused Cly of raping his slaves, but . . . "Your father?"

"It is a source of considerable shame and embarrassment. I'd wanted to wait, before burdening you."

Her stomach burned. *So it's Grandpa who was the rapist. This finding out about your heritage thing gets more fun by the minute.*

Pinna still had her by the hands.

Sophie tried out a smile. "Do you speak . . . Fleet?"

"Little."

She turned to Cly. "Ask her—"

"Oh, no," he said. "I shan't have you bursting in on me in court in six months' time, accusing me of deliberately botching the translation and thereby influencing your conversation." With that he walked off, head high, all but whistling.

Smug bastard. But . . . aunt. Freed slave aunt! She'd been trying to speak to one of the bonded since she learned Sylvanna was a slave nation.

She looked at Pinna. She was younger than Cly, by perhaps as much as a decade.

"May I?" She indicated the room and got a go-ahead.

The shack had nothing to mark its exterior or make it a target—unlike freeborn Sylvanners, these people didn't emblazon their status on their doors. The outside had been shingled in drab brown wood, but within the house itself everything was in first-rate repair and there were plenty of creature comforts. Pinna's kitchen table was made of a plain-looking hardwood that Sophie recognized as quite fine, and her fireplace was compact and well made. The table was piled with accounting ledgers—she had paying work, then—and there was a pot of herbs from a doctor.

Medicine . . . I bet the freed don't all get that.

Pinna was waiting for Sophie to complete her inspection of the place, murmuring "Zophie, Zsssophie," to herself.

Sophie was about to turn back to her when her eye lit on a page, tucked under some of the other papers, marked with symbols like hieroglyphs.

"I've seen these before."

"In my kindling bin?" Garland had taken a seat near the window, taking the weight off his feet and fiddling with the cuff of his shirt.

He didn't add *When you were rifling through my quarters?*, but she blushed anyway.

"Yes. But also on—"

He glanced out the window, seeming to assess how far away Cly had gotten, then spoke so quietly she almost found herself straining to hear. "They're called pictals. Pictal is the written language of the bonded."

"Why were you writing in it?"

"I hoped to ask a friend if Kev and his friends were truly acting as their allies."

"A Nysa friend? Why?"

"If it's true . . . well, it makes a difference, doesn't it? If Kev is with them?"

She nodded.

But for raising her brows at the mention of Nysa, Pinna had waited silently throughout this exchange. Sophie tried out a bow on her, getting a grin in response. "Um. Me. Cly," she said. *"Dottar, patter."*

The woman nodded and imitated her moves. "Pinna, Cly, *litteren, y patter.*"

"Brother and sister, right. Same dad?"

Pinna gestured at two spice shakers on table, indicating they were on same plane, then held a bowl above them. *"Patter."*

"Same dad."

A nod.

With gestures and simple words, and occasional resort to Garland's partial knowledge of pictal writing—his familiarity with the symbols seemed to disturb Pinna, but she went with it—they pieced together the story.

Cly had apparently freed Pinna, upon his marriage to Beatrice, to his elderly father's considerable displeasure. He'd set her up here and got her into some kind of bookkeeping racket.

Pinna shifted one of her ledgers, laying it none too subtly over the pictals. It appeared to be a list of names, jobs, and cash amounts.

"She does accounting for the freed when they find paying work, looks like."

Garland agreed. "These are records of invoices."

"Beatrice," Pinna said, tapping the page. "Beatrice, Beatrice."

"Beatrice taught you to write and do figures?" She mimed the question and got an excited *"Yehyeh!"*

Sophie took a deep breath. "You talk for a sec, Garland."

She left him to query her, using a mix of Sylvanner and Verdanii vocabulary.

So Cly has at least one sister because his father—my grandfather—was a slave-raping—

There were no words.

Cly was horrified by it. He claimed.

He did free Pinna.

She was starting to want, badly, to believe in him.

Garland was showing interest in Pinna's pot of medicine and was getting assurances that her aunt was getting over some minor cold. Cly—sainted Cly, according to her—had ensured that this whole village got regular visits from a physician.

Sophie shivered. *This is Cly's go-to strategy. Find a woman who adores him, and have them try to bring me around. Like this summer, when he asked Tenner Zita to befriend me.*

The thought felt small, maybe unworthy.

On the heels of it, she remembered Annela saying *One can only fight nature for so long.* It was true that people had deep-set behavior patterns. Loops they kept running. Behavioral fingerprints?

This is an opportunity that may never come again, she reminded herself. *We have to ask Pinna the right questions.*

Which were?

Beatrice married Cly? Why?

She wanted to study at the Institute.

Oh.

She dug out her book of questions, unfolding from its pages Bram's printed copy of the last Beatrice spell.

She spread it on the table, finding the symbols in the middle, the ones that weren't spellscrip letters. The black fox, the eye with chain links, all written on birch bark in bright green.

Pinna's reaction was a horrified gasp. Round-eyed, she glanced at the door.

So she doesn't trust Cly wholeheartedly, Sophie thought.

"Beatrice?" Pinna rasped.

"Beatrice. Beatrice, this spell, on me. Sophie." She circled the symbols again. "Pictals?"

The woman closed the ledger book, her hands shaking, pushing the spell at Sophie and gesturing—*Put it away. Get it out of my sight.* She paced, fingers to her face, fighting for calm, obviously thinking.

Finally she barred the door, closed her curtains, opened an old-looking umbrella, and withdrew a scroll. Unrolled on the table, it revealed a series of pictals, perhaps five hundred of them, crammed into a table-size space. She laid bowls on its corners to hold it flat, and thought again.

Garland drew in a shocked breath. "This could be a dictionary of all the pictals commonly used by the bonded. It mustn't fall into slaver hands."

Pinna had clearly decided the risk was worth the ability to communicate more efficiently.

"Beatrice," she said. She began pointing at pictals, one after another. Point. Point. Point.

Garland said. "Beatrice knowledge books to . . . I don't recognize . . . oh. Beatrice taught her to read and write in Sylvanner."

Then: "Beatrice." Point, point, point.

"Open gift . . . discovered inscription bonded. I'm not—"

"Beatrice learned that pictals could be used in inscriptions," Sophie said.

Garland looked profoundly uneasy now. "If the bonded were found to be writing any spells—never mind if they were able to write intentions unknown to Fleet mages or the Spellscrip Institute . . . Seas, the portside nations would . . ."

"Overreact. Freak out?"

"There would be slaughters."

Pinna was picking out words at a feverish pace.

Back in the day, Beatrice had wanted to study inscription, but the Verdanii hadn't thought her talented enough. She'd gotten engaged to Cly, defying her family, and had come to study at the Sylvanna Spellscrip Institute.

At some point, another of the bonded women on Cly's estate had offered her a straight-up swap: the slave got to learn the same things Beatrice was learning at the Institute, and Beatrice learned pictal inscription techniques.

Pinna had found out.

Pinna understood what that other, younger slave had not: if it came out that the bonded had *any* access to magic, let alone to spells the Institute didn't understand or control, there would be executions and purges.

"She was terrified," Garland said, following along as Pinna continued to point out pictals. "Beatrice vowed quiet—she promised to keep the secret. Then . . ."

He frowned, then touched a series of pictals, essentially repeating what Pinna had just said, asking her something.

She nodded vehemently, and he pointed at Sophie's book of questions, at the scroll. "*Yehyeh!*" she said.

"What is it?"

"There was nothing Pinna could do about Beatrice having learned that the bonded were practicing inscription. They had to trust that she would keep the secret. But she had the other girl—"

"The one who spilled the beans?"

He nodded. "Pinna had her teach Beatrice an inscription. The one . . ."

"The one she worked on me."

"They told her it would strengthen their bond, hers and His Honor's. She appears to have sold Beatrice on the spell by indicating that it would give your father the strength to free Pinna before the wedding."

"Right!" she said. "So Beatrice misunderstood what the spell did because Pinna lied."

"Yes," Garland said.

"What does it actually do?" She raised the notebook, giving Pinna a pleading look.

"Cly," Pinna said, and took up the spice shakers she'd used earlier to represent him and his father. She put Grandpa's shaker atop Cly's, pressing, then tapped her scar, where the bangle had been.

"Cly had been under his father's thumb?"

Pinna seemed to understand that she'd got this. She held out her hands at the same height and said, "We balance. Inscription balance. Cly bound fire fear, Cly bound obey rules. We—Beatrice, make Cly to follow nature inside rules. No worries *patter* feeling."

She tapped a pictal that looked like a Möbius strip.

"It means twisting, reversal," Garland said.

"I see it. The spell without the pictal makes you love your family unreservedly—you consider your parents' every whim and wish. You put them first. It's a guilt trip on steroids. Reversed, you do exactly as you please, without regard to what anyone else wants?"

"He sails his own wind, wherever it's inclined," Garland said. "He's like you."

"What?"

"In that you follow your own nature."

She swallowed. This had a ring of truth. She'd spent her life diving, swimming, caving, putting herself at risk, and never quite giving in to her parents' distress over it all. *Hard-hearted*, Dad had called her once, when he thought she couldn't overhear.

It had hurt, but she hadn't changed.

"It frees you," Garland said. "Breaks the bonds of obligation, guilt, national pride. Sets you asea with nothing but your own judgment for breeze."

"Yeah, okay, but Cly wasn't cut free of anything at the time when Sicko Grandpa sent him to the Fleet. Sent him single, against Sylvanner custom. He came back with a Verdanii fiancée and everyone pretended to be unhappy with the arrangement."

"Meaning?"

"If his will was still shackled when he married Beatrice, it means the Bannings ordered him to marry into the Nine Families."

"Why?"

"Same reason as the pirates. To get an eragliding daughter."

Which he did, but then Beatrice extricated him from Daddy's influence. He freed Pinna—

That would have been his own choice, then, she thought.

"Beatrice, Clydon . . ." Pinna still had something to say. She pointed at crossed swords.

"They kept fighting," Sophie said. Magically altering Cly hadn't kept him and Beatrice from clashing. Pregnant, with no option for divorce, Beatrice had run off to Erstwhile.

"His Honor's coming," Garland said.

Pinna rolled up her Ouija board dictionary, stashed it in the umbrella again, and unbarred the door, busying herself making tea and creating the illusion of a nice visit.

"One more question, please."

An agonized glance.

"His Honor is returning. We have, perhaps, a minute," said Garland.

"Cly," Sophie said. "As a kid—" She held her hand low. "Little Cly. He set fires."

Dammit, what to say? "Cly, Cly," she repeated, and then stuck a piece of kindling in the blaze.

"Ah!" Pinna's face cleared. She glanced at the door, then handed Sophie a wafer of coarse brown paper and a bit of brown rope. "Cly—" She mimed tossing them in the fire. "*Patter—*" Now a mime of fury. Last, she touched her bangle scar.

"Hemp," Garland said. "Bonding inscriptions. He was burning bonding inscriptions. Perhaps looking for Pinna's?"

"They scribed him to make him stop?"

He'd been rebelling, and they'd made him pyrophobic. Later, they'd scribed him again, made him obedient, gave him his marching orders, and sent him to Fleet.

A rap at the door. "May I come in? Pinna?"

"*Yehyeh.*"

He stuck his head inside. "If you're done, child, we should get back to the rooms before it's light."

Sneak into the slum while it's dark; get out before you're seen.

But there was nothing more they could ask Pinna with Cly present. Sophie glanced at Garland. He was smiling at her in a keen-eyed and appreciative way that felt immensely flattering.

She gave Pinna a hug, and Pinna returned it wholeheartedly; her aunt's grip was strong. Then Sophie followed Garland back out to their creaky jalopy of a carriage, with its pudgy, exhausted-looking team and a driver whose expression said he wanted to be anywhere else.

CHAPTER 31

Cly lagged for a second to say a few last words to Pinna, to hand her a few gifts, all of which left Sophie free to cuddle in beside Garland on the rear-facing seats. His cuff had popped its button again; she refastened it, a tricky task. It was a nice excuse to touch him, to fuss a little and take in his skin, the graceful proportions of his hand. To stop thinking about the political ecosystem of Stormwrack and just feel a little lovestruck.

"I know you," she whispered, and she felt a jolt in him, an intake of breath, like a gasp or chuckle.

A cough: Cly's way of warning them before he swung in, ducking hard to avoid the roof, and settled with a scowl equally intended, she thought, for the carriage's overall scruffiness and for her indecent daughter behavior.

Just for that, she declined to let go of Garland's hand.

They got under way with a jerk.

"Well?" He sounded tired.

Was he? Or was it a ruse? She took him in, boots to crown. Not a hair out of place, sash with its status signifiers glimmering and perfect.

"Does this change anything?" he said.

"I'm thinking." She wanted it to, wanted it to very badly indeed.

The city was above them, up the long, winding road. She could see the lights, and the blue-edged shadows of the mountains. Somewhere east of them, dawn was breaking.

The carriage jolted over a bump. She heard the driver trying to soothe the horses with a murmur.

She began, "Seems like you're asking me to believe you're against slavery. Not just cocktail-chatter, *Ooh, I'm such a dangerous liberal, ha-ha, give me another shrimp* against, but working against."

"I would never say that," Cly said.

"Why?"

"My position, within Fleet and out, would be precarious if I were to take a formal position against bondage." He frowned as they lurched again. "Without my privileges as a landowner, I cannot be effective."

"You do like your privileges."

"Show me someone who doesn't." Cly steepled his fingers. "You know Fralienne Erminne has entered politics. She is an abolitionist. If Sylvanna's laws were to change, we would take other nations with us. Other votes within the Convene."

"Just like that?"

"Over the years, we have cultivated certain international relationships. There are nations in the Convene who owe us favors. Their votes would travel with us."

"You have an international voting bloc?"

Garland nodded, confirming this. "What truly matters is the military imbalance. As Annela Gracechild has recently reminded me, no alliance of pirates and rabble can stand against Verdanii and Sylvanna united."

"But why, Cly? Why do you care?"

"Pardon?"

"Is it that you're a stealth peacenik? Is it Pinna? Are you besotted with Beatrice, after all these years?"

That got a bark of laughter.

"Are you just kicking dirt on your father's memory?" she continued.

"Tormenting your elders is your brand of perversity, child."

"Tormenting. Really?" *What am I doing?* She should be happy, no matter his motives. A Cly even somewhat committed to abolition was a vastly cheerier prospect than a contented slave-owning bastard. "Why do you *care*?"

"It's complicated."

"It shouldn't be."

"Nudging Sylvanna onto a better path is the best possible outcome for a potentially appalling conflict—"

"That's just pragmatism."

"Well, yes." Cly waved his hand in dismissal. "Kev Lidman must be stopped, Sophie."

"He's locked up and pacified. He's pretty stopped."

"Lidman is connected to your conspiracy. He or his allies are gaming with you."

It was true. But Kev seemed completely depressed half the time and scared to death the rest of it. None of which had shaken the truth from him.

The carriage jolted sideways. Cly rapped at the sliding panel between carriage and driver, barking out orders in Sylvanner like a drill sergeant.

No answer.

Cly frowned, and tried the panel. It didn't slide.

"Use this." Garland produced a thin knife, about nine inches long. Cly used it to pry the panel off.

Their driver was gone.

Garland and Cly, on either side of Sophie, opened the carriage doors without hesitating.

They were picking up speed. One of the mares began to make a sound, a jittery, agonized whining that rose and fell. *EeeEEEeeeEEE!*

The horses' backs and flanks were ballooning, rippling in peculiar ways, as if something under the skin was trying to get out.

"Frights," Sophie said. "The stolen horsehair sample. Frights."

"We must cut the team loose," Cly said.

"We'll lose the road," Garland pointed out.

Cly leaned far out of the carriage, looking up and down the mountain. Scanning for other threats?

"We should jump while we're running uphill," Garland said. "Otherwise the horses will get up more speed. And up ahead, at that switchback . . ."

EeeEEEEeeee!

"We'll crash," Sophie said.

"You first," both men said.

There was no time to argue. She clambered over Garland to get to the door, picked what she hoped was a soft-looking ditch, and sprang.

It wasn't soft. She hit a sapling and pulverized it, rolling over the tree. As pain radiated out from her shoulder and hip, she heard the clock again.

Tick, tick, tick. For the barest of moments, she thought she could see, of all things, a view of the Tower of London. Then she staggered to her feet, before she'd even recovered her equilibrium.

"Garland! Cly!" She limped uphill, her first steps unsteady as she broke into a drunken trot, then an actual run.

The horses hurtled uphill, screaming.

Sun broke over the ridge, brighter than everything, blinding her. A shadow seemed to leap from the carriage. Wishful thinking? Spots in her eyes?

She was squinting and half-blind when the carriage tilted to one side and plunged off the road with a horrifying sound—things breaking, splintering, and inhuman shrieks.

"Sophie?" She'd caught up to the shadow. Cly. He had a smear of dirt on his shoulder and was holding his saber in his left hand.

"You pop those stitches again?"

"I'm well enough," he said. "You?"

"Yeah, same."

"I should have switched carriages as soon as the replacement driver showed up." He scooped a small dagger off the ground. "Parrish! Parrish, are you there?"

The hair-raising screams of the horses were loud enough to drown out anything.

"Stay back, child," Cly said.

She ignored him; she'd spotted Garland.

He had jumped or fallen clear of the carriage maybe fifty feet before it went off the road. From the looks of things, he'd cracked his head on something—his face was bloodied.

"Breathing?" Cly asked.

"Yes," she said, hoping it was true.

"Wait here." He strode past her, toward the orgy of thrashing hooves and breaking wood.

Sophie rolled Garland carefully, feeling his skull, guessing whether anything was broken. His shirtsleeve had burst at the shoulder seams. *I know his middle name; I can have him cured if I need to. He's alive, he's alive. . . .*

She didn't even have a handkerchief to wipe his face, or a rope to hoist him up into the relative safety of the trees. If the thing tearing its way out of the horse took out Cly, they were dead.

"Garland," she said. "You have to wake up. Please, wake up."

His eyes opened.

"Are you hurt?" he asked.

"Am *I* hurt? Teeth! Can you move?"

The shrieks culminated in a sustained equine wail of agony and then a wet ripping noise that made her wish she was deaf. Cly backed into view. The horse followed, staggering. Backlit by the morning sun, they were both silhouettes. The mare was two-headed and gouting blood. Its horse head dangled, limp, almost dragging on the ground.

The raised head of the creature within, the one shedding the body of the horse in bloody hunks, had a familiar shape. A cat?

Marsupial lion, Sophie decided, *with tabby fur. This would account for the cat hair, the cat claws, the stolen braid of horse hair . . .*

Cly ran at it, bellowing, saber extended. It had just shaken a paw clear of the horse before it was impaled.

The creature sprang upward, jerking Cly with it like a toy. The saber fell, and Cly went with it. He rolled as the cat swiped a paw at him. Its rear haunches were tangled in the corpse of the horse, like feet caught in a dropped pair of jeans, but otherwise it was free. Cly retrieved his blade and stabbed again, grunting with the effort of shoving the blade home.

My birth father, the killing machine. The thought had bloody edges. Was this what going mad with fear felt like?

As Cly pulled his sword free and retreated backwards, the oddity considered him, lifting a paw. A massive, flame-eyed mouser, slick with blood.

Cly did not give it time to disentangle its back legs, instead darting in to chop at the thick wrist with the big, throat-cutting claws. The cat sprang sideways, trying to make room for an attack, and Cly followed.

Sophie scrabbled on the ground for whatever she could grab up and throw. Her first stone went wide, but she hit the cat in its flank with a second. The fright roared, turning to face her.

A mistake. The long stonewood blade cut an arc through the air, scything into the fright's belly. The lion lashed out, catching Cly with the back of one big claw, and the two of them tumbled to the road.

Cly leaped up, wobbling a bit, but ready for another attack. The creature shuddered, gouting blood. Then it was still. After an endless minute with his blade raised, Cly checked the other horses, one by one.

Sophie spun, focusing on Garland, helping him to sit.

"There, there," Cly murmured. A hoarse panting sound she had barely registered earlier turned into a sigh, then petered out. A keening whinny rose and was cut short. "What a waste."

When she could bear to look, he was cleaning his blade.

"You're both all right?"

Sophie nodded.

"Yes," Garland said, getting carefully to his feet. "You?"

"Yes. That could have gotten ugly," he observed. "It's well we'd headed out of town. If the carriage hadn't gone off the road and the oddity had got free of the mare faster, we'd have had much more trouble."

Garland nodded, as though this was a perfectly reasonable thing to say when they were standing over the remains of a carriage and horses. *Reminds me of that Sigourney Weaver movie,* Sophie thought, and her eye fell on the stomach-turning remnants. Alien, *that was it.*

"Birth stuff," she said. Her voice sounded calm, too. Maybe it was chill-out hour in crazyland. "Another fright spell. I figure it used that braid of lion hair stolen from Exhibits."

"The same spellscribe?" Garland seemed dubious.

"Few could muster the requisite hard-heartedness to do this," Cly said. "And given the effort to stamp frightmaking out . . ." He indicated the mess behind them. "It does suggest a specialist."

"Because people follow certain patterns," she said, remembering her earlier thought about Cly and Pinna. Find a woman, get her to argue his case.

She remembered Kev, apparently offended: *I'm not the frightmaker.*

The frightmaker. Someone specific; someone he knew.

"That," Cly agreed. "Besides, how many different spellscribes are likely to be after us right now?"

On that happy note, they began the trudge up the switchbacks to the city. The exercise of the uphill climb, and her worry that Garland's injured feet weren't up to the march, were welcome distractions from the gory scene they were leaving behind. The farther they got, the more she wanted to cry.

After an hour, a cart filled with firewood came toiling up the incline. Cly commandeered it, settling Sophie on the logs first, then Garland after her. Its owners seemed perfectly content to switch over to hiking as her birth father took up the reins.

"We'll be on the edge of the city in a quarter hour," Cly said. "I'll send a fast cab after them and they'll barely have lost any time at all."

She was too tired to question whether this was true, but it turned out to be; they pulled up to a stable on the edge of the city and Cly dispatched someone to fetch their benefactors.

He favored them with a wry grin. "Dare we risk another carriage hire?"

"Pick the skinniest horses," Sophie said. "Remember how fat the mare was?"

"Indeed. A spell like that one takes time to gestate."

She tried to work out how long they had been at Pinna's. "Would we have been back at the Mancellor, if not for the side trip?"

"Unlikely," Cly said. "With so many carriages, the main route through Hoarfrost becomes impossibly congested. People line the streets to throw grass wreaths at the betrothed."

"So the fright would've burst out into a crowd," Sophie said. "Do you think a slaughter on National Sex Ed Day would be good for interisland tensions?"

"Frivolous question," Cly said, choosing a carriage with a distinctly bony-looking set of pintos.

She flopped back into position inside—the carriage was just about identical to the one they'd wrecked—and the men crowded in with her. If you ignored the bloodstains and mud painted across their snow-white party garments, they were more or less back where they'd started.

"This provides new avenues of investigation," she said. "We can look into whoever arranged for the carriages to get switched."

"Lidman remains at the heart of this," Cly said. "We need to discover where his accomplices are."

"He has to have been in touch with them, don't you think? Since he got off *Docket*."

"The spellscribe was on *Nightjar*?" Garland said.

"Something made Kev believe his allies would come and get him."

He nodded, conceding the point with obvious reluctance. "I'd taken on new crew since Gale died. I can't vouch for everyone. I've generally been lucky—"

"I'm sure you are an excellent judge of character," Cly said, in that tone that left it open as to whether he meant it or was being condescending.

"There were four whom I don't know well."

"We can see what they've been up to since landfall," Cly said.

"I released them from their contracts. They might be difficult to trace."

"No need," Sophie said. "Here's our next move. . . ."

After she explained, they fell silent, watching the city bustle with early morning work crews, slaves stringing banners between the trees, gauzy strips alight with tiny pinpricks that winked like stars. Lanterns depicting the various phases of the moon were erected on stakes in the public squares and the middle of intersections; kindling and small chunks of wood were piled at their bases.

"Burning the moon," Cly said. "It's part of the High Winter Festival.

Children attempt to stay up all night to greet the new year. It's a significant accomplishment when one is old enough to hold out against sleep on the longest night."

Festival preparations. Sophie's eyes met Garland's. Would Cly march them to the altar on the solstice? There was no way to ask.

Garland was smiling, and she sensed he was remembering the two of them in that little catering tent. Damn it, now she was smiling, too.

Don't laugh, don't giggle, think about the killing machine over there. . . .

Cly was looking over the construction work on the bonfires. Giving them a moment, or merely lost in thought?

She owed her life to the killing machine, twice over. It was hypocritical to label him a serial killer, on no evidence, while benefiting from his skill set.

That's not about you, Sofe, her brother's voice said. *It's about Stormwrack being a violent and insane place.*

She missed Bram so much it hurt.

Five violent and insane, she thought. "I'm going to free Kev," she announced. "Anything else—transferring him, selling him—"

"Having him killed?" Cly suggested.

"Is basically owning up to owning him."

"We'd better work out what he's up to, then, hadn't we?"

They were almost back to the hotel district. "I'll get right on that," she said. "Can you have the driver stop at the Black Fox?"

"I'd ask you to change first, if you don't mind," Cly said.

"I know we're a mess, but what happened to 'Hurry up and crack the case'?"

Cly's lips curled. "The two of you," he said, speaking with almost Garlandlike precision in his diction, "are wearing each other's shirts."

CHAPTER 32

She'd meant to simply dash upstairs and change to a Sylvanner sports suit, buying time both to get over her mortification and to firm up the plan. But as she plunged through the suite doors, she almost plowed right into Krispos.

She skidded, wobbled, and, in the end, stopped herself from trampling him by enveloping him in a hug. He smelled of beeswax and something faintly grassy, like cilantro. "Didn't I send you to Autumn?"

"They let me take the magical path between Institutes," he said. His black beauty-queen sash was weighted by a few new pins, presumably symbols that identified him as a foreign scholar and scribe. He was carrying a sheaf of mail and a latched wooden box.

"What's all this?"

He handed over the letters. "Congratulatory messages from your father's cousins and the woman who's running for governor—"

"Fralienne Erminne."

"Your colleagues in the Watch had directed your mail to His Honor's estate."

She opened a note from Salk first.

Sophie Hansa
Stormwrack Forensic Institute

Kir Hansa,

I have read your summary translation of the Things Go Boom *book, as has Convenor Gracechild. The idea of terror it describes is, of course, an ancient concept. The scale of the attacks recommended, however, and the cold-blooded preference for symbolic targets and large numbers of victims, is something I find appalling.*

It appears that secrecy surrounding the full names of incoming cadets, as practiced by the Fleet, has been lax in recent years. Everyone, we'd assumed, would have held their names close before they came to service. This is proving untrue. I have embarked on a full audit of the bureaucracy to find exposed individuals. In the meantime, we continue to keep a close eye on anyone who might threaten Constitution.

You have asked about alternate targets for these operatives, and note that the spellscribe who made the frights is now active in your vicinity. Do you think there is any chance he will go to Haversham? Their capital city is home to the original documents of the Fleet Compact. There is also a holy site about ninety nautical miles east of Autumn, important to a number of islands.

If the target was Sylvanner (a notion I would normally dismiss, but given the tenor of their current election, it bears consideration), the obvious symbolic locales would be the spell vaults at any of the Spellscrip Institutes, Hoarfrost Harbor, and the great Zoo. Bear in mind, however, that Tug Island and the Golders claim Sylvanna as an ally. Your chief suspects would not want to be blamed for an incident there.

Yours very faithfully,
Erefin Salk

Sophie handed the letter over so Krispos could absorb it. "What's in this package?"

"It's the followbox Bramwell made."

She unlatched it, releasing a smell that reminded her of catacombs, and pulled out the goat's skull, which had reshaped itself into a cube. Its teeth appeared fused, impossible to open.

"I believe it will only unlock for its maker," Krispos said.

She let the bone warm in her hands. Could it have worked? If Bram had it delivered to her spelunker friend, and it got to a cave in Tennessee . . . how long had it been there?

If Stormwrack truly was a future Earth, some of the answers might be inside. Despite Krispos's comment, she tried again, straining every muscle to open it.

Nothing. She might have been trying to crack a diamond. A blackened and smelly diamond, at that; despite its refusal to crumble, it was leaving a film of old soil on her skin.

She rubbed it on her slacks, adding another layer to the horse blood and road dirt.

Okay. Get out of the lady suit. Wash. Catch the terrorists before they send another giant cat after us.

She pulled off the suit jacket, discovering a colorful bruise on her shoulder from her rapid bailout from the carriage, and showered quickly. Then she chose one of her three sets of casual Sylvanner day wear, a royal-blue jacket and slacks cut like a riding habit. As she changed, she nursed, for a moment, a dense sense of homesickness. All of her American clothes had gone down with *Nightjar*; she would have paid in blood for a pair of blue jeans.

The thought was followed by a pulse of guilt. What had she really lost? A few scraps of clothing and a camera. Garland's whole life had been aboard the ship.

Cly had been buying presents again. A biggish satchel, embroidered with a night sky and a moon in a style that reminded her of a Vincent van Gogh painting, was lying on the bed. She tucked the bone box, her book of questions, and the rest of the mail inside. Then she glanced at the bird, Uhura. "Verena? You there? Pick up."

No answer.

Heading back downstairs, she strode across the hotel courtyard, passing more moon pyres in various stages of construction. As agreed, Cly was stationed on a bench near the Black Fox, watching the entrance.

"Parrish has gone around to the rear," he murmured.

"Thanks."

She headed inside, sought out the head concierge, and got him to prove, with a tippable flourish and just a hint of stuffy offense, that Kev was properly under lock and key in the room Cly had rented her. He was working his way through a bowl of citrusy-smelling porridge as they came in, eating with every appearance of zest.

Her arrival put an end to that; he nearly choked.

Thought I'd be dead, huh? What she said was, "You must be bored. Let's go for a walk."

He heaved himself to his feet before the concierge could yank him up, mumbling some phrase which probably meant "As you wish, my lady and mistress," but which was blessedly not in Fleet, and therefore incomprehensible to her.

The Sylvanner concept of a hotel matched almost perfectly the same idea at home, lacking only the electronic conveniences. The Black Fox was no exception. It kept a front desk where guests checked in, writing their names in a big ledger. It had a small tearoom, where visitors to the city were, even now, frowning over ostrich eggs and morning correspondence. A lounge area, near the great staircase, offered guests comfy chairs from which to partake of the ambience.

As Sophie paused in the lounge, Kev shifted nervously.

He probably couldn't speak without permission.

"What's up?" Sophie said.

"Why are we here?"

"I thought you could use a break from the tedium. You've been off kitchen duty since I had you inscribed, right?"

"Oh—" He foundered. "I might go back to it today."

"I didn't know you were into the pain. I'm sorry."

"You had to do it," he said, scanning the lobby. "Where are we going?"

"Nowhere." A muscle jumped in his jaw. "We're going to laze around by the fire and catch up."

"You said a walk," Kev offered, a little feebly.

"Disappointing when people lie, isn't it? So! I'll take this chair, and you can park on the floor, by the hearth. Want a cushion? Here's a fan. If anyone looks at you funny, you can wave it to ventilate me."

"Well—"

"Now. Entertainment. You're not allowed to read, unfortunately, or I'd give you a book. And they don't do newspapers here, so I can't drape one over the chair for you to scan."

"I don't know 'newspapers' . . ."

"Unless you have a better suggestion, I think you'll have to settle for people-watching."

"What will you be doing?"

"Oh," she said, "the same."

He swallowed convulsively, Adam's apple bobbing in his doughy neck. "I'm accustomed to the kitchen."

"Not gonna happen," Sophie told him.

It was gratifying, in a sense, to see him fighting to smother his anxiety.

It meant that this would work. She felt a twinge about making him squirm, and then made herself remember the shredded horse and the marsupial lion. If Cly hadn't diverted to the slums outside of town, the fright would have gone berserk amid a parade in the heart of Hoarfrost.

Was Cly's decision to take them out to the sticks then, just then, another fortunate consequence of Sophie's magical luck?

A uniformed staffer came by, offering tea and biscuits. Sophie slipped a cookie to Kev when nobody was looking. He played with it, seeming to mean not to eat it, but eventually giving in and nibbling.

Stress eater, she thought, giving him another.

Her hip and shoulder, where she'd landed after the jump from the carriage, were stiffening as she sat.

One of the junior concierge types drifted past, once and then twice. The second time, he met Kev's eye, then walked away rapidly. Were they in cahoots? Had he been bribed?

Kev slumped, miserable.

The next time the junior concierge came by, Kev piped up, "I could use a relief break."

"The chief concierge can take you to pee."

"Perhaps *you* might like a break. . . ."

"Rule number one of the stakeout is don't leave your post," she said.

He mouthed the word "stakeout."

The clock struck the hour and he flinched.

Ten minutes later, Mensalohm's law clerk, Sophie's former fake fiancé, came through the door.

Daimon was dressed as a foreigner, with a sash denoting him a citizen of a slaveholder state—qualifying him to stay in the hotel. The garments were nondescript; he was as inconspicuous as any outsider could be. He exchanged a few flirtatious words with the woman at the front desk, tossed his pre-Raphaelite locks, and let his eyes roam the lounge with a casual air that hinted he wasn't expecting to see anyone he recognized.

When his gaze connected with Sophie's, and then he saw Kev seated on the floor beside her, there was a moment of puzzlement, just a breath. Then he dropped his pen.

Kev shouted, "*Smitt! Fenza mey! Net ba treaten—*"

Daimon burst into motion, running so suddenly his hat was left behind—very Bugs Bunny. He bolted for the main doors of the hotel, dodged around a veiled woman dressed all in white with a crimson sash—

And promptly ran into Cly, who tripped him with one elegant toe and then caught him by the scruff before he could fall on his face.

"Gotcha," Sophie murmured.

CHAPTER 33

Daimon. Daimon was the frightmaker. Daimon had sunk *Nightjar* and made that horrible cat-monster.

Daimon hadn't been eaten by a lizard oddity at all. He had almost certainly tried to get Kev away from Selwig.

Daimon murdered Selwig.

Sophie was sucking wind over that as Cly offered them a bow and hauled his prize back out into daylight. He had that pleased crocodile gleam about him. And why not? This was real progress.

Torture. They'll probably torture him.

She turned to Kev, who was starting to hyperventilate. "You told me he was dead."

He huffed, bending almost double, and she relented. "Cell or kitchen?"

"Kir? I mean—"

"Don't you dare milady me right now."

He gulped.

"Oh, I'll be back with a stack of questions, don't you worry," she said. "But right now, the cat's away, hauling your frightmaker off to jail. It is him, isn't it? Daimon's really Smitt the frightmaker? He made that thing that attacked us last night?"

Kev's jaw worked, but no sound came out.

"You weren't afraid of him before," she said. "He told you he could take you off *Nightjar,* any time—well, that his eragliding friend, Pree, could. What changed the deal?"

"You shut off the clock in your cabin."

"He could have restarted that in a pinch."

"You were going to compel me to talk."

"Liar. We agreed I'd pacify you, no more than that."

He spread his hands, bowing his head.

"Was it all bull, Kev? And if so, what was it for?"

"When this began, I hoped, truly, just to save my own skin." He stared at the doors, where Daimon and Cly had vanished. "But my part in this is fixed now. I'll say no more."

"Fine. I have games of my own to plan. Would you rather be locked up, or do you want to wash dishes?"

"Dishes, please."

She dragged him off to the chief of staff, who got an earful about the underling she suspected of being in cahoots with Kev and Daimon. Once everyone understood that Kev needed extra-close guarding and that Cly would be the one checking up, she rushed to the hotel's back door. In a little garden, for guests, Garland was holding up the third post of their stakeout.

"We caught Daimon," she said.

"Daimon's alive?"

"Daimon was Smitt the spy." *Daimon sank* Nightjar. "Now Cly's got him."

Garland had been sitting in a dark corner of the arbor, carving a little flute from a stick of wood. Now he stood, making an ineffectual swipe at the wood curls and shavings, which tumbled down his pants.

"Come on," she said. "Unless you want to end up married tonight, we've got an escape to plan."

They hurried over to the hotel suite, where Uhura was doing an acrobatic dance on her perch. "Hailing frequency," Sophie said. "Anyone there? Rodger dodger?"

"That is obnoxious, Ducks."

"Bram!" Hearing his voice, she welled up. "Where are you guys? Are you here?"

"Let me get Verena." There was a minute or so of nothing; the bird hopped around, tootling. Then it said, "Verena here. We're laying anchor outside the Hoarfrost harbor, aboard *Capo*, maybe a mile and a half out."

"So close! How did you—"

"Magic, of course," Verena said. "Problem is, Sylvanna's customs office has tagged us for a goods and contraband search. They aren't planning to let us dock anytime soon. It's a holiday, they say."

"A mile and a half's not so bad," Sophie mused. "We might swim out to join you."

She glanced at Garland.

"The tide would be out," he said. "I doubt the swim would be very difficult, even—"

She put a hand over his mouth before he could say something about her bruised shoulder.

"I don't like your chances of getting safely through the harbor of a bonded nation," Verena said. "They'll have mines, probably mermaids or shark oddities, too. And if we take you aboard and they search us, they'll catch you."

"That could be awkward, but we're not criminals."

"No swimming," Bram said. "You saw how they booby-trapped the northeast coast. If there's any chance they've done that to the harbor to prevent runaway slaves . . ."

"Okay. No swimming. We'd need a rowboat, then. Or we slip onto some other ship berthed in the harbor, wait out the ceremony, and then sneak out to *Capo*."

"If we do that," Garland objected, "we're involving some other crew in our troubles."

She paced the hotel room as he updated the others on the latest developments and tried to rough out an escape plan. If they could go into the ocean somewhere other than the harbor. If they climbed down the cliffs and someone met them.

All of which assumed they could get away from the ceremony itself, after the wedding banquet.

"His Honor will know we're making for *Capo,*" Garland said. "All he has to do is . . . what was the term? . . . stake us out."

She interrupted. "I have a better idea."

"Shoot," said the bird—she wasn't sure if it was Bram speaking or Verena.

"It's a lot to ask, Garland."

He made a gesture: *Go ahead.*

"We go, we eat, we free Kev. Then I distract Cly—"

"How?"

"By being an awful, embarrassing outlander, of course. And you—"

She got stuck. Her mouth opened, but breath wouldn't sustain the words.

Comprehension dawned . . . and to her relief, Garland broke out a dazzling smile. "I could abandon you before the ceremony!"

"Would that be horrible for your reputation?"

"I've been a disgrace to society for most of my life." Garland grinned. "Sophie, it's perfect."

"Hey, baby, wanna slink off and leave me at the altar?"

"Oh my God, are you kissing?" The bird made a sound that was eerily like a snort. "You guys are completely weird. You know that, right?"

Sophie felt, again, that sense of complete confidence in Garland. It radiated, like sunshine, and she wasn't sure which of them it came from. "He would have refused to get hitched anyway."

"Would I?" He raised his eyebrows, pretending surprise.

"You're too honorable to vow a lifetime commitment if either of us was under any kind of duress."

"I wouldn't, as you put it, slink off."

"No, you'd reject me openly. Right there in front of everyone."

"If left with no choice—"

"Guys, this is verging on foreplay," Bram said. "We're getting off the phone."

"No, wait! We need stuff."

"Like what? *Runaway Groom for Dummies*?"

"I don't know . . . 'runaway groom'?" Garland said.

"Bram, Verena, make a huge fuss about the customs search. Do everything you would do if the plan was for us to run for *Capo* together."

"Sure. But what are you going to do with Kev, once you free him?"

"I don't think spiriting him off Sylvanna's an issue anymore. Willing participant or not, he's in on whatever's going on here. He may not have stabbed Selwig, but he by the Seas didn't bother to tell us that Daimon did."

"So he'll be arrested?"

"Yeah, that's my guess." *And tried. And sentenced to death again, probably. In the end, all I bought him was a few months.*

"Okay, Sofe. Go sleuth, and don't get hurt."

"Let's get all this political maneuvering over with so we can raise *Nightjar* and go do some proper science."

"Go, Team Science," Bram agreed. It was, apparently, a farewell. Uhura shook herself back into birdlike indifference.

"Come on, Garland. Time to go back to the Black Fox and see if we can shake any facts out of our conspirator."

He caught her by the arm, spinning her to face him. He waited until she had stopped—stopped moving, stopped thinking about Kev—until he had her full attention.

"Someday, Sophie Hansa, when there's no duress involved, I will ask."

She put her finger on his lips. "Garland. We understand each other."

"Do we?"

"I meant what I said to Cly," she said. "You can jilt me just as hard as you want. If they march us up to a priest or whatever and ask if I *want* to be with you . . ."

"Yes?"

"I'm a motormouth, remember? And do you think I'm gonna take up lying now?"

He all but glowed.

"Come on. Let's figure out what they've been up to and go humiliate ourselves publicly. This time tomorrow, we can be having illicit, scandalous, celebratory breakup sex on *Capo*."

He drew her closer. "We can't keep sailing this pace. We were out through the night."

"Yeah, Garland. Because things are *happening*."

He kissed her, moving again with that maddening, focused sense of leisure. "You must at least pause."

"That?" She kissed him back. "Is not the way to slow me down."

"No? What about this?"

"Vroom." She giggled. "Vroom, vroom! Do not pass Go!"

"None of that makes any sense at all," Garland said, and then he was lifting her, pivoting so her kicking feet were aimed at the door of her room, trusting that she'd boot it aside as he pointed their bodies—they were both laughing now, so hard she could feel his legs shaking—at the bed.

CHAPTER 34

Later—after—they did catch a few hours of sleep.

She found herself stirring at just around noon, awakened from a dream of Verena's voice that turned out to actually be Verena, muffled by a closed door and speaking again through the bird.

". . . always had this idea of what my life would be, you know? And it was Gale's life, sort of. You and me and *Nightjar* and all the intrigues. Now everything's changed. Gale's gone and the ship's sunk—"

Sophie felt a triple punch of guilt. One on the chin, for getting *Nightjar* sunk, one in the gut, for her half sister's heartbreak. Plus a third, for eavesdropping.

She glanced around the bedroom. No way out that wouldn't take her past Garland. She toyed with putting a pillow over her head.

Garland answered, sotto voce, "I always thought that, too."

"You did?"

"Of course," he said. "It's what we made provision for. Gale and I talked of it, often. How it would be, where I would take you. Verena, you must see that but for the romantic question—"

"The tiny matter of the romantic question," she said, but Sophie was relieved to hear a thread of humor in her sister's voice.

"Aside from that tiny matter, are we not together? Sailing? Amid the intrigue?"

There was a long silence. "Yeah, we are. Of course we are. And speaking of romantic matters, I should go do you guys that favor."

There was a whistle, and then Garland crept back into the room, holding the bird on his arm. His bare feet were looking a little pink and peeled, but there'd been a lot of healing. He was walking normally.

He hesitated when he saw that her eyes were open.

"Sorry," she said. "I heard the tail end of that."

"No harm done," he said, giving her a quick kiss and then, almost before she reached for them, passing over her clothes.

"What time is it?"

"Well past noon."

A sound, outside: Cly returning.

He made a great pretense of hanging his cloak with his back turned, allowing them to imagine he hadn't noticed them emerging from her room together. "Daimon, it turns out, isn't the real Daimon."

"Is he Smitt?" Sophie asked. "One of those last-minute additions to the *Incannis* crew?"

Cly nodded. "He must have waylaid Mensalohm's law clerk before the clerk could board *Nightjar.* The clarionhouse has been in touch with your fingerprint man, Humbrey. There's a body, found asea, that may be the true Daimon Tern. Humbrey is working on proof."

That was what Selwig meant when he'd mentioned Daimon's prints, before he died. He'd been trying to tell her Daimon was an imposter. "It would have been him, then, collecting the cat claw clippings for the fright spell when we were all aboard *Nightjar.*"

"Yes. The lion fright that attacked us is intended, he claims, to target slaveholders."

"He had access to Kev the whole time he was on *Nightjar,*" Sophie groaned. "No wonder Kev wasn't worried about what I'd do with him. Daimon could just slip into his cabin, toss those red curls of his, and make all kinds of promises. 'Oh, Kev, we'll rescue you . . .' And you know when it was that Kev got all angry and uncooperative?"

"Right after you told him Smitt and Pree had infiltrated his group of liberation activists on behalf of the portside nations," Garland said.

"If we hadn't been in the middle of trying to save *Nightjar,* he might've told me what was going on."

"Can you prove ill intent on Daimon's part?" Cly asked. "He refuses to admit to espionage, or to being an agent of any government."

"He claims to be a true abolitionist?" Garland asked.

Cly nodded. "He says he's at odds with his own government. They've disavowed knowledge of his activities."

"But he admits he was on *Incannis*?"

"Yes. According to Daimon, Kev was both the scheme's mastermind and, in essence, the ship's captain. He planned to sink the smugglers and liberate the slaves they were carrying—free them and send them to Nysa."

"He said Nysa?" Garland interrupted.

"Yes," Cly said. "Why?"

"Nobody in league with that island would refer to it by name."

"*Incannis* was too far from Nysa in any case, wasn't she?" Sophie said.

Garland looked surprised. "What makes you think the distance—"

"The questions you asked at the weather office on Ylle," she said. "You wanted to know about winds to the far south."

"*Incannis* could not have been running freed slaves and prisoners to the uncharted seas," Cly said. "Given where she was operating when she attacked my ship, she simply didn't have the time."

"So . . . Daimon's claiming allies he doesn't even have."

"It's an unconvincing lie," Garland said.

"Only to someone in league with said island," Cly said drily. "The interrogation will continue. He's been inscribed so that he doesn't register physical distress—it's a common spell with spies—but we will learn more."

Cly's certainty, and the thought of what the Sylvanners might be doing to Daimon even now, made Sophie shudder. "Let's pull out our bag of Forensic Institute tricks and see if we can dig some truth out of an actual crime scene."

"What scene?"

"They bribed a concierge at the Black Fox, to get access to Kev," she said.

"Yes," Cly said. "He's fled."

"But they couldn't have removed Kev from the hotel without us noticing," she continued. "So I'm guessing Smitt's got a room there."

They landed on the slaver hotel like a hammer. Daimon had indeed had a suite, and the desk clerk was happy to take them up.

The space had been converted into a magical workshop.

Cly glanced at the pots of ink, the sheets of vellum, a clay pot filled with robins' eggs, and a flask that appeared to hold blood. There was a catalog of ingredients and a makeshift writing table crammed beside the bed.

"Send to the Spellscrip Institute immediately," he said to the clerk. "We need the Winter Mage or a first-tier apprentice."

The clerk was openmouthed. "I had no idea Master Smitt practiced inscription."

"He'd been here before?" Sophie asked.

"Many times. I thought him a master cobbler." With a bow, he left them.

Sophie handed Cly and Garland each a pair of cotton gloves. "Go through a pile. Tell me everything you find; I'll write it down."

"Red wax," Garland replied immediately, carefully peering into the bowls. "Dried placenta, hooves, and—yes, here's a spoonful of cats' claws."

"Banana claws," Sophie said, scribbling madly.

"Banana?" Cly asked.

"The shipboard cat, the one now on *Sawtooth,*" Garland said.

Cly's lip was curled into a snarl. "Daimon was the one who inscribed you, Sophie."

"That's circumstantial evidence," she said.

"So?"

"So, basically, don't kill him."

He pointed at a stub of burned sealing wax. "You don't doubt it, do you?"

"No. He's totally the frightmaker. I'm just saying it's not proof. Remember proof? Proof in court?"

"Burden of proof is a Fleet custom, and naturally I hold it sacrosanct," he said softly. "But here at home, child, I would be within my rights to have him minced."

She swallowed. "That's all very well, and I'm mad at him too. But if you want to preserve the Cessation, we need to understand the master plan."

He seemed to weigh that: his oath, the peace of the world, or a bit of tasty revenge. "Fair point."

They continued to search in silence. Then Garland held up a page. "I believe this is a list of horse names."

"How many?"

"Six."

They turned that over. Animals were easier to inscribe, for a lot of reasons. You could name them yourself, and manage their magical load. If the horses were used to incubate frights, the countryside might become overrun with slaver-hunting lions, like the one that had attacked the three of them. Meanwhile, if Daimon kept claiming to be in league with Nysa, abolitionists would be blamed for any deaths the lions caused.

"We'll have to have the animals destroyed," Cly said.

She felt a stab of something like despair. Innocent working animals, blameless pawns in a bloody political game. *What a waste.*

It didn't feel right. It didn't feel like enough.

"Puzzle pieces," Garland murmured, as if he'd read her mind. "Not a picture."

Sophie flipped through her book of questions, running her finger down the list of frightmaking ingredients stolen from the evidence lockup in Fleet. Most of the stuff was accounted for. "Any sign of a jar of salamander eggs?"

Head shakes from both men.

"Cly, what have you found?" He had moved on to examining a table covered in sheets of stiff-looking, unbleached cardboard. These had been meticulously folded, back and forth, into little accordions.

"This would be where they had Lidman working," he said. "The materials here resemble those used in the spell that induced my . . . you called it pyrophobia?"

"Right. Influencing the behavior of kids is his specialty," she said. "So. Daimon makes frights over here. Kev sits across from him, writing spells to do something to the Sylvanner kids whose names they've stolen. Probably his go-to: getting them to burn bondage scrolls."

"That's what they wanted with him, then. To have children on the plantations unshackling their slaves while frights roamed the countryside attacking their parents."

"Would that start a war, Cly?"

"Perhaps, if they killed someone prominent."

Her eye fell on a spyglass propped against the sill of the window overlooking the courtyard. "Meanwhile, someone's sitting here making sure we don't head over to the Black Fox and catch them by surprise."

"A third conspirator?" Cly perked up with typical predatory optimism.

"Smitt's partner, maybe? Pree." She continued to examine the room. "Where do you sleep? You're working like a crazy person on all these spells. Everyone's jammed in here together, scribing. Kev goes back to his room at night, in case I check on him, but . . ." She opened a door. Inside was an alcove, with a mattress and a threadbare blanket. Bending to examine the mattress, she ran her gloved hands over it. One, two, three . . . inch-by-inch examination . . . "Ha!"

She held up a single red hair, as long as the stretch from her wrist to her elbow, and tipped in black.

"What's that?"

"The messenger from Isle of Gold." She groaned. "Oh, I'm so dumb. Golders like to face their enemies. She brought me that letter from Brawn. It started with something like 'You see before you all I can share about our spy.' I was reading it and looking her in the face the whole time. She's Pree."

Things clicked together. *Pree has Verena's build. She could have been the one who broke into Mom and Dad's place.*

Which means I have a photo of her thumbprint on Bram's hard drive at home.

Cly scanned the courtyard, using the spyglass. "So Kev's compatriots are infiltrated by two portside intelligence operatives, one of whom is still at large—"

"Daimon's insisting he's against slavery," Garland reminded him.

Sophie took a step, realized there was no space in which to pace, and instead shut the door to the little sleeping alcove for slaves. "What if the various hawky nations have caught wind of this plan where Cly and his quasiliberal Sylvanner friends are working with Verdanii to upset the balance in the Convene? To really put a pin in the war they've been all but begging for?"

Cly didn't seem to react. He leaned against the windowsill, posed as casually as a magazine model showing off the crease of his well-cut slacks. He ran a thumb over the pommel of his sword, thinking.

"The raids on the slaver ships created controversy within Fleet," Garland said.

"Who cares about a bunch of smugglers?" Sophie said. "Nobody—it's not enough. So they go for a second set of sinkings, targeting portside merchants, within Fleet, where people can see it happening. Higher profile, plus honest merchants make better victims. All so they can build up to sinking *Constitution*."

"All of the injured parties on the portside," Cly said.

"Then you just need someone to do the injuring," Sophie said. "Antibondage agitators from the starboard side. Like Kev Lidman, who Daimon's claiming is their mastermind."

"Yes!" Garland said. "That's why they entangled him."

"Are you saying Kev's primary value is merely that he's a Haver?" Cly asked.

"As everyone's been telling me from day one, where you're from matters a lot here. Kev's no idealistic kid from Tug Island. He's from across the Baste, a citizen of Sylvanna's hated enemy. He really was freeing people . . . and now, thanks to me, he's here on Sylvanna and lion frights are roaming the hills."

"It's not your—"

"No, but it'll play," Sophie said. "Daimon's claiming Kev was the boss of them. He's convicted of sinking slavers. They'll say he got me to bring him here so he could force the local kids to burn their families' slave inscriptions."

"If the Piracy wanted Lidman here," Cly said, "why did Brawn offer to buy him from you?"

"Theater," she said. "They knew I'd say no."

"Knew?"

"It's my nature, isn't that what you'd say? Willful? Uncooperative?"

"Yes," Cly agreed, but he smiled a little. "Speaking of willful and uncooperative, I suppose you're going to insist on going through with freeing Kev?"

"I have to," she said.

"Why?"

"If I don't, you've already got the right to 'mince' him, don't you? At least if I free him he's entitled to due process."

"The result of such an exercise in jurisprudence will merely be another guilty verdict."

"Maybe it shouldn't matter, but even if the difference is he gets another trial, that's a big deal to me. Proof in court and all that."

"It's not the only difference."

"No?"

"If I simply killed him, you'd be due some financial compensation for property loss."

"Teeth! Yes, Cly, we're totally freeing him."

Cly let out the gleamiest yet of his gleaming, sharklike grins. "In that case, dear Sophie, you must go have a fitting for your wedding dress."

Momentum got her moving toward the door before the words sank in. "Wait. I have a wedding dress?"

CHAPTER 35

It wasn't that Sophie hadn't tried to get Cly to tell her how the mass wedding would go.

Oh, she had asked. Repeatedly. At meals, during all the riding to and fro, even first thing on the previous morning, in case there was a chance she'd catch him groggy or off guard. The first couple of times, he'd diverted her with questions about the Kev situation.

The third, he'd flat-out said, "I shouldn't like to spoil the surprise."

Which meant, *Why help you wriggle out of the trap?*

Would they be back at the couples counseling park? In a town hall, or in the equivalent of the high school gymnasium, like a graduation? Was there a temple, a ballroom? He wouldn't say.

The attack by the lion fright, and Daimon's capture right afterward, triggered a whirlwind of police activity. Local investigators had found the body of Cly's carriage driver, Latasha; she'd been poisoned at home and buried in her backyard. Her replacement, the man who'd picked them up after marriage class and drove the inscribed mare to her death, was still at large. A full-fledged manhunt was on to find both him and the junior concierge who'd sneaked Kev upstairs to work in Daimon's rented room.

They filled the remaining time until solstice with a peculiar mix of legitimate investigation and wedding preparations. The horses Daimon had inscribed had to be found and euthanized. Letters were prepared for everyone at Cly's estate and for all his acquaintances, announcing the blessed event. A second batch of notes went out to Erefin Salk and the Watch, inquiring about the true identity of Pree, in her guise as a Fleet page. Sophie had to go to a government-sponsored lecture on her responsibilities as a soon to be newly minted legal adult of Sylvanna and a voter. Then she had to attend a second session on the political landscape of Autumn District.

On the day of the solstice itself, it turned out the Institute had, as a courtesy to Cly, offered one of its own carriages and teams to fetch the Banning party. It was oversize and very round, putting Sophie in mind of the pumpkin carriage from *Cinderella*.

Her birth father had remanded her that afternoon to the custody of a pair of hotel maids for coiffing and dressing, before announcing that he needed to grab a quick nap—he had been up all night, and then through the morning, once again overseeing Daimon's interrogation.

She tried to ask the hotel's in-house lady's maid about the wedding ceremony, but she didn't (or wouldn't) speak Fleet and was far too busy clucking over Sophie's short curls and wayward eyebrows—not to mention her refusal to wear body powder—to play pantomime.

All I have to do is admit we're not really engaged, she thought, with every bite of brush and tweezers.

Once she was coiffed, plucked, begowned, and released, she'd been sent to collect Kev, who was waiting in the Black Fox, under guard, clad in an apparently ceremonial toga. His wrists were, once again, loosely bound by Selwig's white ribbon.

"Last chance, Kev," she said. "Anything you want to say to me? Anything I can do to help you?"

He shook his head, making a point of tucking himself behind her so he could do an ostentatiously servile perp walk to the pumpkin carriage. The sight of Cly made Kev shrink a little; he wedged himself as far from the judge and his sword as he could, and fished in his robe for a cracker. Crumbs spilled onto the starched-white drape of cotton over his chest as he munched, squirrel style, with his hands bound together. He wore a weary, faraway look.

"You aren't in pain, are you?" Sophie asked.

Long-suffering sigh. "I got into this to free a woman, you know."

"I didn't."

"She belonged to one of my mentors on Tug. Jalea, her name was. For her, I created the bondburning spell. Creating an intention . . . it was the pinnacle of my spellcrafting career. I could have sought a place in Fleet as an apprentice spell developer. Instead I found Eame and his group, and we hatched a plan. But Eame said, How can we free one person and ignore the rest?"

Sophie nodded.

"They handled the actual escapes. Getting people away, putting them aboard boats . . . I never knew who was renaming them. Months passed, and I finished school. I'd gone home to Haversham and Eame kept sending me children's names. For years, I helped from a distance, far from any consequences."

"Did it work? Did . . . Jalea escape?" Garland asked.

Ghost of a smile. "Her. Perhaps twenty others."

"It was a good thing," Sophie said, shooting Cly a look, before he could make one of his disparaging gestures.

Instead Cly said, "It is often a personal tie that sets us against the currents of family and nation."

Once they were under way, it was clear from the direction they took that the High Winter Festival, like the summer event she'd attended six months before, would be held at the Spellscrip Institute.

The Institute carriage bypassed much of the traffic, and soon they were being conducted into a banquet hall within the cored-out mountain. It was an open and perfectly circular chamber, with balconies extended into the Institute's parklands, on one side, and toward the ocean, on the other. The incoming tide roared, pounding black boulders and tidal pools twenty feet below, flinging little drabs of sea foam over the lip of the circle.

Moving inward, under the lip of rock that served as the roof of the chamber, banquet guests found themselves sandwiched between two disks, a floor and ceiling of creamy alabaster, supported by what looked to be enormous *pithoi*—the big urns used in the ancient world, back home, for shipping goods. Curvy as ancient goddess totems, the urns were decorated in images that celebrated the iconography of winter: bare trees, thin figures, hibernating animals in burrows, travelers in heavy garb, and ships navigating ice-strewn waterways.

"What do you think?" Cly asked as she looked around.

"It's a symbolic representation of a winter storehouse, isn't it?" Sophie said. "The hole in the ground where you store excess harvest to get through the darkest, coldest months."

"Less symbolic than you might guess," Cly said. "The stores are real enough."

"It's a working larder?"

"Such places are our traditional hedge against a return to the days of war and starvation, when the Havers would raid us across the Butcher's Baste.

Our fields were once quite poor for agriculture, before we drained the swamps. . . ."

He was dressed in his full Fleet Judicial colors: cape, sword, sash, and gleaming, newly polished boots. Added to this was one accessory she hadn't seen before: a stonewood gauntlet, worked to resemble an alligator. It ran from his forearm to just beneath his left hand, leaving the fingers free. The spikes on the green-tinted plates were barbed. It was exceedingly ornamental, appropriate to a fancy dress party. It also looked pretty lethal.

Extra weapons for the wedding.

"I think our table might be over here."

The banquet tables were overhung with chandeliers, arrays of milk-white candles arranged so the flames formed a crescent moon. Each table setting was laid with a shallow bowl that held a bluish, moon-pocked cheese. Cly glanced at the place cards, confirming their table arrangement, and then drew Sophie back into the crowd, indicating with a gesture that Garland should follow.

"Allow me to introduce you to some people," he said.

"What people?"

"Sylvanners who think as I do."

"Slow-mo abolitionists, in other words?"

"Quietly, please. People who may elect Fralienne and her political allies, tomorrow."

"When can I free Kev?"

"After the soup, before the meat."

"Seriously?"

"There is a speech as well."

She had been obliged to check the wilting Kev at the entrance, as if he were a coat. He had been one of a roomful; more than fifty people were slated to be freed tonight.

There was nothing to do but let Cly swan her around, making introductions. "You know a lot of people here," she said.

"I was schooled in Winter for a time," he said. "It is a more politically active place than Autumn. Less rustic."

"Town mouse, country mouse," she said.

"Yes, if I understand your meaning."

At least a lot of the elite spoke Fleet. The conversations were shallow: *Oh, so you're Cly's Verdanii daughter. How terribly quaint!* It was better, though, than wondering what they might be saying about her in Sylvanner.

Suddenly, Cly let out an "Aha!"

Sophie's muscles bunched as he put a hand on her shoulder, turning her slowly.

Bram and Verena were just stepping past a uniformed waiter. Verena was wearing Verdanii traditional dress, a drapey green sarong. Bram was, as usual, rocking the Gap catalog.

"Surprise," Cly said, his voice warm.

"Oh!" She loped over, best as she could, to bundle them both into an embrace.

"That's quite the getup, Ducks," Bram said.

It really was. Cly's tailor had worked up a close-fitted bodice of deep-blue velvet, shot through with silver threads—little flecks intended, she imagined, to look like stars. The skirt got darker as it belled down to her feet, coming to black at the bottom, an obvious representation of the darkening night sky. A clangy belt of silver moons was latched around her hips.

For Garland, Cly had acquired a private captain's sailing uniform: longcoat, breeches, and boots, all in black. He'd been primped and combed, as she had, and looked as though he'd wandered away from a fashion shoot. The only reason he wasn't blinding to look at, straight on, was that gorgeous was so very much Garland's default.

She shut out everything, locking eyes with her little brother. "How's it sitting?"

"The news about Daimon?" He shook his head. "I can't believe I didn't realize."

"I didn't either. Bram, seriously, are you okay?"

A mix of emotions crossed his face. "Okay . . . ish. Three okay."

"If you need *anything* . . ." she began, and he squeezed her hand.

"How did you come to be here?" Garland asked Verena.

"Cly had us bumped to the front of the inspection line," she murmured in English. "The better to keep an eye on us?"

"What's the game?" Bram added.

"Chicken. If Cly can get me to admit there's something hinky in me marrying Garland, he wins. If I can free Kev and wiggle off the nuptial hook, I win."

"Is there a grand prize and a new car?"

"If I get married here, like this, I'm a proper Sylvanner woman, at least on paper. If I get caught, I've committed fraud, broken my oath, and Cly's got leverage."

"Leverage for what?"

She glanced around. "Not here, okay?"

"Well. I brought you a wedding present."

"Jerk!"

"You don't want it?" He grinned, dangling a new DSLR camera. "Look, now we're both in debt."

Tears pricked her eyes. "I have something for you, too, as it happens."

"Gifts. For *moi*?"

Cly had given her a purse of sorts, to go with the gown. He'd been conceding to the obvious, since she never went anywhere without, at minimum, her book of questions and a few test tubes. To these basics she had added the skull containing the magical followbox Bram had made, more than a month ago, back in Fleet. It was bulging out the line of the purse, clonking into things, and seemed every bit as indestructible as advertised.

She pulled it out, extracting it from a wrap of linen napkins. The skull was blackened, fragile looking, disturbingly square and smelled faintly of long-dead moss.

Bram touched the skull, quietly mouthing the ram's name. The bone crumbled away, adding a burned odor to the reek. All that remained on his palm was the small stone box.

He opened it.

Inside, unaffected by time, as far as either of them could tell, were the bone, the piece of lava, and a folded piece of messageply. On the paper were two words: TIME CAPSULE.

Sophie's mouth actually watered as she looked at the rock and the bone. Something they could carbon-date, at last! As for the paper . . .

"Shall we?"

Bram vibrated like a tuning fork. "Got a pen in your handbag, milady?"

"Don't tease." She held one out. He wrote ZOMG!

Sophie opened up her book of questions, paging through until she found the right page of messageply. ZOMG! had appeared on the page, right under TIME CAPSULE.

SOPHIE OPAL . . . PARRISH, Bram wrote. The words formed on the second sheet as he wrote.

She snatched the pen and wrote back, JERKY JERK.

"K-I-S-S-I-N-G," he muttered.

The paper felt hot in their grasp, as if it was about to burst into flame.

"That's it," she said. "It's truly our world that turns to all . . . this."

"That, or the parallels are so close they might as well be the same." He sounded breathless.

"Never mind the hairsplitting, Bramble."

"Things go *boom*."

Boom. Gone. All of America east of Memphis. New York underwater. San Francisco . . . She swallowed.

"We have to find out when the comets hit," Bram said. "If it's within our lifetime—"

"If it's even comets—"

Before they could power up a full-blown shared anxiety attack, bells rang throughout the hall. Cly returned, herding them back to the table.

Marriage. Right. Getting abandoned at the altar. One disaster at a time.

"Sophie, you'll sit beside me. Parrish, on my other side. Bram is to be seated beside Sophie, and Verena by Parrish."

Then he froze, momentarily floored by, apparently, the sight of the camera.

"You okay, Cly?"

"It's exactly the same as the other!"

"That's Erstwhile manufacturing for you."

"For as long as it lasts," Bram muttered.

"What a marvel!" Cly let his finger drop to the lens cap. Then, recovering, he got them arranged at the table as a stuffy-looking older woman claimed the podium, declaiming in perfectly modulated Sylvanner.

"I should translate the speeches, don't you think?" Cly said.

"Is it worth it?" Sophie asked.

He blanked. Then his face took on a quizzical expression as he weighed the question.

It was a weird moment, Sophie would think later, a tiny capture of everything about her birth father that seemed so dangerous while simultaneously leaving her with a thread of hope. That initial expression, quicksilver fast, that blank, *Does-not-compute* reaction that made her sure, deep down, that at least part of Cly was emotionally hollow. Then the quick reversion to a real face: raised eyebrows, and so much apparent good humor.

And then? Was he trying to parse her idea of worth? Looking for a socially acceptable answer? Trying to score points in their ongoing game?

"You'll be less likely to act out if you know what's going on," he concluded, and with that he began to murmur along with the speaker, offering up a text that had all the character of a graduation address.

"Young people! This is an important day. As maturity beckons and you stand on the verge of commitment, remember your civic responsibilities and the debts you owe to your nation. . . ."

What I owe my nation, Sophie thought, *is to find out if it's going to get pulverized by comets anytime soon.*

She caught Verena stealing a look at Garland. There was a sadness in her expression, but the desperation seemed to be gone. She met Sophie's gaze and raised three fingers, whispering as she quoted Bram. "Three. Okay . . . ish."

"Glad," Sophie whispered back. "Five glad."

Despite the weird, foreign, and incredibly formal setting, there was a sense of rightness, solid comfort in being together, with everyone in sight, safe, and accounted for. Bram was listening intently to Cly's translation of the prewedding speech. No doubt he was practicing his Fleet and comparing the Sylvanner vocab, even as he mathed or practiced inscription or did who knew what other work with the remainder of his brain.

"How are the parents?" she whispered to him.

"I sat them down and said I knew it was tough but you'd discovered something important. Manhattan Project important. Discovery of penicillin—"

A thrum of gratification. "And . . . what? They should just suck it up?"

"I didn't use those words."

"How'd they take it?"

"How do you think? They're sad we'll be gone so much, and incredibly proud of you."

She tried to imagine that. "No other break-ins at the house?"

He shook his head. "The spell took."

Magic. Another thing Bram was going to be good at. The thought didn't come flavored with the angst she'd have felt even a year ago.

Garland was looking, with apparent touristy interest, around the room. Figuring out escape angles and ways out of the hall?

I'll have to give him his chance to run before we get marched to the . . . well, it's probably not an altar.

After the opening remarks, table slaves appeared, clad in monkish robes that made them nearly invisible in the dim light. They poured carrot-colored soup over the moon cheese. There was a hiss and a rush of bubbles.

"At least taste it," Cly said.

Sophie shook her head. It had a faint scent of the weird peaches, and a whiff of hot pepper.

Garland and Bram likewise demurred, but, to Sophie's surprise, Verena took a token sip and uttered a ritual-sounding phrase in Verdanii.

They had to wait for everyone else at the banquet to finish the soup before the decumbering could take place.

Finally, *finally,* the slaves began to clear the bowls. Cly indicated a line of couples forming at one end of the room. He handed Sophie a slip of paper. "The text of your declaration, in case you've forgotten."

She had memorized the syllables, but it was a peace offering, and she seized it gratefully. "Thank you. Come on, Garland."

Freeing Kev entailed picking him up at the coat check and then lining up for a turn at the speaker's platform. There, they waited in line as earnest young adults read property transfers, decumberings, and other transactions.

The waiting slaves, Kev included, were in white smocks that made them—men, women, and children alike—look like a bunch of extras for a movie set in ancient Rome. Like the others, he was holding a sash; once he was bonded, he would be required to wear the designation of a freedman. His belly strained against the smock, and he seemed almost dopey. Dark circles bruised his eyes.

"You're going to be arrested," Garland told him. "It's apparent you're involved in an intrigue to influence the Sylvanner election."

"Arrested? It's not straight to the axman?"

"Once you're liberated, your right to a fair trial is restored. You'll have a defense adjudicator."

He slumped a bit. Disappointed?

"A few months ago, you were all about not getting beheaded," Sophie said. "What changed?"

"Back when this began and I freed Jalea, I thought myself a gamer." Kev shook his head. "I was never but a piece on the board."

"You could still help us catch Pree."

"I've crossed that Golder twice already," he said. "Time to leave well enough alone. That way, there'll be a small mercy, when they catch me."

"I'd be more worried about the Sylvanner justice system." Sophie looked back at the banquet table. Verena was making determined chitchat with Cly—from their gestures, they were talking about swordcraft. Bram was examining Kev.

Catching his eye, Sophie puffed out her cheeks, then raised her eyebrows. Asking: *Just taking in the weight gain?*

He nodded.

"I think it's our turn," Garland said.

Kev paused at the base of the platform, head bowed, as they climbed up together—two kids, in the eyes of the law, added up to one responsible adult. The officiator looked at them skeptically. His gaze passed them, moving in Cly's direction, and he stiffened to utterly proper attention.

Bet Cly bared his teeth or something.

The officiator gestured for the two of them to take hands and go ahead. Sophie read the decumbering.

There was no fanfare, no thunderclap. In a world so awash in magic, you would think at least that Kev's symbolic shackles would fall off. But all that happened was that the officiator nodded.

"I think you're free now," Sophie said.

She untied Selwig's ribbon. Kev bowed, clumsily. "Kir Sophie."

The emcee was shooing them.

Garland drew them off before the next couple could elbow through. "If you would like us to contact an advocate on your behalf—"

Kev shook his head. "No need."

They walked him past the lineup and back in the direction of the coat-check. Two Hoarfrost police constables were waiting.

"Hold on," Sophie told them, digging out a robe and sandals Cly had given her, for after. "Let him dress before you haul him off in irons."

Kev shuffled into the sandals, then donned the robe. He smoothed the identity sash over his chest, emphasizing his gut. He was all gut—his legs and arms were still skinny.

She looked at Garland, at the open shaft leading out to the rest of the Institute. Would he take off now?

Let the jilting begin! She was about to suggest it, then he bowed. "Your Honor."

Cly, naturally, had come along to see Kev turned over to proper custody. "Well, Lidman? Is freedom everything you imagined?"

Sophie gave her birth father a *Shut up* scowl. "It's not too late, Kev, honestly. If you leveled with us now, as a free man, we'd still try to help you."

"I was never free. But at least now I'll do no further harm." Kev shook his head. "It's done, Kir Sophie. My family can— Thank you for trying. And for all your kindnesses."

He turned his back on her, lumbering away, stoop-shouldered, with the guards.

"He's no longer your problem, dear one. Come." With that, Cly ushered her and Garland back to the banquet, to watch as the Sylvanners devoured eight more courses of premarital midwinter fare: roasted mushrooms, a salted fish dish, a pickly thing that smelled of kimchi with cherries—and not in a good way—and alligator flesh. They didn't seem to do dessert at the end of formal meals; instead, there was a tiny mouthful of cookie or cake after every dish.

"This is how they feed you before sending you off for a wedding night? How do you move, let alone—"

"Don't be coarse," Cly said, but his expression was indulgent.

Of course he was amused. It wouldn't take a rocket scientist to figure out that Garland was fixing to bolt.

I'll have to look for a chance to be extremely distracting.

Garland himself seemed calm enough, undisturbed by the prospect of being frog-marched down the aisle.

"At home we call this a shotgun wedding," Verena said.

"Wrong," Bram said. "Shotgun is when you're pregnant."

Garland coughed. "There's no question of—"

Pregnant. An uneasy roil of thought within Sophie's mind.

"What's up?" Bram asked, reading her expression. Garland and Cly had leaned forward in the same instant, probably to ask the same thing.

"Daimon," she said. "Or Smitt. Whatever we call him. Frightmaker. Specialist in gross pregnancy spells."

"Daimon?" Bram said. "What about Daimon?"

"Go on," Cly said.

"The bleeding ships," she said. "Amniotic fluid and birth stuff. The mare full of cat monster. She was fat." Nobody was following her. "I'm just thinking . . . Kev . . . He's been belling out." She held her hands out from her gut.

Cly arched an eyebrow. "Is this a ploy?"

"I thought it was inactivity, stress eating."

"You changed his name, child. He can't have been inscribed after he was enslaved and pacified."

"The bigger the fright spell, the longer it takes to bake," she said. "He was getting bigger . . . Seas, as far back as *Docket*."

"What are you saying?"

"Kev was done with Daimon, once he realized he was a spy. But Daimon trailed him here, to the Black Fox, and persuaded him to write those compulsion spells. Why'd Kev agree?"

Garland said, "Daimon blackmailed him?"

"Threatened. He'd have said . . . oh, let's see. That if Kev kept his mouth shut, and wrote the inscriptions they wanted on the kids, they'd rip up the spell that's making him fatten up." Sophie's heart was pounding. "Guys, that cat monster tore the horse to shreds from the inside."

Bram was already on his feet, attracting glares from their near neighbors. "Cly, where will the guards take him? Which route, do you know?"

"There's a secure floor." Cly rose, triggering more scowls and a few disapproving clucks, and ignoring it entirely as they all got moving.

CHAPTER 36

They hurried through the park at the Institute's ground level, skirting a botanical garden and a spectacular zoo—cage after cage filled with creatures as exotic as lemurs and as ordinary as sheepdogs; bright, sun-filled chambers with daisies as big as Sophie's head; and a guarded plot of bristling, thorny poppies.

Maybe I'm wrong, Sophie thought. "Maybe I'm wrong."

"Does that happen often?" Cly inquired.

"The doubting, or the actually being wrong?" Bram said.

"Don't help him, Bramble."

Up ahead—a cry for help.

She broke into a run, outpacing everyone but Verena, and came upon the two guards. They were on their knees, dragging something out of a swampy, moss-lined pool.

Not *something. Him.*

Water flowed into the pool from a crack in the blue stone retaining wall; the pool was one of five in a row, each containing a slightly different species of lesser bulrush. Kev had pitched into the first of these pools—face-first, from the look of it—and they were muscling him out. His cheeks were smeared with mud, and he was gurgling.

"Kev!" The belly of his white shift had split its seam. Flesh pulsed through the ripped fabric, straining against the tears like rising bread. The skin had a bubbly look to it, as if marbles lay beneath.

Sophie knelt, touching them. "Hot."

The others had caught up by now. Cly handed Sophie a small stonewood dagger. "He's unconscious. He won't feel it."

Small poke. She fought back an almost hysterical titter and made a small incision, digging a bead out of Kev's hip.

It was an amphibian egg, a red-tinged capsule of gel, long as her little finger. Inside was a tiny homunculus. As they watched, it grew larger.

A second egg dropped from the cut she'd made, falling into the mud. And another. Garland caught the next with a cupped hand. The ones that had fallen right into the wet were growing faster than the others; it, and the little man-shaped forms within, were suddenly as big as a fist.

"They need the water," Sophie said.

Cly took Kev's feet and hauled him uphill, away from the pond. Gooey amphibian eggs poured from his mouth and from the widening tear in his hip, leaving a glistening trail. They shivered and wiggled, straining toward the pond.

Kev let out an agonized groan, slitting his eyes. His watery gaze met hers.

"Kev," Sophie said. "Kev, can we stop this?"

He gurgled, spitting eggs, clearly terrified, then let out a low, miserable wail.

"It's all right. Lidman, you're all right. Try to breathe. Through your nose now. One, two." Cly had him on the driest point in the trail now. He rolled Kev onto his side as the man continued to moan, flailing, but only feebly. Kev's body was softening, his flesh loosening, like a balloon losing air. Amphibian eggs were pushing their way out to the ground from under the bloody trapdoors of his toenails.

"Close your eyes, Kir." Cly brought a knee down, sharply, across Kev's neck. There was a terrible snap. Kev jolted, right down to his swollen toes.

Oh Seas, holy shit! But what else could Cly do? He was dead. It was obvious he was dying in agony.

Kev let out a long, relieved-sounding exhalation. What was left of him went limp. Eggs began to slide out from under his eyelids, gooey tears with red, man-shaped nuclei.

"Contain the oddities!" Cly said. "They're of water; we'll need fire."

"I'll get oil." Verena sprinted off.

The body was losing coherence, turning to a spilled-custard mass of bloody, mobile amphibians—soap-slippery, hard to catch, the smallest of them as fine as foam. She, Bram, Garland, and Cly scraped at them in a mad fury, trying to block their access to the water, the pools of cattails.

It was impossible to catch them all. The water was roiling, splashing. The stems of the bulrushes vibrated as if in a stiff wind.

"Here." Verena came bolting up with two cruets of oil and a moon torch—to judge from its ribbons. She poured the fluid over the biggest pile of eggs, and Cly touched the flame to its heart. There was a frying sound, a stench of cooked egg. Flames licked with weak enthusiasm at the pile of biomatter.

"Institute security's bringing more," Verena said.

Bram was stamping cherry-size tadpoles and retching. A few were as big as pugs now, and were growing arms. They scrabbled away, trying to escape.

"Moon salamanders," Cly said. "They lay their eggs in the body of a dead fish or reptile. They hatch in the dead of winter. Tug Island was nearly overrun, sixty years ago, by a mob of ten thousand men with frog eyes. It was that incident that led to the ban on frightmaking."

Sophie said, "Salt! Amphibians have delicate skins. Maybe—"

"Over there." Garland pointed at the crest of the hill, along the line of cattails. A few of the things were struggling uphill, out of the other side of the pond, on spindly legs. They were coming to look, more or less, like men.

"They're headed that—"

Bram was interrupted by a surge of energy from the torch they were using to scorch the oiled eggs. A sizzle went through the air. Sophie felt her arms break out in gooseflesh, and her whole body itched, just for a second.

"Teeth! What now?"

"That was spell reversion," Garland said.

They looked around, hoping to see the mini Kevs turning—back into Kev? No such luck.

Taking the torch from Cly, Sophie doused it in the bulrush pond. Then she pulled it up, peering into the fork of its branches. "There's an inscription in here."

"Is it hemp paper?" Cly leaned close. "This will be somebody's obedience scrip, I'm betting."

"A handmade torch with a bondage scrip in it," she said.

"Seems to be."

"Who makes the torches?"

"Children. For the moon pyres. It's a festival activity."

And it was kids Kev had been forced to inscribe. "What's up that way, where you got this, Verena?"

"The children's vigil."

The rustlings among the bulrushes were getting louder, more frantic, as the frights absorbed the pondwater and continued to grow. Boy-size frights continued to tramp their way out of the muck.

Guards Verena had summoned were rushing down to join them now, each carrying heavy urns of oil and, acting on Bram's mimed instructions, using them to spread the fire across the remainder of still-squirming fright eggs.

Cly turned to one of the original pair of guards, a twentysomething woman who looked a bit small for her uniform. Her hands were splashed with slime and gore from destroyed eggs, and her eyes were overly wide, unblinking. "Contain as many of these as you can, do you understand?"

"Yes, Your Honor."

"The rest of you, come with me."

They dashed back uphill, toward the vigil.

How was this meant to play? Sophie mulled it over as she kept pace with Cly's long strides.

Kev compels the children of slaveholders to start burning the bondage inscriptions. Then, tonight, a bunch of slaves go berserk at the Institute.

Ten thousand rampaging frights at the Institute. A mob like that would do a lot of damage. Add to that an intention laid on your children, slaves at home who've suddenly had their free will returned . . .

Cly paused at the crest of the hill. Below them stretched a grassy plain, encircled by moon pyres.

It was suddenly a good thing that "children," on Sylvanna, merely meant single people. It meant that, although there were lots of actual children, tiny kids as young as three, on the green, there also were cohorts of teens and young adults, hanging out, trying not to seem too bored.

The toddlers and little kids danced around the fires, throwing in torches, balls of paper, dried flowers, crumpled hemp accordions—anything flammable that might raise the flames high enough to reach the moon-shaped wooden frames. Burning the winter moon.

Spell reversion energy sizzled whenever one of the bondage inscriptions burned.

"Uh—" Bram pointed back toward the bulrush pools.

The amphibians who'd survived the fire were gathering in a crowd maybe fifty strong. They had Kev's face but were considerably more muscle-bound. Flaps of dried amphibian egg clung to their shoulders and hips, in some cases forming reasonable facsimiles of togas or robes. Others were nude, or clad in patchy tatters of egg skin.

Fake slaves for a fake rebellion.

With a little smoke and confusion, they certainly could be taken for a revolutionary horde. They were making for the hill.

Cly bellowed, "Fleet recruits! All Fleet recruits!"

Two dozen of the elder "children" separated themselves from the pack immediately, running to rank up in perfect formation.

"Anyone in service, up the hill—there's going to be a fight. The rest of you, gather up the younger children and take them to the central tower."

The cadets arrayed themselves as indicated, facing off against the approaching Kev clones. Cly plucked the stonewood dagger from Sophie's hand and gave it to the most strapping of them.

Garland had a knife, too, it turned out. He handed it to another of the recruits. Verena drew her sword.

"They're unarmed. We should be able to keep them from harming the younger children until Institute security mobilizes," Cly said.

This doesn't have to be so bad, Sophie thought. *We got a lot of them while they were still eggs. This is dozens—it would've been thousands.*

Thousands of Kevs and Kev is dead and Cly broke his neck and what could he do? He had to, he had to. . . .

"Use these as clubs." Cly gave her a hunk of smoothed wood—a torch handle—and handed a second to Bram.

The bunch of Kevs advanced uphill, pushing over the moon pyres in a sort of slow-motion calm, finding torches abandoned by the children and taking them up, putting them to the flame.

The first of them reached the top of the hill.

Cly stepped out, blade-first. "Stop!"

The fright paused at the tip of Cly's sword, looking mildly curious, like a dog that isn't sure if it has done something wrong. It tried to take another step, testing the press of the point, and let out a faint, dismayed croak.

Behind it, the other Kevs were fanning out, trying to just muddle their way past the gathered line of defense. One bumped up against an eighteen-year-old Sylvanner boy who, with a shudder of disgust, hauled off and punched it.

That Kev fright fell backwards against a couple of its fellows, its mouth bleeding clear jelly. It gabbled—meek, wide-eyed, and wounded looking. Everyone gaped at each other, the identically muscled frights with Kev's face, the hodgepodge of young Fleet recruits, and the remnant of *Nightjar*'s people.

The Sylvanner cadet let out a bellow and launched himself at the Kev he'd hit, ripping it out of its buddies' arms, shaking it, and then pounding it.

The pacification spell.

"He can't fight," Sophie murmured.

By now, one of the Kevs had turned to flee. He was chased down by another of the teens, the one with the knife.

"They can't fight!" she shouted. "Stop! They're harmless! Their template was pacified—the copies are too!"

That's why Daimon had tried to sink *Nightjar,* she thought. He'd been perfectly happy to let Sophie transport Kev to Sylvanna, until he realized she was going to make his army of frights harmless.

My migraine began just hours after he found out I meant to pacify Kev.

It was a stroke of good fortune, but it might not be enough to prevent a riot. Everyone was in motion. Cly had sheathed his sword and was trying to force his way over to the berserking Sylvanner cadet. A few others had followed the lead of that first boy and were celebrating solstice by beating on the apparently helpless frights. More of the Kev frights were fleeing down the hill, toward a marching squad of well-armed Sylvanner constables, twenty strong. Some of the others were trying to get around the fight, to keep on bumbling toward the smaller kids.

Garland was moving, swiftly, liquidly, sweeping his leg out to trip three of the Kevs at a shot, just enough to knock them off their legs. They goggled at him with hurt expressions; he mimed for them to sit, head down, hands up.

They obeyed.

Bram, after a second, copied him, giving the nearest Kev a gentle shove and then pointing at his seated pals.

They're as tame as puppies. Sophie hiked her sodden skirt to her hips and sprinted toward the squad of constables.

Getting ahead of the muddled Kev frights wasn't hard, mostly. They were mobbing down the hill, unclear about the danger they were in. She skidded through a little slick of mud just as the leader of the constables was slicing through one of the frights' necks, beheading the lead Kev, who'd beelined for the path down toward the pond.

It was a terrible sight, the sword chopping into the body, the spray of pinkish blood, the awful collapse, and the sound—imagined, she knew—of the head bouncing on the ground.

Big breath. "Stop!" Sophie shouted as loudly as she could. "Stop, stop, stop!"

The squad leader gave her a withering look.

Sophie hurled herself in front of a fleeing Kev who was about to meet up with a sword-wielding soldier. When the Kev tried to gently push past her, she slapped its face as hard as she could.

It froze in its tracks, looking at her with huge, hurt, froglike eyes. Then it wilted, like a plant denied sun.

"See?" She shouldn't be crying. It would keep her from bellowing, and she needed to bellow. She marched up—*No time, no time; the others are coming*—and pushed the squad leader's sword down. "They're harmless, they're pacified, they're no damned threat. Just round them up!"

No reaction.

"Doesn't any of you speak Fleet?" Her throat was raw. "Tell them to put their swords down! Please!"

A breath later, two voices rose at once, calling out in Sylvanner.

Another of the Kevs was getting close, and she bolted toward it, tackling him before he could get within beheading distance.

They're never going to listen. Who the hell am I?

But the leader was ordering his team to put away their blades. There was a whisk of blades into sheaths and they came up bare-fisted. They spread out, slapping the Kevs—some with more enthusiasm than others—and then began herding them to a nearby corner of the zoo, penning them in a corral with a pair of anxious-looking, braying zebras.

Sophie stepped around the gelatinous, rapidly decaying body of the first Kev.

I brought him here, she thought. *I brought him to this.*

But no. He'd gotten into something bigger than either of them, long ago. She'd just been a pawn in someone else's big spy game. Again.

I'm gonna find every last one of them and take their toys away, she vowed. *Every spell, every slave, every stupid murderous spy plot.*

Garland came loping downhill to her. "The frights are under control," he said. "There are children burning inscriptions, here and there, but the adults are confiscating torches. His Honor says there'll be trouble tomorrow, when everyone goes home. Everyone will have to check whether their slaves remain under compulsion."

"Tension, bad press, crackdowns," she muttered.

"Seems likely."

"Can he find a way to spin it all so it isn't as bad as all that?"

"If we can prove foreign tampering." He scanned the field. "It would have been thousands of them, Sophie."

"And they weren't meant to be harmless."

"If nothing else, this must have disrupted the festival," Garland said.

"Not at all." Cly strolled up, a big grin on his face and his hand on the pommel of his sword. "We're a carry on, carry on kind of people."

"Meaning?" Sophie said, though she already knew the answer.

"Are you ready to get married, children?"

CHAPTER 37

Of course, Sophie thought. Cly wouldn't give up on a good game of chicken just because of a little bloodbath.

She stood between her birth father and Garland, feeling almost weak-kneed. The sensation reminded her of the watery exhaustion that followed a long swim, that sense of being barely able to carry the weight of consciousness, never mind holding up tissue and bone. Mixed sadness and horror rolled through her, and she felt an intense longing for America, for Mom and Dad and a society without random, arbitrary rules and horrible magic and all the rest.

Nightjar was sunk. Everything Garland had in the world was underwater.

She reached for Cly's hand, and then, with her other, grasped Garland's. "Come here, both of you."

"Sophie—"

"No, Garland," she said. "Shush."

She aimed for a quiet spot on the trampled meadow, near one of the unlit moon pyres, a delicate arrangement of wood and straw that hadn't been touched by the chaos. The meadow looked out over the cliffs and the sea, the star-studded velvet of the long solstice night.

The sky that her dress, now muddied and covered in swamp and monster blood, was meant to evoke.

She took in the sight, breathing it in, trying to clear away the awful memories of the past few minutes.

"We gotta decide, Cly," she said. "Are we going to pile a personal disaster on top of all this . . . carnage?"

"Explain."

"I could marry Garland tonight. I could vow—" She looked straight into Garland's eyes. "I could vow anything. I love him. I think, if I asked, he'd go along. Our feelings . . . there's plenty there. There'd be no lie."

That alert, steady gaze.

"But we're not ready, Cly. Do you get that? There is no marriage where he comes from, and on my world, we . . . wait."

"You haven't waited on much," Cly observed.

"Yes! We've had sex. Thanks for bringing that up. And we'll live together for a while. Raise his ship, sail around, be a couple. You can give me a passport, but that doesn't make me Sylvanner. That's a wish you can't have."

"No," he said at length. "I suppose not."

Someone's got to get off this merry-go-round. "You know what's been going on here. You've known from the beginning. I was afraid you'd torture Kev, so . . . I lied when I said getting married was the plan all along."

"You freely admit it?" Cly's jaw clicked. "You weren't engaged. You committed fraud in order to assert ownership rights over Lidman."

"Broke my almighty Fleet oath, too," she said. "Come on, stop dancing. You *knew* this. The question is, what do you want to do? You can have me arrested, or deported all the way home to Erstwhile."

She felt a thrum in Garland at that point, a tightening of his hand around hers.

"Is that all?" Cly asked.

"Yeah, pretty much." She didn't add that Annela had been waiting for just such an opportunity; she wouldn't use Cly's dislike of the Verdanii to influence him. "Do what you think is best. No . . . wait. There is something."

"Which is?"

"I'm sorry. I should've asked you to help me."

"Indeed you should." Cly nodded. "I need to think."

With that, he walked away.

"You've put our fate in His Honor's hands," Garland murmured.

"I had to."

The smile he gave her was radiant. "I do understand."

"Even if he deports me?"

Any answer he might have made was interrupted when Bram and Verena ran out to join them. "What's going on?"

"She told him," Garland said.

"Everything?" Bram goggled. "Sofe, what are you doing? You just handed him all the ammo—"

"Cly doesn't want me jailed, sued, or deported," she said, keeping her voice low.

"You're the shiny new thing. I know. But what happens when he gets bored?"

She shook her head. "There's a master plan here. He says it's liberating Sylvanna and preventing a Fleetwide war."

Verena frowned. "You believe that?"

"It might not be all of it, but . . ." She shrugged. "Everything he's done since we got to Sylvanna was about stopping this—the mess here."

"He's failed," Verena said. "We're not going to see any relaxation of Sylvanna's bondage laws now."

"Fight's not over yet," Sophie said. "We can prove the Piracy and the Tug Islanders were out to manipulate Sylvanna's election."

"Which brings us back to Daimon . . ."

"No," Sophie said. "It brings us to his accomplice. Pree. Whatever we call her—"

"Sophie." Cly had returned from his amble. "Thank you for trusting me."

She nodded.

"The simplest way to dissolve your engagement is for me to forbid the match."

"Can't Garland just jilt me?"

"I would feel obliged to challenge him."

"Oh." She felt her face get hot. "Challenge . . . as in, ritual exchange of blows?"

"Sophie." A purr. "You know I think he's unworthy of you."

He might have been joking. Who could tell?

She looked at Garland. His expression was untroubled; if he was intimidated by the prospect of fighting the Fleet's preeminent duelist, it didn't show.

"Forbidden it is, then. Garland, my pops here says I'm not supposed to see you anymore."

A bubble of laughter escaped Garland's lips.

"But, Cly . . . You know we'll do what we want, right?"

"Believe me, if there's one thing you've made abundantly clear—"

"Okay!" No point in letting him finish that sentence. "Garland, are you good with this?"

He nodded. "I suspect it's what His Honor would like to do anyway."

"I cannot help my nature." He held out a hand, unleashing one of those irresistible thousand-watt smiles. "I suspect I'd have enjoyed fighting you, Parrish. But it's allies for now, alas."

"Indeed," Garland said, clasping his hand. "What a . . . shame?"

"Can we go looking for Pree now?" Sophie asked.

"Yes, we really ought. Where do you want to start?"

"Where are the marriages happening?"

Cly inclined his head—*Follow me*, he meant—and led them around the children's park, past a band shell that had been packed with another hundred captured Kev frights, and into a spiral staircase leading up and through the mountain.

They came out on a cloud.

It wasn't really, of course; they must be using magic or dry ice or some type of fog machine. But the illusion was perfect: stepping out onto something rock solid, only to find her feet swirling in mist, dimly illuminated, as if by the slightest tinge of moonlight on a black sky.

The about-to-be-married couples were lined up along the length of the cloud floor, facing each other at a distance of about a yard—just a hair too far to reach across the gulf and touch fingertips. At the front of the line, a pair of young men stood before a floating disk that looked like a tabletop made of moon. It had no physical substance, just a lambent, silvery glow. Behind it stood an impossibly tall individual in a sash whose sole ornament was a glimmering pin representing marriage—the clasped hands that Cly had worn on his sash, briefly, before his official divorce.

The nearest handful of bystanders, Sophie guessed, was the family of the groom and groom. The table was throwing so much light that the tops of their faces were in shadow—they were just bodies and chins.

The two men clasped hands as the officiator murmured words in Sylvanner. The family members repeated the words, then the couple did. It was a little singsong; it rose and fell, passing from the officiator to the relatives and then to the couple themselves.

Sophie felt an unexpected stab of regret.

The officiator took the clasped hands of the two young men and pressed them against the moon table. It was liquid, as it turned out. Their hands were submerged in what looked very much like moonlight. There was a reverent pause, and then the couple raised their hands again, still clasped, dripping with the light of the moon. Each laid his hands on the other's heart, and the illumination soaked in. For a second they were young moon men, lit from within. Through their exposed skin, Sophie saw the shape of the bones in their hands, rib cages shining within their clothes, and shadow-organs nestled in perfect order within. Their hearts were beating in sync.

The light faded and they embraced, quickly, before they turned into the warmth and congratulations of their jubilant relatives.

The officiator swirled his fingers in the lunar surface, rippling its waters. As the next couple and their witnesses stepped up, the fluid settled to stillness.

"Sofe, why are we here?" Bram asked.

"Rees Erminne," Sophie said. "Rees and his veil-wearing foreign girl, Cleste. She was the one who told me we could bring Kev here to free him."

Cly spun on his heel, searching the crowd, then chose a direction, making for the edge of the clouded floor. There was an impressively huge contingent of people waiting quietly in the darkness, clustered around expectant pairs of engaged Sylvanners.

"Liquid moonlight," Garland murmured. "Did you see?"

"Cool, huh?"

Cly was whispering with one or two of the waiting family members. Then, putting a hand on Sophie's arm, he led them, a little human chain, to an almost pitch-black corner behind the crowd.

It turned out there were walls here after all—her hand encountered a curtain. Cly drew it aside and they filed into an anteroom filled with newlyweds and their kin. Their hands were sprinkled with luminescent glitter—moon dust, Sophie thought. She was reminded again of graduation ceremonies, the clutches of people gathered afterward. A hundred individual celebrations within a greater crowd.

Rees Erminne was off to one side, all alone, arguing with a uniformed official in whispered Sylvanner.

"Rees?"

The guard made a shooing gesture, but a word from Cly stood him down.

"What gives?" Sophie said.

Rees said, "Cleste is missing."

Not a big shock. She cast about, looking for a sensitive way to break the news.

Then Cly bulled in. "Your intended is an international agitator. She's been coordinating the unsanctioned inscription of several children and the debonding of their family slaves."

Rees buried his face in his hands.

"We haven't time for your emotions, child," Cly said. "When did you last see her?"

"She slipped away after the banquet."

She might be anywhere. Sophie wormed in between Cly and Rees, took Rees's hand, got his attention. "Rees, tell us about her."

"Ah . . . she claimed she was born on Gellada, the daughter of a merchant family. A mutual acquaintance, a shoemaker from Tug, set it up. The Gelladans marry out—they like to raise children with doubled national ties, to calm the seas for trade. Cleste was going to bring in money so that Mother could hire people to work our orchards. It was meant to help us recover from . . ."

"From freeing all your slaves, yeah?" Sophie said.

Rees nodded, looking plaintive. "Is this about the election?"

"Partly." *Poor guy.* That feeling returned: slow-burning desire to scorch the conspiracy—all the conspiracies—to their roots.

"The question," Verena said, "is where's Cleste now?"

Sophie said, "Krispos told me that once pirates set a course, it's a point of honor to never deviate from it."

"Her course is to cause chaos here," Cly said. "Release the frights and set them rampaging through the Institute. To sow murder and destruction at the heart of our most cherished cultural symbol."

"The rampage is more or less thwarted," Bram said. "Can she regroup?"

Sophie scratched her head. "The stuff in the hotel room, the stuff that belonged to her, it was thief stuff. Climbing equipment, that crowbar . . . Is there something she could break into, or steal?"

"There's a great deal here," Cly said.

"Something upsetting," Sophie said. "Something to drag Sylvanna further from any kind of liberal agenda. Something to make Rees look horrible and tank his mother's bid to govern the Autumn District. Something to send every Sylvanner here home in a *Crack the whip and crush the opposition* frame of mind."

"Trouble is, it's a target-rich environment. The whole Institute is full of treasure, isn't it?" Bram said. "Spells, components, relics?"

"Rees," Sophie said, trying to ignore the way Cly and Parrish were both turning over the phrase "target-rich environment," soundlessly, with disturbingly similar expressions of linguistic pleasure. "You spent time with her."

"We don't have time for this," Verena said.

"We can't guess wrong," Sophie countered. "Think, Rees. Every conversation she started. Every time she led you in some direction. What was she most interested in?"

"It was this: the wedding; being here," He closed his eyes. "Where will the banquet be held, where will Kev Lidman be taken after he's freed, will we see the children burning the moon, where do we promenade afterward, how old are the banquet hall *pithoi* . . ."

"Is there anything important in the *pithoi*?"

Cly shook his head.

"She asked who would conduct the ceremony—" Rees suddenly paled.

"What is it, child?" Cly demanded.

"The officiator," he said. "They had a long conversation—Cleste is very charming. She asked about the carving of the Institute."

Cly's hand dropped to the haft of his sword. "Nials isn't a fool."

"He told her no more than what everyone knows," Rees said, and then realized the foreigners probably didn't. "The first Winter Mage wrote a mining inscription to dig out the core of the mountain, then used the stone to build the Winter capital."

"You're sure that was what she was asking about?"

"No. There were so many people . . ." Rees swallowed. "She cannot know where Hoarfrost is entombed?"

"What if she does?" Sophie said.

"We should evacuate the Institute," Rees said.

"What do you mean?" Sophie said.

"You have two minutes to reach minimum safe distance," Bram said, in his movie-quoting voice.

She rounded on him with a glower.

"Inappropriate humor moment," he apologized. "But if they destroy the inscription that dug this facility, the rock used to dig out this complex will return, won't it? From the city?"

"Yes," Cly said.

"Hundreds of tons of rock," Bram said.

"Indeed. The core of the city will collapse, and all the stone used in the buildings' construction will resume its original position within the mountain. We'll be crushed."

"And the nice antiabolitionist from the Autumn District, and a guy from Haversham, will be to blame," Sophie said. "Terror accomplished. Where's the inscription?"

"Come with me," Cly said, already leading them away.

They left Rees sitting in the anteroom, slumped against a wall, a lone, forlorn figure in a room full of newly married adults and their happy parents.

CHAPTER 38

Cly headed for a necropolis deep within the mountain, shortcutting along a corridor radiating into the core of the Institute. Its stone walls, magically wrought, were as smooth as if they had been machined and buffed. The ceilings were high, and the walls met at perfect right angles, but it was all of a piece: varnished blue-tinged rock above, below, and to either side. There wasn't a smudge or a cobweb to be seen. The unmoving air smelled of soap and something like freshly mown clover.

Recesses in the wall, cut at ten-foot intervals, held glowing colonies of softly humming bioluminescent insects. The tombs gave off an air that seemed less sepulchral and more like that of a university building—one of those big monoliths of learning, with endless rows of faculty offices.

They didn't even try to be stealthy as they trotted after Cly, rushing past door after door. Each door bore a plate, set at eye level, on which was carved a cluster of names, and birth and death dates. They were further adorned by some of the same symbols live Sylvanners wore on their status sashes.

"Why does the magical institute have a crypt?" Sophie asked, mostly to remind herself to write it down later, when they weren't midway through trying to prevent a disaster.

"Some of us leave our bodies to the Institute for research purposes," Cly said. "Magic, using human remains . . . as you've seen, it can be very potent."

"So the big cheese founder of the Institute is down this way?"

"Hoarfrost, yes. In the furthest tomb."

The first Winter Mage, as he'd initially been known, was one of an early group of brilliant spellscribes who revolutionized Sylvanna's economy by developing unheard-of inscriptions for sale on the international market.

To hear Cly tell it, the Winter Mage was a mash-up of Leonardo da Vinci and Merlin.

When the revenue started coming in and Sylvanna grew in power, her government and the scribes knew they were, in essence, building themselves up as a great big target for raiders. The fastest way for an enemy nation—Haversham was the big worry, but any aggressive country with a big navy might be tempted—to put an end to Sylvanna's upstart tendencies would be to destroy the Institute and plunder its intellectual treasures.

So the Winter Mage, who had taken the name Hoarfrost and who was by then pretty ancient, ordered the building of great magical fortresses in each quadrant of the nation.

"As I understand it, the digging out of this complex wasn't an overly complex spell; it was merely a matter of scaling up a precision mining inscription. It is written on the inside of—" Cly froze just shy of the entrance to a big subterranean atrium, putting up a hand.

Garland drew Sophie against the wall, gesturing to Bram to retreat into a corner.

Footsteps.

Six Kev doppelgangers shuffled into view, grown eight feet tall, their muscles straining under the weight of a rock-encased conker. The burden was fully one and a half times the size of a normal coffin, but they bore it, naturally, without complaining.

A quartet of grenades was duct-taped to the top of the sarcophagus. Their pins were strung to a chain that led to an iron manacle held by the woman in white.

She had shed her skirts and stood before them, masked, in what would have looked like a Hollywood thief's catsuit if not for its pristine white color.

Her instincts were only a hair less sharp than Cly's. She uttered one word, bringing the Kevs to a halt, and drew her sword, while still clasping the iron bangle with her gloved right hand.

Cly, too, had drawn his blade.

"Perhaps the outlanders can tell you what will happen to the sarcophagus if you run me through," she said.

Cly understood grenades well enough—he'd had Sophie explain them. Yet he pretended ignorance. "Bramwell? What are those objects?"

Stalling, Sophie thought.

"She drops the ring, the pins in the grenades are dragged out by its weight, and *boom,*" Bram said. "They're more of an antipersonnel device than a real bomb, though. Shrapnel. We'd die, but I'm not sure they'd put much of a dent in that stonewood sarcophagus."

"It wouldn't take much of a dent, would it? We'd just need for one little shard to penetrate to the scroll inside the coffin. What would happen to your prize, Your Honor—"

"You'd die too," Bram said. "You're closer to those grenades than we are."

"If I have to give my life for the cause of liberation, so be it."

"You're no abolitionist," Sophie said. "You're forcing those Kevs to haul the coffin."

"Kev Lidman offered his life to the cause."

"You forced him," Sophie said. "You made him write those compulsion spells on the kids. You promised you wouldn't kill him with a thousand parasitic frights if he obeyed."

A half shrug. "As bounty due the doomed, we'll give Kev's family a handsome payment."

"*Bakoo* shine, huh? Very nice."

"It's our way."

"Liberating the bonded isn't truly your goal, girl," Cly said.

"Is there anyone who will believe that, once your capital lies in ruins and the spells in this great vault are reverted by the Institute's destruction?"

Okay, Cly was *definitely* stalling. What did he think would happen?

Sophie didn't have a play of her own; backing his was all she could do. "It hardly matters, Cly. If the inscription inside that sarcophagus gets nicked, the whole Institute refills with rock?"

Cly nodded.

"It'd be a massacre. The cream of your nation, international guests. All these Kevs and the trouble they caused, all the kids who've burned the scrips so their family slaves aren't brainwashed anymore. The buildings in Hoarfrost collapsed. *Boom.* Your government will be out for blood."

"Listen to your daughter, Your Honor. She may be a savage, but she understands the situation," Cleste said. "Why not sheath your sword so we can continue our journey to the ballroom?"

"No," Sophie said. To her surprise, she sounded almost pleasant. "I think if you're going to go all weapon of mass destruction on this place, you should be standing right here at the heart of the implosion."

"Do you think I won't do it? Do you think I'm afraid?"

The Kevs were tiring as they stood there, mute and uncomplaining. Was this why Cly had been stalling?

More time. She examined the woman. The white mask hid everything, of course—expression, eye movements. She had that band around her wrist. A watchband?

Time to play to my strengths, Sophie thought, *and spill everything.* "What if I gave you an absolutely killer piece of intelligence? Something real, not all this stagey Stormwrack smoke-and-mirrors mummery? Something that would get you your crackdown on the bonded, here on Sylvanna and pretty much everywhere else on the portside?"

Everyone stiffened . . . including Cly.

Now that *was* interesting.

"Crackdowns," she said, dangling the bait. "Roundups, interrogations. Any of the freed who might be agitators, or even somewhat educated, would definitely get arrested and examined."

An outright glare from Cly now. Despite the danger they were in, she felt an upsurge of satisfaction. He knew she meant Pinna.

She matters to him. He's not faking that.

"Your 'killer intelligence' hardly avails me if I'm captured," Cleste said.

"You have no real fears on that score, do you? You're gonna glide, glide away, tick tick tick, with your magic wristwatch."

Verena shifted beside her. She got it then. Good.

"We're not so different, you and I," Sophie said. "The Golders sought out your father. Was it Pharmann Feliachild, Bettona's dad? They'd hoped he'd knock up your . . . mother? grandma? . . . and thereby allow them to get a finger onto the genetic legacy of the Verdanii."

"How do you know that?"

"It's what the Sylvanners and Cly's dad did. They were after a Feliachild baby who wasn't just Verdanii, someone with a Sylvanner passport who might have access to the . . . what do you call them, Verena?"

"Wild magics."

"Yeah, that," Sophie said. "Just another round of magical monopoly breaking, with a baby for a prize. And it worked: you approached Bettona and talked her into helping you awaken your latent eragliding ability. She fed you bread made from the sacred Allmother flour."

The Kevs were trembling now. If they set the sarcophagus down, it changed things only slightly, as far as Sophie could see—Cleste could no longer just drop the iron ring and let its weight drag the grenade pins out.

She could still yank it, couldn't she?

"This isn't intelligence."

Wordy. Be wordy.

"This family—our family," Sophie stressed. "The Feliachilds. Your family and mine and Verena's, and Cly and my brother here—we're an ecosystem. When you add inputs to an ecosystem, there are reactions. You put the wrong plant in your garden, something from afar, soon it's all over town, crowding out the local flora. You Wrackers understand this."

"So?"

"Beatrice Feliachild and Cly Banning saw something in each other. They liked each other, at least at first, but what drew them together wasn't infatuation. What they saw in each other was opportunity. Cly's parents ordered him to try to acquire Verdanii genes. And Beatrice had an agenda, too."

"Beatrice Feliachild couldn't manipulate a dancing doll," the girl said scornfully.

"Don't get me wrong—I'm sure she was fond of Cly."

Cly coughed. Taking offense?

"But she'd been told she wasn't good enough to learn magic at home. Her little sister was this ubergifted spy, and—well, who knows what else was going on there?"

"Do we need to psychoanalyze my mother right now?" Verena said. "Because, frankly, this is a little weird." Her tone was mild, lacking any hint of defensiveness. Was she helping Sophie drag this out?

"My point is, she had plenty to prove."

"Meaning what?" Verena said.

"Beatrice came here, to Sylvanna, and Cly bumped her to the head of the line for magical apprenticing or whatever, because that's what he does. Always to the head of the line—"

"Nobody will believe that a Verdanii was given access to Spellscrip Institute secrets," Cleste said.

"No. They taught her little baby-blessing spells and family luck spells and veterinary inscriptions."

"You seem to be saying that Beatrice was using me," Cly said. It was clear to Sophie that, unlike his ire of a moment earlier, this bit of outrage was playacting, an extension of his gambit to keep Cleste focused on them.

"It was a two-way street, wasn't it?" Sophie said.

"Indeed," Cly agreed. "Of course I saw how lonely and out of place

Beatrice was. My father and the Institute had asked me to make myself agreeable to her. Their resistance to the match, when we became engaged, was part of the . . . you'd call it a scam, probably."

"My point is that when it was obvious the Institute was never going to teach her anything significant in terms of inscription, Beatrice went looking for whatever coaching she could get her hands on. She wasn't going to be balked by a bunch of mere Sylvanners. And she found out there were other ways to work magical intentions."

Oh, that got them, Cly and Cleste both. They were all ears.

"Sophie!" Garland said. "This is extremely ill-advised."

"Beatrice found out there were other letters in the magical alphabet."

"Sophie!" Garland protested again. Emphatically not playacting.

"What letters?" Cleste demanded.

Drag it out, keep her attention . . . She rounded on Garland. "What? We let her blast the Institute and half the city apart? End result's the same, right?"

"What you propose to reveal— The consequences for all the portside—"

"What letters?" demanded Cleste. The excitement in her voice was unmistakable now. "Whose letters?"

One of the Kevs buckled. His knees collapsed as he folded to the floor. As he crumbled out from under the sarcophagus, it lurched, and two more of his fellows folded, too. The thing tipped like a spiny submarine.

Time's up, Sophie thought.

Cleste instinctively jerked backwards, toward the grenades, taking the slack out of the chain holding the pins. Maybe she thought she was ready to die, but her survival reflex was too strong to overcome.

Garland lunged forward, grabbing for the iron bangle.

He got it, but not her. Cleste leaped, vaulting over the sarcophagus and the falling Kevs, landing lightly in the far corner of the room. Cly sprang after her, becoming momentarily entangled with one of the frights.

"Here!" Bram urged the Kevs back, away from the fray, making soothing noises.

Cly shoved the fright aside, still pursuing Cleste. She parried a swing; their swords met with a *boom* that sounded more like a drumbeat than any kind of metal-on-metal clash. The impact vibrated up through Sophie's shoes.

Cleste stretched out her free hand toward the sarcophagus.

Wind rushed over Sophie's face. The pulse of clocks beat in her eardrums, against her skin.

"Verena, the coffin!"

Verena grabbed for the spines on its outer shell. Garland worked around her, cutting the grenades free, one by one.

Tick, tick, tick. It was deafening this time. It was more than one clock, and the stone chamber amplified the resonance. Sophie could hear the grandfather clock at Beatrice's house, the metallic clink of tiny gears in a safe-deposit box in San Francisco, and that resonant *boom boom* that she suspected might be Big Ben. She heard Bettona's timepiece.

She heard again what must be the Worldclock, on Verdanii, a *brrum, brrum, brrum,* paced like a human pulse, beaten on something like a drum.

There was one other clock, something aboard a ship. She could sense Cleste pulling toward that one, trying to bring as much as she could: Verena, a Kev or two, and of course the sarcophagus.

She takes it with her, she can blow it up at her leisure. Or just hold it hostage, the way they were going to do with Temperance*'s scroll.*

Bettona said I ended up in the wrong place, that one time when I eraglided, because I yanked away from her.

Make her yank.

"Her wrist," she shouted. "The watch is on her left wrist!"

Cly pivoted, disengaged, and brought his sword around. Cleste deflected again, trying to circle back toward the sarcophagus.

Garland threw one of the grenades right at her free hand.

Bram promptly hurled himself at Sophie, bearing her to the stone floor.

The sarcophagus split in two with a snap, like the spiny conker it resembled. Cleste vanished with the top half of the thing.

The coffin within the sarcophagus fell, rolling to the floor.

A blast of seawater filled the room, knocking everyone across the atrium.

Cly's killing stroke fell on empty air.

There was no explosion from the grenade; Garland must have thrown it with its pin still inside.

For a minute, they all simply coughed and sputtered. Cly recovered first, crawling up and examining the inner coffin. "It's intact," he said. "Obviously the spell within is untouched, or we'd feel the reversion."

"Thank the Seas for that," Verena said.

They spent a second letting relief sink in. Sophie gave Bram an especially ferocious hug.

"I don't suppose you'll tell me what letters you meant?" Cly asked her, wringing out his cape.

"Sure I will," Sophie said. "I'm all oathed up, remember? I pretty much have to. The letters are called pictals."

"Sophie," Garland protested.

"They're how the bonded write to each other."

Cly's eyebrows climbed practically to his forehead. Garland looked appalled. Bram was trying to catch up. Only Verena had her attention elsewhere, as she wrapped her hands around two of the sarcophagus spines, pulling as if into a cat stretch.

"There's a full dictionary at your sister Pinna's place, Cly," Sophie added. "Go ahead, send the goon squad over. She's connected, I think, to whatever resistance the bonded have going locally. The Institute could be interrogating her within the hour. Let the pogrom begin."

"You think I won't?" Cly said.

"I'm hoping—trusting, I guess—that you are who you claim to be. That your oath to protect the Cessation and your family are the things you care about."

The silence stretched until one of the Kevs sneezed, making them flinch.

Come on, Sophie thought. *Are you going to let a bunch of meddling kids screw with your life plan? Would you send them after Pinna?*

Cly seemed to reach a decision. "As the senior Fleet officer on the scene, I'll have to direct you all to keep this confidential while I sort through the implications and report back to the government."

"No problem," Sophie said. She felt Garland, beside her, relax.

Cly pulled off his cape, wrung it out more completely, hung it so it draped properly and hid, somewhat, the waterlogged state of his slacks. "I'll fetch some soldiers. Wait here."

With that, he turned and disappeared down the corridor, leaving them in the catacombs to guard the pacified frights and the old magician's corpse.

CHAPTER 39

Cly sent them ahead to the hotel in the pumpkin carriage from the Institute, into a traffic jam of celebrants and tired newlyweds bottlenecked on the switchbacks that led back to the capital city. Moon pyres burned in the streets of Hoarfrost, smudging columns of smoke skyward, filling the cold air with a smell of crisped aromatic wood and apple chips. Happy chatter and strains of music drifted up from the streets; the whole city was up, apparently, to see out the longest night.

Cly had stayed behind to do mop-up, to consult with the Spellscrip Institute and the Sylvanna government about possible responses to the attack.

Sophie could have been worrying that they'd embark on a hovel-by-hovel search for pictals in Innobel.

She wasn't worried.

The carriage had plush, comfortable seats, and Garland had an arm around her. Verena and Bram were seated across from them. Her sister looked thoughtful; Bram seemed a little shell-shocked.

She nudged his foot with her own boot, caught his eye. "Doing okay, Bramble?"

"Still trying to wrap my head around Daimon doing that horrible thing. To Kev."

"Poor Kev."

Verena said, "You couldn't have saved him."

Sophie shook her head. "No."

"You fought hard." Garland laid his hand over hers and she snuggled closer. He was just as muddy as she was, but he smelled a little of citrus oil; one of the banquet dishes must have tipped onto him.

Verena was watching carefully. Was she expecting a meltdown? Sophie didn't feel like melting down.

Instead she said, "It occurs to me that seeing people get murdered makes me super happy about having gone into hunting criminals."

"Even if it keeps you from diving the Nine Seas in search of new marine mollusks?" Verena said.

"You know, if I wanted to be diving mollusks, I think I probably would be."

"Yeah." Her half sister let out a little bubble of laughter. "Well, they'll keep, right?"

"I see *Capo,*" Bram said suddenly.

They had inched around a curve in the mountain, revealing a view of the harbor. The ship Tonio had brought from Erinth was long and big—thrice masted, low in the water, with black swirls on its sails and a glint of lava-colored spellscrip around its waterline.

"That's what you got as a loaner?" she said. "Looks pretty posh."

"Erinth valued Gale highly, and it supports the Cessation," Garland said.

"I bet they value you, too." Sophie scanned the water, picking out *Sawtooth,* sending a silent thrum of affection toward Watts and Sweet, somewhere aboard. *Nightjar*'s absence from the tableau ached, like a missing tooth.

Above the pall of smoke from the moon pyres, the sky was stunningly clear. Stars shimmered brightly, directly above and all the way to the horizon.

The carriage bumped forward steadily for another ten minutes before getting jammed up again.

"What a mess," Bram said. "At least after Superman defeats the bad guys, he flies home."

Home, she thought. "We'll get *Nightjar* raised and repaired. Prove that Daimon and Cleste were operating on orders from Tug and Isle of Gold. Make a case to prove Daimon stabbed Selwig. And then, hopefully, tie Convenor Brawn into it."

"Is that all?" Bram said.

"We're up to the task."

After a second, he nodded. "We are. But doesn't all this assume Cly doesn't decide to spill his guts to his Institute pals about the pictals? He could be launching a big old slaver crackdown right now."

"He won't." She wasn't worried about Cly. There would be layers to his plans, things that he was yet hiding. But a slaughter didn't fit. He didn't want to get pulled from the Fleet and into a local war with Haversham. He didn't want to be a big fish in a backwater, and he didn't want his sister exposed and arrested.

Garland had followed the direction of her thoughts. "If need be, we'll arrange an offer to smuggle Pinna to a certain safe harbor."

"The aunt? She's not a slave anymore, I thought," Bram said.

"Sophie may be right about her involvement with a true resistance movement," Garland said. "It's one reason why she might have had a full pictal dictionary in her house."

Sophie let out a long breath. "We need to roll things closer to calm before Isle of Gold figures out its next move or unravels what I told Cleste."

"You didn't tell Cleste the whole truth."

"I gave her a clue. They won't waste it."

A raccoon emerged from a stand of spruce along the road, saucily watching as the traffic got moving again.

"You really think we can do it?" Bram said. "Cool things off enough to keep the Fleet from imploding?"

"We're one little pocket of air within a big weather system," she said. "Maybe it's already got too much energy. But if anyone can do it . . . Come on, guys, I'm not being Pollyanna here. Look what we pulled off just now. All those Kev doppelgangers would be on the rampage."

She waved in the direction of the Institute, accidentally tapping the carriage window, and the raccoon's gaze came up, meeting hers.

For a second, Sophie saw something bigger in the woods behind it. A wolf? A pack? Or was it just a moving shadow, enhanced by smoky Erinthian glass?

"We did come off well," Garland agreed.

"We are gonna steal their whole damned war out from under them and leave 'em choking on peace and love," Sophie said.

"Spoken, a little, like a pirate," Bram said. She nudged his ankle with her toe, not quite kicking, and he grinned.

They had been in the traffic jam for an hour and had covered perhaps half of the distance to the hotel when Cly joined them, mounted on a gray mare. True to form, he began obliging the traffic cops to pass the pumpkin carriage forward, bypassing the line at every intersection. Soon they had cleared the congestion and were circling into the Mancellor's spacious drive.

Dismounting, Cly waved off a servant and helped Sophie down from the carriage.

"So?" she said.

"Sylvanna has filed a suit against Tug Island and Isle of Gold, naming Daimon, Cleste, and Kev Lidman as instigators in a plan to sabotage Sylvanna's High Winter Festival and rob or destroy the Spellscrip Institute."

"Strong accusations," Garland observed.

"I have put my faith in your ability to prove enough of them to save us from a counterclaim. Of course, if they can find someone who wants to challenge me—" He whisked his sword carelessly. "The phrasing of the suit makes it clear Sylvanna regards the Golders and Tug Islanders as instigators—not any Havers, nor any local abolitionists or freedom fighters. In fact, Rees Erminne is one of the plaintiffs."

"We've got a strand of Cleste's hair and a room full of latent fingerprints," Sophie said.

"And Daimon himself, don't forget. We'll wring something out of him."

Bram winced, ever so slightly, at Cly's zesty use of the word "wring."

"I'm off to the Black Fox to take custody of the hotel records," Cly said. "I'll be examining the staff for other conspirators. You won't leave, will you, before I return?"

"Of course not!" Sophie shook her head. "We've work to do, you and I. And deals to make. About cases and estates and politics and your cherished national institutions. So many things."

"I'm glad to hear it." He took her in—rumpled, bloody dress and all—and then he smiled and passed her one of a quartet of thin paper lanterns, a ball of illumination lit from within by featherlight candles. "You should go up to the roof garden," he said. "Bringing back the sun at dawn is one of our lovelier traditions."

It was a good suggestion—she felt too wired to contain herself in a room, even one as big as their suite.

Cly passed out the remaining globes, bowed to them all, and strode away, head high, on the hunt.

She took the spiral staircase he'd indicated, zigzagging like a fire escape, up three floors, on the outside of the hotel.

She was expecting another cascade of architectural marvels, like all the things she'd seen at the Institute, but the Mancellor rooftop was more of a tea garden—tables under umbrellas stitched from repurposed sails, all facing the sea. A line of planters fronted the whole thing, filled with little willows whose spindly branches had been woven into a loose diamond grid. It would be spectacular when the weather was below freezing; the frost crystals would razor out from it.

Garland and her siblings had followed, trooping up, likewise laden with the globes.

They stepped up to the deck, setting the lanterns out on the deck to warm. They started to float quickly as they heated, bobbing on short strings tied to two-akro coins.

"So," Bram said. "What now?"

"I believe we release them at dawn," Garland said. "To celebrate the new year and signal the opening of the voting stations."

"I wasn't asking about the lanterns."

Sophie's mind whirled. There were so many things, still, a whole book of questions, her ever-growing list. Most of them, possibly, would never be answered. It was messy, maybe—eight thousand shoots of curiosity, twisting in different directions, some leading all the way to home and her parents, some to Beatrice. Too many to rip out.

Rooted, she thought. *I'm rooted.*

"Yes," Verena said. "What now?"

She reached for Garland's hand. "First things first. We raise *Nightjar.*"

"Nightjar," he agreed, tucking her against him.

"Then what?" Bram demanded. "The rest will take care of itself?"

"No," she said. "We're not leaving anything to chance. You confirm how long we have before Earth goes *boom. Sploosh.* Whatever. Make sure we don't have to evacuate the parents, or . . . you know. Figure out how to manage an apocalypse."

"I do that, you raise the ship. Easy as pie. What about you and Sylvanna and Cly and working for the Fleet? You know, your entire future?"

"If Sylvanna can be tipped . . ." She felt the truth of it. "I'll be Sylvanner if it means breaking the Fleet stalemate on slavery."

"Embrace your accident of birth?" he said. "And Daddy, too?"

"Cly keeps his word. We've tested him and he's come through. Until he gives us reason not to trust him, he's earned probation."

Bram looked skeptical.

"Whatever his underlying motives, Cly is out to derail Brawn and his allies. He wants to steal their stupid war out from under them, too."

"Outpirate the pirates?"

"He can be trusted to act in the Fleet's interests. And, I think, in mine."

"Especially as long as you're working for the same thing, huh?" Bram said.

He took the same oath as me, Sophie thought. It was, strangely, comforting. "Verena, you in?"

"Yeah, let's take away all their toys." The look on her face was both pleased and hungry. "Gale would've wanted us to."

"Garland?"

He said, "It's a fair wind. I look forward to sailing it together."

"Wherever it leads?"

"Sailing's not about merely drifting to wherever you're blown."

"No," she agreed. "It didn't blow us to the altar."

"Not today."

She remembered him saying it: *One day, I will ask.*

A pang. It might've been nice, in its way. Shazam. Married. Done deal. Like some improbable sitcom couple. Off to the honeymoon, throw the confetti, and start racking up anniversaries. "Just so you know, there's a place called Vegas where we can do the deed pretty much overnight, if we ever get the urge."

"Don't be a dork, Ducks," Bram replied. "You're too young to get married."

"Not true, Bramble," she said. "In fact, I think I'm plenty grown up."

She spread her arms wide, reaching around them all, pulling them into a clumsy embrace: brother, sister, and this ridiculous, amazing guy.

They were still standing there, five minutes later, when the first sliver of light began to show on the horizon and the sun globes began to rise over the city, bright glowing circles, miniature suns, drifting upward to mark the beginning of the cold, bright march into spring.

ACKNOWLEDGMENTS

They say nobody is an island, and the Hidden Sea Tales trilogy (and related Gale Feliachild stories) would not exist if it weren't for the generous and inspiring people who support and assist me every day. Chief among these, the emotional and intellectual heart of my world, is a brilliant author and amazing human being—my wife, Kelly Robson.

I owe much to my family—Tuckers, Millars, and Robsons, I thank you!—and especially to my thoroughly wonderful siblings: Michelle, Sherelyn, Susan, and Bill. My friends read drafts, explain research concepts, house me on book tours, and provide moral support when I am flailing. Shout-outs are due to so many: Ardi Alspach, Beverly Bambury, Charlene Challenger, Denise Garzón, Nicki Hamilton, Dawn-Marie Pares, Chris Szego, Caitlin Sweet, and Matt Youngmark.

I am grateful to all the folks at Raincoast and Tor Books, especially Stacy Hague-Hill, Christopher Morgan, Marco Palmieri, and the *Tor.com* team. They are but a few of the editors, writers, and mentors who've guided me: Alexandra Renwick, Linda Carson, Ellen Datlow, Don DeBrandt, Claude Lalumière, Gardner Dozois, Jessica Reisman, Nancy Richler, Rebecca Stefoff, S. M. Stirling, and Harry Turtledove.

Even a book about magic needs the occasional fact. Mark Bowman and Gordon Love checked my scuba diving details, while Peter Watts has shown extraordinary patience, over the years, with my drama-geek approach to physics. Walter Jon Williams got me started on resources for tall ships. Any errors in what passes for science, language, or sailing procedure within this book are all mine. They tried, I swear!

I am one of those people who do much of their creative work out in a café environment, and all of the Stormwrack books were drafted in the remarkable Café Calabria, on Commercial Drive in Vancouver, and finished in Portland Variety, on King Street in Toronto.

Without you all, I would yet be in dry dock. Or, even worse—marooned.

ABOUT THE AUTHOR

Kelly Robson

A. M. Dellamonica is a transplant to Toronto, Ontario, having moved there in 2013 with her wife, author Kelly Robson, after twenty-two years in Vancouver. She has been publishing short fiction since the early nineties, in venues such as *Asimov's Science Fiction*, *Strange Horizons,* and *Tor.com* as well as in numerous anthologies. Her 2005 alternate history of Joan of Arc, "A Key to the Illuminated Heretic," was short-listed for a Sidewise Award and a Nebula. Her first novel, *Indigo Springs,* won the 2010 Sunburst Award for Canadian Literature of the Fantastic; she is also a Canada Council grant recipient. The first novel in this series, *Child of a Hidden Sea,* was a finalist for the Lambda Literary Award; its sequel, *A Daughter of No Nation,* won a Prix Aurora Award in the Best Novel category.

Alyx teaches creative writing courses through the UCLA Extension Writers' Program and at the University of Toronto. *The Nature of a Pirate* is her fifth novel.